Nadeem Aslam was born in Paki͏ the author of two previous novel͏ *Maps for Lost Lovers* (2004), whi͏ Encore Award, was shortlisted for was nominated for a British Book

Further praise for *The Wasted Vigil*:

'A novel of acute psychological and political insight and sympathy. Aslam has emerged as one of the most exciting and serious British novelists writing now.' Colm Tóibín, *Guardian* Books of the Year

'Beauty as well as terror in a polyphonic novel.' Boyd Tonkin, *Independent* Books of the Year

'I loved this novel . . . It is wonderfully written and imagined – he has the most delightful eye for colours and textures, small gestures and human incomprehension. He knows what he is writing about and is impatient with ideologues and belief systems, while always patient with human weakness. The book changes the reader. Aslam is an important writer.' A. S. Byatt, *Financial Times* Books of the Year

'Remarkable . . . Nadeem Aslam's stark, outraged, thoughtful novel, with its unsettling, sorrowing beauty, is a universal book . . . Aslam confirms he is a writer of singular genius.' *Irish Times*

'Nadeem Aslam is a master of words and arresting images.' *The Times*

'What the reader finds, in Aslam's exquisitely written, gripping narrative, is that although war destroys lives and shatters families, and people are capable of the greatest brutality, love and humanity still survive.' *Daily Mail*

'Marrying breathtakingly beautiful imagery with the ugly brutality of violence, Aslam navigates the troubled history of Afghanistan over the past two decades . . . A brave, devastating book.' *Marie Claire*

'The power of this novel lies in the explosive adjacency of brutality and love, the poison of fanaticism diluted by the perfume of Persian lilacs . . . When hope breaks through, it's blinding – a beam of life.' *Oprah Magazine*

'A book that confronts the most painful issues with compasion and humanity, and conveys them in prose of exceptional beauty.' *Metro*

'Aslam's unforgettable novel is a brilliant story ripped from the pages of current events. Few contemporary writers have mixed such horror and humanity in so powerful a narrative.' *Outlook India*

'A harrowing yet beautiful depiction of an Afghanistan mutilated by war and oppression . . . With astonishing lyricism and compassion Aslam creates unforgettable characters while telling a story that is as gripping as it is affecting.' *Boston Globe*

'A searing, multifaceted novel . . . Its polyglot characters inhabit seething cauldron of human drama.' *San Francisco Chronicle*

'Unafraid of political complexity, Aslam is also unflinching in his examination of depravity. Yet his writing also encompasses tenderness . . . This novel seeks to reveal the psyche not just of one rural village or one immigrant community but of Britain, the Soviet Union, the United States and Afghanistan. The revelations throughout are artful.' *New York Times Book Review*

'An intense, empathetic, magisterial interpretation of clashing beliefs and entwined fates, in a harsh and ruined, yet lovely place . . . Complexity, beauty, violence and tragedy mark the pages of Aslam's affecting story . . . The novel has insight and somber impact.' *Kirkus Reviews* (starred review)

'Kiriyama-winner Aslam takes an ambitious and moving look at the human cost of Afghanistan's war-torn reality . . . An unflinchingly clear picture of a country whose history of strife is still being written.'
Publishers Weekly (starred review)

'Arguably the best novel available on the current situation in the Middle East. The jihadists, the warlords, the crusading Americans – all are given voice in calm, relentless, shatteringly beautiful prose that reveals the essential wrongness of the current conflict from every angle. There's no whitewash or caricature here, just authentic writing that delivers the world – and a range of extraordinary characters. Highly recommended.'
Library Journal (starred review)

Nadeem Aslam

THE WASTED VIGIL

ff

faber and faber

by the same author

SEASON OF THE RAINBIRDS
MAPS FOR LOST LOVERS

First published in 2008
by Faber and Faber Ltd
Bloomsbury House, 74–77 Great Russell Street
London WC1B 3DA
This open market edition published in 2009

Typeset by Faber and Faber Ltd
Printed in the UK by CPI BookMarque, Croydon

A CIP record for this book
is available from the British Library

ISBN 978–0–571–23879–8

2 4 6 8 10 9 7 5 3 1

for Sohail and Carole

What is more important to the history of the world –
the Taliban or the collapse of the Soviet empire? A few
agitated Muslims or the liberation of Central Europe and
the end of the Cold War?

ZBIGNIEW BRZEZINSKI, President Jimmy Carter's National
Security Advisor, asked if he regretted 'having supported
Islamic fundamentalism, having given arms and advice to
future terrorists', *Le Nouvel Observateur*, 15–21 January 1998

And the poet in his solitude
turned towards the warlord a corner of his mind
and gradually came to look upon him
and held a converse with him.

DAULAT SHAH OF HERAT, *Tazkirat-ush-Shuara*, 1487

Contents

BOOK ONE

1

The Great Buddha

HER MIND is a haunted house.

The woman named Lara looks up at an imagined noise. Folding away the letter she has been rereading, she moves towards the window with its high view of the garden. Out there the dawn sky is filling up with light though a few of last night's stars are still visible.

She turns after a while and crosses over to the circular mirror leaning against the far wall. Bringing it to the centre of the room she places it face up on the floor, gently, soundlessly, a kindness towards her host who is asleep in an adjoining room. In the mirror she ignores her own image, examining the reflection of the ceiling instead, lit by the pale early light.

The mirror is large – if it was water she could dive and disappear into it without touching the sides. On the wide ceiling are hundreds of books, each held in place by an iron nail hammered through it. A spike driven through the pages of history, a spike through the pages of love, a spike through the sacred. Kneeling on the dusty floor at the mirror's edge she tries to read the titles. The words are reversed but that is easier than looking up for entire minutes would be.

There is no sound except her own slow breathing and, from outside, the breeze trailing its rippling robes through the overgrown garden.

5

She slides the mirror along the floor as though visiting another section of a library.

The books are all up there, the large ones as well as those that are no thicker than the walls of the human heart. Occasionally one of them falls by itself in an interior because its hold has weakened, or it may be brought down when desired with the judicious tapping of a bamboo pole.

A native of the faraway St Petersburg, what a long journey she has made to be here, this land that Alexander the Great had passed through on his unicorn, an area of fabled orchards and thick mulberry forests, of pomegranates that appear in the border decorations of Persian manuscripts written one thousand years ago.

Her host's name is Marcus Caldwell, an Englishman who has spent most of his life here in Afghanistan, having married an Afghan woman. He is seventy years old and his white beard and deliberate movements recall a prophet, a prophet in wreckage. She hasn't been here for many days so there is hesitancy in her still regarding Marcus's missing left hand. The skin cup he could make with the palms of his hands is broken in half. She had asked late one evening, delicately, but he seemed unwilling to be drawn on the subject. In any case no explanations are needed in this country. It would be no surprise if the trees and vines of Afghanistan suspended their growth one day, fearful that if their roots were to lengthen they might come into contact with a landmine buried near by.

She lifts her hand to her face and inhales the scent of sandalwood deposited onto the fingers by the mirror's frame. The wood of a living sandal tree has no fragrance, Marcus said the other day, the perfume materialising only after the cutting down.

Like the soul vacating the body after death, she thinks.

Marcus is aware of her presence regardless of where she is in the house. She fell ill almost immediately upon arrival four days ago, succumbing to the various exhaustions of her journey towards him, and he has cared for her since then, having been utterly alone before that for many months. From the descriptions she had been given of him, she said out of her fever the first afternoon, she had expected an ascetic dressed in bark and leaf and accompanied by a deer of the wilderness.

She said that a quarter of a century ago her brother had entered Afghanistan as a soldier with the Soviet Army, and that he was one of the ones who never returned home. She has visited Afghanistan twice before in the intervening decades but there has been proof neither of life nor of death, until perhaps now. She is here this time because she has learnt that Marcus's daughter might have known the young Soviet man.

He told her his daughter, Zameen, was no longer alive.

'Did she ever mention anything?' she asked.

'She was taken from this house in 1980, when she was seventeen years old. I never saw her again.'

'Did anyone else?'

'She died in 1986, I believe. She had become a mother

by then – a little boy who disappeared around the time she died. She and an American man were in love, and I know all this from him.'

This was on the first day. She then drifted into a long sleep.

From the various plants in the garden he derived an ointment for the deeply bruised base of her neck, the skin there almost black above the right shoulder, as though some of the world's darkness had attempted to enter her there. He wished pomegranates were in season as their liquid is a great antiseptic. When the bus broke down during the journey, she said, all passengers had disembarked and she had found herself falling asleep on a verge. There then came three blows to her body with a tyre iron in quick succession, the disbelief and pain making her cry out. She was lying down with her feet pointed towards the west, towards the adored city of Mecca a thousand miles away, a disrespect she was unaware of, and one of the passengers had taken it upon himself to correct and punish her.

Her real mistake was to have chosen to travel swaddled up like the women from this country, thinking it would be safer. Perhaps if her face had been somewhat exposed, the colour of her hair visible, she would have been forgiven as a foreigner. Everyone, on the other hand, had the right to make an example of an unwise Afghan woman, even a boy young enough to be her son.

Marcus opens a book. The early morning light is entering at a low angle from the window. The fibres of the page throw their elongated shadows across the words, so much so that they make the text difficult to read. He tilts the page to make it catch the light evenly, the texture of the paper disappearing.

Within the pages he finds a small pressed leaf, perfect but for a flake missing at the centre as though chewed off by a silkworm. The hole runs all the way through the pages also, where he had pulled out the iron nail to gain access to the words.

He has given her only the purest water when she has been thirsty. This country has always been a hub of things moving from one point of the compass to another, religion and myth, works of art, caravans of bundled Chinese silk flowing past camels loaded with glass from ancient Rome or pearls from the Gulf. The ogre whose activities created one of Afghanistan's deserts was slain by Aristotle. And now Comanche helicopters bring sizeable crates of bottled water for America's Special Forces teams that are operating in the region, the hunt for terrorists continuing out there. Caches of this water are unloaded at various agreed locations in the hills and deserts, but two winters ago a consignment must have broken its netting – it fell from the sky and came apart in an explosion close to Marcus's house, a blast at whose core lay water not fire, the noise bringing him to the window to find the side of the house dripping wet and hundreds of the gleaming transparent bottles floating on the lake in front of the house. A moment later another roped bundle landed on the lake and sank out of sight. Perhaps it broke up and released the bottles, or did it catch on something down there and is still being held? Water buried inside water. He skimmed many of the bottles from the surface before they could disperse and found others over the coming days and weeks, split or whole, scattered in the long grasses of his neglected orchard.

He lowers his pale blue eyes to the book.

It is a poet's diwan, the most noble of matters, dealt with in the most noble of words. As always the first two pages of verse are enclosed within illuminated borders, an intricate embroidery in ink. Last night she clipped his fingernails, which he normally just files off on any available abrasive surface. When she leaves she should take a volume from the impaled library. Perhaps everyone who comes here should be given one so that no matter where they are in the world they can recognise each other. Kin. A fellowship of wounds. They are intensely solitary here. The house stands on the edge of a small lake; and though damaged in the wars, it still conveys the impression of being finely carved, the impression of being weightless. At the back is the half-circle formed by the overgrown garden and orchard. Shifting zones of birdsong, of scent. A path lined with Persian lilac trees curves away out of sight, the branches still hung with last year's berries, avoided by birds as they are toxic.

The ground begins to rise back there gradually until it reaches the sky. The broad chalk line of permanent snow up there, thirteen thousand feet high, is the mighty range of mountains containing the cave labyrinths of Tora Bora.

At the front of the house, a mile along the edge of the lake, is the village that takes its name from the lake. Usha. Teardrop. Thirty miles farther is the city of Jalalabad. Because Lara is Russian, Marcus's immediate fear regarding her illness was that she had been fed a poison during the hours she had spent waiting for him in Usha, her country having precipitated much of present-day Afghanistan's destruction by invading in 1979.

In the darkness soon after four a.m. one night, Lara had got out of bed. Accompanied by candlelight she went into the various rooms of the house, moving under that sheath of books, needing movement after the countless hours of being still. She avoided the room where Marcus was but entered others, looking, enclosed within the sphere of yellow light from the flame in her hand. Somewhere very far away a muezzin had begun the call to the prayers of dawn, defined by Islam as the moment when a black thread can just be distinguished from a white one without artificial light.

When enough light began to enter the house, she placed mirrors on the floor to look at the books overhead, though not all of them had been nailed with the titles facing out, and any number of them were in languages she did not possess.

Some years ago, at a point when the Taliban could have raided the house any day, Marcus's wife had nailed the books overhead in these rooms and corridors. Original thought was heresy to the Taliban and they would have burned the books. And this was the only way that suggested itself to the woman, she whose mental deterioration was complete by then, to save them, to put them out of harm's reach.

Lara imagined stretching a fishing net at waist level, imagined going to the room directly above and banging her feet until all the books were dislodged and caught without further harm in the net. Marcus said the deep rumble of the B52s had shaken loose every book from one side of a corridor when Tora Bora began to be bombed day and night up there in 2001. The intermittent rain in the whole house had intensified during those weeks in fact.

The Englishman said he had bought the house more than forty years ago, just before he married his wife Qatrina, who like him was a doctor. 'I used to say she brought me Afghanistan in her dowry,' he said. The house was built by an old master calligrapher and painter in the last years of the nineteenth century. He belonged to what was almost the final generation of Muslim artists to be trained in the style of the incomparable Bihzad. When the six-roomed building was complete, the master – who had painted images on the walls of each room – brought to it the woman he wished to make his companion for life. Beginning on the ground floor, each of the first five rooms was dedicated to one of the five senses, and as the courtship slowly progressed over the following weeks, the couple went from one to the next.

The first was dedicated to the sense of sight, and on the walls, among other things, Subha in a dancerly gesture presented her eye to a rogue in the forest.

Allah created through the spoken word, read the inscription above the door that led to the interior about hearing. Here the walls showed singers and musical gatherings, a

12

lute with a songbird sitting on its neck – teaching perhaps, perhaps learning.

From there they moved to the faculty of smell, where angels bent down towards the feet of humans, to ascertain from the odour whether these feet had ever walked towards a mosque. Others leaned towards bellies, to check for fasting during the holy month of Ramadan.

In the room about the sense of touch, there was a likeness of Muhammad with his hand plunged in a jar. He was someone who would not shake hands with women, so in order to make a pact he would put his hand in a vessel containing water and withdraw it, and then the woman would put her hand into the water.

Then it was on to taste, and from that room they ascended to the highest place in the house: it contained and combined all that had gone before – an interior dedicated to love, the ultimate human wonder, and that was where she said yes.

The imagery was there on the walls still but, out of fear of the Taliban, all depictions of living things had been smeared with mud by Marcus. Even an ant on a pebble had been daubed. It was as though all life had been returned to dust. Consolation of a kind could be had from the fact that most of the rest of the images had survived – the inanimate things, the trees and the skies, the streams. And since the demise of the Taliban, Marcus had begun slowly to remove the swirled covering of mud. The highest room stands completely revealed now.

Marcus took Lara to one corner and pointed to the foliage painted there. When she looked closely she saw that a chameleon was sitting perfectly camouflaged on a leaf. She leaned closer to that lovely fiction and touched it. 'The Taliban would even burn a treasured family letter because the stamp showed a butterfly,' said Marcus. 'But I missed this, and so did they.'

Roaming the house at night, her shadow trembling in accordance with the candle flame, Lara had entered the topmost room. The walls were originally a delicate faded gold, painted with scenes of lovers either in an embrace or travelling towards each other through forest and meadow. They were badly damaged by bullets. When the Taliban came to the house they had proceeded to annihilate anything they considered unIslamic within it. What they had heard about this room had enraged them the most. This they wanted to blow up, even though the lovers had been made to disappear behind a veil of earth by Marcus.

Lara's eyes moved across the shattered skin of the walls, the light picking up hints of gold here and there. This country was one of the greatest tragedies of the age. Torn to pieces by the many hands of war, by the various hatreds and failings of the world. Two million deaths over the past quarter-century. Several of the lovers on the walls were on their own because of the obliterating impact of the bullets – nothing but a gash or a terrible ripping away where the corresponding man or woman used to be. A shredded limb, a lost eye.

A sound originating in one of the other rooms startled her where she stood, her heart speeding up at the possibilities.

14

It was not a thief, she reassured herself, nor a Taliban fighter looking for somewhere to hide. Nor an Arab, Pakistani, Uzbek, Chechen, Indonesian terrorist – seed sprouted from the blood-soaked soil of Muslim countries. On the run since the autumn of 2001, al-Qaeda appeared to be regrouping, to kidnap foreigners, organise suicide bombings, and behead those it deemed traitors, those it suspected of informing the Americans.

'What fool drew this?' the Tsar had demanded to know of a fortress that a student at the Academy of Military Engineering in St Petersburg had drawn inadvertently without doors. The young man was Fyodor Dostoevsky, and Lara wished this house was similarly devoid of entrances as she slowly moved along the corridor, the drops of molten wax sliding down the side of the red candle in her hand.

No one came near the house, Marcus had told her, because the area around the lake is said to contain the djinn. Lake wind, mountain wind, orchard wind collide in the vicinity, but to the Muslims the air is also lastingly alive with the good and bad invisible tribes of the universe. If that was not sufficient, a ghost said to be that of his daughter Zameen had appeared in one of the rooms the day the Taliban came here, the apparition putting them to flight.

After the sound, she was aware of the completeness of the night's silence.

Perhaps Marcus, fumbling, had dropped an object. The word 'lame' described what happened when a foot or leg became damaged or was missing, but she could think of no specific term for when an arm or hand became unavailable, though the body was just as out of balance.

She entered a room and stopped when she saw the book that had detached itself from the ceiling and fallen with the thump she had heard. The disturbed dust of the floor was still in movement around it.

She picked it up and, setting the candle down, wrested out the nail. Opening the book on the floor she began to read, sitting chin-on-knee beside it.

> *Tell the earth-thieves*
> *To plant no more orchards of death*
> *Beneath this star of ours*
> *Or the fruit will eat them up.*

In the garden Marcus opens his eyes, feeling as though someone has drawn near and blocked his sunlight, but there is no one. Letters and messages, and visits, are received from the departed. And so occasionally, and for a fraction of a second, it is not strange to expect such a thing from those who have died. It lasts the shortest of durations and then the mind recalls the facts, remembers that some absences are more absolute than others.

It was in the darkness of the night, in 1980, that the band of Soviet soldiers had broken into the house to pick up Zameen. The cold touch of a gun at his temple was what awoke Marcus. The darkness was cross-hatched with the silver beams of several flashlights. Qatrina, beside him, came out of her sleep on hearing his sounds of confusion. In those initial moments of perplexity she thought this might be a repeat of what had happened the previous week, when a patient was brought to the house in the middle of the night, the victim of a Soviet chemical weapon from the day before, his body already rotting when he was discovered in a field an hour after the attack, his fingers still looped with the rosary he had been holding. He must have been in unimaginable pain, and though he couldn't speak the stare from him was so strong it verged on sound.

The couple were not allowed to switch on the light but there appeared to be about ten soldiers. From their voices Marcus could tell they were in their teens or early twenties. He wondered if they were deserters, frightened young boys running away from the Soviet Army, running away from the Soviet Union. People from East Germany, even from as far away as Cuba, came to Kabul and then defected to the West. His mind was jolted out of this consideration when they asked for his daughter by name.

Qatrina's grip on his forearm tightened. There had been reports of Soviet soldiers landing their helicopter to abduct a girl and flying away with her, parents or lovers following the trail of her clothing across the landscape and finally coming across her naked bone-punctured body, where she had been thrown out of the helicopter after the men had been sated.

Two of the soldiers could speak a broken Pashto and they were asking for Zameen and would give no explanation as to how they knew her or why they had come for her. There followed moments of rancour and violence towards Marcus and Qatrina. The men had searched the house before waking them, and had been unable to locate the girl.

A soldier stayed with them while the others spread out through the house once again, their voices low: it was a time of war and they always had to be alert to the possible presence of rebels near by. Some were searching the garden and the orchard, others Marcus's perfume factory which stood beyond the garden, a voice drifting up now and then. There was great urgency in them, and Marcus thought of the night the previous year when the Soviet Army had entered Kabul, the Spetsnaz commandos running through the corridors of the Presidential Palace looking for the president, whom they immediately put to death when they found him.

Marcus and Qatrina managed to engage the Pashto-speaking soldier in a conversation.

'Your daughter is sympathetic to the insurgency. Her name is on the list we have been given by an insider.'

'There must be some mistake,' Marcus said through the cut mouth.

'Then where is she at this hour? We are here as part of a big operation in Usha tonight, to capture those who attacked the school earlier this month. We'll make them pay for the twenty-seven lives we lost.'

The sun was beginning to rise outside when someone came in and said Zameen had been apprehended.

The lapis lazuli of their land was always desired by the world, brushed by Cleopatra onto her eyelids, employed by Michelangelo to paint the blues on the ceiling of the

Sistine Chapel, and, from the look of certain sections of the sky above Marcus and Qatrina as they came out into the garden, it could have been Afghanistan's heights that were mined for lapis lazuli, not its depths.

The couple searched their surroundings and then went into Usha, trying to understand what had happened.

Hours later, as dusk began to fall, Qatrina stood beside an acacia tree, holding with both hands the clothesline tied around the trunk. Marcus thought it was for balance, but then saw that the section of the rope between her hands was tinted indigo, where one of Zameen's dresses had once seeped colour into it, the dress she must have been wearing when they captured her because it was missing from her room.

He led her back to the house, the perfume from the acacia clinging to her. The djinn were supposed to live in the scent of acacia blossom, making themselves visible only to the young in order to entrap them in otherworldly love.

FOR A LONG TIME before Lara came to the house the kitchen was Marcus's living quarters. There was no electricity so the refrigerator was used as a clean white cupboard to store clothes. He seldom visited the other interiors, the doors fastened, a muffled thud indicating that a book had detached itself from the ceiling. Qatrina and he had built up this collection over the decades and it contained the known and unknown masterpieces in several languages. Up there Priam begged Achilles for the mutilated body of his son Hector. And Antigone wished to give her brother the correct burial, finding unbearable the thought of him being *left unwept, unsepulchred.*

He went on a journey whenever he received word about a young man somewhere who could possibly be his lost grandson. Though he feared there was no hope of locating someone whose face you had never seen, whose face you didn't know. The last excursion was to a city in the south of the country during the Taliban regime, and like the other times it was fruitless. There he saw an abandoned and locked-up school for girls into which, he was told, every book to be found in the city had been thrown on Taliban orders. When he put his ear to the keyhole he could hear the sound of worms eating the millions of pages.

*

While Marcus was digging in the garden one afternoon last month, the sunlight falling deeper into the small pit inch by inch, his implement struck something hard. He pulled out the cassette player wrapped in canvas, interred there during the time of the Taliban. He tried to remember where he had buried the cassettes. Sound fossils! There is hunger that declares itself only while it is being satisfied, and so for the next dozen hours he listened to music without pause, cassettes on every surface around him.

A recording he himself had made two decades ago – of the long lifting notes from the throat of a red-vented bulbul, the bird known as Asia's nightingale – was followed by Bach and then American jazz.

'Duke Ellington visited Afghanistan,' he would tell Lara when she came to the house. 'He performed in Kabul in 1963.'

'The year of my birth.'

'And my daughter's.'

He worked in the garden, or, book in hand, sat on the threshold where there grew five cypress trees as tall as a house fire, or he wetted a small piece of cloth in warm water and carefully lifted away the earth smeared onto the men and women on the walls, layer by patient layer, taking three hours to uncover the arm entwined around the stem of a small-blossom-laden tree. A red vein in a petal, like a mild thrill. Rubbing off the thick crust from the woman's wristband he discovered an emerald painted underneath. He felt like a gem miner. He thought about David Town, the American dealer in gemstones his daughter had loved in the months before she died. He wondered how long it had been since David last visited him.

Carrying a lantern in his only hand, he went along the path enclosed within the Persian lilac trees. The perfume factory he had built soon after buying the house was in that direction, women and men coming from Usha to work there, harvesting the acre of flowers from the adjoining fields. It now stood disused and he let himself in, his feet rustling the dry leaves on the floor. Crossing the small office he carefully began to descend the long staircase that was a funnel of trapped warmth.

The factory had to be below ground for the coolness and the softer light to help preserve the ingredients. And soon after the digging work began, they had encountered a large boulder, an indentation at the top of the mass the first thing to come into view, a hollow no bigger than the clay bowls in which Marcus cultivated the ferns of Nuristan. As they worked away the earth, a slender ridge was found snaking around the small depression, and then they saw that the whole was in fact a large human ear. Continuing downwards and around the mass, they understood that they were excavating the head of a great Buddha, lying on its side. Vertically it measured ten feet from one ear to the other. Horizontally it was fifteen feet from the topknot to the decapitated neck.

A face from another time.

Though he knew that this province was one of the most important pilgrimage sites in the Buddhist world from the second to the seventh centuries AD – over a thousand Buddhist *stupas* in the area echoing to the incantations of monks back then – Marcus would never learn when this particular statue had been buried or why. Too heavy to move, he decided to continue with his plans for the factory with the head in it. It lay on the floor and into the wide rectangular space that they cleared around it they constructed work stations and storage areas and shelving.

Eyes two-thirds closed in meditation. The smile of serenity. The large dot between the eyebrows, perfectly circular like a guitar's round mouth. The head covered entirely in the incised ripples of hair. Marcus journeyed around him now, his sleeve absorbing warmth from the hot glass of the lantern. A stone stillness. He wondered if the rest of the body was buried near by, whole or fragmented.

The place was dusty. In the air lit by the bud of flame there were countless motes as though fur dislodged from a clash of moths. Under the staircase there were cages in which Nepalese civet cats were once kept – three ferocious blue-and-white felines, the buttery secretions scraped from whose perineal glands were a prized fixative for perfume.

Bracing his arm against the stone mouth he bent down to retrieve a small vial of glass from the floor. So much destruction and yet this had survived. A four-line poem in Dari was etched on it. He removed the stopper the size of a lark skull and sniffed it, remembering that containers discovered in Egyptian tombs were still fragrant after three thousand years.

*

Where was Zameen on the night the Soviet soldiers came to the house? Marcus wouldn't know the answer to this question until he met David Town many years later.

She would disappear from Marcus's life but enter David's at a point farther down the line, and then, time moving on, David would meet Marcus. *How stories travel – what mouths and what minds they end up in.*

The girl had slipped out of the house in the darkness when a pebble was thrown against her window pane, the sound like a bird's beak accidentally striking the glass. A boy in the garden. She went with him along the lake, towards Usha. She was unafraid of the djinn, Marcus and Qatrina having taught her to quietly disregard the many rumours about that place – quietly, undemonstratively, because Marcus with his outsider's nerves did not wish to injure anyone's sensibilities.

Just the previous week a man was said to have trapped a green bee-eater and taken it to his bride, but the pious girl who was versed in all seven branches of Islamic knowledge had veiled her face immediately, exclaiming that that was no way for an honourable husband to behave, bringing a stranger into the presence of his wife. She explained that the bird was in fact a human male who had been given his current form by the djinn.

Zameen and the boy were in the demon-strewn expanse of trees when they saw the cleric of the Usha mosque, a torch burning beside him. He was a powerfully built man in his late thirties who had four wives, the maximum simultaneous number allowed to a Muslim. His back was towards Zameen and the boy, and they were about to change direction when he looked over his shoulder. Later she would think the perfume she was wearing on her skin had reached him. But the disturbed soil from the grave he was digging must have released much stronger odours. Their eyes met, and then the two young lovers turned and hurried away, ran, unsure of whether or not they were being pursued.

They knew what he was doing, because he had done it before.

Soon after buying their house, Marcus and Qatrina had learned that the myth of the djinn was only a decade or so old, dating from around the time the cleric's eldest wife – a woman in her forties who had pulled him out of poverty – had vanished. That was when he began insisting that the area around the lake was a nest of malevolent beings, forbidding anyone from venturing there. He married a thirteen-year-old within a month of the disappearance. His insistence proved to be a great problem for Marcus and Qatrina who would have liked their home to serve as their surgery and clinic. But virtually nobody from Usha, no matter how ill, was willing to brave the journey because the spiritual leader had forbidden it. Qatrina and Marcus had to acquire two small rooms in Usha and drove there every morning. The cleric was to prove just as intractable when Marcus began thinking about the perfume factory, but he changed his mind when Marcus offered to produce the *sat-kash* rose perfume for him: the extract of the best blossoms was distilled seven consecutive times to produce this, and the very few people who could afford it took it with them to Arabia to sprinkle on

Muhammad's grave. An immense honour. The cleric agreed to issue talismans to the workers of the perfume factory, to protect them on their journey towards Marcus's house, providing they kept to the one main path along the lake. Later he began to issue them to the very desperately ill also, warning them in no uncertain terms that they must not stray.

All her life, Zameen had heard Marcus and Qatrina air various theories about the djinn, but it was always obvious to them that the missing wife was interred there.

And now Zameen herself had proof.

The two of them emerged on the path along the lake, the water so placid tonight it could have reflected even the thinnest of the moon's fourteen faces. Seeking reassurance, she stretched her hand in the darkness until it was pressed against the boy's face. At one time there would have been thin silk between the palm of her hand and his features. So great had been his beauty a few years ago that, fearing abduction, his parents had confined him to the house. A second Joseph, a second Yusuf, he was draped in diaphanous material if ever he was allowed into the street. There had been several attempts to seize him, the house shaken by the ferocity and the organised nature of some of the assaults.

Zameen and the other young girls of Usha had kissed the adolescent through the veil, his mouth the mouth of a doll for them.

Now he was older – eighteen years of age, the delicacy of the features beginning to coarsen into handsomeness – and was truly loved by her. He came regularly to her house to borrow books and she saw him frequently in Usha, writing in his notebooks – sometimes very rapidly as though using a quill whose top end was on fire, but slowly at other times, as carefully as an embroiderer intent on delighting a sultan. In the beginning she was too timid to say anything to him and had consoled herself with what Muhammad had said about those who died of secret love – that they would be granted immediate admission to Paradise as martyrs – but a fortnight ago she had revealed her feelings to him. What she hadn't known was that when he shyly removed his cap in her presence it was so she could see him better.

Now, in a dark grove of trees near the lake, she shook as they tried to think of something to do. They were sure the next day the news would come that one of the cleric's older wives had vanished, and then in a few weeks he would marry a young girl.

'She was still alive.'

'I heard her too. We must go back.'

They went past the burnt remains of the school that the Communist regime had opened in Usha last month. The first one in the area, Zameen herself being a boarder in Jalalabad, coming home at the end of the week. Following the sermons from the mosque, and with the active involvement of the members of the two rich landowning families – whose wealth and lands the Communists promised to distribute among the deprived and unfortunate majority of Usha – the teachers and their families had been savagely massacred a week ago and thrown into the lake, the poor of Usha doing their worst to announce their loyalty to the landowners and to Allah – their only protectors. They had wanted to kill Zameen's lover too, because he was always reading and a young man who spent that much time with books had to be a Communist. He had managed to flee, revealing himself to Zameen only tonight with that sparrow peck on her window.

Now they led each other back to the djinn's lair, but despite an hour and more of searching they were unable to locate the burial site.

Neither of them knew that during their search Usha had filled up with soldiers. Among the murdered teachers had been the Soviet headmaster of the school and his young family. And tonight the Soviets had retaliated.

Zameen was holding the boy's hand in the thinning darkness at the end of the night when she felt her arm being suddenly tugged downwards, and only then did she realise that he had been shot, the sound of the gun also reaching her now. The Soviet soldiers surrounded her and took her to Usha where the cleric confirmed her identity to them with a nod. She saw the mud on the hem of his trousers.

The mosque was among the first places the soldiers had visited upon entering Usha, rightfully suspecting it of being the possible centre of the resistance, and the cleric – just back from interring his wife – had provided them with a list of names to save his own life. This was a chance for him to eliminate the two lovers also, to make sure what they had seen would go no further. He said Zameen and the boy had participated in the massacre, that they were among the people who had marched through the streets carrying the severed heads of the school's staff, the headmaster's wife and three fair-haired children among them.

LARA STANDS in a corner of the abraded golden room at the top of the house, considering with her serious eyes the expanse of empty floor lying before her. A candle burns in a far alcove. Beside her is a cardboard box and she dips her hand into it without looking. She brings out a piece of plaster on which a set of lips is painted. Taking five steps, she lowers herself into a crouching position and places the smile on the floor.

The hand entering the box again, she brings out this time a painted sprig of foliage. She looks around and decides where this fragment should be placed. A distance of two feet from the dark red mouth.

There is coloured dust on her fingers as though pollen.

Next comes a section from a woman's ribboned hair. She consults her imagination – the outline of the picture she is trying to construct – and then positions the piece on the floor accordingly. Marcus must have saved these from when the room was attacked, the strafing of guns tearing out these details from the walls. How carefully he has washed away the mud even from these fragments. Moving backwards and forwards she positions further pieces. Some are as large as her hand. One has half a face on it, a beauty mark on one cyclamen cheek. There is a whole moth in flight, wings patterned like a backgammon board.

From the candle comes the smell of burning wax and a twisting line of smoke. The image on the floor develops section by section. It is a kind of afterlife she is constructing for all those who have been obliterated from the walls. A young man and a woman made out of the ruins of the dozens in this interior.

He should have brown eyes, she tells herself, and she exchanges them, moving the green irises to the girl's face. Now suddenly he seems disbelieving. A lover is always amazed.

She takes out another fragment and looks at it – a black tulip, a rare flower native to northern Afghanistan. She closes her fist around it until it hurts. In the spring of 1980 a Soviet lieutenant had died holding this blossom, having picked it moments before a sniper's bullet found him. A comrade threaded it into his collar and he came home with it on his chest. Later in the war the large transport planes flying dead soldiers home took the name of Black Tulips, this flower becoming a symbol of death in the Soviet Union.

This is her third time in Afghanistan. Over months and years she tracked down soldiers who knew her brother, gathering vague clues, and then planned a trip. The number of Soviet soldiers still missing here is 311 but that could be one of Moscow's lies, just as the true figure of the dead is closer to fifty thousand, four times the official number. It was said that the general who supervised the initial invasion had shot himself soon afterwards, but for the first several years of the war the Soviet Union would all but deny any casualties. When the dead multiplied, the relatives were discouraged from holding funerals and no mention of Afghanistan was made when occasionally a soldier's death was reported in the newspapers – he simply *died whilst doing his International Duty.* When losses could no longer be denied or stifled it was judged best to make them fantastically heroic, and so wounded Soviet soldiers kept blowing themselves up with grenades in order to take thirty Afghan rebels with them. Lara didn't know at the beginning but Benedikt hadn't died or gone missing in battle – he had defected. Lara herself was under great suspicion as a result of what her brother had done, if things weren't bad enough already because of the activities and opinions of their mother. They wouldn't even tell Lara where in Afghanistan he had been based at the time of his disappearance. Later, as the years progressed and the Soviet Union began to be dismantled, they continued to tell lies or sent her from person to person to exhaust and frustrate her.

But by now a part of the story is clear. Benedikt was with another soldier when he defected, a seventeen-year-old. They both ran away from their military base together but Piotr Danilovich eventually lost courage and went back before he could be missed. He was the last Russian person to have seen Benedikt. By tracking down Piotr Danilovich she has managed to collect Benedikt's last known movements. Their plan, he said, was to simply walk into the nearest Afghan village in the middle of the night carrying weapons stolen from the base to present to the Afghans as a sign of good faith. Thieves of food, of medicine, of the photographs of sweethearts – every soldier had some skill when it came to picking locks; and so Benedikt was to get the guns from the armoury while Piotr Danilovich went into the bedroom of one of the officers, a colonel. In Afghanistan there were deserts whose names conveyed everything about them. *Dasht-e-Margo*, Desert of Death. *Sar-o-Tar*, Empty Desolation. *Dasht-e-Jahanum*, Desert of Hell. And a few months earlier in one such desert, where the temperature had gone beyond fifty degrees, and on the dunes the spiders stitched together sand grains with their silk to make sheets to shelter under, the colonel had come upon an ancient skeleton with a mass of gems scattered on either side of the spinal column, where the stomach would have been. On the night of the desertion, Benedikt sent Piotr Danilovich to the colonel's room – he was to find and swallow these gemstones. When he couldn't get into the safe, he made his way through the darkness to where, having successfully stolen seven Kalashnikovs, Benedikt had emerged from the armoury and run into the colonel. The man was in all probability on his way to help himself to some weapons, Piotr Danilovich told Lara years later, to sell to the Afghan enemy. Piotr watched from the shadows as Benedikt and Colonel Rostov stood looking at each other in silence.

Always hungry, always ill, the weak Soviet antibiotics of little use if ever they were to be had, many soldiers had thought of and talked about deserting, about defecting – an arc of movement in their minds, from Afghanistan to a country in western Europe, perhaps even the United States of America. They had been conscripted and sent out here and they drank antifreeze to escape from life for a few hours or left shoe polish to melt in sunlight and then filtered it through bread to obtain a sip of intoxicant. There were stories about what the Afghan rebels did to captured Soviet soldiers, loathing them as much for being non-Muslim as for being invaders – they who in trying to wipe out one Dashaka machine gun, or a journalist from the West, would literally flatten an entire village. Having dreamt that they had fallen into the clutches of the Afghans, the soldiers sometimes woke up screaming and were unable to fall asleep again for hours. Pillows of thorn. But there were other stories about how the Afghans welcomed defectors, especially if they agreed to convert to Islam.

Time slowed down around them as Benedikt and Rostov faced each other, Piotr watching from the darkness. Rostov had sold a ZPU-1 anti-aircraft gun to an Afghan warlord recently, writing it off as lost in combat, but he had begun to suspect that one of the captains at the base intended to expose him, and so he had ordered the captain and two other men chosen at random – Benedikt and Piotr Danilovich – to carry out a dawn reconnaissance mission in a nearby area, an area notorious as a hive of the most dangerous guerrillas. It was to be tomorrow. And although for safety reasons it was customary to take two vehicles, Rostov insisted the three of them take only one. Benedikt and Piotr had dreamed about desertion often but tonight was truly their last chance.

Piotr watched as Benedikt lowered the Kalashnikovs from his shoulders, time accelerating now. A forward lurch of Benedikt's body towards Rostov. Piotr would tell

Lara that he felt the slam of the body, saying he knew it was packed solid with fury at the abuse and drunken humiliation suffered by all the young soldiers at the hands of the officers. The blade moved back and forth three times. Twice in the stomach, and then again in the ribs. The man fell onto his side on the ground, one arm pinned under him, the other raised half-way in the air, the wet index finger trembling.

When Piotr and Benedikt were more than a mile from their military base, running towards the village they knew lay ahead in the darkness, Benedikt had stopped suddenly. 'We have to go back.' And he wouldn't take another step, just shook his head when Piotr asked him to forget about the gemstones.

'No, not the jewels. We have to go back for the girl.'

'No.'

'She'll die.'

'Better her than me.'

'Most of Rostov's blood is on my clothes. He was alive when we left him so we either go back to make sure he is dead or we get the girl. They'll kill her in trying to save him.'

Death by exsanguination. The Soviet Army would kill prisoners by draining them of blood whenever transfusions were required for its battle-wounded soldiers.

The girl, Zameen her name was, had not provided any information regarding the rebellion after she was captured, though others had been made to talk successfully, and then it was discovered that Rostov and she had the same rare blood type. She was separated from the other prisoners. On one occasion Rostov even took her with him when he visited another city in case he sustained a serious injury there.

Benedikt led Piotr to a small wooden bridge and told him to wait underneath it, and, astonishingly, he was back with the girl in just over two hours. Rostov, he said, had dragged himself into the armoury, smearing red on the floor as he went, and though he was still alive at the end of that path of blood Benedikt had gone to the small room where Zameen was kept.

She was as dazed as she had always been – she had not uttered a word or made a sound since her capture – but now she spoke, startling them, saying Piotr and Benedikt must change the direction of their journey. She said she would take them to a place called Usha and then a little further beyond that to the house of her parents. Piotr was certain she was leading them into a trap – a month ago three Soviet soldiers were found hanging cut up in a butcher's shop. The time he had spent alone in the darkness had altered him, when he had felt like a castaway on a vast black ocean, fears accumulating around him. Now terrified, he wanted to go back to the base. He arrived just before Rostov was discovered, and he was among the soldiers who were sent out into the night to hunt for Benedikt and the girl – but they were not to be found.

The breeze rustles through the branches of the silk-cotton tree. Lara has heard this sound captured on the recording of the bird that Marcus had made in this garden decades ago.

Another few days and then she'll leave, another few days of sitting beside his aged form as they both drink the bright red tea he loves, a vague smile occasionally on his lips when he glances up from a page to tell her something. A Prospero on his island.

The mountain range looms above the house. On those quartz and feldspar heights at the end of 2001, American soldiers had ceremonially buried a piece of debris taken from the ruins of the World Trade Center, after the terrorists up there had either been slaughtered or been made to flee. Before these soldiers flew out to attack Afghanistan, the US secretary of defense told them they had been 'commissioned by history'.

We sharpened the bones of your victim and made a dagger to kill you, and here now we lay the weapon to rest.

No. Perhaps something sacred is meant to grow out of the fragment of rubble. She thinks of the Church of the Resurrection on the banks of Griboyedov Canal in St Petersburg. It is known also as the Saviour of the Spilled Blood, built as it was on the spot where a bomb thrown by a member of the People's Will revolutionary movement had mortally wounded Alexander II in 1881. The canal was narrowed so the altar could stand exactly where the royal blood had stained the pavement.

Always like a distant ache within her is the thought of landmines, so she cannot bring herself to go too far into the garden. She has seen single shoes being sold in Afghanistan's shops.

She goes back into the house. Dusk, the hour between the butterfly and the moth. Standing in the dark kitchen she drinks water from a glass. She places the glass on the table and remains still, listening to her breath.

She has told him everything she knows about Zameen and Benedikt, all that Piotr Danilovich related to her.

'Did they come to this house?' she asked. 'They were on their way here at the point where Piotr Danilovich's story breaks off.'

'Qatrina and I were not here at that time – the house was taken over by others,' he replied, looking at her. The bereaved glance. 'I don't know if she brought him here. I had gone to a village to the west of here, where a battle between the Soviet Army and the rebels had left almost a hundred civilians wounded. Women and children mostly. The Cold War was cold only for the rich and privileged places of the planet. Qatrina remained here while I was away. There was no knowing when a doctor would be needed *here*. I returned to find her missing and was told that she had been taken away by the warlord Gul Rasool, the man from Usha who was one of the resistance leaders in this area. He wanted her to accompany his men into battle to treat the wounded. Nabi Khan, the other resistance leader from here, a great rival and enemy of Gul Rasool then as now, had the same idea soon enough and came to get *me*. There was nothing left here, no one in the house.'

'Then as now, you say?'

'Yes. Only the dead have seen the end of war. Gul Rasool is the sole power in Usha now, and Nabi Khan is out there somewhere plotting to unseat him.'

She looks at the moon caught in a windowpane, great in size and brightness both. It seems that to shatter it would be to flood this room and then the entire garden and orchard with luminous liquid. In the 1950s, when the Soviet Union was ahead of the United States in the space race, the US Air Force had asked scientists to plan a nuclear explosion on the moon. People would see a bright flash, and clouds of debris would probably also be visible. Higher than they would be on Earth because of the difference in gravity. She knows from the tales of her cosmonaut father, someone who fell towards Earth in a burning machine, that Moscow had also had the idea of a nuclear blast. Yes, after such a demonstration who wouldn't cower beneath a nuclear-armed Soviet moon, a nuclear-armed American moon? It never happened but she wonders if the terrorists didn't come close to something like it in 2001, an enormous spectacle seen by the entire world, planting awe and shock in every heart.

She leans against the wall and closes her eyes.

Even if she hadn't fallen ill she would have considered asking Marcus for a short refuge when she met him, letting a portion of her weight onto another, being held. While almost everyone else gave it to understand that shame must accompany failure, because you obviously weren't wise or strong or brave enough to have prevented a derailment of your life, Marcus seemed one of those few humans who lent dignity to everything their gaze landed on. Like a saint entering your life through a dream. To him she would have admitted that the years have left her bewildered by life.

In the topmost room she looks at the fragments she had arranged on the floor. The two lovers summon up an army of ghostly lovers, the man embodying every other man, the woman symbolising every other woman, all imperilled.

In Usha they know Marcus Caldwell by his Muslim name. He believes in no god but had converted to Islam to marry Qatrina, to silence any objection. Like him she would have been satisfied with a non-religious ceremony, indifferent to the idea of supreme beings and their holy messengers, but she had agreed on condition that a woman perform the rites. 'We have to help change things,' she said. 'Nowhere does the Koran state that only men may conduct the wedding.'

These days, Marcus seldom says more than a few words to anyone in Usha, communicating in the bazaar with just nods and gestures as much as he can and then leaving. He knows he is not the only casualty in this place. Afghanistan had collapsed and everyone's life now lies broken at different levels within the rubble. Some are trapped near the surface while others find themselves entombed deeper down, pinned under tons of smashed masonry and shattered beams from where their cries cannot be heard by anyone on the surface, only – and inconsequentially – by those around them.

Yes, he knows he is not the only one who is suffering but he cannot be sure who among the inhabitants of Usha had been present the day Qatrina was put to death by the Taliban. A public spectacle after the Friday prayers, the stoning of a sixty-one-year-old adulteress. A rain of bricks and rocks, her punishment for living in sin, the thirty-nine-year marriage to Marcus void in the eyes of the Taliban because the ceremony had been conducted by a female. A microphone had been placed close to her for her screams to be heard clearly by everyone.

He began to avoid the light of the sun, keeping to the hours of darkness as much as possible. He took every clock and watch in the house and put them away in a drawer. At first the ticking was amplified entreatingly by the wood but one by one they all came to a standstill, as though suffocated. In this way he removed the sense and measurement of time from his surroundings. He knocked onto its side the pedestal bearing the sundial in the garden. A time of deepest darkness. The numerals painted on the sundial might as well have been dates engraved on a tombstone. The food in the cupboards ran out and he had nothing to eat. The entire world it seemed had fought in this country, had made mistakes in this country, but mistakes had consequences and he didn't know who to blame for those consequences. Afghanistan itself, Russia, the United States, Britain, Arabia, Pakistan? One day he thought of capturing a bulbul that had flown into the house. In the end he knew he could never eat anything he had heard sing.

He recalled the desolation that used to occasionally overpower his mother, a sadness at whose very centre lay his father's death. Marcus's father was a doctor in the

Afghan frontier and was murdered by a tribesman in 1934, a few months before his birth. The motive for the killing was never established though the killer had a son who had recently declared an interest in Christianity. The family had tried starving him, but when it didn't have an effect the father tied a grenade to the son and threatened to pull the pin if he did not renew his vow of faith in Islam. Having murdered his son this way, he set out to take revenge on the doctors at the missionary hospital where the boy had come into contact with ideas that made an unbeliever of him. No attempt at conversion was made at the hospital but a chapter from the Gospels was indeed read in the wards every night.

Marcus's mother continued as a nurse in the heart of the British Empire's most turbulent province, returning to England only when Marcus was five years old. Kabul, Kandahar, Peshawar, Quetta – some of the earliest words he heard were the names of these cities of Asia. And he visited them during the years of his young adulthood, meeting the stately Qatrina in Kabul and continuing the friendship and romance when she moved to London to study medicine. Coming to live with her beside the lake near Usha, thirty miles from the city of Jalalabad, the city that sent its narcissus into the snow-bound Februaries of Kabul four hours away.

Flour and other basics. That red tea. Kerosene for the lamp. He rarely goes into Usha now, left alone by them all, his first reaction that of mild incredulity whenever someone approaches him. They can see me. And then this week a man drew near and told him about Lara, told him about a woman who was waiting for him two streets away, having come on the daily bus from Jalalabad the day before. They can see me. Some aspect of this he had sensed in the woman he was brought to, her inwardness so intense she could scarcely bring herself to speak or meet another's eye. She stood up and smiled at him weakly. He saw the unslept eyes, the blue-black neck. The tiredness and the large bruise were physical but they seemed connected with her spirit somewhere.

He picked up her suitcase and they began the journey to his house. There were no words during the walk along the lake's rim. Later he discovered that the clothes in the suitcase were damp. She explained that during her long journey towards him she had seen a girl raise a fire in front of a house and heat a basin of water to bleach some fabric. After she had finished and was about to pour away the leftover liquid, Lara had moved forward and asked if she could submerge her own three spare sets of clothes into it. Wanting that white suddenly, that blankness. The sole ornament on her now was a necklace of very fine beads like a row of eggs laid along the collarbones by insects.

Her gaze on the Buddha's giant face, Lara sits on the lowest step of the staircase in the perfume factory. She looks at the features of the beautiful young man. He feels vulnerable and intimate, as if facing someone in bed.

Dressed in black, the Taliban that day in March 2001 were preparing to dynamite the head when one of them had contemptuously fired a round of bullets into the stone face smiling to itself. In some versions of the events of that day, a ghost had appeared in Marcus's house to put the sinister malevolent figures to flight. But others insist it was the occurrence down here in the perfume factory. They carried Qatrina away with them, to her eventual public execution, and would have taken Marcus also if not for what happened here.

After the gun was fired into the horizontal face it was noticed that a small point of light had materialised in each bullet hole, a softly hesitating sparkle. Over the next few instants, as more and more of the men took notice and stared uncomprehendingly, each of these spots grew in brilliance and acquired a liquid glint. Welling up in the stone wounds, the gold eventually poured out and began to slide down the features very slowly, striping the face, collecting in unevenly spaced pools on the floor.

As though they had come out of a trance, the men in defiant rage sent another dozen bullets into the idol but with the same result. In addition he now seemed to be opening fully his almost shut eyes, the lids chiselled in the stone beginning to rise without sound in what felt like an endless moment.

2

Building the New

THE AMERICAN MAN, David Town, is awakened just before sunrise by a muezzin. The first two words of the call to the Muslim prayer are also the Muslim battle cry, he remarks to himself as he lies in the darkness, never having seen the connection before.

The voice is issuing from a minaret three blocks away, dissolving into the air of Jalalabad, the city that surrounds him. He has travelled through most of this country over the decades, his work as a dealer in precious stones bringing him to the amber mines of Kandahar, taking him to Badakshan for the rubies that Marco Polo had written of in his *Description of the World*. The war-financing emeralds of the Panjshir Valley. He found the River Murghab to be so full of rapids it could have been the Colorado.

He listens to the voice continuing as he falls asleep again. *Come to worship*, it says, *Come to happiness.*

An hour later he gets up and walks out to a nearby teahouse. There is a samovar, and bread is being pulled out of the clay oven buried in the ground in the corner. He remembers Marcus Caldwell telling him tea is an ingredient in some perfumes. Maybe it was Zameen, passing on knowledge absorbed from her father. We learn in detail that which is most insistent around us. The desert people make good astronomers.

To the left of him a *chakor* partridge bites the bars of its cage. They are a gregarious bird, moving in large family groups in the wild, but are kept like this all across Afghanistan. The place becomes more and more busy as daylight increases, the road full of traffic. Vans and lorries, animals and humans. Wrapped in a coarse blanket he occupies a far chair, nodding and saying *salam-a-laikam* whenever someone new arrives to take a seat near by. He sits with his quiet watchful air. A cap unscrewed from a missile serves as a sugar bowl in this place. He can see the words *Death to America* and *Kill Infidels* daubed in Pashto, in two different paints and two different scripts, on a near-by wall. A news hawker enters, a child of six at most, and a man buys a magazine with Osama bin Laden on the cover, photographed as always with the Kalashnikov of a Soviet soldier he had killed here in the 1980s.

'Marcus?'

David, walking back from breakfast, calls out towards the figure on the other side of the narrow lane.

The man with the white beard stops and looks up and then comes to him, taking him into his arms, a long word-less hug. Just a few smeared noises from the throat.

'I didn't know you were in the country,' Marcus says when they separate.

'Why are you in the city?'

'I came yesterday. A shopkeeper in Usha, who recently visited Jalalabad, told me about a boy in his twenties who could be . . . our Bihzad.' That was the name Zameen had chosen for her son. Bihzad – the great fifteenth century master of Persian miniature painting, born here in what is now Afghanistan, in Herat. 'David, he remembers a lot of things, remembers her name.'

'Where is he?' He looks at Marcus, the eyes that are the eyes of a wounded animal.

'I met him yesterday. I spent last night with him.' Marcus points to the minaret with the high domed top in the distance, a brass crescent at its pinnacle. 'Up there. He makes the call to prayer from up there.'

'Then I think I heard him at dawn.'

'We spent almost the entire night talking, or rather I talked. He is a little withdrawn, distant. There was something fraught about him occasionally.' From his pocket Marcus takes out a key with a cord threaded through its eye. 'He gave me this. Come, I'll take you up there.'

'What about the scar?' The child had burned himself on a flame.

'Yes, I saw it.'

'He's up there now?'

'He said he had a few things to do but he'll be back. I came yesterday morning, thinking I'll go back on the evening bus but the service was cancelled. So I had to stay.'

'I'll drive you back this afternoon.' A journey along vineyards that produced bunches of grapes the length of his forearm. 'I was going to come see you in the next few days anyway.'

'I should have returned as planned. She spent last night

49

alone.' Marcus stops. 'David, there is a woman back at the house.'

'Yes?'

'She's Russian.'

He'd kept on walking and is two steps ahead of Marcus, but now he halts. 'A Russian?'

'Larissa Petrovna. She says her brother was a soldier who knew Zameen.'

David nods. The older man does not say the Soviet soldier's name but David hears it in his head anyway. Benedikt Petrovich. The man who fathered Zameen's child through repeated assault, the child David later called his own son, who it is possible has grown up to be the young man at the top of the minaret over there, the sunlight making the crescent appear as though it's on fire. At the military base Benedikt Petrovich guarded the room where Zameen was kept, and he unbolted the door night after night and went in to her.

'David, did Zameen ever talk about a Soviet soldier, about twenty-four years old?'

'No. Never. So what kind of things does this Bihzad remember?'

A camel goes by with the burnt-out shell of a car fastened upside down to its back, the high metal object lurching at every step.

When David met Zameen, in the Pakistani city of Peshawar, Bihzad was four and was taught to think of David as his father. It was a matter of months after that that Zameen died and the boy disappeared. Lost as he was at such an early age, how surprising it seems that he has

50

managed to carry with him even his name. Holding onto that one possession over the violent chaotic years.

'He remembers Zameen telling him Qatrina was a doctor, seemed to have forgotten that I was one too, though he knew I had some connection with England. He remembers you, remembers Peshawar – all very vaguely.'

David has looked for him for nearly twenty years, making a number of journeys towards hints of him, always unsure about how much someone can remember from when they were four or five. It must be different for different people. There have been several leads in the past, one or two as compelling as this one, but nothing came of them. He is forty-eight this year, and from among his own early memories the earliest is of experiencing a strong emotion – which he would in later life learn to call love – towards what a set of coloured pencils did on a piece of paper, those brilliant lines and marks with a thin layer of light trembling on them. He always wanted those pencils near. He has calculated that he must have been about three. But he has no personal recollection of something that is said to have occurred at a slightly later age, something that is family legend – of him sinking his teeth into the leg of the doctor who was about to give his brother Jonathan a vaccine shot, Jonathan weeping with fear at the needle.

Marcus unlocks the door at the base of the minaret and they enter in silence, climbing the staircase that spirals upwards at the centre. Most minarets are narrow, merely architectural details these days, but this staircase is wide enough for horses. Half-way up there is a large hole that must have been caused by a stray rocket during one of the many battles the area has seen in the previous decades, one of the many wars. It is as though someone had bitten off the side of the tower.

At the very top is the landing and then a door opens onto a balcony that runs around the minaret, a circular terrace just under the dome, exposed to the sunlight at this hour.

'Does he actually live up here?' They passed a cotton mattress on the landing. A small tin trunk stood open to reveal things for making tea. Powdered milk spilling from a twist of newspaper headlines. And out here there is evidence on the floor of a small fire of splintered wood, of burnt thorn and twig. There is a cot for sitting, its ropes frayed. He thinks of the summer months with their dust storms, palls of them rising up and burying the city for twenty minutes each time.

'This area is without electricity at dawn so they can't use the loudspeaker to make the call to prayer. Someone has to come up here and do it physically. He does that, but he actually lives somewhere else.' He points to the east. 'In that neighbourhood.'

They are standing on the balcony, looking at the city below. Above them is a roof of corrugated iron on which the claws of pigeons can be heard.

'He said they used to give lessons in the Koran to the djinn up here, a long time ago. They came to the mosque down there at first but their presence was too overwhelming for humans, a child or two fainting with awe. So this minaret was built for them to walk up to without being seen or felt by humans. Bihzad says no one wants to be the muezzin, afraid in case the effect of the djinn still lingers.'

'What does he look like? And when will he be back?'

'Around noon. I told him I must go back home before night falls.'

David nods. 'So this Russian woman – Larissa Petrovna, you said her name is.'

'Lara. She'll go back in a few days. She won't say much but she lost her husband two years ago and is obviously in a time of darkness. She keeps apologising for being a burden on me even though it's not a problem in the least. She is an art historian at the Hermitage in St Petersburg. You are sure Zameen never mentioned a Soviet soldier named Benedikt?'

'Absolutely.'

'You'll meet her. But you haven't told me what you are doing here. Listen to the birds, David, their wing beats.' He is sitting on the cot, his back against the wall. 'It feels strange to be away from the house after so long. I look at this ceiling and for a second expect to see books nailed up there.'

David looks at the panorama of the city while listening to him, the mountain range in the hazy distance.

'The large book of Bihzad's paintings had required three nails to stay in place on the ceiling. Such brutality had to be inflicted on it to prevent it from being burned to ashes – and here was a man so subtle he painted with a brush that ended in a single hair picked from a squirrel's throat.'

David's first concern is Marcus: how much has his Russian visitor told him about her brother's assaults on

Zameen? The shock would be devastating to him, but how much does she know herself? Zameen had hidden nothing from David but he has always been careful not to reveal too much to Marcus – or to Qatrina when she was alive. Qatrina who died in 2001, the long-ago spring of 2001 when the United States believed itself to be at peace, believed itself to be safe and immune from all this.

The Englishman's eyes are closed now, the birds coming and going on the roof.

Zameen told him how she heard the door open that night, heard Benedikt enter the room in the darkness. Strangely he didn't approach her bed as he had done over the previous nine occasions. He closed the door behind him but didn't bolt it. A chain, hanging from a ring on the wall beside her wooden bed, was attached to an iron band around her wrist, so she couldn't rush for the open door. His breath was rapid and shallow as though he'd been running. He whispered her name and struck a matchstick alight. Speaking in English, a language he knew brokenly from his mother, he said he was defecting and that she must go with him, said he had made it out of the base safely earlier tonight but had turned back for her.

When during his assaults she had wanted to scream but had been unable to, her hands – out of humiliation and rage – had flown at him, raking his skin, but now she listened, looking at his face in the yellow light which soon ran out.

'Here is the key for your wrist.' She heard something land by her feet. Like a raindrop on a leaf. He drew closer. One time he had fallen asleep beside her for a few seconds after the act and she had heard that breathing stretch much deeper.

She did not move towards the key, shaking her head even though it was dark. And so he lit another match and told her that Rostov lay bleeding out there and that she must know she would be drained of blood to save him. 'Don't make me go and kill him.' There was pleading in the whispered voice, as when, his thirst quenched, he sometimes asked her to forgive him for what he had just done. During the daylight hours he was ashamed of what he did to her, but again and again in the darkness he found himself approaching her, ready to subdue, dizzy and almost sick with longing and desire and power.

Picking up the key she released her hand from the chain.

Out there, after an hour's running through the darkness, they came to another soldier, another defector. Zameen persuaded them that they must go to Usha, but Piotr Danilovich left them soon after they set out. From within the darkness of an orchard, the flowers and the perfume of apricot trees, Zameen and Benedikt watched the small group of soldiers from the Soviet base arrive to look for them. After they had gone and the two of them were thinking of continuing towards Usha, they became aware of another possible danger, another set of voices close by. It was dark but the sky was beginning to lighten in the east, a few very faint lazuli strokes. The sound and movement of the Soviet soldiers must have attracted people from the nearby village, or perhaps they had been here among the apricot trees all along and had stilled themselves earlier. To avoid Soviet gunships many farmers went to work in their fields and orchards only at night, accompanied by small lamps.

Benedikt told her to wait as he went forward on his elbows to investigate, raising himself to a crouching position and then disappearing from view. She would never see him again or know what happened to him, what kind of life he walked into, what kind of death. The orchard was vast, and there were many others around it, but he had said he would find her easily because somehow they had ended up within a clump of three trees that were the only ones among the hundreds that were not in flower. She curled herself in the high grass and perhaps fell asleep beside the stolen Kalashnikovs. When next her mind focused, the voices out there had grown in number and dawn had arrived, and now she saw, as though hallucinating, that the branches above her had blossomed with the first rays of the sun, the late buds opening at last, hatching white-pink scraps against the clear blue of the sky.

David walks around the circular balcony and looks out at the distant peaks in that direction. The city of Jalalabad is flanked to the north by the Hindu Kush and to the south by the White Mountains, the chain standing over Marcus's house. Looking at a relief map David always feels that if you grabbed Afghanistan at the borders and pulled, so great is the number of hills and mountains here, you'd end up with an area ten times its current size.

Marcus comes and joins him on this side of the minaret, both of them looking towards where his house is. The Buddha is said to have visited this valley to slay the demon Gopala, and Chinese pilgrims have written of the sacred relics once housed in shrines here. A fragment of the Buddha's skull entirely covered in gold leaf. A *stupa* erected where he clipped his fingernails. The city resisted the spread of Islam until the tenth century.

'She spent the night alone in the house,' Marcus says quietly. 'I should have gone back.'

'I am sure she's fine,' David replies; he has nothing to base that on but he doesn't know what else to say. He is in Jalalabad because he is financing a number of schools in the country. He has kept himself in the background, just letting a group of committed and intelligent local people get on with the details. Even the selecting of the name has been left to them and they want Tameer-e-Nau Afghanistan School. Building the New Afghanistan. The branch in this city became operational a fortnight ago, and he is here to see it, spending last night there, the dog in the building next door disturbing his sleep throughout. Before leaving the United States he tried to contact Marcus, and then again repeatedly on entering Afghanistan, but the satellite phone he had left him on one of his previous visits wouldn't ring.

'There is no electricity to recharge it,' Marcus says in reply when he raises the subject now.

'What about the generator?'

'It seems too much to turn that on just for the phone.'

Present in his voice is the fear that he would not be

understood, would appear contrary. So David touches his sleeve, 'It's all right. I worry about you. I won't lie and say I don't sometimes wish you would leave Afghanistan, but' – he raises his hand – 'I know, it's your home, and if you weren't here we would not have been able to learn about this young man.'

It's minimal, his life, requiring adjustments on a weekly if not daily basis. Once David arrived from the USA to find a camel tied in the orchard for her milk. Once there was a ewe and a lamb. Some ducks, a stand of ripening corn. Items from the house are taken or sent to Kabul's antique merchants sometimes. Most of the money David forces on him every year is, he's sure, still around untouched, or has been given to others.

'Can we see your school from here?' His skin is dyed to fawn after the decades of strong sunlight and heat, making him look almost like a native of this country, maybe someone from the Nuristan province.

'Yes. It's not far from here. Just follow that curved street, then along that road – see those palm trees? It's the yellow building just beyond them, next to the big white one.'

'I see it. So great is the love of a male palm tree for the female palm tree, that it always grows leaning at an angle towards it, even if it is in a neighbouring garden. Did you know?'

The city centre down there is full of citrus trees, this valley being famous for its orange blossom, verse makers from across Afghanistan gathering in Jalalabad in mid-April every year for a Poets' Conference to recite poems dedicated to the blossom.

David rubs his face with his large hands. 'We have a view of all sides from here, like the Pentagon in Washington, DC.'

'And the wooden O of Shakespeare's Globe Theatre.'

They stare at the mountain range, the blue and white ridges. The air can be very thin on some of those heights. The US Army has discovered that at times the blades of its helicopters cannot find enough purchase to get airborne from there, the machines swaying a few feet off the ground.

Even the air of this country has a story to tell about warfare. It is possible here to lift a piece of bread from a plate and, following it back to its origins, collect a dozen stories concerning war – how it affected the hand that pulled it out of the oven, the hand that kneaded the dough, how war impinged upon the field where the wheat was grown.

PARTICIPATING IN some battle when he was about ten years old, Bihzad had seen a fire break out in the long dried grasses of the meadow where the dead and the dying lay. He remembers feeling ashamed because his pangs of hunger had increased with the smell of roasting meat.

He now opens his eyes onto opium flowers. He moves along the edge of the field, the white-streaked pink blossoms swaying in the late-morning breeze. From Jalalabad up until a moment earlier, he was blindfolded. The man who had uncovered his eyes is now guiding him towards a building beyond the expanse of poppies.

He has been brought here before. It was three days earlier, another journey with the sense of sight disabled. Now too he is delivered from person to person inside the building. At one door there is a coded set of knocks. Three times, pause, twice, then a final twice. It's been changed since the previous occasion, he notices.

'So you are clear on all the details?' says the man who leads him down a dark staircase. 'You are to drive the truck out of here and park it outside the new school, between the tree with the red flowers and the large signboard that shows the public how to recognise different landmines.'

Bihzad has not been introduced to anyone by name here but, during an unexpected moment of tenderness during the previous visit, he had felt emboldened enough to ask this man if his name was indeed Casa, having overheard one of the others refer to him as that. The man had agreed with a quick almost-soundless 'Yes', and then gently grabbed Bihzad's collar, telling him he mustn't try to be too clever. Everyone else he has encountered here is dour and tense, exuding unrelenting distrust and hostility.

Now Casa tells him, firmly, 'Do not deviate from your instructions in any way.'

They enter a room below ground where on a shelf, lit by a small bulb from above, there are two square frames containing the calligraphed names of Allah and Muhammad, peace be upon him. Between them, in a glass box, is a mounted mongoose with its teeth sunk into the edge of a cobra's hood, the serpent's black length wrapped three times around the body of its adversary. A figure sits crosslegged on a bed in the dimly lit other side of the room. The Kalashnikov in his lap has a second magazine taped to the first. Casa deferentially presents Bihzad to him and takes a few steps back.

His power and authority within this group is obvious, and he addresses Bihzad in measured tones: 'You have been shown what to do? You'll press the button attached to the red wires and get out of the truck and walk away.'

'It won't go off while the children are still inside the school, will it?'

'Do not doubt our word,' the man says quietly but with an edge to the voice. Earlier Casa had said Bihzad was being given the honour of doing this for Islam and for Afghanistan. 'Aren't you troubled that boys are being brainwashed in there,' Casa asks now, 'and girls taught to be immodest?'

The man raises a hand towards Casa. A thin blanket is draped on his shoulders, open in the middle as though to expose his pure transparent heart. He must have been writing something earlier because there is ink on his fingers. 'We have no remote controls, and the timers we have are not very sophisticated either. Otherwise we wouldn't have had to involve you, would have just left the truck outside that school built and owned by Americans. Someone has to park the vehicle and set the timer going on site. The explosion will happen hours later. You must know that Allah and the prophet Muhammad, peace be upon him, will be greatly happy with you.'

Bihzad has been told how this operation is just the beginning, a demonstration to attract and obtain help for bigger things. The man in this basement room, once a great fêted warrior, cannot return to his native village, a place Bihzad has overheard being referred to as Usha. An enemy has appropriated power there, having accepted money and weapons from the Americans at the end of 2001 to help uproot the Taliban and al-Qaeda. But soon this enemy – these men called him a traitor to Islam and Afghanistan – would be made to regret everything, happy though he is for the time being because he has been given a place in the government of the province. A large-scale raid is being planned for Usha, a spectacular offensive to drive out that unbeliever and his American-paid fighters and bodyguards. There will be a war.

The building next to the school was their original target, a warehouse belonging to their great enemy, but they would be delighted to see the school reduced to rubble as well.

Someone from inside the school has informed them, Casa told Bihzad, that the school's American owner is visiting, staying in the building for a few days. That is why they are keen to go ahead with this operation, unable to wait for the proper equipment to arrive. To kill an American would send out a big message.

Every American who dies here, said Casa, dies with a look of disbelief on his face, disbelief that this faraway and insignificant place had given rise to a people capable of affecting the destiny of someone from a nation as great as his.

The Americans too had blindfolded Bihzad when they took him to their detention centre at the Bagram military base, one of the many prisons they have established here to hold suspected al-Qaeda members. Someone had betrayed him to them in exchange for reward money. Night and day every prisoner cursed those Muslims – the *munafikeen!* – who had sold them to the Americans for $5,000 each. Though at one level everyone in there was happy because Allah had especially chosen him to suffer for Islam. There wasn't a speck of dust in that place that didn't make Bihzad want to scream – apart from anything else there was the constant fear that he might be transferred to Guantanamo Bay – but he had felt very close to Allah during those months, everyone spending every spare minute in prayer, the environment there much more spiritual than anything he has been able to find on the outside. Every day, his life shifting its centre, he slips into worldly longings and wants instead. May Allah forgive him but, the reward so alluring, he has even fantasised once or twice about approaching the Americans and telling them someone innocent in his neighbourhood is a member of al-Qaeda.

His main reason for agreeing to carry out today's task is the money these people will pay him afterwards.

The smell of disturbed earth is intense around him, this airless sunken chamber.

'Don't forget that not only did the Americans imprison you, they caused your sister to die. This is how you'll repay them,' says the man. 'She wasn't your real sister though, right?'

'No.' They had met in an orphanage when they were children and he began calling her sister. He had always treated her as though she was.

From his pocket the man takes a folded piece of paper and hands it to Casa. 'It's a statement I have prepared,' he says. 'The statement that will be issued to television and radio after the blast. And, you'll notice, I have decided to give our organisation the same name as the school. Building the New Afghanistan – I approve of what it conveys.'

He invites Bihzad to sit beside him and, taking his hand in his, begins to read aloud verses from the Koran – not always accurately, Bihzad notices. Muhammad, peace be upon him, had appeared in the dreams of many at the Bagram prison. And one night Christ had visited Bihzad, carrying the Koran in his right hand, the Bible in the left.

When Bihzad made to kiss his forehead, Christ asked someone, 'Who is he?' Upon learning that Bihzad was a prisoner of the Americans, the great prophet came forward and kissed *his* brow. He apologised for the Christians who had incarcerated Muslims in various locations around the world. Bihzad was shaken awake at that point by the other prisoners: they had been brought out of their sleep by the concentrated fragrance issuing from Bihzad's forehead. He told them that that was where Christ had placed his lips, and they wiped the scented sweat from his brow and ran it over their own clothes.

'The desire to rid my country of infidels and traitors,' the man says upon coming to the end of his recital and releasing Bihzad's hand, 'has made a fugitive of me. I would have loved to have carried out this task myself, but I cannot even step outside without fear of being apprehended, cannot even use a phone because the Americans are listening in and could send down a missile.'

Back at ground level, Casa says of him, 'He skinned alive a Soviet soldier with his own hands before you and I were probably even born. It was done slowly to increase the suffering. They say it took four hours and he was alive for the first two. Apparently some parts are simple like skinning a fruit, others tricky. Around that time he had had his photograph taken whilst shaking Ronald Reagan's hand, in whose infidel heart Allah in His wisdom had planted a deep hatred of the Soviet Union.'

As they walk out of the building Casa produces a set of keys. Bihzad understands they are for the truck, suddenly terrified more than ever, no strength in any of his muscles.

He has to go through with this, he tells himself. Later he'll go and talk to the Englishman, continue to pretend to be his missing grandson. Nodding sometimes vigorously, sometimes uncertainly, when the old man attempts to jog his memory. I do remember that. No, I have no recollection of that. The aged man must be rich – a doctor. He'd heard about the Englishman a while ago, and sent a message out to him saying he was his grandson Bihzad. He had been told that the missing child had a small scar due to an accident with a candle, and he had duplicated the burn on himself, the flesh taking a month to heal. The name is the only real thing he shares with the lost grandson.

Maybe he'll get to go to England. A chance at last to make something of his life. Even find love: become someone's, have someone become his. There was once a girl he had loved, a girl he still thinks about, but because he had no means and no prospects, her family had humiliated him when he brought them his proposal.

The truck is parked, as docile-looking as a cow, against a nearby wall. Bihzad and Casa walk towards it, going past two figures sitting on stationary motorbikes under a mulberry tree. A black pickup van arrives through the entrance gate and Casa raises his hand to stay Bihzad. Men appear from all corners of the building now, the vehicle coming to a stop, and from the back seat an old man is pulled out by the chain around his neck, a look of absolute horror on his face. His hair, beard and clothes dusty, he is led away like a reluctant performing bear, held by that chain, and Casa tells Bihzad that he was an employee with the organisation until his sudden disappearance some years before. A dollar note was found stitched in the lining of the coat he had forgotten to take with him. 'There is a chance he is an informer, obliging the group to relocate to this farm,' Casa says as they continue towards the truck. Bihzad knows the punishment for betrayal. With a funnel and a length of tubing they'll pour acid or boiling water into the man's rectum. That and much more, and then they'll slit his throat. Nor would a confession mean freedom – it would just mean they'll kill him sooner, it would mean less torture.

The motorbikes wake to noisy life, the smell of fumes recognisable in the air within moments. The two riders will guide Bihzad towards the city. And Bihzad understands now – as though the pungent scent has brought the knowledge with it – that he will be followed into the city as well by these armed men, right up to the school, in case he changes his mind and tries to abandon the truck or inform the police.

The men bring the motorbikes over to the truck. They use the trailing ends of their turbans to cover the lower halves of their faces, just the eyes showing, as riders must to avoid the exhaust and dust of traffic. Bihzad climbs in behind the steering wheel, trying to control the rhythm of his breathing. He has been shown how the cushion of the passenger seat can be easily detached and lifted: underneath is the pair of insulated wires leading to the switch he has to throw upon parking the truck outside the school. There is a button he must press after the switch, and then he must walk away from the vehicle.

Casa had demonstrated and explained everything on the previous visit, sitting on the floor in a back room. Bihzad and Casa – in that interior filled with crates of rocket-propelled grenades, packets of explosives that smelled like almonds, and boxes full of DVDs and CDs depicting jihad as Allah the Almighty saw it and not as the world's media distorted it – had then talked about their childhoods: the hunger, the refugee camps, the deaths one by one of the adults around them due to various causes, the orphanages, the beatings and worse, the earning of daily bread as beggars or labourers in the bazaars. Neither remembered the date or place of his birth, nor had any firm memory of his mother and father. Pointing to the lengths of blue, green, red and yellow wires that lay around them, Casa said:

'When I was a child I had knocked over a basket of silk embroidery threads, probably belonging to my mother. That's the only thing I remember of her. The threads suddenly unspooled along the floor in many brilliant lines and then went out of the open door and down a staircase.' He fell silent and then said through a sigh, 'Yes, that's the only thing I remember.'

Now Casa comes forward and shuts the truck door, sealing Bihzad in.

With the vehicle just beyond biting point, he rolls out of the gate set in the boundary wall of the farmhouse, the wrinkled colour of the thousand poppies now behind him.

The road is lit by the late-morning sun. One of the riders is in front of him and the other he can see in the

68

rear-view mirror. It seems it is of no concern to these people that Bihzad now knows where the farmhouse is
situated. On the previous occasion he was picked up at the
outskirts of Jalalabad and blindfolded before being
brought to the farmhouse, and the procedure was the
same again when he was taken back to the edge of the city.
But this time they have let him drive out of there with full
knowledge of how to find the place again. An additional
few moments and everything is perfectly clear to him: the
instant he throws the switch the bomb will be armed – and
the instant he presses the button the truck will explode. It's
not a timer, but a detonator.

He feels as though his heart is clamped in someone's
fist. And when, at a gentle curve in the road, his shadow
begins to inch towards the passenger seat, the feeling
intensifies. He experiences this dread whenever he is in an
area not yet swept for landmines – wanting always to pull
his shadow closer to him, thinking the weight of it is
enough to set off whatever death-dealing device is hidden
there.

He has no choice, and nothing but Allah's compassion
to see him through this. Perhaps he should swerve and try
to disappear down a side street, try to dismantle the bomb.

He wishes the road and landscape would stop unwind-
ing before him, wishes it were only a painted screen to
arrive at and burst through to the other side, emerging
into another kinder realm. Just some place that is not this
Hell. To ask for Paradise would require someone less hum-
ble. But the truck continues its journey, bearing down on
the city in the distance.

DAVID WALKS OUT of the minaret of the good djinn. Marcus is asleep up there surrounded by the millennia-old mountain vista.

He must go back to the school, to take care of some paperwork. His car is parked under a *chinar* plane tree within the school's enclosure wall. He'll bring it here and then, having met Bihzad, drive with Marcus to Usha. From the foliage of the *chinar* trees in a miniature painting, said Zameen, it is possible to tell if it was painted in the Herat of the late fifteenth century. Distinctive serrations and ways of colouring.

David will have to carefully question the young man to see if he is who he claims to be.

Bihzad Benediktovich Veslovsky.

There is a faint continuous rumble from the sky above the street. An unmanned Predator drone collecting intelligence on behalf of the CIA, he thinks, or a fighter jet the Special Forces have summoned, calling down a missile strike on a hiding place of insurgents. The information that selects the target isn't always without its faults, he knows. In Usha at the end of 2001, the house of the warlord Nabi Khan was reduced to rubble from the air, everything and everyone inside a hundred-yard radius was charred, but later it turned out that he had not been in the vicinity. His rival, Gul Rasool, had lied to the Americans just to see the building decimated, to have as many of Nabi Khan's relatives and associates killed as possible. Gul Rasool now has a position in the ministry of reconstruction and development, installed as the chief power in Usha. Nabi Khan is at large, though there have been rumours of his death, rumours of him having moved to Iraq to fight the Americans there. Both men are little short of bandits and the cruellest of barbarians, seeing all of life's problems in terms of injured self-esteem, their places in infamy well earned.

He makes his way through the press of bodies in the bazaar, the bustle of any of these Asian cities. The orange-blossom air. A little girl goes by, walking possibly towards the day when she will disappear behind the burka, her face never to be seen again. Perhaps nowhere is the *Mona Lisa* loved more than here in Asia, and he remembers Zameen telling him that on seeing it for the first time as a child she had wondered what that black line was, high on Mona Lisa's forehead. It was, of course, the edge of her veil. Zameen was seeing the picture in a poor reproduction that missed the thin gossamer fabric covering the head. At that age, she said, it didn't occur to her that women in the West could wear veils.

Instead of going towards the school he has taken a short detour and entered this bazaar, looking for a place that sells satellite phones. With the landline to Marcus's house rotted away, David has decided he'll buy a phone for Larissa Petrovna which she must keep with her while she is here.

He stands at a crossroads and looks around, suddenly finding himself lost, surrounded by noise and talk. The men and women of Afghanistan share between them a store of tales so extensive, so rich and ancient, that it has been said it is unrivalled by any other land. Alexander passed through here in 329 BC with thirty thousand troops, and so now a man selling what look like centuries-old Greek coins approaches David. The years of war and civil war have emptied this country's museums. One 190-carat diamond in the sceptre of Russia's Catherine, bought by her from an Armenian gem merchant, was first the eye of a god in a temple in India, and so it is that no one can be certain where most of Afghanistan's looted treasures have ended up.

He turns and goes back along the street, thinking of how a long time ago, when they were both schoolchildren, his brother Jonathan had asked him to make his way out of a maze in a puzzle book. Only when he failed was it revealed that by drawing a small line in black ink across the correct path, Jonathan had mischievously blocked the only way out. Bringing him nothing but dead ends.

With a smile Marcus raises a hand when he realises that Bihzad is – that Bihzad was – the driver of the vehicle that has just gone past him. He hopes he has been quick enough, that the greeting can be seen in the rear-view mirror. The boy's apparel is patched and dirty, his mouth full of crooked teeth, but he is young and, as Qatrina once said, two things make everyone appear beautiful: youth and the light of the moon.

Marcus is walking towards the school. He woke up in the minaret and found David gone, but he knows where he must be.

Bihzad's truck is going in the same direction as him. The hand of a traffic controller, at some intersection located further up, has released a flood of vehicles just ahead, and now Marcus's view of the truck has become obstructed, though he can see the school building.

He cannot stop thinking of Lara. The thought of her alone in the house last night. A night of stone. He sees in his mind the pitch-dark surroundings, the lake filled with the blackest ink, and the shiver of pale candlelight in one window, sees her figure dressed in white, which is all she has worn since she came. The set of clothes she was wearing when she dropped the rest into bleach is the only one with colour, and that she has folded away out of sight.

It was a mistake for him to have come here yesterday. Could this have waited until she had gone back to Russia? The children's game of hangman – where one has to guess a word letter by letter, each wrong guess meaning that a friend draws a scaffold and then a noose and then a person suspended from that noose – has always terrified Marcus, the idea that every time one makes a wrong choice someone else gets closer to disaster, to death.

The traffic has thinned and he sees that Bihzad's vehicle is stationary outside the school building. Perhaps he has seen Marcus and is waiting for him to catch up. He quickens his pace, going past the cluster of palm trees David had pointed to from the minaret, the loud chatter of birds coming to him from the fronds. For the next fraction of a second it is as though the truck is in fact the picture of a truck, a photograph printed on flimsy paper, and that the rays of the sun have been concentrated onto it with a magnifying glass. And then the ground falls away from his feet and a light as hard as the sun in a mirror fills his vision. The tar on a part of the road below him has caught fire. *Soon they will feed you the entire world.* The explosion has created static and a spark leaps from his thumb towards a smoking fragment of metal flying past him. Then he is on the ground. Beside him has landed a child's wooden leg, in flames, the leather straps burning with a different intensity than the wood, than the bright blood-seeping flesh of the severed thigh that is still attached. A woman in a burka on fire crosses his vision. He hears nothing and then slowly, as he gets to his feet in the midst of this war of the end of the world, scream soldered onto scream. He thinks the silence was the result of momentary deafness but the survivors had in all probability needed time to comprehend fully what had just taken place. The souls will need longer still, he knows, and they may not begin their howls for months and years.

ONLY IN THE EARLY EVENING do Marcus and David leave Jalalabad for Usha, journeying under the first constellations.

David had heard the truck explode from a mile away. Elsewhere he would have thought it was thunder, but in this country he knew what it was, what it had to be.

At the site he found Marcus and gathered him into his arms amid all the black smoke. There were no injuries on him, just a few grazes to the skin. A woman carried a severed hand up to them and had to be told that Marcus had lost his own years before today. David went deeper into the soft black talcum of the smoke, to learn all he could about the event. Around him the word 'fate' was being used in reference to the chance passers-by who had been killed along with the staff and children. Fate – it is the nearest available word when the name of the destroyer or the destroying thing is not known.

When Marcus told him he had seen Bihzad at the wheel of the truck, David had gone to the police. The boy's house was searched and they learnt that he had spent time in captivity, under suspicion of being al-Qaeda. The story of his sister's death last year also came to light. A sister in possession of a love letter: while the brother was giving her the beating he thought she deserved for being shameless, she had escaped from his grip and run off into a field near a former Taliban weapons depot that the United States had repeatedly struck in 2001 with cluster bombs, some of which had failed to explode and still lay undisturbed – in that field and also elsewhere within the already mine-laden cities and countryside.

David and Marcus were also told by the neighbours that Bihzad was in no way related to doctors or Englishmen of any kind. Though he grew up in various orphanages and madrassas, his lineage was known to everyone – both his parents were Afghans and had died in the Soviet bombing of a refugee caravan back in the 1980s.

The statement from the terrorists appeared after four hours, the group calling itself *Tameer-e-Nau*. David and Marcus listen to the words as they are repeated on the radio during the journey towards Usha:

> *A passionate servant of Allah has carried out a glorious act in Jalalabad. He wrote this declaration personally to be read after his death. We have hundreds more young men like him, lovers of Muhammad, peace be upon him, who are willing and eager to give their lives in this jihad against the infidels . . .*

Scarcely anything can be seen in the deepening darkness outside. David thinks of night as a creature that licks objects into oblivion.

> *We regret the loss of the children's lives. But those children were already worse than dead because they were being*

taught to forget Islam in that American-funded school.
They were bound for Hell but because of our actions have
now become flowers of Paradise . . .

David remembers how back in the 1980s, when the Salang Tunnel to the north of Kabul was an important supply route for the Soviet Army, there were several plans by the US-backed guerrillas to blow it up. But because the tunnel was of such key importance, the Soviets guarded it day and night and nothing was ever allowed to obstruct the traffic inside it – you couldn't just park a truck full of explosives in the middle and then walk out, having set the timer going. The only possible way of collapsing the tunnel was for someone to blow themselves up in there. The Afghans were appalled when the Americans suggested this to them. No one volunteered because suicide was a sin. The path would not fork at the moment of the explosion, sending the bomber to Paradise, the infidels to Hell. No, the Afghans told the Americans then, it would deliver both parties to Allah's Inferno.

The statement now continues:

The blameless Muslim adults who have died are like the
blameless Muslims who died in the attacks on the Twin
Towers: Allah has sent them to Paradise . . .

The age David is, in the middle years of his life, he is equally responsible for the young and the old. Those above him and those below. As he drives he places a hand on Marcus's arm to transmit comfort. The bones of the Englishman are thin under the weight of his palm.

It was in the Pakistani city of Peshawar that he had met Zameen, when he was twenty-seven years old, a dealer in gems. Someone who knew by heart the co-ordinates of where to locate various stones. Spinel: 34° 26'N, 64° 14'E. Emerald: 35° 24'59"N, 69° 45'39"E. Someone who knew that Kublai Khan had paid as much as 170,000 ting for Afghan rubies. And that the world's earliest known spinel was discovered in a Buddhist tomb near Kabul in 101 BC.

In Peshawar a ruby had suddenly materialised at his feet one day at dusk. He leaned closer because of the lack of light and saw that it was a sphere of embroidery silk. There were others around him. Emeralds. Sapphires. Opals. They had leapt out of the door at the top of a stair-case a few yards from him, unravelling as they came in a waterfall and then a river of loveliness. A young woman stood there holding the other end of the red filament that was in his hand, and for a few seconds they had remained linked by it, looking at each other.

Pure distilled life, a beautiful child behind her was stretching his body in a high-armed yawn, his shirt rising up to reveal his navel.

CASA IS FOLDING a sheet of paper in half. In the light of the lantern resting on the ground near by, the paper is bright in his hands. He is swift though careful. A series of ten folds – some small, others spanning the entire length of the sheet – and the plane is ready. Gripping it between his forefinger and thumb, he walks towards a clearing. He releases the plane a few times into the air to test its arc. After a number of adjustments, he walks to another section of this disused expanse of land behind his home.

He raises the small white plane above his head and puts his other hand into his breast pocket. He strikes the match against the bark of a nearby tree without looking, introducing a smell of smoke into the air, and brings the fire to the aeroplane's tail. The flame touches it almost caressingly and the white paper ignites.

He releases the burning shape, watching it glide along the low tree branches.

He walks away then, travelling in the opposite direction to the airborne fire, turning around only when he is fifteen or so yards from where he was, his eyes all intensity and seriousness. The plane – or what remains of it – comes to rest precisely where he had wanted it, and the surrounding dry grass begins to burn. The flames grow quickly in size and strength. He covers his ears and the ground erupts in an explosion, a fountain of earth or a small cypress tree rising seven feet into the air. The stones and the larger pieces of soil fall back immediately but particles of finer dust float sideways, slowly drifting with the breeze.

He had found the mine thirty minutes ago, had immediately warned the others in the surrounding houses against venturing out, telling women to make sure all the children were in, and then set to work. It was from the time of the Soviets. Perhaps as old as he was. He dripped petrol onto the grass above it. After an early childhood spent in the company of bird-stunning catapults, and the later years with various guns in the jihad training camps in Pakistan and Afghanistan, he knew he could make the paper plane land on the target precisely. At several locations around him are planes whose trajectory he had been unable to hone, those that had looped or corkscrewed away towards this or that high branch.

Once he had seen a mine detonating in a grove of pomegranate trees with such force that the skin of every fruit on every branch had cracked, the red seed spilling out.

He enters the small brick building he shares with seven others, mostly taxi drivers – like he used to be – or day labourers who work in the centre of the city not far away. After the US invasion, he – someone with links to the Taliban and al-Qaeda – had begun to drive taxis, first in Kabul and then here in Jalalabad. One day he took a passenger to a poppy farm beyond the northern outskirts of the city and ended up being introduced to the people there, Nabi Khan's men, and he has been with them since.

Even though he wishes to take off his shirt and enter his

bed, he performs his ablutions and begins to wait for the time to say the night prayer. Today was a long day and he is tired, but Nabi Khan's organisation has achieved all it hoped. A message had come from Pakistan that if they could arrange this spectacle – the proposal had been sent to Peshawar last month – then they'd have funding and support for other greater missions, culminating in the eventual taking of Usha, Nabi Khan's home base somewhere to the south of the city. Though nothing was made explicit, the message that came down the Khyber Pass from Pakistan was from a former Pakistani Army officer by the name of Fedalla. He had been at the ISI, the Pakistani spy agency, but when Afghanistan was attacked in 2001, he had resigned in protest because the Pakistani government had chosen to side with the Americans instead of the Taliban. Some say he had not resigned but had been forced to leave. When the Taliban were uprooted he had smiled and said that the Americans should not exult: 'The war hasn't ended. The *real* war is about to begin.' He is renegade, they say, a rogue. He and other like-minded individuals in Pakistan are indispensable in the jihad against the Americans and their Afghan supporters. The message he had sent ended with an exhortation not to lose heart, never to give up the struggle against Islam's enemies:

When Nimrod built a pyre to burn Allah's prophet Ibrahim, the hoopoe carried water in its beak and released it onto the flames from above. An onlooker, some Dick Cheney of his time, asked the hoopoe whether it thought the two drops of water would put out the mighty blaze. '*I don't know,*' replied the bird. '*All I know is that when Allah makes a list of those who built this fire and those who tried to put it out, I want my name to be in the second column.*'

Casa listens to the muezzin and spreads the prayer mat on the floor. Night has fallen and the call to the last prayer of the day has begun to issue from the minarets. The mechanism of the Islamic world functioning with precision.

3

Out of Separations

THE SOUND OF AN APPROACHING VEHICLE brings Lara to a window. A tree quivers and shakes in the glass pane, its leaves outlined in bright light against the sky. Walking away from the book she has been reading and the lamp that burns in an alcove beside her chair, she emerges from the house to meet the Englishman in the darkness. She stops upon drawing near and, burying her face in her hands, begins to weep silently. She hears him cover the distance between them. Placing her face on his chest she releases the sobs, her hands clutching the lapels of his jacket, the fabric drenched in smoke. When he did not return yesterday she was certain he had died somewhere. The long hours of imagining the absolute worst, too afraid to approach the radio.

He puts his arms around her and at their touch she tightens her grip on the lapels, thinking it is an attempt at separation. A brief squeal-like sound of protest, until she realises he wishes to hold her. They stand joined like this for two minutes. In the darkness surrounding them, her white clothes seem to glow. Light from the lamp had soaked into them.

Going past the rosemary plant that is said never to grow taller than Christ, she brings him into the house. She knows now from one of his notebooks on perfume that rosemary increases in breadth rather than height after thirty-three years.

He requests with a gesture and she dilutes condensed milk in water and brings it to a boil for him to drink. Through all this they do not say a word. She is still trembling with sorrow. Only when she is in another section of the house to wash the tears off her face does she think of the man who had driven Marcus here. She returns to see him standing beside Marcus. He holds in his earth-covered hands a bottle of whisky. He must have gone off into the night to dig for it the moment he arrived. Like a gold muscle or sinew he pours a measure of it into Marcus's milk.

Past midnight, and all three of them are motionless, her fingers interlaced with Marcus's where he lies in a bedroom on the ground floor. David in a chair on the other side of the room.

'A daughter, a wife, a grandson,' Marcus had been saying earlier. 'You could say this place took away all I had.' She was sitting beside him on the bed, as now. 'I could so easily appear to be one of those unfortunate white men you hear about, who thought too lovingly of the other races and civilisations of the world, who left his own country in the West to set up home among them in the East, and was ruined as a result, paying dearly for his foolish mistake. His life smashed to pieces by the barbarians surrounding him.'

David's eyes seemed fixed on some random detail in a corner.

'But, you see, the West was involved in the ruining of this place, in the ruining of my life. There would have been no downfall if this country had been left to itself by those others.'

'Don't do this,' Lara had said quietly. 'You must try to sleep.'

Now she stands up and turns the small wheel at the side of the lamp, reducing the diameter of light so that darkness appears to take a step closer. A thought she dislikes. 'I'll be in the room next door tonight in case you need something. Just on the other side of this wall, I'll listen for you.'

'So it is that we make links out of separations,' he mutters.

Books are stacked high on the bed in the adjoining room, and as she is clearing them David enters and begins to help. They have exchanged only a few words so far, and now too they work in silence.

Through stories we judge our actions before committing them, said the Englishman, and so this was a house of readers, declaring a citizenship of the realm of the mind. She has seen five different editions of *The Leopard* here, four each of *In a Free State* and *Rustam and Sohrab*. Each beloved book has more than one copy – some small with the text crowded into perhaps too few pages, others where the print and the page are both generously proportioned. At first she hadn't understood but by now she does. Sometimes there is a need to take pleasure in a favourite book for its story line alone, and the smaller editions facilitate this because the eye moves fast along a closely printed page. At other times one wishes to savour language – the rhythm of sentences, the precision with which a given word has been studded into a phrase – and on such occasions the larger size helps to slow one down, pause at each comma. Dawdling within a landscape.

When the bed is free she thanks him, and he glances at her and then she watches him disappear along a darkened corridor, towards the distant painted wall which is covered in the long wash of moonlight from the window, the numerous pinks and reds. The soles of his shoes are worn the way the edges of erasers become rounded with use. As though he walks around correcting his mistakes.

She wonders if his eyes and the quality of his gaze are always those of someone on the verge of sleep – or are they of someone who has not finished waking up?

During the first fever-haunted hours and days, her mind had shimmered with the things she had encountered in this house. They were desert mirages. Phenomena she could not really be sure she had seen. She would separate herself from the sheets and go down the darkened staircase just to check. In the kitchen cinnamon sticks were indeed being stored in a plastic box that had once contained a video cassette. Marcus must have dropped the jar accidentally and then placed the spice in whatever came to hand. *It is 1573*, she read the summary printed on the box, by the light of a struck match, *and Japan is being torn apart by a bloody civil war* . . .

*

Becoming aware of movement during the night she comes out to find David at the kitchen table.

She turns to leave, thinking he might wish to be alone. His back is towards her but the amount of light in the room has increased at her approach, the candle reflecting brightly off her white clothes, the brightness flung up the walls. He turns around.

'Forgive me, I thought it was Marcus,' she says.

'No, it's me.'

Hesitantly she enters and stands across the table from him and he gestures towards a chair.

'I thought he needed something,' she says.

There is no movement from him. *To you, insane world, only one reply: I refuse.* She thinks of this line from a poem by Marina Tsvetaeva.

'I am sorry to hear you have been unwell,' he says. 'Quite a tough journey you made to get here.'

'Marcus has been kind. I'll leave in a few days.'

'He said you work at the Hermitage. Qatrina made beautiful paintings when she had the time.'

She knows. The bottles for Marcus's perfumes, and their stoppers, were designed by her, as well as the mazes of calligraphy and flowers to be etched on the glass.

'Sometimes I shudder at the books up there,' she says. 'They are after all a reminder of someone who lost her reason in the face of cruelty. Did you know her well?'

'I loved her. She was endlessly kind in her personal conduct. But there was something very hard about her intelligence at times. She would not have agreed with what Marcus was saying earlier.'

'No?'

'The cause of the destruction of Afghanistan, she said to me towards the end of her life, is the character and society of the Afghans, of Islam. Communism wasn't the ideal solution to anything but, according to her, her fellow countrymen would have resisted change of *any* kind.' He stops, no doubt given pause by his remark about Communism in the presence of a Russian. 'Whenever Marcus spoke the way he did earlier, she would ask him to remember the circumstances of his father's death.'

He has opened the outside door and is standing framed within it, looking up at the sky. According to the Afghans each star represents a victim of the wars of the last quarter-century.

'Did Zameen ever mention to you a Soviet soldier named Benedikt Petrovich?'

'Not that I recall.'

'Or someone called Piotr Danilovich?'

'I'm sorry, no.' He looks at his wrist watch and switches on the radio, the volume low. 'I couldn't sleep so I thought I'd come and wait for the next news bulletin, to see if there have been any developments in Jalalabad.'

It is four-thirty. The radio informs them that the gangs who roam the streets looking for children to kidnap, to harvest their eyes and kidneys, had attempted to drag away several of the half-dead ones from the site of the explosion.

'Maybe I shouldn't have started the school,' he says after switching off the radio. 'A provocation to the jihadis.'

She doesn't know what to say.

'I'll go back to Jalalabad very early in the morning but I'll return in the evening. Would you please tell Marcus?'

'Of course.'

'Thank you. Goodnight.'

After he has gone up to his room, she sits in the chair, looking out now and then at the silhouettes of the trees, the sudden startling bats that appear out of nowhere like flickering ink blots. *Quite a tough journey you made to get here.* In her room she looks through the sheaf of letters Benedikt sent home from this far country. *Princess Marya, learning of her brother's wound only from the newspapers and having no definite information, was getting ready to go in search of him . . .* When her courage had failed just before an earlier journey to Afghanistan, Lara had encountered this sentence in Tolstoy's great book and become resolute again. As she is putting the letters back in a pocket within her handbag, her fingers slip through a tear in the lining and touch something. She closes her eyes the moment she pulls out the small cellophane-wrapped sweet into the light. Unable to bear the sight of it. They were loved by her husband, the colour of strawberries. After she made him give up cigarettes he had become addicted to these. She doesn't know what to do with it now, her breath awry, and then in great hurry she extracts it from the crackling wrapper and places it in her mouth, her teeth working very fast, consuming it, letting it go down into her body.

As in a lyric the moon glitters like a jewel. Through the pane she watches the pomegranate trees, the blossoms and the foliage that would be dripping with dew in the morning.

She had taken with her the gift of a single pomegranate when she went to visit Piotr Danilovich last December, having located him after all the years. When he returned from Afghanistan he had failed to adjust to life, becoming silent like all soldiers who come back from a war. There was a period about which he would speak somewhat vaguely to Lara, but which she knew from other sources to be a time of mental collapse. Now he lived a hundred or so kilometres outside Moscow, in a place known as the House of Ten Thousand Christs.

Bringing with her the crowned, brass-coloured fruit wrapped in black tissue paper, Lara had gone to meet him through the thickly falling snow, to that monastery whose central icon of Christ had been lent at one time to armies, to be carried into battles against the Crimean Tartars. Faith going to war. The Soviet soldiers in Afghanistan had called the rebels *dukhi*, Russian for ghosts, never knowing when they would arrive, never understanding how they could slip away suddenly, the only explanation being that they had otherworldly assistance.

Piotr Danilovich's responsibility at the sacred House of Ten Thousand Christs was to repair damaged images, his fingers smeared with resin and ink and pigment, dissolved gold under his fingernails. There was a period during the Soviet rule when the great mosque at Leningrad was turned into a weapons depot. And so wheat was stored at the monastery during the Soviet years, the icons rotting away out of neglect in the back rooms, being eaten by rats.

'How did you find me?' he asked.

'My husband, Stepan Ivanovich, was in the military. One of his friends told me about you, about the story – or rumour – that you had tried to defect with Benedikt but had changed your mind and returned.'

'You say your husband was in the military. Has he left?'

'He died this time last year.'

'So you are the wife of that Stepan Ivanovich.' His voice remained low throughout her visit and he kept his head very still when he talked.

Three officers had been put on trial for killing prisoners in Chechnya, torturing those suspected of being guerrillas or supporters of the rebellion against the Russian government. Stepan Ivanovich had served as character witness for two of them. *If we have in our custody someone who knows where a suitcase full of explosives is planted, set to go off in a few hours, but who refuses to talk, do we not have the right to hurt him into revealing the information – burn him, freeze him?* This would have been his line of defence.

'I am sorry for your loss,' Piotr said.

She had nodded, looking out at the snow lying in front of the building, then turning to him. With his thinness, and the darkness of his eyes, he seemed to her a figure stepped out of the margins of one of the icons, aged beyond his years.

The pomegranate was on a table close to the fireplace.

She slit it open now. The outer layer of scarlet seeds had been warmed by the flames. The temperature of menstrual blood, of semen just emerged from a man's body.

'Afghan fruit vendors would sometimes inject poison

into the oranges, melons and pomegranates they sold us Soviet soldiers.'

The orchard is a lace of linked greenery around them as Marcus and Lara walk between the trees in the morning. A paw of mist comes down from the mountains above the house.

Marcus inhales the green scents of the spring morning. 'One year when we visited England there was pollen everywhere, everything coated yellow. A wet April followed by a dry May had caused the pollen cloud to float over to eastern England from Scandinavia. It was thirty years ago but I remember it suddenly now.'

'Stravinsky in his seventies remembered for the first time the smell of the St Petersburg snow of his childhood.'

'Is it something distinctive?'

'Unforgettable. Benedikt mentioned it in one of his letters home.'

There are butterflies in the trees around them. Some have green underwings so that – visible invisible visible invisible – they seem to blink in and out of existence as they fly amid the leaves.

'Look there, Lara. That tree with pink blossoms.'

She comes and stands beside him. 'It's as though lightning struck it.'

'Qatrina did that. A man from Usha kept making his wife pregnant year after year. The young woman was twenty-two and had had seven children in six years. He never allowed her body to recover, despite warnings and pleadings from Qatrina. When he brought his wife to us for an eighth time, she was almost dead. The tree was small then, a sapling, but still rather robust, and while I was trying to stabilise the woman, Qatrina came out here. In giving vent to her rage she tore the young apricot plant in two. It's possible she wanted to break off a branch to thrash him.'

They look at it where it is split down the middle. The pink splash-pattern of its flowers.

About five years ago Lara herself had failed yet again to carry a pregnancy to full term. For a Russian woman an abortion was one of the more obvious options when it came to birth control, the men not agreeing to consider any preventative methods themselves, and the ones Lara had had in her youth had damaged her.

'You mustn't think badly of Qatrina from what I have just told you.'

'Of course not.'

'Women were always dying in repeated childbirth because the husbands didn't listen – Qatrina had to struggle with the mosques because they said birth control was the West's attempt at reducing the number of Muslims in the world. And then the Communist regime came and closed down the family planning centres, saying they were an Imperialist conspiracy to detract attention from the real causes of poverty.'

Last month in Usha he overheard a child of about seven say to another, the pair obviously at a loss for something to do, 'Or shall we go and throw stones at the grave of

Qatrina?' Marcus wishes he hadn't heard it, had heard it inaccurately.

She used to say she did not want any mention of God at her funeral.

They move towards the tree through the sunlight. Easy to imagine, at such an hour, how Qatrina could have filled notebooks with the colours she found in a square foot of nature. An olive grove outside Jalalabad – *grey, white, green*. A mallow blossom – *red orange, sulphur, yellow bone, red-wine shadow.* The mountains above the house – *silver, evasive grey, blue, sapphire water.* She'd use these notes as reference when painting. Muhammad had said, 'Verily there are one hundred minus one names of Allah. He who enumerates them would get into Paradise,' causing Muslims to search them out in the Koran so that a list was compiled. And Qatrina's life's work was a series of ninety-nine paintings concerning these names – 'the Artist' among them. They are now lost because of the wars.

'She worked with the patients for longer hours than I did,' Marcus says. 'Travelled to remoter areas than I ever contemplated whenever she heard about an outbreak or epidemic. But she would at times feel utterly helpless at the state of her country's people.'

'I am surprised the tree has survived.'

'It even produces some fruit, later in the year.'

'Then I won't get to taste it. A few more days, at most, is all I'll spend here.'

'If you are in no hurry to get back to something, you can stay here longer. And I'll talk to David so we can accompany you to Kabul airport, we'll try to walk right up to the plane, when you do decide to go.' The night she had spent alone in the house has deposited the blue of fearful anxiety under her eyes.

'There is no need,' she shakes her head but then murmurs a thanks.

For the next three days, David leaves for Jalalabad early each morning, the song of the birds entering his ears like gentle pins, and he returns to the house in the evenings. The electricity generator is actually broken, he discovers, and he takes it to Jalalabad to be mended, the house continuing to live by candle- and lamplight, moving between weakly illuminated pools.

One morning there is a demonstration in Jalalabad, the placards and shouts expressing contempt for the people who had planned and carried out the bombing of the school. Pakistan's government has denied suggestions that current or former members of its secret service were involved in the crime. Another day, the weeping father of one of the eleven dead children insists the Americans leave Afghanistan because if they had not come the atrocity would not have occurred. And a woman, broken with grief at having lost a girl and a boy, approaches David and wants to know why the Americans had released that criminal from custody. She demands they catch his accomplices and take them away to be slowly tortured to death somewhere.

He sits on the stone steps that descend into the perfume factory. As night arrives he can barely see the Buddha's head, save for slashes of minimum light that define his hair and mouth. He spreads ambergris onto his hands. His head filling up with sea odour. He discovered a small amount of it in a jar here like a dab of black butter. It is obtained from the insides of sperm whales but the Arabs who peddled it along the Silk Road always disguised its origins, protecting a trade secret. For a long time the Persians believed that it came from a spring beneath the oceans, and the Chinese that it was the spit of dragons.

They are saying that the building next to the school was a warehouse for storing heroin. It belonged to Gul Rasool, the man who is the court of appeal in all matters in Usha. If the intended target was the warehouse, then Nabi Khan must be alive. It must be him, trying to strike a blow against his enemy. But the statement left behind by the suicide bomber had hinted strongly that the school was the target. It had ended with the words *Death to America*.

A rumour has also spread that the bombing was carried out by the Americans themselves so that the concept of jihad can be blamed and discredited.

He sits quietly at the table with Lara and Marcus, listening to their talk. Twice during the months he knew her, Zameen woke up screaming from a dream of being assaulted by the Soviet soldier. Memories rising in her like bruises as he held her. A dream of lying lifeless on the floor, the attacker manipulating her body 'as when a corpse is washed before burial', arranging her limbs before beginning. 'Of course he committed a crime,' she said, 'and if these were normal times I would have liked to have seen him brought to justice. What else can I say? That doesn't change the fact that I am grateful he helped me escape from the military base. He may have saved my life. When I think of that I hope he's all right, wherever he is.'

When he is not with the other two inhabitants of the house, David walks through the orchard and the garden, some younger stems as slender as *nai* flutes. One night he builds a fire at the water's edge. As a young man he had gone to Berkeley for a university interview and, having stood on the roof of the astronomy building and looked out at San Francisco Bay with its sailboats, had made his decision. He bought an ancient twenty-seven-foot boat and for the next four years lived on it in the Berkeley marina. And every time he has visited Marcus, this lake has begged to be paddled on. This time he has brought with him from the United States the basic materials to construct a birch-bark canoe, having contemplated spending a week or so building it here; from a storeroom in the half-ruined school in Jalalabad he brings it all to Usha one day, unloading it into an unused room. Visiting the lakes of the northern United States as a child, in the company of his brother Jonathan and an uncle, he had seen a sea of wild rice engulf an Ojibwa woman seated in a canoe. A slide into harvest: she gently bent the slender stalks that were sticking out of the water's surface and knocked the grain into her vessel, to sell for twenty-five cents a pound. The last armed conflict between the United States military forces and the Native Americans had taken place right there on Leech Lake in 1898. White officers and troops – and around them in the forest, circling quietly on the icy ground, nineteen Natives with Winchester rifles.

He walks around the house, reacquainting himself with it. The broken painted couples enclose him when he enters the room at the top. On the walls of muted gold, they are either in union or keeping vigils for each other in grove and pavilion. Waiting. On first walking in he has to halt mid-step – seeing the hundreds of coloured fragments arranged on the floor. Initially he is not sure what they mean but circling around them he discovers the vantage from where they do not appear arbitrary and the image is the right way up.

A man and a woman.

'I'll pick these up. Do you wish to use the room?' Lara has come in.

'Don't put them away on my account, please. I was just going around the house, reminding myself of things.'

Having removed an oval piece on which the strings of a harp are painted – just a few black lines made as though by ink-dipped twigs – she lets her hand remain some inches off the floor, the limb suspended in the air irresolutely, and then she puts it back and stands up.

They look at each other, and he doesn't know how to fill the silence and then she withdraws.

He moves towards the windowsill to gaze at that vast sky of Asia, caught between inside and outside.

*

It was here in this part of the world that David had heard for the first time the call for America's death. A mob fired by visions of a true Islamic society, shouting, 'Kill All Americans!', 'President Carter the Dog Must Die!' It was in Islamabad, Pakistan, in November 1979. He was twenty-two.

At the beginning of November a group of protesters in Iran had stormed the American embassy in Tehran, taking forty-nine Americans hostage. And seventeen days later David had arrived in Islamabad, very late in the evening, falling asleep almost immediately in his hotel room owing to the exhaustion of the travel. He had finished college for now and intended to spend the fall months travelling in northern Afghanistan, something he had wanted to do for some years. His plan was to go from Islamabad to Peshawar, and from there – one long road full of twists, veering like a kite's tail – move on through the Khyber Pass to the city of Jalalabad and then on to Kabul. The languages around him were still many-lettered lumps in his mouth and ears but he was sure he could get by. Seven days a week for eight weeks – he had taken a course in ancient Greek during the summer, discovering suddenly that he had a gift for languages, and he carried with him a copy of the oldest surviving Greek tragedy, the *Persians*, Aeschylus contemplating the East's grief and shock at finding itself defeated by the West.

While he slept, Saudi national guardsmen encircled the Kaaba, the Grand Mosque in Mecca, Saudi Arabia. A delusional fundamentalist had declared himself the Messiah and, having barricaded himself inside the mosque with his followers a few hours earlier, opened fire on the worshippers. The fanatics – they wanted a purer Islam implemented in Arabia, calling for song, music, film and sports to be banned – had smuggled in their assault rifles and grenades in coffins, the mosque being a common place to bless the dead. The Saudi government did not tell anyone who was responsible for the invasion of the holiest site in Islam, the place every single practising Muslim turned his face to five times a day. Not long after David Town got up on the morning of 21 November, the rumour spread through all the cities of Islam – from country to country, continent to continent – that the killings in the Kaaba were carried out by Americans as a blow against Islam, perhaps in retaliation for the Tehran embassy siege.

He didn't know about this rumour when he left his hotel. He had to visit the US embassy to be updated on the situation in Afghanistan. The rebellion against the Communist government, begun back in the spring, had now spread to most provinces there.

At a pedestrian crossing he reached into his pocket and pulled out a small notebook to check something. Last night while having dinner at the hotel, he had had a brief conversation with a Pakistani man at the next table. Upon learning of David's interest in gems, the delightful pedant told him that the Emperor Shah Jahan's wealth had included eighty-two pounds of diamonds, 110 pounds of rubies, 275 pounds of emeralds, fifty-five pounds of jade and two thousand spinels. David had written it all down, but now, this morning, he wanted to confirm that another detail had been committed to paper: the treasury also contained four thousand living songbirds.

He glanced at the page and just at that moment the car that had come to a halt to allow him to cross, with its front fender only two feet away from him, jerked forward by six inches. The driver had decided to startle him for sport. He gave the windshield a cursory look and continued without breaking his stride – not in all honesty due to strong nerves, but because he was distracted by the four thousand birds and hadn't really seen the car move until it had already come to a stop, knew he wasn't about to be run over.

The car drove away but it was back minutes later, coming to a screeching stop beside him on the sidewalk and disgorging four men. They were friendly, more or less his own age, and they invited him to a nearby teahouse, very pleased to have met an American, asking him how they could migrate to USA the Beautiful. When he regained consciousness about two hours later, in a back alley, the skin on his head was split open in two places. There were cuts and bruises on the rest of his body too. He had no coherent memory except a faint impression of the car driver's features filled with malice, of an arm locking onto his neck from behind to choke him. By not reacting how he was meant to when the car jolted forward suddenly, David had obviously caused the driver to lose face with his companions.

David thought he'd never encounter this man again, but he would see him only a few hours later under circumstances even more murderous. He'd learn that his name was Fedalla. And, some years from now, he would be one of the first people David would suspect of being involved when Zameen and Bihzad disappeared.

Blood on his face and clothes like a wild cursive script, he arrived at the US embassy around noon and was admitted when he produced his passport. The nurse had just finished attending to him when buses began pulling up outside the main gate. Hundreds of armed men streamed out in wave upon wave and began jumping over the perimeter fence, firing guns and hurling Molotov cocktails.

There were six Marines at the embassy but they were not allowed to open fire. They were in any case massively outnumbered. Within minutes, one of them, a twenty-year-old from Long Island, had caught a bullet in the head.

The rioters were led by a gang of students from the fundamentalist Islamic wing of the city's university. Inspired by the events in Tehran and the fire-breathing triumph of Ayatollah Khomeini, they had been waiting for a chance to demonstrate their own power.

David, and 139 embassy personnel and the dying Marine, found themselves behind the steel-reinforced doors of a vault on the third floor as they waited for the Pakistani government to send police or military troops.

The vault echoed to the sound of a sledgehammer coming down on CIA code equipment that could not be allowed to fall into the hands of the mob, a mob now fifteen thousand strong.

Around and below them, the building was on fire, the floor of the vault beginning to get intensely hot, the tiles blistering and warping under their feet. The other Marines were still out there but the request from them to open fire was repeatedly denied as it would only incite the riot further. When the ground floor had completely filled with smoke the Marines retreated upstairs to join the others in the vault, dropping tear-gas canisters down each stairwell as they came.

Despite pleas from the ambassador and the CIA station chief, hour after hour passed without any rescue attempt by the Pakistanis. Giant columns of gasoline-scented smoke issued from the building, visible from miles away – miles away where rioters arriving in government-owned buses were also attacking the American School while children lay cowering in locked rooms.

The mob at the embassy climbed onto the roof and pounded on the hatch door that led down into the vault. David, looking up at the ceiling, watched it buckle and twist from the blows over the course of an hour, the oxygen running out, many around him fainting or vomiting. But the hatch door held and as the sun set over Islamabad the rioters dissolved away into the darkness.

From the vault they emerged with the body of the dead Marine. Two Pakistani employees of the embassy lay on the first floor, killed by asphyxiation and then badly burnt. An American airman had been beaten unconscious and left to die in the fire.

Climbing onto the roof David saw the arrival of a few Pakistani troops at last. They stood around, and David thought he recognised one of them – the young man who had been behind the steering wheel of the car. The photographs that were taken of these moments would later confirm his suspicions. Fedalla. So he was in the army.

Later that evening David, and most of the others who had feared for their lives in the vault for over five hours, were amazed to learn that President Carter had just telephoned Pakistan's dictator General Zia and thanked him for his help.

In the near future, upon joining the CIA, David would know that the explanation for some events existed in another realm, a parallel world that had its own considerations and laws. As he watched Pakistan's ambassador in Washington accept the gratitude of the United States and claim that Pakistani Army troops had reacted 'promptly, with dispatch', he had little idea of the larger things at stake, didn't know why the United States could not afford to dwell on the issue. Khomeini's revolution had meant the loss of important listening posts in Iran that had been trained on the Soviet Union. General Zia had accepted a CIA proposal to locate new facilities on Pakistani soil.

Strange sacrifices were required in that shadow-filled realm, strange compromises. In another month the Soviet Union would invade Afghanistan, and Pakistan's corrupt and brutal military dictator would become a fêted ally of not just the United States but of most of the Western world, David himself present on a number of occasions where the man was extravagantly celebrated and flattered, his own voice adding to the dishonest chorus.

'LARA CARRIES WITH HER a leaf from the Cosmos Oak that grows in the Kremlin,' Marcus tells David. 'Her cosmonaut father was killed when his spacecraft malfunctioned during the return to Earth in 1965.'

The two men are at the lake, beside the small fire that David has built. Night insects, knees and elbows of finest wire, cross and recross the zone of light around the flames.

'There were rumours he knew while still in orbit that he was doomed, that his death screams during the dive back towards the world were recorded by American monitoring stations.'

'Where is she now? Does she know we are out here?'

Marcus points to a lit window on the first floor of the house. 'She knows where we are. I have told her she'll never be left alone here again. One of us will always be with her.' Marcus has a rose blossom with him, and he smells its petals from time to time. It is from one of the plants which he has patiently retaught their former elegance.

David brings more wood for the fire, two sword-length dead branches which he breaks into eight sections, leaning them onto the burning pyramid, at evenly spaced points.

He looks towards her window. The Cosmos Oak was planted to mark the first manned space flight by Yuri Gagarin, he knows.

'Her father's last journey had been timed to celebrate a day of International Solidarity,' Marcus says, 'and the Kremlin ordered the launch despite the chief designer's refusal to sign the flight endorsement papers for the re-entry vehicle.'

'I remember when we landed on the moon in 1969. Jonathan took me to have what they were calling "moon burgers". There was a small American flag planted on top of the bun.' He smiles at the memory. 'I was about twelve, he must have been eighteen.'

A few minutes before midnight they walk up to the house to collect Lara – waiting for her by the threshold's cypress trees until she emerges with a lamp – and then the three of them go to David's car to listen to the news bulletin. The batteries of the kitchen radio are lifeless due to use and David will have to pick up new ones tomorrow. A night journey, along the curved sequence of Persian lilac trees. Marcus says that when Muhammad's disciples were leaving his house, he would put his hand out of the door and the light from his palm would light their way home.

There is a trace of acacia scent in the air as there is the faint presence of Alexander's name in the word Kandahar, as there is the presence of Ahmed in Anna Akhmatova's surname, she whose lines Lara had quoted during a conversation yesterday: *As if I was drinking my own tears from a stranger's cupped hands.*

They get in and close the door against the sound of the lake water and the million leaves, against insects hungry for light.

The news tells them that an angry statement has appeared, purporting to be from those who choreographed the bombing. They wish to point out the hypocrisy of the Americans who condemn this killing of the children but whose president had shaken hands with the people who in the 1980s had blown up a passenger plane just as it took off from Kandahar airport, carrying Afghan schoolchildren bound for indoctrination in the Soviet Union.

'Is that true?' Lara asks, turning towards David, but he doesn't answer.

Apart from that there is nothing about the Jalalabad bombing in the bulletin. Afterwards they sit in the darkness for a while, the various metals and mechanisms of the car cooling around them, Marcus having gone to the house.

'In the States we call them chinaberry trees,' David tells her as they slowly walk under the Persian lilacs, going towards the lake. 'The berries are poisonous. My brother and I would dissolve their pulp in a deep slow-moving part of the river and when the fish passed through those waters they'd be stunned. We'd just pick them up with our hands.'

'Marcus told me about your brother.'

A 180-person military task force scrutinises the hills, fields, and jungles of Vietnam to determine the fate of more than a thousand Americans unaccounted for there. In Vietnam, as well as Laos and Cambodia, witnesses are interviewed, crash sites are excavated, ponds are drained, and bone fragments are sifted from shallow graves.

Men lost in long-forgotten ambushes.

Men lost in falling B52 bombers.

Men last seen alive in the hands of their captors.

'He was twenty. 1971. Last month I was looking at a photo of him from that time. How young he was, how amazingly young we all look at that age!' Like one of those miniscule new leaves found at the very tip of a branch, the ones that can be crushed into a watery green smear between thumb and forefinger – so unformed, so . . . resistanceless.

The fire is out when they arrive at the lake, just an exhalation of the red embers and a column of smoke that changes direction every few instants.

'I read somewhere that there once existed in Burma a ruby so large and vivid that when the king placed it in a bowl of milk, the milk turned red.' She is blowing into the fire while he looks for pieces of wood that might be lying around.

'The watch my father gave Jonathan when he left for Vietnam had a tiny spinel inside it, attached to one of the plates that held the mechanism. He said it was from Afghanistan. That was one of the reasons I came to this country, all those years ago. Always wanted to visit Afghanistan because of that small jewel. And then of course the Soviet Union invaded and my interest deepened.' He'd visit Afghanistan's gem mines even during its Soviet occupation when no Americans were permitted. Slipping in from Pakistan and out again without leaving an official footprint anywhere.

'You helped the anti-Soviet guerrillas, the *dukhi*? Yes?'

Nothing from him. The sound of the wood splitting as the fire comes back to life. The water swaying.

'It's okay,' she says. 'The two empires hated each other. I know that when Soviet troops entered Afghanistan, the reaction in the United States was, "We now have the chance to give the Soviets their Vietnam." Revenge.'

But he is shaking his head. 'It's possible that everyone else was fighting the Soviets for the wrong reasons, was mercenary or dishonest, faking enthusiasm due to this or that greed. Even wanting revenge, yes. But I never doubted that my own reasons were good, genuine.'

Just as it doesn't matter to a person when he is in a hall of mirrors – he himself knows he is the one who is real. The confusion is for the onlookers.

He says: 'How I feel about the mayhem I helped unleash, how I live with that, is a separate matter, but my opposition to the principles behind the Soviet Union is still there when I look – my opposition to what the Soviet empire did to those who lived in it, those who were born in it.'

MARCUS TAKES DOWN Virgil from the shelf. On the cover is a painting of Aeneas fleeing the burning destruction of Troy. The great broken heart of the city in the background. Aeneas is accompanied by his young son – a path to the future – and is carrying his aged father over his shoulder – the reminder of the past. The old man clutches the statues of the household gods in his right hand, and because the other hand is out of sight in the folds of his cloak, absent beyond the wrist, Marcus thinks for a moment of himself. If so, then David is Aeneas – he had offered to carry Marcus up the tall minaret in Jalalabad. The little boy, is he Bihzad?

He opens the book to the contents page and lets his eye slide down the list of chapters, moving deeper into the story rung by rung, Aeneas establishing an empire but along the way losing his soul. A flicker in Marcus's eye: something slides out from between the pages and falls onto the floor. It is one of the pieces of absorbent white card on which he tested perfumes. He raises it to his face and convinces himself that it smells of Zameen, however faintly, of the fragrance he had blended especially for her.

After being forced to accompany Nabi Khan into battle, to tend to his wounded soldiers, he had ended up in the refugee camps in Peshawar, surrounded by millions of other traumatised Afghans, displaced by the rebellion against the Soviets. He didn't know where Qatrina was, hadn't seen her since Gul Rasool took her with him into his battles. Then one day in 1986 he discovered where in Peshawar Gul Rasool was based: he was living in a mansion in the wealthy University Town area of the city with his family and band of fighters. The blossom sitting heavy as flocks of white birds on the branches, Nabi Khan also lived near by in that area wreathed by magnolia trees, as did other tribal leaders and warlords, holy warriors all, all made rich by the hundreds of millions of dollars pouring into the jihad. Marcus went to see Gul Rasool to ask where Qatrina was, and towards the end of their conversation he felt a sweet strong stab from somewhere. Thinking back sequentially, moment by moment, he connected it to the faint sound of glass shattering in the room next door. Outside he had to lean against a palm tree for support – a vial of Zameen's scent had been broken behind the thick mahogany door. She was letting him know she was there.

He couldn't have asked Gul Rasool anything about the women in the house and now didn't know how to proceed. The scent was a message from her – a call, a prompt. Through one of the servants in the house he discovered that a young woman had recently been brought there, that she was from the Street of the Storytellers in the centre of Peshawar.

Marcus went to the fabled Street and, after an hour or so of questions and answers with the locals amid the manic activity and noise, climbed two flights of dark stairs, finding himself at a small flat. Almost in tears he knocked several times and then forced his way in, suddenly past caring. Only a short while later he heard someone follow him in. He placed his hands and an ear against the wall. Feeling along it over many minutes, as though trying to locate the heart of a live organism. He silenced his breathing as much as possible and resisted the scrape of fabric and skin against the wall. Then suddenly he was overpowered and pinned to the floor with a foot on the side of his face. He strained up to see a gun pointed at his temple, the metal gleaming even in the small amount of light coming in through the window.

'What are you doing here?'

'I am looking for my daughter.' His mouth crushed against the floor. 'A young woman named Zameen.'

The pressure of the boot slowly eased off his head.

'I have reason to believe she lives here,' he continued.

'What's your name?' he was asked, in American-accented English this time.

'Marcus Caldwell.' He sat up. The man had been leaning down towards him and now straightened, his face moving through a rectangle of light from the open window. Marcus saw that he was a young Caucasian. 'Who are you?'

'My name is David Town,' the American said and switched on the light. 'Zameen has told me all about you, about Qatrina.'

David would never reveal anything about the activities hidden behind his gem business, and Marcus knew not to ask, having guessed more or less immediately that he was in espionage. He now said he had been away for a period and had recently returned to find no trace of Zameen and her son here.

'I know where she is. She has a child?'

'Where is she?'

'Are you the father?'

'Where is she?'

Marcus told him where he thought she was, accepting the younger man's scepticism that the clue had been provided by perfume.

They eventually learned that since the day of Marcus's visit, Nabi Khan had carried out a raid on Gul Rasool's mansion in University Town. There were regular pitched battles between rival warlords in Peshawar's streets, car bombs and assassinations, missiles and rocket-propelled grenades fired into buildings and crowds. Nabi Khan had carried away several of Gul Rasool's women and children during the attack, to be exploited or sold, Bihzad among them. Several people had died, including Zameen.

All this knowledge was incremental, years in the acquiring.

Marcus smells now the few molecules of the perfume that still inhabit the fibres of the white card, Virgil open on his lap. Qatrina had designed the container – a map of the world and the word *Zameen* acid-etched onto the glass. The space inside him seems to expand when the fragrance enters him.

Stamen and flint and petal and river moss. Afghanistani women, in the songs they sing, do not desire Allah's Paradise after death, wishing instead to become streams and grasses, the breeze and the dust. The soil placed upon them in the grave, they sing, they'll take as their lover.

The nail had gone through the card. A hole the size of a cell in a beehive. He puts it back in the *Aeneid*.

LARA TURNS THE PAGES of the atlas until she holds the United States of America in her hands. Milk is a river in Montana, lit by her candle. Heart is a river in North Dakota. Rifle, Dinosaur, Delhi. These are towns in Colorado. Antlers. Two Medicine. Twentynine Palms. Talking about Usha, Teardrop, the lake outside this window, he had said a lake named Tear of the Clouds is the source of the Hudson River. She searches for it now. New York City. Marcus has told her that David was there in 1993 when Muslim terrorists tried to blow up the World Trade Center for the first time. Oldland, Montana, was where he was born in 1957.

She follows him with her fingertip: to university in California and then back to Montana. One grandfather was a watchsmith, the child David coming into contact with gemstones through him. The father – originally a farmer's son – had been encouraged by his schoolteachers to apply to Harvard, and the mother was a doctor's secretary and eventually a nurse, rolling her hair into the car window so it would jolt her awake if she fell asleep during the long commute to the nursing school. As he spoke, had she detected something like satisfaction in him? A contentment at how his family had been given the chances to improve themselves over the decades and generations, slowly and patiently encouraged to thrive by America in American sunlight?

She looks up, at the possibility of a sound from Marcus's room, fully alert. She inclines her head for the best angle, recalling the aunt who when attending the Mariinsky Theatre always sat high up at the back of the house, saying the acoustics were better up there even if she couldn't make out the expressions of the singers or the details of the costumes.

Nothing but silence from the other side of this wall where Muhammad sits dressed in Islam's green with his hand plunged into a clay pitcher of water – consolidating and expanding the Islamic empire by sealing a deal with a woman.

She has noticed how Marcus tries to hide his missing hand. She wonders if 'hide' is still the correct word. She releases her mind into this small consideration. Can you hide something that is not there to begin with? He is trying to hide *the fact of* his missing hand.

She closes the atlas and moves towards her bed. These are the rooms where Qatrina had lost her reason, Marcus having to tell her there was no need to be afraid just because the bar of red soap was producing white lather. Benedikt and Lara's own mother, someone who graduated from the Philological Faculty of Leningrad University and had worked as an engineer and a translator, was declared schizophrenic and confined for six years to a psychiatric hospital prison where drug treatment was administered. She was a civil rights activist and was arrested in 1969 for participating in a demonstration

117

against the Soviet invasion of Czechoslovakia. Lara and Benedikt, their father already consumed in fire above the planet, were billeted with various relatives from then on, some as powerless as them, others well connected – in these houses even the brooms were softer. But nothing could be done, no network of influence and protection available, when Benedikt was summoned by the army.

To be sent to the feared war against ghosts in Afghanistan. To become a ghost himself.

4

Night Letter

CYANIDE CAN BE EXTRACTED from apricots, Casa knows. He had distilled it at a jihad training camp, injected it into the bodies of creatures. The memory comes to him as he walks past a flowering tree at the edge of a street in Jalalabad city centre, the flowers still not finished emptying themselves of scent this late in the afternoon. An ant travels up the trunk at the speed of a spark along a fuse wire.

Pencils. Lemons. Corn syrup. Dye. As he walks through the street he knows he could fabricate explosives from many things on the carts and in the shops around him. Sugar. Coffee. Paint. He even knows how to make a bomb out of his urine.

Three international military patrol vehicles go by containing khaki-clad soldiers, a clamorous knot developing in the traffic because all others have to make way for them. There are women and blacks among the soldiers, an attempt, Nabi Khan says, by the USA-led Western world to humiliate Muslims by having sows and apes be their new monarchs.

Word has come that the explosion outside the school has delighted the Taliban, al-Qaeda, and the covert grouping of Pakistani military officers led by Fedalla. They have promised further help.

Casa himself has never attended a school, just various religious institutions. Attached to a number of which there was a military training camp. At about ten he had wanted permission to fight in Bosnia but he was told it was too far for someone so young. And the response was the same at eleven when he wanted to pursue martyrdom in Chechnya. By then he had been holding a Kalashnikov for three years. He knew the finger on the trigger was steadier during exhalation as opposed to during inhalation. He knew how to strip and clean the rifle blindfolded, and he could do it in sixty seconds. He had fired it from moving vehicles and had fired it in the darkness, had fired it after running for an hour to simulate the banging heartbeat of a battle. He was proud of the fact that it was a Soviet gun. The Koran told of Daud, the raw youth with no weapons or armour who had used Jaloot's own sword to slay him, Jaloot the giant whom the Christians call Goliath, having felled him with a sling first; and so the Afghans had used captured Soviet weapons as the instruments of the evil Godless empire's own destruction. The Koran being a guidance for all time, this method continues to be relevant. Of the sixty-six Tomahawk missiles fired at Afghanistan's training camps in the 1990s, across thousands of miles from an American warship in the Arabian Sea, a number had failed to detonate – and these had been sold by al-Qaeda to the Chinese for millions of dollars.

Casa was present at a camp at the exact moment the missiles landed. He had been bowing before Allah and had just raised his forehead from the prayer mat. The needle of the small compass fitted at the head of the mat – to allow the faithful to always find the direction of Mecca – had started to spin at great speed just as it did in lightning storms. He was severely injured but Allah had spared his life, having better plans for him.

Because no true Muslim should shrink from killing in cold blood, his jihad training had included slitting the throats of sheep and horses while reciting the verse from the holy Koran which gives permission to massacre prisoners of war: *It is not for the Prophet to have captives until he has spread fear of slaughter in the land.* In the laboratories of the camps, stocked with labelled drums of various acids, acetones, cellulose, wood composite and aluminium powder, he had learned to mix methyl nitrate, had hit a small drop of it with a hammer to see it shatter the hammer. He blew up a car with a sack of fertiliser and ammonium nitrate fuel oil, the burning chassis travelling in an arc through the air to land a hundred yards away. He crumbled a boulder with twenty pounds of US-made C-4, and, for comparison, others with C-1, C-2, and C-3, and also with Czech Semtex. He knew the Americans were trying to get back from the Afghans the Semtex they had supplied for use in the Soviet jihad, so dangerous was the substance. During all this he chanted the sacred words of the Koran. *I will instil terror in the hearts of the Infidels, strike off their heads, and strike off from them every fingertip.*

The faces of women are on display around him but he keeps his eyes off them as he walks. Nowadays he doesn't think of such matters but at one time he had dreamed of a wife, preferably one of the thousands upon thousands of Bosnian women who had been raped by the Serbs, many of them becoming pregnant so that the Bosnian men banished them. These men couldn't contemplate raising a child who was half enemy. But Casa and his brothers at the camps and madrassas had felt it their duty to marry these women, and raise their children to become jihadis, who could go on to slaughter the Serbs whose blood they shared.

He arrives at the crossroads where someone is to pick him up. To take him to Nabi Khan at the poppy farm. There they'll get ready and wait. Tonight, under cover of darkness, he and four others are going to Usha.

IN *CITY OF GOD* St Augustine records his belief that the peacock's flesh has the God-given property of resisting putrefaction after death. Marcus withdraws his hand from deep within the bird's breast, having plunged the scissors into the topiary figure to snip at a branch. He is in the shattered glasshouse to the west of the house, most of its panes missing. The candle flame shudders as he turns around, suddenly aware of the three men standing at the lake's edge. He walks to the house where Lara sits reading by lamp at the kitchen table.

'Stay in here, Lara,' he says to her without stepping in. 'But could I please have the light for a moment?'

She stands up perhaps too fast. In a moment of vertigo she has experienced before with the books in this house, she feels as though the things printed on the paper would drain away through the hole in the centre of the page. From the door she sees him disappear along the curved path, catching the last hint of his greyed blue jacket amid the rustle of the long grasses.

She is in darkness. She switches on the cell phone she brought with her from St Petersburg, though there is no signal for it here. In the silver haze of its light she goes out and moves along the path until she can see him in the distance, talking to the three figures near the tree split in two by Qatrina's despondent love for her countrymen.

She stands there and then David arrives from his day in Jalalabad, the beams of the car scattering on the low foliage. He gets out and joins the group, a voice from there drifting towards her whenever the wind spins around – she realises she has begun to recognise the voices of these two men.

'The doctor in Usha is away for a few days,' David walks up and tells her. 'One of the old men out there got injured last week but the wound he thought was healing is suddenly giving him trouble today. He's hoping Marcus can help.'

They will not come into the house, she knows, afraid of the ghost of the perfume maker's daughter. Of the Buddha, the suffering stone that had bled gold, that had been granted life by bullets.

'I'll get more light, to make it easier for Marcus.'

When she had appeared at Usha and asked for Marcus, she was mistakenly brought to the current doctor's house, and his young daughter – the teacher at the one-roomed school Gul Rasool has permitted in Usha to please the United States – had lovingly taken charge of her. Before leaving for Russia she intends to visit the girl.

She follows David towards the lake, bringing a hurricane lamp and a flashlight. All things considered, the Afghans she has met have been helpful and kind towards her – with the exceptions of the boy who attacked her with the tyre iron, and the guide she had hired to bring her from Kabul to Usha, who had absconded with most of her money one night.

Marcus is leaning towards the bloody shoulder of the man sitting on a tree stump, and now with a sound of astonishment he extracts a piece of paper from within the gash. It is blood-soaked and folded tight to the size of a coin. The man attempts an explanation while Marcus tries to spread it to its full size: what appear to be verses of the Koran are written on the paper. As she doesn't understand the language the aged man is speaking, Marcus explains,

'It is a talisman. Given to him by someone at the mosque to make the wound heal. Instead of just wearing it around his neck he has inserted it *into* the wound, thinking it'll speed up the process! That is why the bleeding won't stop.'

She can smell the injury, the small percentage of blood in the air.

The man takes the paper from Marcus's hands and begins to fold it again, both of them shaking their heads at each other and talking very fast – he obviously wishes to slot the holy words back under his skin.

The three strangers steal glances at her from time to time, their faces lovely to her, the beard of one fox-orange with henna, the eyes of another an uncontainable grape-blue. And Islam and its love of flowers! They have helped themselves to a pink rose from somewhere and are passing it between themselves.

One of the men, his skin the colour of violins in this light, says something in her direction. She realises it is 'Rus.'

Russia.

She nods.

'*Rus*,' the man says again, grinning. And he makes a comment which elicits an identical reaction of surprise from David and Marcus. They ask him questions and soon the other visitors begin to contribute – a discussion with many gestures.

'What are they saying?' she asks, smiling. Old timers. Perhaps one of them had visited Russia in the past. She tells herself to restrain the expression on her face – her guide had told her that she smiles too much for a woman. One of the men shakes the rose in his hand, thrusts it at the others.

The talk continues and then she hears one of the men clearly and carefully utter the name Benedikt, syllable by syllable.

She is suddenly numb.

'What did he just say?'

'Nothing,' David replies but she catches him exchange a glance with Marcus.

'Didn't he say Benedikt?'

'No, no.'

A man is now drawing a shape on the dust between his feet. A lobed oblong with a stalk. An oak leaf? Like the one she has, like the one Benedikt carried with him. Or is she mistaken? It could just as easily be a quick map of Afghanistan.

David quickly rubs away the drawing with his hand, avoiding her eye, while Marcus pretends busyness, the face determinedly turned away from her.

'They are just talking about a visit to Russia,' Marcus says to her at last. 'The Afghans are great travellers.

Farming the valleys of California or journeying across the Australian deserts for trade.'

'There is more than one Giovanni Khan in the Italian villages that their fathers saw in the battle heat of the Second World War,' David adds; and, turning to Marcus, says, 'Now, we must try to persuade him to keep the paper in the layers of the bandage and not in the wound itself . . .'

She can't help but feel shut out. There is a profound uneasiness around them. Even the air and light feel different to her, and after standing at the edge of the group for a while she walks back to the house. Not sure what has just happened.

She is silent and subdued all evening, and retires to her room earlier than usual.

'Do we tell her what the men said, David?'

'She knows we are keeping something from her.'

One of the three men had said that Gul Rasool and Nabi Khan had all those years ago fought over the possession of a Soviet soldier. And that the soldier, named Benedikt, had had a leaf in his pocket. But his companions – contradicting him and offering alternatives – had made Marcus and David uncertain about every detail.

'Did Benedikt bring a leaf with him?'

Marcus nods. 'I think she mentioned it.'

Marcus is sitting against the painted lyre on the wall and it appears as though the instrument is strapped to his back, its frame showing on either side of his body, the curled ends protruding above his shoulders.

'We have to tell her, David. That is why she is here, to know the truth about him.'

'Let's try to find out a little more on our own first. There is no need to worry her if it isn't true.'

And if the truth is too terrible? David has allowed Marcus to believe that Zameen died at Gul Rasool's villa in Peshawar, during a raid by Nabi Khan. That was what David was told originally. But the real facts – when he came upon them later, years later – weren't something he could have revealed to Marcus.

'Do you think Gul Rasool and Nabi Khan killed him, David?'

'No, that's not what they said. The two had just fought over him – probably over his pistol though they themselves had huge arsenals by then. They just needed an excuse to clash.' Ancient tribal rivalries.

They are in the kitchen, David sitting on the doorsill, the moths feeding near by on the small blossoms that grow at the base of the cypress trees.

The candle stub goes out with a hiss. No light except the stars now, the moon not yet up. Each star is a drop of transparent nectar, just large enough to fill a moth's stomach.

'Is it possible Benedikt ended up in a Western country? Looking for him, she says, she came into contact with the parents of a soldier who did manage to make his way to America. They distrusted the letters he wrote to them from Chicago, convinced they had been written by the CIA.'

'And the letters they sent him, he must have thought were dictated by the KGB.'

'On American trains and buses he took snapshots of children and sent them for his sister's little girl in Moscow.'

There was disagreement between the three men about what kind of leaf it was. One of them said he had heard it was a dried flower. Another that the soldier's name was Ivan, was Nikolai. The fate some captured Soviet soldiers and defectors met at the hands of the Afghan warriors like Gul Rasool and Nabi Khan was horrifying. To save bullets they were buried alive. Or repeatedly hurled from a roof until dead. Thrown off mountainsides, nothing remaining of them but bones at the base of a cliff after the wolves had been at them. Many of these conscripts were mere children and the beautiful ones were raped and traded between persons, for a good knife or a bad gun, before being shot in disgust by an owner somewhere down the line. The Afghans could remain suspicious of the loyalty of the defecting Soviets and refuse to give them guns, and so, dead weight, they would be executed when a major offensive drew near. And given the chance the rebels of today would do all that and more to American soldiers, to the enemy cities and towns of their bodies.

Two a.m. and Lara steps out of the house quietly, not lighting the lamp until after she has gone some distance along the lake's edge, in case a particle of light or a scrap of smoke alerts David or Marcus. She had felt distraught all evening and now the feeling has spilled over into something like determination, perhaps defiance. If they won't tell her what the three visitors said earlier, she'll go to Usha and try to find out for herself. The doctor's daughter in Usha will help, help her locate the men who visited Marcus earlier. She is quite certain she will remember how to find the house where the father and daughter live. A house with apple trees in the courtyard. A nocturnal insect occasionally decides to accompany her then disappears back into the night. To the right of her is the lake. When they wished to end their lives, Afghanistan's women often chose water instead of the noose or the knife in the breast. It was a final assertion of dignity, one last proclamation of their humanity. Why choose ropes or blades, the things used by men to overpower and kill animals?

She stumbles and the glass globe of the lamp, lit a moment ago like a jar of honey, is lost, the flame disappearing into fumes of oil and hot glass. She stands so still she imagines that even the flow of blood inside her body has been suspended, but then she forces herself to continue, arriving at Usha's outermost house and then on into the maze of lanes towards the dark centre. She realises soon that she is lost and in a panic she turns back, her breath jagged, wondering how to align herself. A mosque, she knows, has a niche pointing towards the west, the direction of Mecca. Perhaps she should present herself at the biggest house in Usha, Gul Rasool's mansion, and ask for help there.

When Marcus was away and she was alone in the house, she had looked out at dawn and seen a dog crossing the space between two trees with a bird in its mouth, the small head swinging from the limp neck, the hide on the animal's snout corrugating in a snarl when it caught sight of her at the corner of its eye. She'd only just woken up and later wasn't sure she had seen the disturbing sight. She now tells herself she is only imagining the low canine growl from somewhere up ahead. The mastiffs here are wolf battlers. The Afghan hounds can kill leopards.

The religion of Islam at its core does not believe in the study of science, does not believe the world runs along rational and predictable laws. Allah destroys the world each night and creates it again at dawn, a new reality that may or may not match the old one of yesterday, the Muslim clerics demanding a ban even on weather forecasts since only He can decide such a thing according to His will. And so in the darkness Lara feels as though she is buried alive under the ruins of the universe, under the weight of the extinguished and smashed suns and moons.

David plunges into waist-high grass in his hurry to reach Usha, to find Lara, his body scoring a deep black trench in the mass of grass blades silver-lit by the moon, the beam of the flashlight swinging wildly in the night. The sun provides heat because it is made of fire, and given the chill tonight it is possible to believe that the moon is carved from ice. He has cancelled the fears of landmines from his thinking. He remembers going out into the night with the Afghan rebels in the 1980s as they planted landmines along roads frequented by Soviet tanks, the explosion a few hours later tearing the turret off a T72 and hurling it and the gun several yards away, the thick heavy steel of the hull perforated like a colander. He had watched the rebels open up an unexploded Soviet bomb found in a field of wheat, a thousand-pounder, and extract the half-ton of explosive from it, using it to increase the power of the Chinese mine.

Hava hu, hava hu – he hears the call of a jackal from somewhere behind him just as he nears Usha. Or is it the djinn? Up there on the mountains are fronds of shining mist in extreme slow motion.

Before entering Usha he stands listening, looking for possible signs of her. In one of the volumes of paintings in the house, he has seen a jewel-like miniature from the sixteenth century, depicting Jalal in his search for the beautiful and winged Jamal, who encourages his quest by visiting him in the guise of a series of birds, by having him encounter trees on all of whose leaves her name is written, by having him converse with talking flowers and a drum, even kill a hostile member of his own family.

The doctor in Usha hadn't brought Lara to Marcus's house when she arrived there because, despite being a man of science, he believes in the djinn and in ghosts.

And now suddenly David knows where Lara has gone – to the physician's house. He stops to orientate himself. The house, he remembers, has a large board outside it with the doctor's name and qualifications painted on it, has the tops of several apple trees showing above the enclosure wall. Zameen said that upon visiting England for the first time as a child she was astonished to discover that the two halves of an apple were always symmetrical there.

He goes past the mosque in whose shadow Qatrina had had stones aimed at her. She had to wear the burka while they were killing her. Afterwards, as she lay on the ground, a man had gathered the hem of the burka and tied it into a knot and dragged her away as he would a bundle, and he grinned at his own ingenuity the while, as did the spectators. Blood was draining steadily through the holes of the embroidered eye-grille.

Next to the mosque is the house belonging to a widow. Marcus has told him how she had run off into the desert with her two teenage daughters at the end of 2001, having heard that the Americans were coming to rape and slaughter everyone they saw. Out there the three women had fallen into the hands of a group of Taliban men. The American soldiers arrived just in time to save their lives and honour, leading them back to this house.

Perhaps he has only imagined it but, a hundred yards ahead of him in this narrow lane, there is a movement, a graphite-grey form traversing the darkness at a diagonal. He raises the hand with the flashlight but there is no one at the end of the tunnel bored by the light. His other hand is pressed against a wall and he senses a wetness there – in the curved valley between thumb and forefinger. A swivel of the torch and the Night Letter, the *shabnama*, pasted onto the side of the house perhaps only minutes ago is revealed, the glue glistening under his light. He stands there reading the text and then turns away. Someone is going around posting these warnings to Americans and their Afghan sympathisers, swearing imminent extermination in the name of Allah. There is another stuck to the house across the lane. In nineteenth-century Montana, the number 3-7-77 would be pasted onto the houses of 'undesirables' in the middle of the night. An ultimatum by the Vigilantes to leave town. No one to this day knows what the number stands for and there are many theories. You have three hours, seven minutes and seventy-seven seconds to get out or face violence? Or are they the dimensions of a grave – three feet by seven feet by seventy-seven inches? One of David's great-uncles was found hanging from a bridge in 1917 with the number pinned to his clothing.

He plays the beam into the next street. Several sheets are revealed on the walls there also.

She is out there, with demonic forces roaming free near her.

The grandson of a watchsmith, he appeals for leniency from the god who decrees the point of no return. The moment the arrow leaves the bow, the moment when sexual climax is unstoppable, the moment when poetic inspiration begins.

Casa moves into the shadow of a wall when the clouds slide apart above him, the moon released. In subconscious reassurance he touches the Kalashnikov slung over his shoulder, the metal cold to the fingertip. *Allah sent down iron,* says the Koran, *so He in the unseen world may know who supports Him and His messengers.*

He uses the last of his fifty sheets to wipe the glue from his hands, crumpling and tossing it onto the water collected in a ditch, making it bounce off his upper arm. All of this without making a single noise. He is a veteran of ambushes that could be called off after three days because someone had just exhaled audibly.

Travelling through the darkened landscape, he and the four others had arrived at the edge of Usha sometime after midnight to post the *shabnama*. Because the Koran calls upon Muslims to create alarm among non-believers. Three Afghans, a Chechen and an Uzbek – they parked the motorbikes in the shadows, and then spread out through these streets and lanes, a pair going in the direction of Gul Rasool's house even though there is every possibility that it is protected by landmines, Nabi Khan's express instructions having been to paste a warning onto the enemy's front door. 'The hypocritical West likes him now, despite the fact that he had shot a Western journalist in the 1980s for having written a favourable article about me.'

The moon is bright above him as he moves through the lanes of Usha. The archangel Jibraeel, he knows, had been asked to blot away some of the moon's brightness with his wings, mankind having petitioned Allah that it was too strong for the nights. The grey markings on the radiant white disc were caused when he pressed his feathers onto it three times.

From shadow to shadow, he walks towards the spot where he is to meet the others to go back to Jalalabad: towards the crumbling stub of a shrine in the cemetery where they left the motorbikes. Enemies surround him here. And they are not just those who carry guns. According to the laws of the jihad the enemy can include the entire supply chain. Those who give them water, those who give them food, those who provide moral encouragement – like journalists who write in defence of their cause. Women too cannot always be innocent. If she prays to God for her husband's safety in a battle against Muslims, she is above blame. But if she prays for him to kill and triumph over Muslims then she becomes the enemy. If a child carries a message to the enemy fighters, he can be targeted and erased.

Lara has decided to ask the dead for directions. Coming to a cemetery, ringed by cypress trees, she has entered it because Muslim graves are orientated in a north–south alignment, ensuring that the face is turned towards Mecca while the feet are pointing away. It's unlikely that she'll forget this fact though the bruise on her neck has almost faded.

A bone forest. Most of those lying around her must have met unnatural deaths, been victims of the wars of the last quarter-century.

Marcus's house is to the south of here, but she finds herself too tired to calculate which direction the south might be, remembering how at times in the dozy heat of a late summer morning she would be unable even to concentrate on picking flowers in a meadow, a task that required concentration because the fresh flowers were mixed in with day-old ones, the pinks and yellows that dotted the swathe of grass behind their dacha. She lowers herself to the ground and leans her head against a tomb-stone. Her Stepan died at the dacha after testifying on behalf of the officers who stood accused of the torture of Chechen prisoners. Two days after the trial ended, Stepan and Lara had come out to their snowbound dacha on the Gulf of Finland, wishing to repair the fissures of the pre-ceding weeks, Lara's fury at Stepan's comments. The couple were there less than a few minutes when Lara – walking down a hallway – heard Stepan talking to some-one in the room just ahead of her. She stopped and stood listening.

'*You don't recognise me, Stepan Ivanovich. I was hoping you would.*'

'*I have never met you. What are you doing in my house?*'

'*People always said my brother and I looked alike, so I thought you might guess from the resemblance. You see, you have seen my brother's face.*'

'*Have I met your brother? What is his name?*'

'*You never met him either. You just saw photographs of him. He was abducted by the military to force me to come out of hiding, to make me go back to Chechnya from Afghanistan. Please stay where you are. I am telling you nicely, but my four friends here won't be as polite if I give them the signal.*'

A breeze in the cypress trees and she opens her eyes. A rustle. The night has entered its second half, she is sure. She'll stay here till daybreak, shoulder pressed against the marble slab. At the touch of the stone she experiences a sensation from childhood – a drawing that has been filled in with coloured pencils, the paper feeling slightly silky. All the colour is down there.

'Lara.'

David has approached and is extending a hand towards her, pulling her upright and away from the magnet of the tombstone. The day Stepan died had become the first day of the rest of her life. She had only a handful of new memories until she came to Marcus's house. Over the months she had just stepped away from everyone, coming back to St Petersburg from Moscow, where she had moved on marrying Stepan. She desired no real communication with anyone, entire days going by without her speaking to even one person.

'Come on, I'll take you home,' he says.

The wind picks up grains of dust from the ground and then releases them.

'I couldn't bring the car because I thought the engine would wake Marcus.' His voice is low in the darkness, bringing energy and focus to her mind with his talk of practical matters.

'How did you know I was missing?'

'I couldn't sleep. Came down and the front door was unlocked. You should have brought your phone.'

In the absence of the electricity generator he charges the phones with his car battery.

'And why not bring a light, Lara?'

'It broke.'

'I was on my way to the doctor's house but then saw you sitting here. The white glow of your clothes.'

'We have to go back the way I came, so we can take home the broken lamp.'

'Okay.' And as they leave Usha behind, he says, 'We are almost half-way there.'

'Benedikt had great difficulty trying to commit the English alphabet to memory as a child. During recitals the letter M would always come as a relief to him, indicating he was almost half-way there.'

She stops. 'David, tell me what the three gentlemen said.'

She takes in what the visitors had claimed about the leaf from the Cosmos Oak, listens to David's reasons for keeping the information from her.

'So Gul Rasool might know about Benedikt's fate?'

'It's a possibility. We thought we'd check first, we didn't want to alarm or distress you needlessly. I am sorry.'

Approaching the house, she goes through the garden while he remains beside the lake, the sky on fire with the stars. Later, sitting with a dying candle at the kitchen table, she hears him enter the house from a side door, through the room that had been the doctors' surgery. When it overflowed the patients could be found in the orchard, lying under the trees, the drip hooked to a flowering branch overhead. Marcus said it would have been appropriate if the room dedicated to touch had been turned into the surgery but that was too high up for the infirm to climb.

She goes up to his room to ask for a candle.

She is there inside its light a while later when she looks up and sees him standing against a blue and red section of the kitchen wall. In a tale she had read in childhood there

141

was an enchanted lamp in whose light you saw what the owner of the lamp wished you to see. *I'll make you think of me.*

Her hand reaches out and douses the candle he had given her.

Mind torn by contending emotions, she takes a step towards the wall in the perfect darkness, to find out.

Casa is going through a stand of acacia trees when he hears a small sweet-edged noise. Coming to a standstill, he lets his hearing pierce the darkness. The noise is like metal coming into contact with something, giving a small ring. A blade or iron nail. He becomes still and parts his lips slightly – a hunter's trick to increase the sharpness of hearing. The world is full of homeless ghosts, and it is said that by the time a house has a roof on it, it has a ghost in it. He switches on his flashlight, sending its gaze – and his own alongside it – out into the night. He sees the gun pointed at him in the high grass and weeds. There are others, he now sees, ranged in a circle around him, each a black grasshopper the length of his arm.

They are flintlock guns, resting on foot-high tripods in the undergrowth, concealed in the foliage. He identifies the tripwire stretching across his path. Two more steps in the darkness and his foot would have landed on it. The gun that this taut wire is attached to would have swivelled on the tripod and fired into his shin.

The entire grove is crisscrossed by these lengths of wire.

Each gun has three of them fastened to its trigger, the central coming at it from the base of the tree directly in front, and the other two reaching it diagonally. To kill jackals or wolves or wild boar, or to maim thieves. These things were first employed during the times when there was a British presence in these parts.

He raises a foot and places it carefully on the wire before him, just holding it there for a few seconds before starting to release the weight onto the metal filament. The branches and leaves of the acacia trees are moved by a sudden breeze just then. It passes and the trees are still again, as though the angel of death had flown down into the grove.

He continues to press downwards with his foot until, to his left, a gun turns towards him like a magnetised needle inside a compass. With extreme caution he lifts the foot off, suddenly aware of the weight of his limbs. A Russian PMD6 mine – just 250 grams of TNT in a cheap wooden box with a detonator – could blow off your legs. Someone he knew had stepped on one, and as Casa had braced himself to lift him onto his shoulders, he had learned at the upward swing that the man had become shockingly lighter.

Knees raised high, he goes over the wire but then stops. What *is* that noise, the small metallic chime? It has never really stopped, some variation of it always present in his hearing. He looks up with the beam – the light separating into shards of seven colours on his eyelashes – and sees the dagger hanging from a cord fifteen feet above him, gently swaying. There are others, dozens of them, and they flash in the canopies when the wind sends them towards the rays of moonlight pouring through the leaves. When one of them occasionally meets a branch it makes a noise.

A second trap.

A moth has appeared, as soft-looking as a pinch of rabbit fur, attracted by his light. He still hasn't worked out how the second trap will be activated when his weight sets off some buried mechanism. The blades are released in unison all through the grove as though they are pieces from a mirror shattering overhead. One of them almost enters his flesh, cutting through the thin blanket wrapped around his body. There is a gust of wind, powerful enough that had it been daytime the bees in the grove would have been thrown off their flight paths.

When he moves forward to avoid the falling knife, he loses his balance and ends up on his knee in shock, his turban falling into the grass. He continues forward because of momentum so that his hand snags the tripwire attached to one of the guns. The result is a blinding flash and an explosion. The hot ball of lead shoots out in a shower of sparks and grazes the back of his skull, tearing off skin and tissue, the dry grass bursting into a line of flames towards him.

Lara's eyes are open in the darkness as she lies beside David, his hand on her rib. She feels a measure of safety here against him, though her mind is at the dacha with Stepan in the grip of his killers.

'Who's that out there? You said you were here alone, that your wife was back in Moscow.'

She had slipped away then, leaving the corridor and rushing upstairs to hide. They began to hurt Stepan, so that his cries would force her to reveal herself.

'Just like my brother was tortured to call me back to Chechnya.'

Of course she presented herself to them, unable to bear it any longer, Stepan's mouth hoarse from shouting at her to stay where she was – to run away into the snow and ice outside – and then just from screaming.

There are tough calluses on many areas of his skin as though part of his body is shell. He can survive this. Under the white lantern moon he runs down the alley away from the acacia grove, casting a long sharpened shadow before him. He feels the night itself had come alive to attack him back there, the air clotting into predator muscle, into bone and razor. The noise of the guns going off will bring men who will give chase. He is not sure whether the sounds he can hear are his own thoughts or something outside him. With one hand he is holding a fold of his blanket to the back of his head to staunch the blood flow, his fingers wet. Allah is on his side. *We have created the human being in the throes of loss. But does he think no one is watching over him? Haven't We made for him two eyes, a tongue, and two lips? And guided him to two places of safety in distress?* He must find somewhere to tend to the wound, mustn't lose focus.

His blood bellowing in his ears. Two places of safety. He is very cold as though his skeleton is made of ice. Now suddenly he knows where he must go: towards the house that belongs to a doctor – he had pasted a *shabnama* on the metal signboard outside it. He'll go and ask for – or demand – help with his injury. As he runs his head spins. The peripheries of his soul don't feel bound within his body.

'How big is the Cosmos Oak?'

'Say that again. My mind was elsewhere.'

'Nothing.'

David is standing at the window.

We and others like us will never stop until we have covered ourselves in glory by reaching Jerusalem and blowing up the White House, says the Night Letter.

He has dressed, and she is sitting on the bed wrapped in a sheet, hugging herself with the fingers that had gently slid into his hair earlier, when they were both searching for themselves in each other.

When he touched her he felt it was not in the present. He was as though a ghost, watching himself place his hand on her shoulder, his mouth on her thigh. Either a ghost or a memory. He is not young enough to believe that a moment can be seized, no longer a child who looked at the hundred clocks in his grandfather's workshop without seeing that the hands were moving like scythes.

'I'll see today if I can find James Palantine and talk to

him,' he tells her, moving towards the door. 'He'll talk to Gul Rasool to find out about Benedikt.'

'Who is James Palantine?'

'His father, Christopher, was someone I knew, though I know him too. He is friends with Gul Rasool – an "associate" is probably a better word. He is responsible for Gul Rasool's security. I knew Christopher Palantine back in the 1980s in Peshawar.'

'When you were in espionage?'

A hesitation.

Both Christopher and he were. He thinks of the CIA's motto. From the Gospel of John: *And ye shall know the truth and the truth shall make you free.*

He opens the door and leaves. Outside the wind rustles in the trees as though trying to speak someone's name.

5

Street of Storytellers

DAVID HAS HEARD it said that no other war in human history was fought with the help of as many spies. When the Soviet Army crossed the River Oxus into Afghanistan in December 1979, secret agents from around the world began to congregate in the Pakistani frontier city of Peshawar. It now became the prime staging area for the jihad against the Soviet invaders, rivalling East Berlin as the spy capital of the world by 1984.

By then seventeen thousand Soviet soldiers had been killed, and David had been living in the city for two years. Because it was once the second home of Buddhism, the city could count Lotus Land among its almost forgotten names, the peepal tree under which the Enlightened One was said to have preached continuing to grow in a quiet square.

The City of Flowers.

The City of Grain.

It was transformed into a city filled with conjecture, with unprovable suspicions and frenzied distrust. Everyone's nerves were raw and everyone had something hidden going on. For most of its history it was one of the main trading centres linked to the Silk Road, and now the United States was sending arms into Afghanistan through here. Wherever David looked he could find evidence of the war in which those weapons were being used. Makeshift ambulances filled with the wounded and the dying raced through the mountain passes towards Peshawar, carrying at times children who had been set alight by Soviet soldiers to make the parents reveal the hiding places of guerrillas. Dentists filled cavities with shotgun pellets in Peshawar.

Having trained with the CIA, David now had an office in the Jewellers Bazaar, his interest in gems an ideal façade. He had met Christopher Palantine during the Islamabad embassy siege back in 1979, when Christopher had put forward the possibility that he might like to answer a few questions upon returning from his forthcoming trip to Afghanistan. To gain information about the Soviet Union, the CIA had been known even to question the pilgrims who arrived in Mecca from the central Asian republics, the Saudi Arabian government allowing this because of the abhorrence it felt for Communism. And David too had agreed readily to Christopher's request. By the time his sentient life began, a hatred and fear of Communism was in the air an American child breathed, and it could have remained as just subconscious animosity, but there was the matter of Jonathan's death. The Soviet Union had supported Vietnamese guerrillas and had thus played a role in the disappearance and probable death of his brother. He was fourteen years old when the news came that Jonathan was missing presumed dead. Even the festive occasions would now be sad ones because Jonathan wasn't there, and everything reminded David of him. He wept into the crook of his arm standing in front of the house: as soon as they reached the age of twelve, both he and Jonathan were allowed in the mornings to take the car out of the garage and down this very driveway while their father collected his coat and briefcase. As the days passed without further news of Jonathan, his father gently began to ask him whether he would be able to control his tears – the two of them had to give strength to their mother. But a fire of immense intensity burned inside his young body. Having trapped a coyote in the woods one day he began to hit it with a club. Who gives a fuck if this is wrong. He needed release, and, as though he wished to obliterate the evidence of what he had done, he continued to beat the animal long after it was dead. And for the rest of my life I am going to do everything I can to fuck up the Reds.

But that was then. By the time he came to Peshawar as an employee of the CIA, his opposition to Communism was the result of study and contemplation. Not something that grew out of a personal wound.

He was in Peshawar as a believer.

An almost blind white-haired poet lived in the apartment next to David's office in the Jewellers Bazaar in 1984, having fled death threats from both the Communists and the Islamic guerrillas in Kabul some months earlier. For most of the day he sat cross-legged on a threadbare rug on the floor, surrounded by books. A god of immutable stone, the entire earth his plinth.

David had slipped into his apartment to check for listening devices: any number of people could have wished to spy on him – the KGB, Pakistan's ISI, the Saudi Arabian spy agency, or the KGB-trained Afghan intelligence service that at the height of the conflict would swell to thirty thousand professionals and a hundred thousand paid informers, maintaining secret bases in Peshawar, Islamabad, Karachi, and Quetta. The jihad was at its fiercest then and had anyone wished to gain access to a conversation taking place in David's office, it would have been a case of just piercing the wall in the poet's apartment with a silenced drill and inserting a microphone.

He found the apartment to be free of any devices but before the month was over its occupant had vanished: while the poet was out one afternoon a five-year-old girl with her throat slit was discovered at his place. A crowd baying for blood descended on the apartment and the man was never seen again.

David learned from _____, his own source within Pakistan's ISI, that a Pakistani intelligence officer had ordered a child to be picked up from the streets of Peshawar, brought to the poet's place, and killed there. The mob and the police were then sent in to discover the crime. The intelligence officer wanted the place empty so he could install a tenant able and willing to spy on David.

'So it was Fedalla who did it?' Christopher Palantine said when David told him.

'Yes. He was among the ones I suspected.'

Five years had passed since Fedalla and his friends had assaulted David in Islamabad, and David had recognised him when he ran into him at a meeting with the Pakistani

154

military personnel not long after coming to Peshawar with the CIA. Back in 1979 Fedalla had been a senior captain aching to make major, which he now was, heavier in both face and body. David waited for his chance and then confronted him but Fedalla denied all knowledge and memory of the assault in Islamabad.

'You have to move out of the Jewellers Bazaar fast,' Christopher told David.

David acquired premises in the nearby Street of Storytellers, the street that in ancient times was the camping ground for caravans and military adventurers, storytellers reciting ballads of love and war to the amassed wayfarers and soldiers. It extended from east to west in the heart of the city, and in April 1930 British soldiers had massacred a crowd of unarmed protesters there, a defining moment in the struggle to drive the British out of India. When the protesters at the front were felled by shots, those behind had come forward and exposed themselves to the bullets, committing suicide in all but name, as many as twenty bullets entering some bodies. The massacre continued from eleven in the morning till five in the afternoon, court martial awaiting the soldiers who refused to pull the trigger.

His new neighbours in this three-storey building were clean, as was the unoccupied apartment on the level above. One day a few months later, as he was emerging from his office, fifty or so orbs of thread leapt down the steep staircase leading to that upstairs apartment, some stopping but others continuing to bounce past him, going down the next stairwell, leaping over the banister until they had fully uncoiled themselves.

The suspicion was immediate: the young woman who stood in the open door at the top of the stairs was a spy.

The hand in which she held the thread was dyed with henna, indicating the possibility that she had recently attended a wedding.

'Thank you,' she said in English after he had helped her gather the silk filaments.

'What's your name?'

She stopped and looked back at him from the staircase, then the haughty face brightened into a smile.

'All names are my names,' she said with something like mischievousness and disappeared.

He was in her apartment the next afternoon when she went out with the child. He found nothing in there that suggested subterfuge then or during the searches he carried out on later dates.

Zameen.

A single word.

How easily a person gave his name to another, and yet how restless he was during the few hours when he didn't know it, finding it out through methods of his own. Discovering for the first time that there could be something magical about someone's name – a mere word but what power it held, as in a fairy tale. It was after all the first thing one learned about another. A way in, and a possibility.

At the moment of the initial encounter he had been on his way to a meeting with Christopher Palantine, and he thought of her during it. He was then away for several days, vanishing once again into schemes he'd set in motion in and around the teeming city, he and Christopher

Palantine both great mavericks of that time and place, a cause of some anxiety to their superiors when they simply became invisible for weeks. But when he returned to the Street of Storytellers he synchronised several appearances at the door of his office just to encounter her, to just see her again. Once when the area plunged into darkness due to power failure, he went up to ask for a matchstick instead of going down into the bazaar. He had known when he began this work that there would be sacrifices. Loneliness was the price they paid for being who they were. And yet as he sat in the light of the lamp lit with her matchstick, he couldn't help seeing how incomplete his life was. There were houses and establishments in Peshawar he occasionally entered to alleviate solitude, and he had a rendezvous with a certain woman each time he visited the city of Lahore, meeting her for a few hours in Falleti's, the hotel where Ava Gardner had stayed when she was in Pakistan filming *Bhowani Junction*. But this was different, seemed to be something deeper.

He listened to her feet in the ceiling above him, following her movements.

And then one afternoon he managed to talk to her openly, running into her in the Street at the stall of a cassette vendor. Before engaging in a battle with Soviet soldiers, the Afghans sometimes inserted a blank cassette into a tape recorder to capture the sound of combat. They played these cassettes to themselves later during periods of recreation and leisure, reliving the excitement. They were for sale, the seller beginning to shout out the highlights of each cassette the moment David picked it up:

The ambush at Qala-e Sultan, April two years ago, a little-known battle but . . .

The Dehrawud offensive, October 1983, the sound of helicopters and fighter planes, the screams of the wounded, contains the famous death by torture of a captured Soviet infidel . . .

Battle for Alishang District Centre, August 1981, on three cassettes. The Soviets are made to withdraw in a hurry but they force the elders of the next village to come ask the Mujahidin for the bodies of the dead Soviet soldiers left behind . . .

He recognised the decorative motifs on the henna-dyed left hand that reached towards a cassette at the same time as him and when he looked up he saw that, yes, it was her. The recording was of a mujahidin attack at a newly opened village school, the teachers and everyone associated with it massacred.

'Something like that happened in the place I am from,' she told him in her apartment later. 'A place called Usha. It means "teardrop".'

He had attempted to talk to her in the crowded Street but she had shaken her head in fear, telling him in a quick whisper to come up in a few minutes.

'Why only the one hand?' he asked now.

'The henna? It takes a while to dry, I have work to do and my son to look after. That's why I kept my right hand free. As it is I grabbed the wrong child one day in the chaos outside.' The boy was moving across the floor on his knees, pushing a toy car along.

They stood facing each other, not knowing what to say

or do. She bent to clear away the sheets of paper bearing the outlines of foliage, flowers, dragonflies, and vines. They were embroidery patterns and he remembered being told how, just before the First World War, patriotic young Germans had entered the French countryside with butterfly nets, catching specimens and sketching wing patterns to take back to Germany. Encrypted in the designs of the butterfly wings were maps of strategic information, such as the exact locations of bridges and roads.

He picked up one of the sheets and looked at it. The French country people were knowledgeable about their local butterflies and soon realised the drawings were incorrect, exposing the spies before the information could be sent back to headquarters.

'You live here by yourselves, the two of you?'

She held out her hand for the drawing.

He listened as she began to speak about her lost parents, and then, his heart breaking, about a young man who as a boy had been so beautiful he had had to be veiled.

'He was shot by the Soviets. I was with him that night, and that was the last time I saw him. I thought he was dead but I have since learned from refugees who have come from Usha that he had actually survived. I don't know where he is.'

One night when David had been standing above her sleeping form in the darkness, having gained access to her place to see if she was involved with intelligence-gathering or surveillance, he had heard her say a man's name in her sleep.

It was that of the missing lover, he now realised.

She wanted his help in finding these three, she herself – being a woman – lacking the ability to move as freely in this place.

As he took his leave her little boy moved towards the kitchen area and, thinking himself unobserved, put back onto the shelf the knife he'd kept concealed upon his person during the entire visit; David had seen him pick it up a few moments after his mother opened the door to him. *What have they been through?*

A few evenings later as he was leaving the office he noticed that the door to her place was ajar, something unusual for that hour. He stood listening and then went up slowly. He raised his hand and knocked. Spoke her name. And when there was no response he looked in.

She was sitting on the bed with her back towards the door – the kid asleep, hardly any light from a weak lamp on a table. He could hear the sobs clearly.

'Zameen,' he said but she did not turn around. The impression he had had of her was that she was quite self-sufficient and tough: after fire she probably wouldn't be ashes, she'd be coal. But this was darkness and solitude. The hidden side of the courage required from her daily.

He spoke her name again.

She turned to him but there was no recognition. He could have been the noise of the breeze against the window.

He stayed there until she had exhausted herself and then he watched as she took up a pair of scissors and began to cut herself out of her clothes, ready for sleep but still in a daze, unable to find the correct path for the given destination.

Her clothing fell from her in pieces.

'Zameen,' he said in a half-voice, afraid she might hurt herself.

He stayed where he was until she got into bed in just her white shift, and then he withdrew and spent the night in his office. Only when he heard her lock her door around dawn did he go home to the apartment he rented a few miles away.

Before the month was out he found the man she was looking for, in one of the refugee camps closest to the border with Afghanistan. He was there on an unrelated matter when a likeable person came forward and began to help with the translation because David was experiencing difficulty with certain dialects.

As they talked, it became apparent that his name and details were the ones Zameen had given David regarding her lost lover.

He didn't tell him she was looking for him.

He arrived back at the Street of Storytellers and before he knew it an entire week had gone by without him having said anything to her either. *I'll do it this afternoon. I'll do it tomorrow. Tomorrow. Tomorrow.* Her son was becoming fond of David, frequently loud with delight around him, the boy who was born under a thorn tree while she was making her way towards Peshawar, and, yes, he had begun to notice signs of attraction in her also. He went back to the refugee camp twice and talked to the young man. It turned out he was a believer in Communism despite the fact that the Soviets were tearing apart his land.

He didn't know what to do.

I'll tell her tomorrow.

He came into her place to see the mother and child out on the small wooden balcony. It was raining weakly, a kind of mist that coated everything, and they were leaning towards a nasturtium plant, observing something with great concentration. She waved him to her, the boy immediately leaning against him when he joined them, a rumble of thunder in the far distance. He saw how on each nasturtium leaf the minute dots of moisture joined up until they were recognisably a drop of liquid, balanced perfectly and brightly in the centre of the circular leaf for a while. But then, in a matter of seconds, it became so overgrown that the leaf stalk could not support it: the leaf began to sway and finally tipped the bead to the ground, becoming upright again for the entire process to be repeated.

She smiled at him – presenting this, one of the unasked-for delights of existence, to him.

His conscience ached.

Today let me stay here, I'll tell her tomorrow.

CASA OPENS HIS EYES to see the giant face suspended above him, the first light of dawn falling gently onto it. He lifts his head off the floor and looks around. He remembers descending the steps in the darkness a few hours earlier, coming to a halt upon seeing the stone object in the centre of this space. A contour of it had caught the edge of the beam from his flashlight. He trained the light on it and saw that it was the face of a Buddha. He approached it and spread his blanket on the ground, with difficulty because his head was numb even though the bleeding was being kept in control with strips he had torn from the blanket. There had been no response to the knocks he had sounded on the doctor's house in Usha and then he had decided that he must make his way to the cemetery. When he managed to get there the three motorbikes were gone – his companions had had to flee without him. The gun going off in the acacia grove had alerted the inhabitants of Usha to the presence of a thief and then the *shabnama* must have been discovered, the place in an uproar.

He doesn't know where he dropped his own Kalashnikov. After spreading the blanket on the floor beside the stone head he had unknotted from around his waist the cloth that had been his turban. He lay down under the fabric – it is actually his shroud, everyone always taking theirs with them on arduous operations, to signal their blissful willingness to die.

Five days ago, the man called Bihzad was sent to bomb the school not because Casa and the others were cowards themselves. They knew that a greater mission awaited them, the coming battle for Usha.

He must get up now and find his way back to Jalalabad.

He tries to sit up but as in a bad dream he cannot manage it. He would at the very least like to choose another spot to lie on – somewhere not so close to this idol – but he feels drained of all force, his mind askew.

He lies there aware of the giant features hovering above him in the half-light.

The almost-closed eyes.

The smile.

Lara is half-way down the staircase when she notices the figure. He is asleep pressed up against the painted wall so that a shrub with small yellow flowers is growing out of his left hip, the Buddha's decapitated head a few yards away from him. She has never been able to find any sign on the stone of the bullet marks that are said to have bled gold. But sometimes she imagines that being nailed to the ceilings in the house had made the books drip brilliance onto the floors in each room.

She takes her eye off the boy only upon gaining the topmost step and then she rushes out into the avenue of

Persian lilacs, the avenue of chinaberries. David's car, always parked here under these trees, is moving towards the lake, taking him to Jalalabad for the day, and she can see Marcus emerging from the kitchen to add a glass to the basket of washed dishes she had left out to dry in the morning sunlight.

David tells the two of them to remain outside and goes into the factory, returning five minutes later.

'He has an injury, a two-inch wound,' he tells them. 'Has lost a lot of blood. He says he was attacked by a bandit last night, up in the mountains. He came down the ridges and stumbled in there, probably losing consciousness.'

Lara and Marcus peer down to where he sits immobile against the wall, the side of the head resting against the flowers. He is thin, dust on his face and clothes and hair, and there is a pad of blood-soaked fabric tied to the back of the skull. A red butterfly three-quarters of the way up the wall makes it appear as though a small quantity of his spilled blood has become airborne.

David brings the car back to the factory and then goes down to lead the stranger up into daylight, supporting him by feeding an arm along the back of the ribs at one point but the young man gently uncouples himself.

'I think you should take him to Jalalabad,' says Marcus after he has had a look at the wound, managing to ease off the fabric stiff with caked blood, his hair glued into it. 'Have the hospital look at him. He'll need stitches – one or two.'

The young man sits on the back seat without a word or glance towards anyone, taking a few sips from the sugar-rich tea he has been brought. The back of his shirt is streaked with blood, but he declines with a raised hand when Marcus offers to find a new set of clothing for him. He hands back the cup without lifting his eyes and then settles down and brings his white cloth over himself. His only other communication is the nod when David tells him in Pashto that he is being taken to the city.

They go through Usha, the place subdued this morning because of the *shabnama*. In other villages, the Night Letters tell people to plant opium poppies, a crop forbidden by the new government, but here in Usha, Gul Rasool is a poppy farmer already despite the fact that he is in the government. As in Vietnam, as in the Afghanistan of the 1980s, where the CIA ignored the drug trafficking of the anti-Communist guerrillas it was financing, the activities of Gul Rasool have to be tolerated because he is needed. Last month he was among the dozens of male politicians who had hurled abuse at a woman MP as she spoke in parliament, shouting threats to rape her. Harassed and fearful, she changes her address regularly and owns burkas in eight different colours to avoid being followed.

The Night Letter is from an organisation that chooses to call itself Building the New Muslim – the bombing of the school was carried out by Building the New Afghanistan. It could be the same organisation: if they have found rich backers outside Afghanistan, people who have Islamic goals, they must have asked for the name to be amended. This isn't about one particular country – it is about the glory and aspirations of Islam. Saladin fought for Allah and for Muhammad and so he won Palestine, but today's Palestinians are fighting just for land, even if it is their own land, and therefore losing.

The Night Letter is offering a financial reward of two hundred dollars to any inhabitant of Usha who might help in the war they are promising against Gul Rasool for – among other things – having allowed girls to be educated here. Yes, it could be Nabi Khan's organisation. He must be alive. The money is an unbelievable sum for most ordinary people in Usha and some could be tempted by it, seeing it as a way out of poverty.

The eyes of David's passenger remain closed throughout most of the journey towards Jalalabad, though he occasionally takes a sip of water, one of those bottles that had landed around Marcus's house. As soon as they near the city, however, he wants to be let out of the car, suddenly all vigour and purpose, darting looks to his left and right. David tries to reason with him, an exchange lasting many minutes with the car brought to a halt by the side of the road and with David reaching a measured hand back to stay him, telling him a doctor should take a look at his injury.

'I have no money for the doctors because the bandit took everything.'

'The hospital is just around the corner.'

'I must leave.'

Does your mother know you are intent on wasting the blood she made out of her own blood, her own milk?

Someone had said this to him after an injury here in Afghanistan, but it's too intimate a thing for him to say to this boy.

'I want to leave.'

'Don't worry about the money.'

He consents eventually and they drive in through the hospital entrance, past the gunmen protecting the building.

Leaving him in the waiting room for the doctor to arrive, David comes out of the building to stand under the pine trees, the Asian magpies in the branches, the crested larks. There is no breeze but a lavender bush is in constant movement due to the bees that land on or fly off the thin stalks. A small boy approaches him with a fan of Pashto, Dari, and English books for sale – *101 Best Romantic Text Messages* as well as a volume entitled *The CrUSAders*, and also *Mein Kampf* translated as *Jihadi.*

When he sees boys like these he sometimes finds himself wondering if they are Bihzad, forgetting that time has passed, Bihzad grown up out there somewhere.

The border with Pakistan is just three hours in the eastern direction. Continue through the twenty-three miles of the Khyber Pass and you arrive at Peshawar. The Street of Storytellers.

Where he had met and fallen in love with her and she with him.

He now knows how places become sacred.

'Where is the boy's father?' he asked her. The kid who had won every arm-wrestling competition with David in recent weeks.

She shook her head, and he knew not to proceed. More than a month had gone by since he met her but sometimes he felt he was still little more than a neighbour. And for almost two weeks now he had known that the man she really longed for was only a few miles away in a refugee camp.

'Who pays for this place?'

'An aid agency. They pay for me to be here so women from the refugee camps can come here and embroider in secret.' The work he thought might be something to do with spying. 'It's secret because we fear the fundamentalists who have constructed mosque upon mosque in the refugee camps and have forbidden work and education to women, so much so that a woman in possession of silk thread is branded a wanton, it being the Western aid organisations that began the embroidery scheme to give war widows a chance to earn a livelihood. The fundamentalists tell them they must beg in the streets – that this is Allah's way of using them to test who is charitable and who isn't – or send their little boys out to be labourers in the bazaars. We have to be very careful in case the women are followed here by them.'

Imagining her loneliness, he had felt wretched, but the man she wanted in her life – the Communist – would only add to her difficulties, he was sure. He decided to visit him for the final time to ask him as openly as possible about his plans and prospects.

'I don't care if Communism has failed in Russia,' he told David. 'It remains the best hope for a country like Afghanistan. Never mind food, some people in my country can't afford poison to kill themselves. There's no other way we can put an end to the feudal lords and the ignorant mullahs who rule us with their power and money, opening their mouths either to lie or to abuse.'

'You don't know what you are talking about. Communism has killed millions upon millions of people . . .'

'Let's just wait until it has killed a few thousand more – the bloodsuckers who control the place I am from – then I'll be happy to denounce it.'

People like these had to be told that Communism wasn't the only way to end inequality. 'We don't have that kind of people – the priests and landlords – in the United States either . . .'

'Then why are your people actually *supporting* them here, giving them money and weapons?'

As he talked to David he was keeping his voice low: around them were victims of Communism, and David could not imagine what they would do if they heard him talk in that manner. In 1917, one of David's great-uncles, a copper miner sympathetic to the far-left Industrial Workers of the World, had made known to everyone his opinions about America's recent entry into the war. He'd call President Woodrow Wilson 'a lying tyrant' and denounce US soldiers as 'scabs in uniform', unmindful of the fact that the state of Montana, in the grip of patriotic fever, was increasingly intolerant of dissent. During the course of one September night, a small group of masked men grabbed him from his house and left him hanging for all to see at daybreak. A piece of paper with the number of the Montana Vigilantes of the nineteenth century, 3-7-77, was pinned to his body, with the initials of four other men threatened with the same fate.

No, David could not allow this man and his misguidedness to endanger Zameen and the boy.

He could see that the man's ardour was genuine, but it was directed at falsehoods. David had learnt as much as he could about his great-uncle's death and had decided that – an outrage and a crime though his hanging was – he could not agree with the man's views. They would have resulted in the United States becoming entangled in the barbed coils of revolution, like the rest of the countries that had adopted Communism and its offshoots. Revolutions that eventually devoured their children and turned half the planet into a prison. They were the early years of the century and he admired the optimism of people like his distant relative, was even proud to have such a person in his bloodline, someone who cared about equality and justice. But at the opposite end of the century, the consequences were there for all those who wanted to see them. In David's time, an end to inequality and injustice meant having to contain and undo those outcomes.

'Just wait until the Soviets are defeated,' David said. 'Then we'll help you Afghans sweep away the landlords and mullahs.'

'The Soviets are helping us now. Building roads, hospitals, dams – which your people keep destroying.'

They weren't building anything. It was all either third-rate or just for show, and either way they were billing Afghanistan millions for it.

'The Soviets are flying thousands of our children to Moscow to be given free education. If I had a child I'd send him happily.' And he said that he and a small group of like-minded young men and women had come together and were planning to journey back to Kabul in a few weeks' time, to offer their services to the Communist regime.

David walked away from him.

And then the next afternoon, Christopher Palantine informed him that the Soviet military would be carrying out an air attack on the refugee camp where the young man lived. The refugee camps of Peshawar were the hub of the anti-Soviet guerrillas, where commanders and warriors came to regroup and recuperate after fighting the Soviet Army in Afghanistan. Tested beyond endurance, the Soviets had violated Pakistani air space to bomb the camps many times before – and that afternoon they would be doing it again.

He and Zameen had kissed for the first time last night, standing in the dark wooden staircase that led to her door, and it was she who had initiated it.

Having learned of the bombing raid in advance, Christopher said, from a mole inside Afghanistan's spy agency, the CIA had arranged for journalists and television cameras from several major cities of the Western and Muslim world to be present in Peshawar, so that the news and images of the carnage would spread around the world.

He sat under a massive tree with Christopher Palantine, in a saint's shrine not far from the Street of the Storytellers, the holy man's grave covered in a lively skin of tiles. He knew there was not enough time to get to the refugee camp and warn the man. So he sat there with his friend and watched the huge crowd in the courtyard before him. They were mostly women. The shrines of the Muslim saints were places journeyed to more by women than men, Zameen had told him, their despair greater, their lacks more essential and urgent. They would come from various places in the land and stay for days around a sacred grave, their saint often the only person in this life they could question with impunity and even accuse of neglect in the language and manner of a wronged lover.

When he got back to his office a note had been slipped under the door. Only he knows how he managed to get to that camp within the sixty or so minutes that remained before the arrival of the Soviet jets. The note, from Zameen, said she'd received word that the boy from her teenage years was living in that refugee camp and she was going there to meet him.

He got there before her, watching her arrive and then leading her and the child away from the site. The place was of course a furnace, smoke issuing from it in enraged billows as though demons had been set free by the bombing. All paths to the part of the camp where the man had his room were impassable, row upon row of burning homes. Leading them away from the deaths of the innocents, he looked over his shoulder. The civilised world would see this and condemn Soviet brutality, Moscow made to rethink its policies.

*

That night David became her lover and within days she was half his world.

He watched her pour water onto her shoulder when she bathed, the water spreading in a thin layer on her skin and then breaking up into shapes that resembled countries and islands, resembled continents. She lifted her hair, revealing the length of her neck, and said she and her school friends had been shocked when the prince climbed up the rope of Rapunzel's hair. 'We had all read Ferdowsi's *Book of Kings*. When the daughter of the ruler of Kabul lets down her hair from a high window, her suitor Zal is unable to bear the thought of using it as a substitute rope.'

The only part of him that seemed alive was where the two of them came into contact. There was no way of identifying many of the bodies after the bombing but it was certain that no one who lived in the bombed part could have survived. And yet initially he remained afraid that the other man would turn up, recognise David and expose his deception. He had already asked her to marry him. They would keep looking for Qatrina and Marcus. And when the Soviets were defeated and Afghanistan was at peace – and her parents were back in the house over there in Teardrop – David, Zameen and Bihzad would move to the United States.

She said her father's sense of smell was so acute he could discern a word written with colourless perfume on a sheet of paper.

The CIA required that he declare anyone with whom he had regular contact for more than six months. Soon that period was about to pass and he would have to mention her in the report he filed, though he had swept her place and knew there was no need to put her to the trouble of being under an investigation. The Agency also made the recruits sign a paper saying they wouldn't mention to their spouses the true nature of their work, but he didn't know of anyone who didn't tell everything to his wife or husband – easier than having to explain those late-night meetings with agents.

It was 1986 and the war was entering an unprecedented stage: the secret services of the United States, Great Britain and Pakistan had agreed that guerrilla attacks should be launched *inside* the Soviet Union itself, in Tajikistan and Uzbekistan, the states that were the supply routes to the Soviet Army in Afghanistan. This was to be done by Afghan guerrillas, but David had decided he would go with them. As he readied himself to meet up with the group, he was aware of the nightmare that would result if an American spy was captured either in Afghanistan or in the USSR, but he was convinced of his ability to avoid detection. When it came to these matters, in adulthood he had never felt himself surrounded by forces larger than himself.

Outfitted with mortars, boats, and target maps, he and the guerrillas intended to cross the River Oxus and mount sabotage and propaganda operations inside Uzbekistan. They poured diesel over the light-reflecting paintwork of their vehicles so the dust of the roads would stick to them as camouflage. The Soviet Union's chief cartographers had, at the KGB's behest, falsified virtually all public maps for almost fifty years. But David and the Afghans were carrying accurate CIA maps of the region. The stars above them were like mirror signals, the rapids of the Oxus giving off a ghostly glow in the darkness, the Arabs having renamed it the 'Insane River' when they met it centuries ago.

As well as weapons, they were bringing thousands of Korans in the Uzbek language, a translation the CIA had commissioned from an Uzbek exile living in Germany. Islam had to be encouraged in the USSR, to make the Russian Muslims rebel against Moscow. Five days – and several explosions in key buildings and on vital bridges and roads – later, David saw a woman in a silkworm village being paraded naked through the streets. She cowered as she was beaten by men for having committed adultery, for having taken a Russian lover. The men who were whipping her were part of the clandestine group that David and the Afghan guerrillas met here in Uzbekistan. Her head had been shaved and a green cross was painted on her forehead. The men were laughing – 'Call out to your lover to come and save you, "Sasha, Sasha, help, help!"' There was nothing he could do to put an end to her torment – they stopped at his outraged shouts but he knew it was temporary – and he watched as a man moved forward and placed around her neck one of the Korans he had brought.

Just before coming out to Uzbekistan, he had returned from a ten-day visit to Cambodia, his search for Jonathan taking him there. Her joy at seeing him when he returned made her suggest they go to Dean's. 'The three of us. Let the world go hang.' They had tried to keep their affair as secret as possible till then, fearing reprisals against her. As it was, she had lied about Bihzad to the world, never disclosing that technically he was illegitimate, claiming she was a widow whose husband had perished in the war.

'Are you sure?'

'Yes.'

A fountain played in tiers like a jelly mould at Dean's. She got up from their table and walked over to it. She had told him how every few weeks a man would come along the lake shore in Usha with a basket of crabs which he emptied into the fountain behind the house. The Afghans did not themselves eat these creatures, calling them 'water spiders', but were willing to catch them for the doctors in exchange for money or medical treatment. The crabs stayed in the stone basin until required in the kitchen, Zameen approaching the water to lift them out, jabbing competitively at their pincers with a pair of tongs.

'Who was that?' he asked distractedly, busy with the child, when she returned. Under an arch he had seen her exchange a few words with someone.

'Who?'

'The man you were talking to.'

'I wasn't talking to anyone.' The voice did not waver. The voice in which she had sung Corinthians to him. *And now I will show you the most excellent way.*

He slowly looked up. Her face was a mask.

'Okay.'

They continued with the meal. Hadn't something similar happened before? She had convinced him he was mistaken, but this time he was sure. She was wearing a light-pink tunic patterned with saffron flowers, over narrow white trousers, and combined with a long stole of white chiffon resting on the left shoulder. It *was* she whom he had seen, even though the light was not clear over there under the arch.

Was it the Communist, had he survived the bombing after all? How will David explain to her that he kept his existence secret from her because he loved her, was afraid of losing her? By now, even to himself, it seemed an incredible thing to have done. In her anger she will turn away from him for ever, never allow him to see Bihzad his son again.

And then suddenly everything became clear. O Christ, she was spying on him. He hadn't hidden anything from her about his activities. And now suddenly everything became dangerous. If it was someone else he would have known exactly what to do. But she wasn't someone else.

Dropping her off at the Street of Storytellers, saying he had to do something but would be back in about an hour, he drove back to Dean's, prowling the corridors to see if the man was still there. Aware of the tight jaw muscles, aware of the handgun under his shirt, his breath loud. He sat until dawn in that arch, then got a bed at Dean's and woke up around noon. What now? He was meant to cross into Afghanistan in a few hours, to enter Uzbekistan through there. She knew that. Would there be an ambush?

He phoned her and said the plan had changed, that he wouldn't be going to Uzbekistan.

'I'll see you in a few hours.'

When he got back from the Uzbekistan excursion nineteen days later he found her apartment empty. He sensed immediately that something was wrong: the silence in the two small rooms seemed deeper than just silence. This was more than mere absence. On the windowsill nine candles had burned all the way down to small coins of wax. Day or night she would light a candle here as indication that it was safe for him to come up, signalling that she wasn't in the company of Afghan visitors, the women who gathered at the place to embroider.

Her fiercest loyalty had been to these women. The one occasion she quarrelled with David had been over a matter concerning them. One of the women had just lost several relatives in a bombing the previous week. Nineteen names of grandparents, uncles, aunts, cousins.

'It looked like the list of guests for a wedding feast,' Zameen said to David.

'How is she? Would she be okay?'

She did not answer him, moving around the apartment silently for the next few minutes, attending to various things.

He stood up to leave – it was time for the women to arrive. 'Are you all right?'

'I have to be, don't I?' she said over her shoulder, the vehemence shocking him. 'We have to be, don't we? Just as long as you Americans and Soviets can play your games over there – nothing else matters!'

She turned to face him, glaring from the other side of the room, eyes red and brimming with tears. Daring him to cross over to her.

The candle didn't burn for a week after that. Then one day it summoned him. One massacre of innocents had driven him away, and another had now caused the reunion. The news that day had been terrible and she needed him. 'I feel so alone.'

Now David sought these women out, to ask them if they knew where she was. Most of them recoiled or let out apprehensive noises when he approached them. But eventually one of them did prove unafraid. In great desperation and hurry he began to question her about Zameen, asked her if she knew who the man Zameen had denied talking to might have been.

'I knew her very well, sir,' the woman said. 'So I can tell you that there is only one possibility why she could have lied to you. The newborn Bihzad was close to death when she arrived with him from Afghanistan. There is supposed to be healthcare for everyone in the refugee camps but the Pakistanis are corrupt. And the camps were ruled by warlords who wouldn't do anything until she registered with one of their parties – the more members each party has the more money they can get from you Americans. She needed to have a card made before they would even look at him and he was dying, she needed money to save him . . . Can you guess, sir, how she obtained the funds? I'd rather not say it out loud.'

Yes.

'She had to do it for about three months. There was no

180

alternative, you must understand. After she gave up she was sometimes accosted by her former . . . clients.'

He sat still, trying to absorb the information.

That night he dreamt of her face full of disappointment at him, perhaps even contempt. The face that had laughed at his impatience with jazz and had told him Tolstoy smelled of cypress wood. The face that had expressed the purest of joys when he found for her a volume of paintings by the Persian master Bihzad, a book her parents had owned but which she had been unable to find in the Peshawar bookstores.

But where was she now? He sat in the apartment where nothing, it seemed, had been disturbed. While he was making his way towards Uzbekistan, she had lit the candles: he'd told her the journey had been cancelled and she must have thought he was avoiding her, that he had somehow found out about what she had had to do to save her child. He was staying away until he discovered what he felt about the information. Trying to see if he could unlove her.

There was no sign of a break-in. The raw jewels Bihzad liked to play with were still here – two sapphires and two emeralds, like someone with blue eyes staring into someone's green eyes. Her books were stacked high in the corner, old stories that came to an end on the last page but hurled their wisdom and judgement decades and centuries into the future, there into the midst of them all. As was everything else, except the bottle of the pale-gold perfume she always kept with her, her father having composed it for her. Maybe Fedalla and the ISI slit her and the boy's throats so they could acquire the apartment for someone who would spy on him. A snake-oil vendor always sat not far from their building, with a large thorn-tailed lizard sitting untethered among the bottles of his wares, the fact that it never made a bid for freedom always a surprise to David until he was told that its spine had been broken by its master. From him David learned that while he was away there had been an explosion just across the road. A bicycle bomb had gone off. David himself had taught the rebels how to rig these up, to kill Soviet soldiers in Kabul and Kandahar, in Herat and Mazar-i-Sharif.

He kept hearing her voice.

If I speak with the tongues of men and angels,
but have not love,
I am only a resounding gong or a clanging cymbal.
If I have the gift of prophecy and can fathom all mysteries
    and all knowledge,
and if I have a faith that can move mountains,
but have not love, I am nothing.

She'd told him how she had left the refugee camp where she had been living and come to the Street of Storytellers: the cleric from Usha had these years later found his way to Peshawar, staring thunderstruck at her when he saw her one day in a lane that came out of the camp. This site was particularly sacred to Peshawar's few Hindu citizens because here a banyan and a peepal tree grew side by side, their roots entwined to signify the coming together of the body and the soul. And Zameen had gone out there on hearing that the people from the camp's newest mosque had attacked the two trees with axes. The CIA didn't care what the religious affiliation of the warriors was – wanting the funds to go to those who fought the Soviet soldiers the hardest – but the Pakistanis made absolutely sure the funds provided by the United States and Saudi Arabia and the rest of the world were channelled only to the Islamic fundamentalist guerrillas, who went on to assassinate the moderate clerics and warlords. Zameen retreated after she recognised the cleric supervising the mutilation of the sacred trees. Within months he had had seven women murdered for being prostitutes. Five were in the camp but two were in the city of Peshawar itself because he was linking up with Pakistani extremists. He was arrested once and confessed to killing two sinful women but walked free after one month. His patrons had paid off the relatives of the killed women and therefore he had been reprieved under Islamic law. He scrutinised the inhabitants of the camp for moral laxity, calling down Allah's wrath on them through his Friday sermons, and Zameen knew he would focus on her fully some day soon. The city's police and the magistracy seemed to enjoy or approve of what he and people like him were doing because soon after each murder, each beating or arson attack, the eyewitnesses recanted their earlier statements due either to threat or inducement.

Zameen began receiving visitors from the new mosque, who asked her to prove that her son was legitimate. She was planning to flee to another camp but then, fortunately, she heard about the aid agency that needed someone to mind and live in an apartment in the city.

Maybe she has been driven out of her apartment in the Street of Storytellers too.

'*Sasha, Sasha, help, help!*'

'David, David, help, help!' He couldn't shut these words out of his mind. A peepal leaf blew in on the wind one afternoon and over the coming days it lay there, became more and more shrivelled and sickly brown, its veins prominent. To him, nightmarishly, it was like a real person dying.

What did they, the Americans, really know about such parts of the world, of the layer upon layer of savagery that made them up? They had arrived in these places without realising how fragile were the defences that most people had erected against cruelty and degradation here. Conducting a life with the light from a firefly.

He now entered fully the hell that was the Afghan refugee camps ringed around the city, searching for the pair of them among the three million people. Children screamed on seeing this white man, thinking he was a Soviet soldier. He was sure he would know her by her shadow alone but panic spread through him at the thought of Bihzad. Each day he grew up more and more, becoming unrecognisable. He couldn't rest because the boy had to be found soon. Some parent birds, he knew, would not recognise a fledgling if it fell out of the nest because they hadn't seen it from that particular angle, only in the nest. And Zameen had told him about the demoiselle cranes that landed on the lake beside her house in Usha, on their migration to and from Siberia each year: how the young lost their high-pitched calls in the first twelve months of life so the parents simply did not respond to them. Unseen though still beside them.

He saw the years stretching ahead of him, the decades of not knowing where the brutal improbabilities of war had taken the mother and child. One of the fears of a CIA case officer in Peshawar was kidnap by the Afghanistani secret service or the KGB, but David didn't care as he moved through the camps, the clerics of the mosque shouting from the minarets that while the USSR was a prison, and the USA a whorehouse, Islam was the answer. Music had been banned in several camps for two or more years now.

One evening he stood to watch a pair of children, participants in a game of hide-and-seek that was in progress in a street of hovels. They were crouching next to an open sewer that spilled black matter, their eyes trained on the door from which the seeker was probably to emerge, the smell of cooking smoke and bread floating in the evening air. David watched as the two children sprang to their feet and grabbed the little boy who had just appeared in the door, chewing, having just finished a meal. They marched him to a corner and then quickly, before David could believe what he was seeing, or react, a finger was inserted into the overpowered little boy's throat, the vomit emerging and being caught in the hands of the two assailants, who then began to eat the still-undigested food. The little boy stumbled away dazed and fell, his eyes bright with liquid even in the dusk. And David was hurrying through the four-foot-wide 'street', trying to find a way out of the maze. He had helped create all this.

No, all this was the Soviet Union's fault because . . . because . . . He could not complete the thought. He had before and he would later but not just then.

The henna blossoms had completely faded from her hand, but she had two mirror-image birthmarks on her shoulder and thigh. And the distinguishing mark on Bihzad's body was the three-quarter-inch burn just above the waist on the left side, one of those windowsill candles having fallen on him one day.

What would become of the child in this place? As they emerged from Uzbekistan into Afghanistan, he and the Afghan warriors had been ambushed by the Soviets and had lost three men. It was discovered that an orphan boy and girl from a nearby village, shepherds, had guided the Soviets across the hills towards them in exchange for food. David awoke the next day to find his companions drinking tea under the bough from which the lifeless bodies of the two very young children were hanging.

Days passed in the search, and then one evening he came back – exhausted as a firefighter – to see that her apartment had been broken into, the door half-open. He slipped into the darkness and stood listening. In the room about the sense of touch in Usha, she had told him, there was a master archer who could put out a candle with an arrow blindfolded, by focusing on the heat from the flame.

'I am looking for my daughter,' said the man he pinned to the floor, the gun at the ready. 'A young woman named Zameen.'

David bent closer to the figure and lifted his foot off the head. The father from England? From Canterbury, the town that produced the saint venerated as the protector of secular clergy. The Englishman was sitting up now, his face moving through a rectangle of light from the open window. After revealing to him that Zameen had become a mother, David told him he wasn't the father, that she hadn't told him about the child's paternity. He should leave it up to her to reveal as much or as little about Benedikt to Marcus as she preferred.

He told David he had sensed her presence at the house belonging to someone called Gul Rasool, that she had signalled to him by breaking the perfume bottle.

David didn't want to approach Gul Rasool and mention that it was Marcus who had told him about Zameen being at his place, putting Marcus in danger. Gul Rasool's car was eventually rammed off a deserted road outside Peshawar. Almost three years had passed by now, two previous attempts to apprehend him having proven unsuccessful. Now Gul Rasool was pulled out of the mangled vehicle and brought to the ruins of a mosque in a wilderness. He was interrogated with David present but out of sight, looking down through filigree on an upper storey.

All this based on something as evanescent as perfume. But he couldn't think what else to do.

The mosque's dome – tiled with blue fragments – had fallen to the ground and was like a giant cracked bowl in which the rain had collected to the brim. When the water moved, the Koranic calligraphy amid the mosaics writhed like a nest of black vipers. With the help of that water, among other things, Gul Rasool was made to talk.

It was just a case of turning one of those trick bottles the right way up – the information just poured out of the man.

Gul Rasool said he had been in one of the shops at the Street of Storytellers when the bicycle bomb had gone off near by and then he had seen Zameen, her head and face uncovered because she had come out in a hurry at the sound of the explosion to look for her son. Gul Rasool recognised the young woman instantly as the daughter of the two doctors from Usha, the Englishman and Qatrina, having seen her any number of times in Usha, Qatrina even carrying a photograph of her when she accompanied Gul Rasool into the battlefields.

He lost Zameen in the crowd of the bazaar, but then saw her face briefly in an upstairs window, lighting a candle.

The vigil she was maintaining for David.

Gul Rasool knocked on the door and, telling her he had a message from her father, brought her to his house.

So Zameen was there when Marcus visited.

David heard all this standing behind the panel of cement lace. A set of elaborate ruses had been invented to get at Rasool's knowledge about Zameen indirectly, letting him think the interrogators were interested in completely different matters. Nor could they let him see David in case Rasool later saw him in Marcus's company.

Gul Rasool revealed that Nabi Khan had staged an attack on his mansion in University Town, a raid during which he carried off among other things the group of women and children he kept for pleasure. Zameen and Bihzad among them.

Soon after that day David learned this to be partial truth. Only Bihzad was abducted by Khan – some of the others, including Zameen, had remained in Rasool's captivity. Despite their best efforts and forethought, the men who had questioned Rasool at the ruined mosque had had to become specific about the women and children, and Rasool must have guessed that they were the reason why he was being interrogated. No longer wishing to be held responsible for any of them, he had said they were all taken away by Khan.

The child's fate has remained a mystery to this day. He hasn't been able to obtain an opportunity to talk to Nabi Khan, these warlords always disappearing into battles, into various hiding places and retreats. He has put out feelers and sent messages through intermediaries but without success. People tell him the boy had probably been sold or given away, jettisoned as Khan and his guerrillas moved from place to place. They are probably right.

Compared with this, how quickly it was, after that day behind the cement filigree, that he found out Zameen's fate. About what happened to her as she remained in Rasool's custody without her son. About what Rasool made her do in exchange for the promise that he would help her reunite with Bihzad.

And following the trail of her murderers, David would realise, he had been stepping on his own footprints.

CASA WALKS DOWN the cold hospital corridor. His reflection caught glasslike in the just-wiped floor. The smell of medicines in the air. It is late afternoon, his stitches in place at last, and he has just borrowed a phone to call for his companions to come and collect him from here. He is glad he had managed to persuade the American to leave some hours ago, his kindness an embarrassment and confusion for him. As they approached Jalalabad he was afraid of being taken to another nearby hospital, a place where there was a chance someone would recognise him as one of the twelve wounded fighters who had been delivered there in December 2001, their bodies smashed in various places, the nurses letting out terrified gasps when they were rushed to the X-ray room and it was revealed that they all carried pistols and knives and had grenades tied to their bodies. Wild with wrath and pain, four were Arabs, three Uzbeks, one Uighur Muslim from China, one Chechen, and the rest were Afghans, and they had warned that they would pull the pins on their grenades if they felt threatened or caught a glimpse of a foreigner.

He looks at the black plastic Casio on his wrist, the digital numbers startling themselves onwards second by second.

They should be here any minute. His other fear as they

approached Jalalabad was that someone would see him in the company of the white man. The attack Nabi Khan has planned for Usha is too important for even the smallest of risks. There are dreams of putting together a large militia with the help of the ISI, using Usha as a base. If they have cause to doubt Casa's loyalty they will torture him. Though he knows nothing beyond the vaguest details, not even the exact date. There is every chance they would execute him out of hand.

Through the window at the end of the corridor he looks out at the road, touching his bandages absently, the long white strips encircling his head. When he was about six and living in a refugee camp in Pakistan, some women upon arrival from Afghanistan would pull out lace that had been wound around their limbs and torsos under the clothes. Smugglers' apprentices, they would step away from the miles of looped softness they had just shed, and the boys would then go into the room to gather them up. They could feel the warmth of the women's bodies still in them, lingering in the haze of colour. The older boys would occasionally pocket one – for, he now knows, moments of arousal later.

He looks up and his heart sinks upon seeing David the American walking towards him.

'Are you well?'

Casa manoeuvres him away from the large window. 'I thought you had gone.'

'Not without seeing if there's anything else you needed, and we have to pay for your treatment. I went off to attend to a few things.'

'I thought you had already paid, I thought you had gone.'

From the plastic bag he has with him, the man takes out three new sets of *shalwar-kameez*. 'For you. I wasn't sure about the size but I think they'll fit.'

Casa takes them from him and just as the man is proffering a sheaf of Afghani banknotes – 'Do you want to settle the hospital bill yourself?' – Casa catches sight of the three figures at the other end of the corridor, watching him. His fellow warriors. They pivot away and are gone in the next instant, Casa's fingers still not fully closed around the money.

They've gone to report to Nabi Khan what they have seen, to ask him what should be done. People at the very centre, like Khan, cannot use electronic equipment, made watchful by the bounty on their heads. Only the external circle can be contacted through the cell phones – they would then convey the message verbally to Nabi Khan and bring out his response and instructions. Casa has at most ten minutes before they return to kill him, spray him from their guns. Those standing near by will die also because bullets are blind. He has to think fast, extremely fast. No location in the city is safe for him. They know all possible places where he might hide for a few days to work out what to do.

He feels thirsty all of a sudden, intensely so, as though he has been force-fed thorns. Where is that bottle of water?

'I am glad you came back,' he tells David. 'Would you be kind enough to take me back with you?'

He still has his shroud. No one has commented on it so far – wrapped around his body under his blanket it just looks like an extra layer for warmth – but he must hide it somewhere when they get back to Usha. The stark white cloth is dabbed with a few syllables of his blood from last night. A Saudi Arabian boy had given it to him as a gift, having soaked it in the holy water of the spring in Mecca which burst forth when the infant prophet Ismael struck the ground with his heel, to quench the thirst of his mother, the pair having been abandoned in the desert by his father at Allah's bidding.

David has to negotiate his way into Usha. As a result of the *shabnama*, armed gunmen have been posted on the road in from Jalalabad. A third of an orchard has been felled and the flowering trees arranged in a barricade, a giant white garland in front of which the men stand with their weapons, the last bees of the day working the blossoms. Gul Rasool was away but has now come back to Usha.

Near by a father is chastising a little boy for playing football, as all that kicking would damage his new shoes.

David had phoned James Palantine earlier today and asked if they could meet. He too was in another province but is making his way towards Usha at Gul Rasool's request. A group of his men, young Americans like James himself, is here to safeguard Gul Rasool in the meantime.

'He'll come and see me here,' David tells Lara when they arrive. 'I'll ask him about Benedikt then.'

They are taking a pillow and a thin mattress and some sheets to the perfume factory for the boy. He is too reserved to enter the house, saying he'll sleep down there.

David looks at her under the evening sky, the leaf-filtered

light from above. All day he had wanted this, had wanted to touch her, but there has been no contact since his return. Marcus always present. There was also the matter of their unexpected guest. And, yes, he must admit, there is a hint within him of shame, of doubt. What makes him think he deserves these moments of gladness amid all this wreckage? Afghanistan will still be there in the morning?

As he and Zameen made love at the apartment in the Street of Storytellers – that thing a woman's long hair does, when it accidentally comes to lie over the face in crosshatched layers, her features seen through the overlapping gauze! – songs would drift in through the open window, words on the night breeze. He hadn't at first understood why in these lyrics mundane observations were mentioned in the first verse – a mosquito's whine, the sound of a twig broom on the courtyard floor – but were coupled in the second verse with expressions of deepest longing. But by then as he smelled the jasmine on her breast, looking into the vertigo-inducing depths of her eyes, he knew that in its obsession the heart responds to everything by echoing back a truth about the lover, by echoing back a truth about love. Everything – everything – reminds you of her. *The pomegranate tree has produced its first blossom*, a woman would sing on a radio in the bazaar downstairs, and as Zameen sighed in his ear, the singer would add, *On the journey towards the beloved, you live by dying at every step.*

Slowly he raises his hand and touches Lara's neck with the back of his fingers as they walk towards the perfume factory.

CASA IS CLIMBING the giant face, using his hands and his toes to seek out holds amid the stone features. The arc of the lip. The nose ledge. The dot between the eyebrows. Reaching the top – which is the side of the head, full of waving locks of hair – he sits beside the horizontal ear, the stone grainy under his palm. The floor is ten feet below him. He looks into the pit of the ear's whorl and reaches for the flashlight in his pocket. Half a minute later he switches off the beam and sends his fingers in there.

He scrambles down and then goes up the staircase where the oil lantern they had given him burns on the fourth step, emerging into the dark corridor of trees, going past David's car. He is carrying before him the old bird's nest he has discovered in the ear. A loose bowl of grass. The bird must have found its way into the factory through one of the many broken windows. Amid the straw and grass blades there is a black feather, a complete diamond-shaped pink rose petal, and bits of brittle moss that he can see. With a tentativeness in his demeanour, trying not to smile, he enters the kitchen and places the woven object on the table where the three of them are sitting. The candle flame giving a lurch in the draught, the light sloshing to one side of the room like liquid. He turns and leaves, a small sound of delight and surprise from Lara behind him.

DAVID MOVES AMONG the shapes in the glasshouse. A sweep of stars above him. The Straw Ribbon, *Keh Kishan*, is what the Milky Way galaxy is called in Persian. Zameen had told him this.

After the Soviet Army conceded defeat in 1989 – the war had lasted longer than the Second World War – Marcus had returned to Usha and David had gone back to the United States, visiting every few months for the next five years. One night at a function at the Islamabad embassy he ran into Fedalla, who was now a colonel, rich with all the money he had siphoned from the guerrillas. A large house, a harem of cars. He was in a group with _____, David's mole in the ISI, and was participating drunkenly in a conversation about Afghanistan. How the influx since 1979 of the millions of filthy Afghan refugees had ruined the once beautiful city of Peshawar. Had led to what he termed the 'Kalashnikovisation' of his homeland. 'Look at the shapes of the two countries on a map and you'll see that Afghanistan rests like a huge burden on poor Pakistan's back. A bundle of misery.'

As the conversation moved on to the ten thousand bombs that had fallen on the city of Kabul the previous month, the civil war having begun, _____ indicated that he had something to convey to David.

'Back in 1986,' David was told when they met the next day, 'Christopher Palantine had arranged to meet Gul Rasool at a location outside Peshawar. Rasool was selling missiles supplied by the CIA to the Iranians. Christopher had the evidence and wanted to confront him, but when he arrived early he saw a young woman planting a bomb there. Rasool had lured him there because Christopher had to be eliminated, couldn't be allowed to expose Rasool and have his CIA funding stopped. Christopher accused Rasool of trying to kill him when he and his men arrived, but he said, "Would I turn up here myself if I had sent her?" He had her shot then and there to prove she wasn't anything to do with him. But he was more than an hour late, so it could have been him. And we actually now know that it was. Definitely.'

For some unknown reason David dreaded the moment the young woman's name would be spoken. *All names are my names.*

'She could have been sent to eliminate Christopher by the KGB or the Afghan secret service.'

'That was one of Christopher's initial suspicions. Fedalla, who has heard of the incident from somewhere, was telling us about it last night, convinced she had been sent by you, by the CIA. And Fedalla was in awe that the CIA allowed one of its own to be killed. He said it is such cunning and resolve that has turned your country into a superpower. That the Pakistani secret service cares too much about its people, cares too much about civilians to be truly effective.'

'What was her name?'

'I don't know. But she pleaded to be let go, telling Christopher she couldn't disclose who had sent her because then she wouldn't be able to see her son again. Obviously too afraid of Rasool.'

The very next day David flew to New York City and telephoned Christopher Palantine and asked to see him.

Christopher was already there at the restaurant when he arrived and took his seat almost wordlessly, his silence cutting off Christopher's words of pleasure at seeing him after such a long period. Friends who loved each other like brothers.

All David could do was stare at him. A cold February noon outside.

'What is it?'

David took out Zameen's photograph from his pocket and reaching his arm across the table placed it before him, swerving it in the air so that it was the right way round for the other man.

Christopher looked at the image and then lifted it off the tablecloth, and his hands disappeared below the table with it, the neutral expression not leaving his features. Perfect composure. They were after all spies, committed to their dark profession, their conversations laced with phrases like 'plausible deniability' and 'I can't tell you how I know that' and 'we never had this discussion'. Such words were spoken so often in Peshawar that they could be plucked out of the city's dirty air.

There followed moments of chilling merciless disbelief as David had his answer. No language was needed. As confirmation there now came the sound of the photograph being torn up under the table. Three long rips that must have divided the rectangle of paper into narrow strips; these were gathered together and there were three shorter, thicker rips that must have carved the whole thing up into sixteen small squares. David remembered her telling him how someone from the mosque in the refugee camp – believing her child was illegitimate – had broken into her trunk and drawn a large dagger on her mirror as warning. She had lifted it out and seen the weapon superimposed onto her face.

David leaned back against his chair and closed his eyes, suddenly drained, Christopher's stare still fixed on him.

He wanted to cry out, the noise a raised welt in the air.

'It's over, Christopher,' he managed to say. 'I am finished.' Homer used the same word, *keimai*, for Patroclus lying dead in battle as for Achilles falling beside his body in grief. And later when Thetis came to comfort her son, the poet had her take his head between her hands – the gesture of the chief mourner in the funeral of a dead man.

It was then, just after 12.17 p.m. that February afternoon in 1993, that the thirteen-hundred-pound bomb exploded a block away in the underground garage of the North Tower of the World Trade Center.

It was a yellow Ryder truck, parked there by a graduate of one of the training camps set up in Afghanistan to fight the Soviets. The explosion was meant to release cyanide gas into the building but the heat burned it away. And one tower was supposed to fall into the other – the terrorists had hoped to kill a quarter of a million people.

The ground shook. Some fragments of the woman's

image scattered from Christopher's hands. They had almost arranged to meet at the Windows on the World, 106 floors directly above the bomb.

They rushed out into the street now. There were flakes of snow in the air, floating like sparse bits of airborne glass, mixing with the smoke. People from all directions were running towards the site – soon there were doctors, ambulances, police cars, bystanders, groups of workmen from a nearby construction site, one of them wearing an *IRA – FREEDOM FIGHTERS* T-shirt. Sirens and cries and shouts.

He could have been up there, the elevators and the electricity having failed, smoke pouring up through the Tower towards him. And he felt as though he was, with devastation all around him and the howling depth outside.

'They are here,' he murmured to Christopher in the shocked recognition of inevitability.

He saw himself clearly, making his way down the black stairwells, and the deeper he went the greater the number of wounded and disorientated people who joined him like shades in Hell, the darkness and smoke increasing. *Wherever you may be, death shall overtake you, though you may put yourself in lofty towers*, said the Koran.

They are here.

Cops with flashlights were guiding people out as they neared the giant hole at the bottom.

Christopher dragged him away into a doorway. 'Who was she?'

But he was still up there with them.

'Who was she, David?'

'I loved her.'

'I didn't know who she was or I wouldn't have allowed her to die.'

'Where are her remains?'

'I don't know. I doubt if anyone does.'

The workers digging the foundations of these buildings years ago had found ancient cannonballs and bombs, a ship's anchor of a design not made after 1750, and one small gold-rimmed teacup made of china but still intact, with two birds painted on it.

He left Christopher and walked away.

The cleric who had inspired the attack – he lived and preached across the Hudson in Jersey City, having sought asylum in the United States – had called on Muslims to assail the West in revenge for the centuries of humiliation and subjugation, 'cut off the transportation of their cities, tear it apart, destroy their economy, burn their companies, eliminate their interests, sink their ships, shoot down their planes, kill them on the sea, air, or land'. The bomb resulted in more hospital casualties than any event in American history since the Civil War. And what did his life resemble from that point onwards? He became fundamentally inconsolable. It was like missing a step on the stairs or losing one's balance for a moment – that sensation extended to hours to days to years.

He looks towards the window of Lara's room, as yet unlit. Midnight, and she is still with Marcus. No one has ever mentioned – anywhere – the dust-and-ash-covered sparrow that a man leaned down and gently stroked on September 11, the bird sitting stunned on a sidewalk an hour or so after the Towers collapsed. It is one of his most vivid memories of that day's television, but no one remembers seeing it. Perhaps he remembers it because he has since read that Muhammad Atta's nickname as a child was Bulbul.

David didn't want to retaliate against Gul Rasool – for killing Zameen, and for lying about her to his men during torture. Too sickened and exhausted, and also because it could have jeopardised Marcus's safety.

And now Gul Rasool is a US ally, James Palantine providing him with security. James must know that Rasool had once wanted to kill his father. In the wake of the 2001 attacks, Gul Rasool was the only one who was around to help root out the Taliban from Usha, to help capture al-Qaeda terrorists, and to keep them at bay, the United States paying him handsomely for his support. The first CIA team that arrived in Afghanistan soon after the attacks, to persuade warlords and tribal leaders, had brought five million dollars with them. It was spent within forty days. Ten million more was flown in by helicopter: piles of money as high as children – four cardboard boxes kept in a corner of a safe house, with someone sleeping on them as a precaution against theft.

Originally the idea of asking Gul Rasool was resisted, Nabi Khan's name being put forward instead. But when Gul Rasool heard of it, he put together a death squad to assassinate Nabi Khan. Khan – who, also scenting money, had dispatched his own men to kill Gul Rasool – was the first to be wounded and was therefore unable to fight with the Americans.

David watches as the light comes on gently in Lara's room, can visualise the candle flame stretching itself to full height. He wonders what news James Palantine would bring for Lara. He hadn't seen the boy for years when he contacted the family after hearing of Christopher's death. He enters the house, going past the bird's nest on the shelf, and walks down the dark green floor of the hallway.

BOOK TWO

6

Casabianca

THE YEAR 1798 was a disaster for Islam. Napoleon Bonaparte's invasion that year of Egypt – the very centre of the Muslim world – was the symbolic moment when the standard of leadership passed on to the West. From that point on, Western armies and Western capital over-ran the lands of the Muslims.

And Casa got his name from a poem about a boy who died in 1798 at the Battle of the Nile. Giocante Casabianca. The twelve-year-old son of a French admiral. He was on board the *L'Orient*, the principal ship of the fleet that carried Bonaparte and his army to Egypt. Cannon fire set the *L'Orient* ablaze and further shooting meant the blaze could not be put out, but Giocante Casabianca remained on the burning deck, unwilling to abandon the post without his father's permission. The flames consuming the sail and shroud above him.

> *He call'd aloud – 'Say, Father, say*
> *If yet my task is done!'*

The father was close to death below and did not have the strength to raise his voice. When the ship's powder magazines eventually exploded, the blast was so large it was felt fifteen miles away in Alexandria.

One day in 1988, the six-year-old Casa, known then

only by the generic 'little boy', had exhibited similar valour and obedience, and one of the adults around him had laughed and called him Casabianca.

Casa would meet that man again in his teens and remind him of the matter. The man would remember it well – he said he'd learned about Giocante Casabianca through a poem at school – but the man would then become angry. He had begun his education at an expensive Western-style school but, because the family circumstances had deteriorated, he was taken out of there and sent to a free Islamic one, and he now believed in the primacy and supremacy of Muslims above all. He said that even back then, only minutes after referring to the brave faithful six-year-old boy as Casabianca, he had become maddened by the thought that he had been required to learn Western history at one point in his life, along with fictional stories where the principal characters could easily be Christian or Hindu. Not minor characters, not villains – but the heroes! Regardless of his bitter fury, the name he gave the little boy had stuck, shortened to Casa.

The full story of the boy whose name had become his has slipped out of Casa's mind. Only a few vague impressions remaining.

> *'Speak, father!' once again he cried,*
> *'If I may yet be gone!'*

*

He rises in the perfume factory just before dawn, the thought materialising in him instantly that he should do his best not to stay here for too long. Nabi Khan and his men are coming to Usha soon.

At the lake he performs his ablutions, the water so still it is as though it has been smoothed by hand, and says his prayers on a boulder, using his blanket as a prayer mat.

He sits wrapped in it afterwards and looks around as the sky starts to brighten above him, the white vapour rising from the lake looking like airborne milk. Under his breath he reads the verses one is supposed to read at the start of day.

O Allah I ask You for whatever good this day may hold
And I take refuge in You from whatever evil it may hold
And ask you to grant me victory, but do not grant victory
over me.
O Allah watch over me with Your eye that never sleeps
And accept my repentance, that I may not perish.
You are my hope. My Master, Lord of bounty and majesty,
To You I direct my face, so bring Your noble face close to me
And wash away my sins, answer my supplications, and
guide my heart,
And receive me with Your deepest forgiveness and generosity,
Smiling on me and content with me in Your infinite mercy.

He gets up and walks towards David's car. He could present the car to Nabi Khan as a token of good will, convince him of the truth of what had transpired at the hospital. Wind-loosened perfume is in the air now from the flowering branches overhead as he circles the vehicle.

The keys are in the house. But David would report the missing car to the police and they might trace it to Nabi Khan, who, in any case, might not see it as the honest gift Casa intends it to be. He doesn't want them to inflict pain on him, though he can understand how Nabi Khan might feel perfectly within his rights to use agony in ascertaining the truth. When the rumours reached Ali about the virtue of Ayesha – the wife of Prophet Muhammad, peace be upon him – Ali had had Ayesha's maidservant tortured to learn if the gossip had any basis in fact. Muhammad, peace be upon him, was aware of this.

The act of courageous obedience that earned him his name had occurred at a weapons warehouse situated in a heavily populated residential area near Islamabad. The United States had given about one thousand Stinger missiles to Pakistan in 1986, to be passed on to Afghan guerrillas. But one of these missiles, in October 1987, narrowly missed a United States helicopter in the Persian Gulf. And three days later, two Afghans were arrested in Pakistan for attempting to sell Stingers to representatives of the Iranian government, for one million dollars each. This led to a United States investigation and it was decided that there would be an audit of the weapons supplied to the Pakistani military. Casa cannot believe it but it is said that the ISI, its alleged corruption and duplicity about to be exposed, had set fire to the massive warehouse with the result that $100 million worth of rockets and missiles had rained down on the surrounding area, killing an estimated thousand people and maiming countless others for life.

In a mosque a block away from the warehouse, the six-year-old boy had been asked to guard the door behind which a prisoner was being kept – a Christian who had been beaten until he confessed that he was responsible for the defaced copy of the Koran found lying in a gutter outside.

He remembers the rockets falling around him again and again, bursting into giant clusters of hot sparks and metal, setting fire to the straw prayer mats that lined the floors. The heat from one blast leaving the blades of the ceiling fan curled up like a tulip. He had remained where he was asked to remain an hour ago, trembling with terror amid all the acrid smoke and ash and light, his trousers soiled and his ears in pain from the incredible noise like hammer blows, screaming for help but realising no sound would issue from his mouth. He was holding a gun that was older than him, and through all this he kept it aimed at the door as he had been shown.

He walks into the orchard on seeing the kitchen door being opened by David. These foreigners – who is protecting them? They are probably attached to a charity or an aid organisation, cogs in a machinery of kindness. Allah – in His wisdom – has planted these compassionate impulses in the hearts of non-believers, for Muslims to exploit and benefit from.

He had let down his guard when he took the bird's nest to them last night. He had been looking for a place to keep his shroud and had found the discovery so enthralling that he had wished to share it with another human, the momentary fascination of it making him act out of his true character.

Having studied manuals for weapons and computers, for microprocessors and motherboards, having taken lessons in passport and credit-card forging, and having carefully examined news footage of almost every attack ever mounted on Western targets, he knows the English language. He had helped put together films at the jihadi camps in that language, to be sold in the mosques of European cities after Friday prayers – propaganda and preaching, the Jihad of the Tongue. But he cannot follow these people when they talk amongst themselves, the words coming too fast. If they communicated through written notes, he would, taking whole minutes to decipher a phrase but deciphering it nevertheless, the way he'd made himself expert on cell phones solely by studying the little booklets that came with them, warning Nabi Khan that even if the SIM card is changed, a caller who continues to use the same phone can be traced – by the police, by the Americans. Khan and his people had been told otherwise by the phone sellers, and that had been Casa's entry into Khan's inner circle.

The shroud, even rolled up tight, would not fit in the stone ear so he hid it in a far cupboard.

He is startled now to see David emerge from the house with a shroud of his own, then realises it is the skin of a birch tree peeled in one long piece, folded and tied up.

'It's the material for making a boat,' he tells Casa. 'I am taking it to the lake, I'll build it there.'

Casa helps him carry to the water's edge a box of implements and also the long pieces of wood for the vessel's frame, the sky brightening overhead.

He examines the two antler-handled awls.

'They are for making holes in the bark. The canoe is sewn together with spruce roots,' David explains. 'With these.' The peeled roots, like thick glistening strings, are in bracelet-size hoops. 'No nails or screws are used to hold the canoe together.'

He unrolls the birch bark, like a length of stiff cloth about a quarter of an inch thick, one side white, the other a dark gold. There are smaller pieces too but the longest is about fifteen feet long and forty inches wide.

Apparently the canoe is an American Indian thing.

'And this is for the finer work,' David says, looking into a bag and bringing out a knife with a blade made out of a straight razor. 'It's called a crooked knife – crooked because its handle is crooked not the blade.' He hands it to Casa. 'The thumb rests along the bent part of the handle – the native people did not have a vice to clamp their work so they held it in one hand and used the knife with the other.'

Casa grips it as demonstrated.

'But, Casa, I think you should rest. Go back and lie down, and you should have something to eat. I am sure Marcus is up – I'll come and join you in a while.'

The missiles that landed in Casa's jihad training camp were named after an American Indian weapon – Tomahawk. Casa knows other words too like Comanche and Apache and Chinook. First the Americans exterminate the Indians, then name their weapons and warplanes after them. What did those Indians do to make the white Americans respect them?

215

HE DRINKS THE RED TEA sitting at the table with David and Marcus – on the farthest chair from them, the one nearest the door. Marcus is expressing his worry about the perfume factory being too cold during the night.

'I don't know why you didn't sleep in the house.'

'You are very kind.'

'And remind me to find you a prayer mat.'

He is grateful for the gentleness they are displaying towards him, and feels he should convey his gratitude to them – show them somehow that he too is mindful of their well-being.

'You are from the USA?' he asks David. 'You flew here?'

'Yes.'

'You should be careful about flying.'

David shrugs. 'Why?'

'In case the Jews repeat the attacks of 11 September 2001.'

David gets up suddenly and pours more tea into Marcus's cup. And the Englishman too becomes somewhat animated, abruptly voluble. 'Look at the three of us here. Like a William Blake prophecy! America, Europe and Asia.' He points to the ceiling. 'I must take down the book one of these days.'

'My hands are already aching,' says David. He has spent

the last three hours with the canoe – it's past nine and he is getting ready to go to the city.

'I'll help you build it,' Casa offers.

For the time being they are his only allies, the only people who would try to act if Nabi Khan were to come through this door right now.

Two hours ago he himself was thinking of taking the car, but the fact now is that if he saw someone trying to steal it he would do his best to prevent the theft.

He now asks about the nailed books, and Marcus tells him it had been done by his wife, the unfortunate woman losing her hold on reality in her concluding days. Using her long hair to dust surfaces. He remembers to make appropriately sympathetic noises, though of course being female it must have been easy for her to fall into madness, Muhammad, peace be upon him, saying, 'Women have less reason than men.'

Marcus has told him he is a Muslim but he must still be vigilant in case the other two try to convert him to Christianity. He walks back to the perfume factory through the sun-heated orchard, a peppermint lizard squiggling away at his approach. Near by a black beetle is trying to maintain a jittery balance on the rim of a tulip blossom, exactly resembling the one that is painted on a wall in the kitchen. Something smells of resin. Something else slow and furry can be glimpsed behind a fern – a striped caterpillar. He hears a flutter and looks up to see a flash of red in a silver-leafed tree. He can't take the car and disappear towards Kabul or Kandahar because Gul Rasool's men have cordoned off Usha. They'll want to know who he is, how he acquired his injury. As he enters the perfume factory, the thought of being close to the idol down there is suddenly a distress to him. Afghanistan is a Muslim country. The entire world has to submit to Islam one day: when the Messiah arrives just before Judgement Day he will issue an invitation for all to become Muslim – those refusing will be eradicated so that the earth is inhabited only by the believers.

The Pharaoh's wife Asiya and Jesus's mother Mary are waiting in Heaven to be married to Muhammad, peace be upon him.

Sitting in an alcove before the smiling statue, to catch the sunlight pouring from above, he looks into the note-books stacked on a shelf half an arm's length away. Each page filled with what appear to be drawings of constella-tions but are in fact the chemical formulae of various perfume molecules. Small palaces of tangled geometry. The bindings are the green of grass stains on white cloth, the colour the world appears through night-vision gog-gles. He had been given a pair of these glasses by someone who had come to the jihad training camp from Chechnya; he had taken them from a dead Russian soldier there and had come to Pakistan with a load of antique carpets to fund the war in his homeland.

He tries to see if the stone head can be nudged in any direction. It should be taken away and sold to non-Muslims to finance the jihad against them.

He is relieved Lara wasn't in the kitchen while he was having breakfast. A woman seen is a Western idea, he had been told by a cleric at a madrassa when he was a child.

These dozens of clerics – the emir, the haji, the hafiz, the maulana, the sheikh, the hazrat, the alhaaj, the shah, the mullah, the janab, the janabeaali, the khatib, the molvi, the kari, the kazi, the sahibzada, the mufti, the olama, the huzoor, the aalam, the baba, the syed – had frightened him as they preached when he was very young, moving unpredictably across the full register of the human voice, from the whisper to the growl to the full-throated shout, now screaming, now weeping, now vituperative and righteous, now plaintive and melodious. At the start they would recite a few verses of the Koran to signify that both the speaker and the listener were now in the realm of the sacred, but what followed was, in fact, history – a lament for Islam's lost glory and power, a once-proud civilisation brought low by the underhandedness of others, yes, but mainly by the loss of faith among the Muslims themselves, the men decadent, the women disobedient. The child Casa was told to supplicate during prayers and beg forgiveness for not loving Muhammad enough, peace be upon him, a man whose sweat was more perfumed than a shipful of roses.

Ay naunehalan-e-Islam, Ay farzandan-e-Tawheed – O children of Islam, O sons of the Sacred Creed . . .

And so Casa and the other children had wept. By the time he was about twelve he and the other boys at the madrassa hadn't seen a woman for five years. There was a rumour that a group of older boys had a photograph of a female face, cut up into ten pieces and hidden in diverse corners and recesses. Travelling assorted distances, the fragments came together now and then to form her.

Casa had longed to arrive at the moment when he'd see her – the thought of it was like a butterfly attached to his heart on a string – and when at last he did lay eyes on her he shook at the very phenomenon of her. Unable to find his breath or control his heartbeat, he had lost consciousness. The first thing he remembered upon coming to was that during the Crusades beautiful girls had been sent to seduce and corrupt Salahudin and his generals, the Christian priests assuring the girls forgiveness for all sin incurred in the service of their religion.

He repented. The madrassa teachers had told the children that women's guile was immense, their mischief noxious, that they were evil and mean-spirited, that all the trials and misfortunes and woes that befell men came from women, that Muhammad, peace be upon him, had said when a woman steps out of the house Satan is delighted. And yet on a bitterly cold night he found himself with a group of others pouring petrol onto a grave and setting it alight, watching the fire leap into the air in a golden dance, their shadows thrown in the shape of a wheel onto the other mounds in the cemetery. The boy in the blazing grave – he had been martyred during a night exercise when, tired and disorientated, his foot had slipped and he had plunged into a canyon – had loved the paper woman's eyes and, in a moment of now-regretted emotion, his friends had placed one of them in his shroud just before burial. They wanted it back now. The icy earth was solid as metal and difficult to dig through so they were employing fire to thaw it. In the absence of spades and shovels, they used the blade bones of animals slaughtered for food or as instruction. There was little hope of getting another picture because the boys were forbidden from seeing newspapers and magazines from outside the madrassa – 'Where is the news in any of them to hearten the faithful? Where is the news that a Muslim army has conquered an infidel land?'

By the time he was about ten he had endured every kind of assault on his body by men or stronger boys, and – because the only way to feel any control was to distress or wound others – by the time he was about fourteen he had done the same to younger or weaker boys. At the very core of him was the belief that human beings had little to offer beyond cruelty and danger.

His apparel was often dirty and in tatters but he had learnt that he must not wish to flourish in men's eyes, only in Allah's.

The important thing was that he knew a gun could be smuggled onto an aircraft by concealing it in a mixture of epoxy and graphite, that he knew how to defend a house and how to storm it, how to kidnap and assassinate and how to kill with his hands, with his feet.

If you do not fight He will punish you severely and put others in your place, said the Koran. He had been hung by his ankles and electrocuted to see if he would break under torture, his body in spasms for hours afterwards as though the current were still running through him. Testing his resistance, trying to see how deep a breakdown they could provoke, his companions had subjected him to confinement without light, without odour or sound or any fixed reference to time and place. He knew that if captured by

Americans he must tell them he was fully aware of his 'rights' and ask for a lawyer, tell them that he wanted to be put on trial in a court in New York or London or, best of all, in a European country, just as the youngest warriors knew what they were to tell the Westerners: that they were not 'war criminals' but rather 'war victims' who had been subjected to 'undue adult influences' and 'indoctrinated' into firing bullets and throwing grenades. Those between the ages of eight and fourteen were made to learn by heart, along with the Koranic verses, English phrases like 'the special protections accorded to captured child soldiers' and 'the violation of international principles'. They didn't know what the words meant but that was no barrier to memorising them; they didn't know what the Koranic verses they chanted day and night meant either, since they were in Arabic. One of the rare entertainments allowed the children was the acting out of a sketch about a holy warrior captured by the Americans, the prisoner's invoking of those English phrases so frustrating to the captors that they were reduced to banging their fists helplessly on the floor, to much delighted laughter from the audience, the prisoner eventually walking free to continue on the path of armed jihad, having executed the Americans before leaving.

He knew that when a bullet hits a body you hear it, an unmistakable unforgettable sound, and knew HE38 meant the grenade was High Explosive and would burst into thirty-eight fragments. He knew gelignite smelled like the sweetmeats made with almond pulp beaten in cream.

DAVID, before leaving for Jalalabad, goes along the corridor towards Lara's room. 'Even to this day', Zameen had told him at the Street of Storytellers, 'my dreams take place in that house in Usha.' She had wanted to bring him here, and after that small place in the Street of Storytellers he wanted to be with her in rooms brightened by rows of windows. Curious about the transformation her face might go through against a different background, in the air of a different temperature. He fastened the small transparent buttons on Bihzad's shirt, no bigger surely than the lens inside a nightingale's eye, and wanted him to run and tumble in a large garden. 'Like legendary heroes he was born in the middle of the night,' she said, 'the hour when the wicked sleep.' Two hours after he was born the night air had filled up with butterflies.

Just about here last night – this wall with its painting of a woman on a horse playing a portable harp – he had decided he couldn't go in to Lara and had continued towards his own room, overwhelmed suddenly by shame and regret – he must be the last thing on her mind in all this disorder. He also wondered how much of the previous night was just her need to feel safe, a desire for security. Perhaps she was in shock. But then he heard the door open behind him.

'I have just phoned James Palantine again,' he tells her now. 'He'll be in Usha tomorrow.'

She nods. Dressed in white.

'You know you have to be prepared for the worst?'

'Yes.' She is looking straight at him, unflinching, then she turns away, busying herself with some objects in an alcove. He brings home newspapers at the end of the day and she is lining the shelves with yesterday's atrocities and small hopes. Most of her face is out of sight. Just a part of an eyebrow is visible, the dark-brown hairs that are fine like embroidery silk – a bird's wing in flight.

'It's my twelfth day as Marcus's guest.'

'I wish I'd come to the house earlier.'

'Marcus must feel his home is so crowded all of a sudden.'

'He doesn't mind.'

She turns to look at him and smiles.

He moves towards her but stops and they both look towards the door because someone is going by outside in the corridor. Though there is no need to hide anything from Marcus, they are awkward at the thought of having to reveal this to him.

Marcus had been concerned for him when – Zameen and Bihzad having disappeared from view, the Soviets having been defeated – he went back to the United States, placing telephone calls to Afghanistan, visiting, writing.

Marcus worried that he might be grieving too much for Zameen and the boy, that he wasn't progressing with his life. Once when David mentioned a girlfriend called Angela, he was very suspicious, saying didn't you say last time her name was Angelica.

Somewhere along the way he had picked up the ability to endure isolation. There were no lovers, only moments of love. It seemed enough. And also he was young and under the impression that – living as he now did in a secure Western country, a place whose rules he knew – he was more or less in control. But he didn't yet know the laws of time. He thought he could waste opportunities or let them go by for now and find happiness or something close to it later. That caught up with him suddenly. A shock. Marcus was older and wiser and knew that some things can't always be guaranteed even in peaceful lands.

When he eventually did marry, Marcus remained distrustful. Wasn't sure whether he could believe him. The divorce four years later must have confirmed it for Marcus: David had finally decided to wrap up the fiction he had created for him.

As he drives through Usha he knows its people are dreading the thought that the Night Letter came from Nabi Khan, fearing a return of the days of the civil war, Nabi Khan and Gul Rasool reducing two-thirds of Usha to rubble in the early 1990s, killing a third of its population as they fought for supremacy, five hundred rockets fired into various parts of Usha in a single day. To visit certain streets was to realise that only the sky remained unchanged there.

THE BUDDHA, Marcus remembers as he approaches the stone head, had denied the existence of the soul.

It's mid-morning and the boy is asleep at a distance from the statue, as still as an effigy.

It was here in Afghanistan that the Buddha had received a human face, the earlier representations of him having been symbols – a parasol, a throne, a footprint. A begging bowl. The Greeks in Afghanistan gave him the features of Apollo, the god of knowledge, the god who repented. The only Asian addition to Apollo was a dot on the forehead and the topknotted locks.

A meeting of continents. When he described the Muslim Paradise, Muhammad in all probability drew on the memories of the Byzantine palaces he had seen during his pre-prophethood days as a travelling merchant.

It seems that the young man has been looking at his old notebooks. Marcus picks one up from the alcove. Qatrina and Zameen and he had loved everything about books. In tissue paper, in cardboard boxes, in paper cups they would locate the scent of stationery, the odour of libraries.

He turns the pages and it all comes back. Cis-3-hexanol smells of cut grass, he recalls with a pang. How can he count the things that are now lost? To him. To this country. Are the forty-seven names by which a lover may address the beloved preserved somewhere? The tablets of etiquette. And the one vital sign, specific to each situation, which exhibits a person's character and intentions: *My friend had hesitated before entering my house, so I knew I could trust him.* Does anyone recall the blue-black curls and arabesques on the water, the yards of meandering lines, when kohl floated away from the eyes of the women washing their faces at the dawn lake? And is this remembered? As though it were the moon cutting into their sleep, the men of Usha had woken one night to discover pillars of shimmering gold descending on them from the mountain range, a midnight breathing in the air as they stared at the hundred columns of light drawing near, as unnaturally real as a dream – and then the women, for it was they, approached and lifted the fronts of their burkas and revealed that the entire reverse side of each garment was studded with fireflies, one for every square inch of the fabric, the women's skin flickering. The wives had gone away and captured these specks of frayed light and come back like living lanterns, the fluorescence streaming through the cloth. Their skin reacted provocatively wherever the wing of an insect brushed against it with any firmness, desire entering the hearts of the men at the sight. The husbands had fallen quickly asleep upon returning from the labours of the world a few hours earlier, fatigue bubbling in them like soda, the exhaustion that at times made them resent even having to drag their shadows around. And if there was anger in any of them now at having been abandoned during sleep, they remembered to check their words because they knew that a woman decides who deserves to be called a man.

Does anyone else remember that night?

There are millions of marks of love on the earth, runes and cuneiforms on the water, on the very air. It is the wisdom of a thousand Solomons. The communal script of belonging. The First Text. In a place where not many can read or write, each person's memory is a fragile repository of song and ceremonies, tales and history, and if he vanishes without passing it on, it's like the wing of a library burning down.

The boy stirs on the floor. For that's what he is. A boy. Visiting the West, Marcus was always surprised to read the word 'man' being used to describe eighteen- or nineteen-year-olds. They are children, who, even if they may already know much about the world, know nothing about themselves yet. Won't for many years.

'I thought I'd have a look at your wound,' Marcus tells him when he opens his eyes. 'I wonder if we should change the dressing.'

'Why do you have this idol here?' he asks, beginning to unknot the bandage.

'It's always been here. It is part of Afghanistan's past.'

He just nods in return. There is a little drowsiness in him, the result of the painkillers.

'For a long time it never bothered anyone, for a very long time.' The Arabs who came to fight the Soviets had called the Afghans 'donkeys', telling them their version of Islam was a corruption, even saying they didn't know how to pray correctly. They fired rockets into the graves of Afghan saints. 'People used to come and work down here, long before you were born. This was a perfume factory.'

He recalls the floor heaped with the frilly hills of roses.

'It seems to me', Casa says, 'that only a bad Muslim would remain unconcerned by this thing.' He speaks very quietly so it's hard to detect if there is ill feeling behind what he is saying.

'The Koran itself says that the race of djinns belonging to Solomon had decorated his cave with statues.'

'Please don't say such things.' He is visibly pained.

'I am sorry.' Muhammad had personally saved portraits of Jesus, Mary and Abraham from the Kaaba shrine while ordering others to be smashed.

'I thought you said you had converted to Islam.'

'True.'

'Then I don't understand why you are disrespecting the Holy Book.'

'I wasn't aware that I was. But I'll say nothing more on the subject.'

'Thank you.'

At breakfast neither David nor Marcus had known how to react to Casa's words. Qatrina, of course, would have gently but firmly challenged him. Sometimes it is important to *say* things, she'd claim. And although, yes, Marcus remembers change taking place in him because of what he had heard someone say, some conviction of theirs that was startling to him, he doesn't wish to argue with the boy now. 'I sometimes wonder', Qatrina once said, 'if one shouldn't let people hear a sentence like, "I do not believe in the existence of Allah." They'll be stunned but will go away and think about it. They might have heard about such people but to have it come from a person with a skin, with a mouth and eyes, a person who is standing at the same level as them – that has a different impact altogether. They must see that I am someone whose pulse they could feel if they stretched out their hand and placed it on my neck vein, and yet still I haven't been struck by lightning because of what I have just said.'

Marcus examines the back of the head in silence and then reties the bandage, their three hands working together, rising and falling. Replace just one carbon atom with one silicon atom in the 1,1-dimethylcyclohexane molecule and the smell goes from eucalyptus to unpleasant. Who knows how the boy ended up with these opinions? What small thing could the others in the world have done differently for a happier outcome, what small mistake was made? Wolves exhibiting strange behaviour – caught in traps and thrashing about, injured by other creatures or by bullets, pups suffering from epilepsy – are attacked and killed by their pack members. But here everyone is human and must try to understand each other's mystery. Each other's pain.

He hasn't said anything about himself except that he is an itinerant labourer from a village in the nearer ridges of the mountain above them.

He thanks Marcus for the bandage and asks if there is anything he can do to repay his kindness. Marcus tells him to just rest.

'Was it a landmine – your hand?'

Marcus shakes his head and stands up to leave.

'Does it hurt?'

'Sometimes.'

230

'I am sorry. What happened?'

'The Taliban cut it off.'

Casa does not miss a beat. The information not even remotely troubling or unusual to him. 'You stole something?'

'Yes.'

'May Allah keep us all on the correct path,' he says and then lies down again.

When Richard the Lionheart displayed brute strength by breaking an iron bar with his sword, Saladin's delicately sharp scimitar countered it by slicing a silk handkerchief in two. What has been lost is the desire to believe in and take pride in Saladin's gentleness.

Marcus goes up the stairs, giving the Buddha a last glance – its stone the light-brown colour of an apple moth found in English gardens, having arrived there from Australia.

He emerges into the clean clear morning. The world is apricot light and blue shadows. In sura 27, Solomon laughs on hearing the conversation of two ants – a rare example of humour in the Koran – and there is a third-century Buddhist version of that tale with two butterflies instead of ants. It's no point sharing with the boy the delightful essential idea that tales can travel, or that two sets of people oceans apart can dream up similar sacred myths.

And yet he can comprehend the believers' anxiety about pollution – of not wishing to be infected or contaminated by their surroundings. On the flight back from India decades ago – he'd gone to visit the fabled suppliers of perfume raw materials along Bombay's Muhammad Ali Road

– he had discerned Hanuman and Ganesh and Radha in the shapes of the clouds below him, so overwhelming had been the sight of the Hindu gods and goddesses, so strongly had their flying and dancing forms imprinted themselves onto his consciousness. Little wonder Sanskrit poetry celebrated *the beauty of the lifted foot* and *the lotus-stalk waist*. All this hadn't been there on the way into India. 'Pollution' had occurred while he was there.

Iris-root butter from Florence. Lemon. Bulgarian rose. The wood of the Indian *oudh* tree that has been eaten by fungus. These were some of the ingredients he contemplated when he blended the perfume for Zameen – the daughter he has been missing now for longer than he had actually known her.

The sweet-smelling putchuk of Kashmir was used in Europe in 288 BC as an offering to Apollo.

When a soldier dies his weapon is referred to by his brothers on the battlefield as 'the widow'. In addition, Casa remembers being told that he must guard his gun 'like his eyes'. Looking for his Kalashnikov, he begins to retrace his path from the night of the *shabnama*. He goes through the orchard, trying to see if his blood is in the dust. Not spilled, but rather given to Allah.

He shouldn't have said anything to Marcus about the Buddha. He should rein in his words when talking to these people, must try to be pleasant. If he's banished from here he'd have no safety.

He has to maintain composure. And he must look for his rifle.

'You have been a thought in the mind of Allah from all eternity.' With these words of encouragement the fourteen-year-old Casa and one thousand others had been sent from his madrassa in Pakistan in 1996. To conquer Kabul from the seven warring factions. To take it in the name of One True God. 'History is Allah working through man,' they had been told. 'You are not new to this: you are taking back what has always been yours.' In the flow of secular Christian time they would have appeared to be just a band of ragged boys, but in the corresponding year of the Islamic calendar – 1417 – they were warriors who were drawing their swords and throwing the scabbards aside for ever, tightening their clothes to themselves in order to fight unhindered, a continuation of a long line from Muhammad onwards, kings of tomorrow, who hated the carnage they must cause but cause it they must.

Swarms of their Datsun trucks with heavy .50 calibre machine guns, cannons, anti-aircraft guns and multiple-barrelled rocket launchers mounted in the beds – all supplied by Saudi Arabia and the ISI, the lovers of Allah – had swept into Kabul. The former Communist president – who, as the head of the Afghan secret service, had sanctioned and overseen the torture of thousands of Afghans during his time – had sought shelter in the UN compound, thinking it sacrosanct, but five Taliban had just walked in during the night, the guards having fled earlier at the sound of the gunfire from the city limits.

Beating the president and his brother until they were

senseless, the Taliban bundled the pair into a pickup and drove to the darkened Presidential Palace. There they castrated him and dragged his body behind a jeep for several rounds of the Palace, and then they shot him dead. The brother was similarly tortured and throttled to death. Just before daybreak Casa's convoy arrived at the scene and – because it was important to terrorise the inhabitants of the city into submission – he assisted in the hanging up of the two swollen and bloodied cadavers from steel-wire nooses on a traffic post, just a few blocks from the UN compound.

He is about to emerge from the orchard when he sees that the old man and the woman are there a few yards ahead of him. Retreating to a safe distance he watches her face through the branches, the leaves glowing bright from the sun. He feels engulfed in a green fire as he looks at her. Anyone can envision Paradise, can try to clothe the other side with the colours of this world. But whenever during his time as a taxi driver the Western passengers questioned him about the Islamic afterlife, their prurience was an offence to him. He didn't know a single Muslim whose first thought on hearing the word 'Paradise' was *Seventy-two virgins.* The trials of the world were so immense and harsh that committing sins was unavoidable, and so on being granted entry into Paradise a believer was first and foremost glad to have been spared Hell. *That* was the first thought, and the second and the third and the fourth and the fifth. Everything else came much later, including the demands of that thing which was the first thing the angels created when Allah asked them to mould Adam out of clay.

Parental figures. Women of Lara's age are what he looks at most closely when he gets a chance. Avoiding the disturbing faces of the younger ones, thankful when the burkas kept them out of sight during the Taliban regime. A residue from childhood – when he was without any sense of time, when he thought adults had come into being the size they were – there is a faint trace of envy in him even today when he sees a boy accompanied by his mother. Her hand must deliver anaesthetic as well as pain when she slaps the child over a misdemeanour.

He wonders about the magnitude of the sin he is committing by looking at Lara's face, even though his thoughts are pure. A wish in him to prolong the tenderness he is suddenly experiencing in his breast. A mother. An aunt or older sister or cousin. He tears himself away from the comfort at last and turns back, to find another path towards the lake.

Lara and Marcus are spreading washed clothing onto a rope in the sunlight. There are no pegs so they are using large safety pins instead. If the pomegranates were in season, she thinks, they could have distributed them among the pockets to weigh down the clothes against the wind.

'Do you miss Britain?'

'I think about it, yes. It's only natural.'

On one of her white sleeves, not fully bleached, one-third of a pale orange-coloured blossom is visible.

'We went almost every year at one point. Zameen knew

the Lake District, knew Edinburgh and London nearly as well as she knew Mazar-i-Sharif and the Buddhas of Bamiyan.'

'The Yorkshire moors.'

'The woods full of bluebells.'

'When David and I are gone you'll be alone here once again.'

'Did you know Turner used sketches he made of the Yorkshire moors when he painted Hannibal's army crossing the Alps?'

'Do you have family in England?'

'A painting of immense power. A sweep of blackness above the soldiers. The stragglers being picked off by the savage mountain-men . . . The book of his pictures is nailed in the corridor on the second floor. Later when he produced a canvas about the victory at Waterloo, there was no glory to be seen there either. Just the dead bodies lying on the battlefield with wives and sweethearts searching among them. And this was the *winning* side.'

Only now does he lift her hand to his lips. He kisses the fingers, cold from the wet clothing. 'Thank you for being worried about me.'

'I'll go back in a few days no doubt.'

'There is no reason why you can't come and visit me again.'

She nods.

'And after you have gone back to Russia, David will be alone too.'

She looks at him, seeing his grin, the pulse of benevolence in the face.

He goes to sit on the threshold, and she joins him minutes later, the light filtering through the hanging clothes. She watches him smoke his one cigarette of the day. A bit of tobacco rolled by him in kite paper. They can be pink or blue or white.

'How could a perfume maker smoke?'

'Smokers actually smell better than non-smokers.'

'That's illogical.' She smiles.

'Not at all. The carbon monoxide in the cigarette blocks the enzyme in the nose that breaks things down – so the smell lingers longer than normal.'

'Next you'll be telling me there are perfume makers who continue with their profession even after losing their sense of smell.'

'There are such cases.'

She laughs. 'Like Beethoven continuing to compose after he lost his hearing.' She looks up into the sky. A cloud appears and dissolves even as she watches – a flimsy wisp, it is gone so thoroughly she finds herself doubting a memory a few moments old. 'My Stepan used to smoke. I made him give up.'

'You needn't feel guilty about David.' He kisses her hand again. 'We must live.'

'I wasn't always like this.'

'Let me imagine.'

'When I was much younger. If I was happy you'd know it, and the same if I was unhappy. Didn't really believe in silent or passive suffering.'

'The Russian Soul, and all that. Right?'

'Tell me more about Qatrina.'

'For a long time I didn't know where she was buried. They wouldn't tell me.'

'You won't see her again?'

'Neither of us believed in an afterlife. When you are dead you decay and become part of the earth. It is no disrespect to the dead to say that their bodies have been consumed by creatures in the soil. It makes us cherish this life and this world more. That is much better than the talk about eternity and the hereafter. Death is *not* greater than life.'

'I would have liked to have seen the ninety-nine pictures she did.'

'Gone.' He raises his hand towards the sky.

'Why that subject?'

'She represented us humans doing all the things that Allah is supposed to do. Her comment on the non-existence of God. We don't have souls, we have cells.'

'There is a tradition of the Buddha having ninety-nine names.'

But his mind is elsewhere. 'It took me years to locate her when I came back from exile. I looked for her, journeying through deserts and forests, along limestone cliffs and granite boulders. Gul Rasool had abandoned her in the mountains, and she went from place to place. Trying to practise her profession as much as she could. Tired like me of the colour red. Everywhere there was the civil war.' He places the cigarette on a pebble, and rubs his scalp with his fingers. 'It then seemed unreal that I had found her, that we two had been overlooked by death and were together in this house once again. During the years of her captivity by

Gul Rasool, she said, his fighters in a hashish haze had beaten her for marrying a white man. She'd sneak off to give medical treatment to the villagers whom Rasool and his guerrillas had wounded for not giving food and assistance to them. She used mountain snow as anaesthesia for amputation after battles with the Soviets. Temperatures low enough to freeze battery acid. Similar things had happened to me with Nabi Khan. But we now counted ourselves among the lucky, with dynamite and rockets and grenades exploding all around us. Then one day the civil war stopped and the Taliban arrived in Usha. 1996.' He shakes his head, looking at her with his light-filled eyes. 'But enough of sad things.'

Life in Usha was blasted-out and silent because of the war between Nabi Khan and Gul Rasool, but the Taliban put both of them to flight within days. And now – only hours after gaining control of Usha – they began whipping women in the streets for showing their faces. They banned smoking, music, television, kite flying, ludo, chess, football. There were bonfires of books and videos and audio tapes. They stood on the sides of the roads arresting men who didn't have beards, taking them to jail until the beards had grown. They ordered shops to close at prayer time, and in the first few hours they nailed a singer of devotional music to the mulberry tree in front of the mosque, for not revealing where he had buried his instruments. Qatrina, on her way to the clinic, tried to intervene and was struck in the face by a young man – so hard she thought he'd shattered her cheekbone – and told to go home and not to venture out from then on. He had raised his hand in the air and held it there for a few seconds instead of bringing it down to slap her. He wasn't hesitating, he was stalling to give her time to become afraid of the coming blow.

They were mostly poor foot soldiers from primitive and impoverished backgrounds. Vulnerable and easy to control, it didn't take much effort to work them up into frenzy over what they had been taught to believe as religious truth, and the domination over women was a simple way to organise and embolden them.

They asked for all windows to be painted black so no one would catch a glimpse of a woman. Earning a living was declared inappropriate conduct for females, resulting in arrest for insubordination against Allah's will. Trying to escape a Taliban beating for exposing her feet, her burka not being long enough, a young woman had in her terror run in front of an oncoming Taliban jeep. She bled to death in front of Marcus's clinic because – being male – he was not allowed to administer to her. Women became afraid of catching even the smallest of illnesses: left untreated, it could grow and cause death – and Marcus did see a twelve-year-old die of measles.

They had banned schools for girls immediately but later they forbade them even for boys, and no one could do anything. Men walking by averted their eyes and quickened their pace if a woman was being lashed in the street – if they tried to prevent it they would be set upon. It was best to see as little as possible. Afghanistan became a land whose geology was fear instead of rock, where you breathed terror not air.

Despite this monstrous thraldom, however, Qatrina and Marcus continued to see patients of either gender in secret whenever they could.

Visiting a patient's home one day he noticed in a corner the large wooden chest in which Qatrina had kept the ninety-nine paintings. The chest was among the many things missing from the ruined house by the lake when he returned from exile in Peshawar. On seeing it now Marcus moved towards it and opened it: the paintings were still in there, still beautiful like jewels. She would paint a picture, allow the paper to dry, and then dip it into a tray of water to dissolve away some or all the colour. After it had dried she would paint for a second time and again take away part or the whole of the pigment in the water bath. The process could be repeated as many as ten or twelve times. On occasion she added an amount of colour to the trayful of water before lowering the picture into it, so that the entire composition was suffused by a very pale redness or by a reticent haze of saffron. A sustained shimmer of blue. Layer by layer she would build a complex painting over many weeks.

The man of the house said the pictures belonged to him but Marcus hauled the chest to the door, appalled at the lie, and out there he looked for someone who would help him transport it back to Qatrina at the house. He and the man were arguing in the street when a Taliban vehicle pulled up. The pair were taken to the mosque.

He had no way to prove that the paintings were his and

so it was decided that on Friday his hand would be cut off as punishment for theft.

The Taliban did not know how to deal with the pictures – each bore one of Allah's names in Arabic calligraphy, the Compassionate One, the Immortal One – but the words were surrounded by images not only of flowers and vines but of other living things. Animals, insects and humans. They wanted to tear out these details but couldn't because the various strokes and curves of the name took up the entire rectangle, reaching into every corner, every angle.

A man slapped Marcus, expressing everyone's feeling of rage at the quandary the pictures had placed them in, and then they had him taken to a small chamber at the back of the mosque. Jars of the best rose essence had been given by him to be added to the mortar when this extension of the building was under way years earlier, still fragrant. He emerged blinking into daylight two days later, weak with hunger and thirst. It was Friday. He had been handcuffed – the thought with him the previous two days that one steel hoop would just slide off when the hand was amputated – and now they walked him out towards the large crowd gathered at the side of the mosque. A woman in a bloodstained burka was on her knees in the dust at the centre of the circle formed by the crowd. Her hand must have been cut off, there was blood all around her, but then he saw that both her hands were intact where they emerged from the folds – and he recognised the wedding ring on her finger. She was Qatrina and she had actually just carried out an amputation. The blood was that of the victim. There was a scalpel in the dust. She must have collapsed and now, rising to her feet and turning her head, she let out a scream on seeing Marcus, realising what lay ahead. A man came and retrieved the amputated hand of the earlier thief from the ground. He held it above the heads of a cluster of children who laughed and tried to grab it as he encouraged them to leap up higher and higher. He went away with it: according to Muhammad's instructions the thief was to wear it around his neck for the next few days. The crowd was chanting the Koran. She tried to run away but the black-clad figures barred her way, pointing her towards the block of wood drenched in redness, glistening in the sun. They brought Marcus to the block, which was a round stump cut from a mulberry log. And a man with large hands, fingernails the size of pennies, reached towards him and held his left hand down on the bloody wood. She was screaming defiance, hurling aside the tray on which there was a butcher's knife and several glass syringes. Lignocaine, he thought, the local anaesthetic. Mixed with adrenalin, to constrict the vessels and reduce blood flow, preventing haemorrhaging. There was a woodworker's small saw and a rust-speckled pair of scissors.

They now held a gun to her head – 'Do it!' – so that Marcus had to plead with her to go ahead, knowing they would kill her without thought. He picked up the scalpel and pushed it into her hands, tried to close her fingers around it. But she kept saying no, enraging them with her defiance, shaming them in front of the crowd. She lifted her burka and looked into the eyes of the boy in front of her. The crowd suddenly silent.

243

'Go ahead and kill me. I said I am not going to do it.'

She stood to full height.

She had told Marcus how, when she was a girl, some women in her family had shuddered as she became taller with each passing year, her height too immodest for a woman, a portent of catastrophe. Her growing body seemed intent on rebellion because this was the country where the term 'white eyes' was used to reprimand a female child or young woman by implying she let the whites of her eyes show, rather than keeping them lowered in deference, as befits a woman or someone of inferior status.

Seconds ticked by.

The gun was taken off her head and moved to Marcus's temple.

'Do it, or we'll kill *him*.'

When the blade came towards him he stretched his fingers to touch her palm. The last act his hand performed for him.

In the months that followed they entered a different geography of the mind altogether. She would not speak, or couldn't, kept her face to the walls, to the shadows. In any room she rushed towards corners. Or she wandered off into the burning noonday sun until he found her, fully expecting her eyes to have evaporated from their sockets in all that heat. In the orchard she feinted at pomegranate blossoms thinking they were live coals, fireflowers. His own wound was full of terrible pain, the pain he had to stifle so as not to terrify her, though he could have howled for entire days. The hand was missing but it still hurt as though he had closed the absent fingers around a scorpion, around shards of glass. The cut muscles, the bones, were not healing properly and he had to go to Jalalabad for treatment, relying on people's kindness to provide a measure of care and safety for Qatrina. At times she was oblivious to him, but at other times, watching him leave, she stretched her arms towards him through the bars of the window – a song of lamentation issuing from a lyre's strings. Twice he had to go to the hospitals in Kabul, the city where plans were being made to make the non-Muslim inhabitants – a few Sikhs and Hindus, a handful of Jews – wear clothes of a specific colour, to make sure their lesser status was immediately apparent on the street. It was a different city once. Two decades ago a group of laughing college girls had discovered that the white car parked on Flower Street belonged to Wamaq Saleem – the great Pakistani poet who was visiting Afghanistan to give a recital of his poems – and they had covered it entirely with lipstick kisses.

Returning from a week-long stay at the hospital in Kabul, Marcus found all the books in the house nailed to the ceilings.

THE HIGH GRASS REACHES up to his pelvis as Casa makes his way towards the lake, the seed heads brushing his hands. Two o'clock in the afternoon.

A roof of sparrows goes by overhead. To save ammunition he would always shoot only when there was a chance of taking two birds at once – aiming at the point where the flight paths were to cross.

He cannot be sure if he took this route to the factory that night. If he dropped the Kalashnikov in a damp or wet place he'll have to wipe off the water from inside it and re-oil the entire mechanism, a task that will take several hours, if he is lucky enough to locate some oil, that is. Walking around, trying to remember, he is put in mind of the time he had practised laying minefields at the al-Qaeda training camp. As the procedure allowed no carelessness, everything was mapped out beforehand with precise co-ordinates: a few days later he would have to come back and find the mines as part of the training. An inattentive holy warrior could be killed by a mine he had laid himself.

He changes direction on seeing the small flock of demoiselle cranes on the lake's edge. Grey and black, with white ear-tufts and crimson eyes. One of them raises its wings a little in order to close them more comfortably.

Several were kept at one of the madrassas in Pakistan as they are better than watchdogs in warning of intruders. The ground delves under his feet and the cranes are obscured from view behind the wall of grass as he walks towards them.

He stops on seeing them. They are perfectly still, looking at him. Three white men, young like him but bigger, one of them without a shirt so that slabs of muscle stand exposed. A couple are armed with third-generation Glock 22s. Then an Afghan man appears and joins them.

'Who are you?' the Afghan asks. He is holding Casa's rifle.

Casa points towards Marcus's house back there, not taking his eyes off the whites, one of whom has his finger on the trigger though the weapon hangs down beside his leg.

'The old doctor's house?'

He gives a nod, trying not to look at the Kalashnikov, betraying recognition.

The questioner turns to the other three and, huddling, says something in English to them. A tense glance directed towards him from time to time.

Casa asks the Afghan – the West's running dog – who his companions are but gets no answer. He repeats the question but it is as though they are incapable of hearing him. They now motion for him to follow as they begin to walk out of the river of grass, and in turning away the half-naked man reveals that he has a life-size tattoo of a Glock handgun at the small of his back, just to the left of his spine's base. Only the tilting grip and part of the trigger are showing, the muzzle hidden beyond the waistband of his trousers – as it would be if a weapon were kept there.

One of the whites hangs back so that he is behind Casa as they emerge onto the path.

With the Afghan translating, the white men want to know how he got his injury.

'A bandit. Are they American?'

A tribe's greatness is known by how mighty its enemy is, the clerics at the madrassas would say, telling them they must plan to inflict pain on America.

And now the whites want to know why he is interested in their nationality.

'No reason.'

He wonders what images the two other white men have inked on their bodies. A serrated knife at the ankle? A .44 Magnum along the side of the ribs, resting as though in an invisible holster – with the grip just under the armpit and the tip of the barrel touching the hipbone?

They want him to show them the palms of his hands.

They know they should be looking for Kalashnikov calluses.

At least they are not negroes or women.

He crosses his arms under the thin blanket wrapped around his body.

Proud as Satan, the one without the shirt watches him narrowly, looking as though about to move forwards and raise a hand towards the blanket, Casa taking an embattled step back, his fingers curling into the slippery hot palms.

The edge of the blanket is woven into fine mosaic-like shapes. He is the mosque these Americans wish to bomb.

He is perfectly innocent – how do they know otherwise? – and yet they are behaving like this towards him. Every Muslim should be told what his fate would be if his sword hand fails. This is his country, but the sense of entitlement he detects in their eyes brings home to him the full extent of the peril and challenge faced by Islam.

Just then David's car appears from the direction of Usha. Casa takes an additional few backward steps to be out of the force field of these persons, who are turning back to look at the approaching vehicle. They are in the middle of the path so must move to the verge. Two on one side, two on the other – Casa remaining where he is at first but then walking to the border extremely carefully as though he is on a tightrope, looking straight ahead. Light is being sieved through a tree on the left, and whenever an insect flies through a ray the sun ignites its wings briefly. David stops the car and exchanges a few words with the Americans – they seem to know each other. He opens the door on the passenger's side and asks Casa to get in but he doesn't move, his eyes two live coals where he's trying to hold back tears. Rage and humiliation, a fury many centuries deep.

The West wants unconditional love; failing that, unconditional surrender. Not realising that that privilege is Islam's.

'What did they say to you?' asks David when the car moves forward.

He just shakes his head and they sit without words for the few minutes it takes them to get to the house. Soon after he stopped being a taxi driver and joined Nabi Khan's group, Khan had sent him to a martyrdom training camp – to give it its correct title, and not 'suicide' training camp as the Westerners and their servants here would call it. And but for the fact that he and Khan are probably estranged now, he would happily carry out the mission he had prepared for.

These days they keep saying, *Why do the Muslims become suicide bombers? They must be animals, there are no human explanations for their actions.* But does no one remember what happened on board flight United 93? A group of Americans – 'civilised' people, not 'barbarians' – discovered that their lives, their country, their land, their cities, their traditions, their customs, their religion, their families, their friends, their fellow countrymen, their past, their present, their future, were under attack, and they decided to risk their lives – and eventually gave up their lives – to prevent the other side from succeeding. He is not wrong when he thinks that that is a lot like what the Muslim martyrdom bombers are doing.

Marcus sniffs one of the smaller pieces of birch bark. He identifies it as *Betula papyrifera*, saying it could grow up to eighty feet high with a two-foot diameter. In the United States cedar would be used for the gunwales, and for the ribs and sheathing. Eastern white cedar – *Thuja occidentalis*. Ideal for building a canoe as it is easy to split and resistant to disease.

There is a large tin and Lara helps him take off its lid.

'Spruce gum, for waterproofing the entire thing,' David says. 'It'll be softened with this': he picks up another container – 'bear fat.' These two, and the bark and the spruce roots, are the things he has brought from the United States; the rest – the wood for the gunwales, the sheathing, the three thwarts, the finger-long dowels – he has acquired here in Afghanistan.

'My brother and I dug up spruce roots from an abandoned Christmas-tree plantation when we built ours. The ground was covered in a sheet of moss and we'd grab hold of a root and lift it – it would just rip itself free through the soft moss, yards ahead of us. It was like a creature was attached to the other end, racing away.'

Casa is holding the long beam-like pieces – the inwales and the outwales, to be pegged with the dowels along the rim of the boat – and Marcus, after remarking on the brightness of the wood, says:

'Mary is said to have beaten the child Jesus for weaving sunbeams into a bridge and drowning three boys. They had refused to play with him because of his lowly origin. He cursed the willow tree from which the switch was made and that is why the willow tree rots easily.'

Casa smiles through this unneeded reference to Christianity. Muslims revere Jesus Christ – peace be upon him – but that Jesus bears no resemblance to the one today's Christians follow. They have perverted the Bible, adding and subtracting stories, suppressing certain sayings of Jesus – like *Think not that I am come to send peace on earth: I came not to send peace, but a sword* – and before the world ends the Muslims will ensure no memory of the false Jesus remains in the world. 'Today's Christians don't want us to know this,' Casa was told at the martyrdom training camp, 'but the God we share with them approves of our methods.' Yes, he knows. He knows how the helpless and debased Samson – who is Shamaun in Arabic – had asked for strength from God. *Then Samson called to the Lord and said, 'O Lord God, remember me, I pray Thee, and strengthen me, I pray Thee, only this once, O God, that I may be avenged . . .'* And with that he grasped the two middle pillars upon which rested the temple where he was being disgraced and humiliated, and he leaned his weight upon them – his right hand on the one, his left hand on the other. Saying, *let me die with the Philistines*, he toppled the two pillars and brought the massive building crashing down, killing himself and three thousand others, an act of which God obviously approved because He must have given Samson the strength he had asked for.

'The chest in which Qatrina kept the ninety-nine paintings of the names of Allah was made of willow,' says the Englishman. 'Each picture rolled up and fastened with a wide ribbon of Chinese silk.'

Casa had seen women wearing Chinese silk during his days as a taxi driver. He'd take young American soldiers to the Great Wall of China, the clandestine house of pleasure that opened in Kabul after the Taliban were obliterated. No Afghans were allowed into the establishment, the white men emerging from there sometimes with women on their arms, the shimmering colours of their dresses like bright wrapping paper around a child's toffee.

He himself has been touched by a woman only five

252

times in his entire life, mostly the nurses handling him at hospitals. Certainly there has never ever been anything of his own volition. The state of affairs is similar among those who intend to carry out Nabi Khan's imminent martyrdom attacks in Usha. And since Allah says that no one must die a virgin, Nabi Khan had arranged for them to know intimacy for the first and last time in this life. It was to have happened tomorrow night.

'I don't know what became of the paintings,' Marcus is saying. 'I see them in my memory, though. For me that is possession enough. She painted on the chest the berry tree that grows above Allah's throne according to the Koran.'

'How long will the canoe take to construct?' Casa asks David.

'You and I, we'll have it on the water in a few days.'

David made a start this morning. The white side of the bark was almost luminous in the lake's water where it was left to soak. He had lifted it out, as well as all the smaller pieces, and brought them dripping to the dry land. And placing that largest piece on the ground, the white side up, he had laid onto it the twelve-foot leaf-like shape that he had fashioned out of plywood – the shape the base of the canoe is going to be.

Now he and Casa get to work – silently on the whole, except for a grunt now and then, and with the million-year-old gaze of the demoiselles watching them from far away.

David had collected large stones from along the lake's shore, some of them covered in brilliant patches of moss, and these are weighing down the plywood leaf.

The main piece of bark is only slightly wider than the widest point of the plywood leaf, so they'll have to use extra pieces at the sides, sewing them on with the lengths of spruce roots soaked in hot water for flexibility, using the antler-handled awls to make holes for the rows of double stitches.

The excess bark has been bent upwards around the plywood template and stakes have been driven along the outline to keep it folded up.

They are doing this in the shade because the sun would dry out the bark, and they are pouring hot water from a bucket – set on a fire near by – to ensure the bark remains workable.

David tells Casa that this type of boat had been in use for at least fourteen thousand years, that torches would be fastened to the canoes when they were taken out by the Native Americans for night fishing on the lakes of North America.

It is an awakening when the generator is installed.

Casa and David work on the bark boat until the sun sets, the gradual disappearance of light in a vast show of overlapping reds above them, sweeping in evenly spaced bands. Then they lift the generator out of the back of the car. And, working together by candlelight for half an hour, they set it going.

Casa tries not to get swept up in everyone's obvious delight. Like transparent eggs, David has brought boxes of bulbs which Casa fits into the socket in each room, putting chairs or stools on tables to gain the heights, someone always holding the column of furniture for his safety. He takes out the dead bulbs and examines them closely. If the filament is broken – as opposed to burnt away completely – he can manoeuvre the two ends into meeting again, snagging the coils together so that the current can flow through once more.

Suddenly the house is lit up with radiant electricity. It's as though they had trapped daylight a few hours earlier and have now brought it into the house, hanging a cage from a hook in every room.

It is his first time in the deeper interiors of the house. When the switch is thrown, light shoots out of the bulb and slams into the walls but then it is as though the walls are glowing from within. They also seem to take a step towards him. Colour. He stands inhaling it. Marcus points out various details to him, his talk confusing him, making him feel at times that he doesn't know much about Islam let alone other religions, that he knows little about Afghanistan let alone the world.

Arriving at the room at the top, however, as he stands in the middle looking around, all he can think of is annihilation.

Fragments of plaster are arranged in the centre of the floor, depicting two lovers with their arms around each other, Marcus carefully removing four pieces for the four legs of the table, so Casa can rise towards the fixture in the ceiling, towering above the image. He stands in a daze: the indecent images on the walls seeming to swell and recede with each thump of his heart.

He had told Nabi Khan that for tomorrow night's necessity they must be given an adult female.

The lilies stretching their jaws, the smaller blossoms hanging in triangular grape-like clusters from high vines – he does like these painted details, he must admit. But the rest. If all this is what is meant by the word 'culture', then culture is not permitted in Islam. So it is that the Devil has the temerity to say to Allah, 'I have added colour to Adam's story,' and – the senses undermining faith at every turn – no wonder the Saudi fighters want all the mosques here in Asia painted white inside and out, like the ones in their desert homeland.

Music issues from a tape recorder in a stone alcove while he sits in the kitchen with Lara and Marcus, helping them peel boiled potatoes. He gets up and half-fills a glass of water and brings it to the table – for them to dip their fingertips into from time to time because the potatoes are scalding hot. His own Kalashnikov was the authentic article, but there were Pakistani-made copies that heated up when they were fired, obliging a warrior to dip his hand into a puddle during battles.

He wonders what kind of instrument produces the sounds they are listening to.

He doesn't flinch when David comes in with a bottle of wine and uncorks it and puts it on the window sill, next to the bowl of water in which there is a fountain pen that Marcus had been cleaning earlier in the day, taking it apart like a rifle.

Before opening the dark-green bottle David asks Casa if he'd mind their drinking it and he shakes his head and smiles. The smell of alcohol reaches him within a minute. That such things are for sale in the cities of a Muslim country.

They weren't until the West routed the Taliban.

Marcus says that in the year 988 when Prince Vladimir was casting around for a religion for the people of Rus he rejected Islam because he knew about its prohibition on alcohol. As though Casa wants to hear it. Perhaps if Russia had been a Muslim country it would not have given birth to the misfortune of Communism. As a child he had wanted to fight in Chechnya because he knew Communism and equality were a direct rebellion against Islam. The Koran clearly states in sura 16 that:

To some Muslims Allah has given more than He has to other Muslims. Those who are so favoured will not allow their slaves an equal share in what they have. Would they deny Allah's goodness?

Marcus, who had claimed he was a Muslim, sits drinking wine at dinner. There is indeed no limit to the cunning of the infidels. He deceived the trusting and amenable Muslims of this land just to marry a woman, but at heart he is still a non-believer. No wonder Allah punished him by deranging her, by taking away his hand.

The food bitter in the mouth, he finishes the meal in silence and quickly, and then, clearing away his plate, leaves for the perfume factory, declining their invitation to stay. Walking through the orchard he passes the large aloe vera plant whose thick serrated fingers Marcus slices up with a blade every day, extracting the pulp for Lara's neck. His head is spinning from the scent of alcohol. He drops to his knees close to the saw-edged plant, putting the lantern on the ground and waiting for the wave of nausea to pass. His left hand is in a mane of wild grass and some irregularity in the blades makes him look at them. He lifts the lamp with the other hand and is suddenly clear-headed. The half-green grass conceals a massive landmine. It is only two or so yards from the aloe plant. He withdraws the left hand slowly and stands up. He must calculate, see how this object can be used to his best advantage. He pinches the corner of his mouth between incisors as he stands thinking. A vision in his mind of the Englishman bleeding to death here. One whole sura of the Koran is dedicated to the hypocrites. *They use their faith as a disguise . . . Evil is what they do . . .*

He imagines laying out the Englishman before the stone idol's head and filling up the entire perfume factory with earth, interring them both.

After Marcus is eliminated he could take possession of the house? But what about the other two?

He continues towards the factory, the sky the darkest of blues above him, almost black, the colour he imagines each of their three souls would be if it were stretched thin and nailed to the corners of the sky. Containing just a few scattered points of light.

He goes down into the factory but, unable to jettison the thought of alcohol from his mind, the smell of it still inhabiting his nose, rushes back up and vomits as neatly as a cat in the darkness, shivering, squatting beside the tall tough stems of a weed. The various components of his soul rebel at the memory of having been so close to the forbidden repulsive liquid.

The cold air hits him now. It's as though he has taken off a metal hat.

He knows he must prevent Marcus and the others from ever venturing near the mine. He cannot bring himself to care about what happens to them, but it's important that the mine remain intact, to be at his disposal if ever those Americans threaten him again. He'll lure them to it. It's his only weapon.

'I read somewhere', says Lara, 'that when Muslims conquered Persia they burnt the libraries as instructed by Omar, the second caliph.'

'That story is probably invented,' Marcus says. 'But it was invented by *Muslims* to justify later book burnings.'

'When the thousands of manuscripts were set alight, the gold used in the illuminations had melted and flowed out. It's odd that they invented this detail too.'

'To make the myth appear convincing, yes.'

Holding a bamboo shaft at either end, they are on their way to the second storey, have been moving through the house to bring down books.

'When in the seventh century', says Marcus, 'the Arabs conquered Persia, Khorasmia, Syria and Egypt, these were rich and sophisticated societies. The ignorant desert Arabs exchanged gold for silver when they entered Persia and made themselves ill by seasoning their food with camphor. One can only wonder, Qatrina would say, at what these lands could have been had they not been set back by

the arrival of Islam. In Khorasmia the Arabs killed everyone who could read their own language. Only Arabic was
allowed.'

He has stopped on the landing and is touching the tip
of the bamboo to a thick volume on the ceiling, brown
leather stamped with gold filigree.

'But time moved on and the two peoples changed each
other. Eventually it would be the Muslims who'd keep the
philosophy of Aristotle alive for the Europeans through
the Dark Ages.'

She thinks he is slightly drunk. Lets him talk, following
him wherever he goes. Perhaps it's ebullience brought on
by all this light. Or it could just be the company. They are
stirring in each other memories of other times.

David has gone outside, saying he remembers burying
wine under the silk-cotton tree one year. She enters an
unlit room to look for him through the window. Over half
the world's mine dogs are here in Afghanistan.

In this room there is a wall of moonlight at this hour.
Something like a flock of hummingbirds sweeps across it.
Mites hide in the nostrils of hummingbirds, the
Englishman has told her, and when perfume begins to
drift over their bodies they know the bird has arrived at a
blossom – they climb down and begin to consume the
pollen and nectar.

'He'll be back soon,' Marcus says from the door.

She nods and joins him.

'Were you always interested in perfume?'

'The factory? I started it to give the women of Usha a
chance to earn money. Qatrina wanted them to know

they could have an independent wage. And this valley has always been known for its flowers. Later when I went to a perfume factory during a visit to Paris, with its large laboratories full of test tubes and pipettes, I told them that my own creations were just a matter of experimenting, of putting things together to see what happened. They laughed, "But that's how we *all* do it, it's all random – don't be fooled by the fancy equipment.'"

They are sitting next to each other on the stairs.

'I think I hear David. I should go to bed.'

'Stay with us, Marcus.'

'No, you go and find him.'

She watches him leave, clutching the new books. The clerics had the brilliant al-Kindi whipped in public for his words in the ninth century, he said earlier. The Father of the Perfume Industry, as well as philosopher, physician, astronomer, chemist, mathematician, musician and physicist – al-Kindi was sixty years old and the crowd roared approval at every lash. Al-Razi was sentenced to be hit on the head with his own book until either the book or his head split. He lost his eyesight.

It is always the case that where there is power, there is resistance, and so a parent came to the house during the time of the Taliban and asked if Marcus would help his eleven-year-old son with his studies, afraid the boy would forget what he learned in the days before the Taliban. Then more and more parents arrived with the same request, wanting to equip their sons and daughters for the possibilities of the world, rebelling against the Taliban's insistence that the wings be torn off the children. That was how it began, Marcus, his hand amputated, deciding to secretly tutor Usha's boys and girls in the perfume factory. Soon it was no longer a case of tutoring. It was a school.

The children were asked to walk to the house in twos and threes to avoid drawing attention to themselves from the Taliban's Religious Police. One group came in the morning, the other in the afternoon. This way the forty children were divided into two groups of twenty, each group sitting around the Buddha for four hours every day. Marcus tried not to talk of danger with the children: they were there to learn, not discuss problems that could not be solved. The youngest ones had little idea of certain forms of play. If a kite flies too high, one of them asked, does it catch fire from the sun? High on a wall in the kitchen, Marcus painted a diamond, with three coloured bows threaded along its tail, and attached an actual string to it: if a child excelled at his lessons he or she could go and hold the string and pretend to fly the kite as a reward.

An entertainment they had devised on their own had to be stopped when he discovered it to his horror. They banged their feet on the ground where the piano and the two rababs were buried, leaping from place to place, managing to strike some of the keys this way, to vibrate some of the rababs' strings, and listening as the notes seeped out of the soil.

For himself, denied music, he carried strips of paper in various pockets on which he had scrawled musical phrases, his fingertip touching the inked score like a stylus making contact with the groove of a record –

– and flooding his mind with the remembered melody. Silently. *I'll lament until Laila emerges from the house. I will lament for mercy from beloved Allah, like a bulbul saddened by her cage.* Centuries-old lyrics granted new relevance.

Four months after he started the school, danger found its way to the doorstep. Qatrina was sitting in the factory along the avenue of Persian lilac trees, holding an English primer upside down and chanting along with the two youngest children, 'A for Apple, B for Ball,' when Marcus saw the four men arriving from the direction of Usha, panicking a swarm of small birds from a clump of tall grass as they came. He had come out to the house to get a cloth for Qatrina's ink-stained fingers, or for the rest of the day she'd leave miniature herds of zebra on everything she touched. She was not the only one who was suffering mentally, he knew. A little boy had told him that his widowed mother, forced now to beg, beat him and his siblings when they asked for food, threatening to kill them and herself.

263

'How can I help you?' Marcus came out of the house and greeted the men. 'Has there been an injury?'

He wasn't sure whether he was just imagining it but he could hear the children's voices like a bit of fragrance on the breeze.

'We think you have been teaching children here – teaching them things other than the Koran.'

'That's not true.'

The men were staring at him. He recognised one of them. He had shot dead a man in the street last week for having missed prayers at the mosque on three consecutive days.

'There's nobody here but my wife and I. She's unwell.'

'I hope for your sake you are telling the truth.' They were looking up at the windows, looking towards the orchard, the Persian lilacs.

'I barely have enough time to take care of her, to take care of myself – how could I teach children at the same time?'

A man leaned forward and said something into the leader's ear. There was a marked change in his demeanour suddenly – he even took half a step back. 'Is it true that she has become possessed by the djinn of late?'

'Only Allah, the Pitying Friend of the Helpless, knows.'

He nodded. 'If you have lied to us about the school, we'll come back and kill you both,' he said and then they were gone.

He was going up the stairs of the perfume factory six days later when he saw the first of them materialise on the top step. Marcus went backwards, not taking his eyes off

264

the black figure. Then there were others, twenty-five of them, all with guns, and they were coming down the stairwell at great speed. In no time they were down there with the Buddha. One of them gripped Marcus's throat and crashed his head against the wall and as the children began to scream in terror a fist connected with his jaw, bone colliding against bone. Marcus wondered how mere meat – the human body – could generate such ripping pain.

In shock and confusion, he raised his hand to his face where the blow had landed but then remembered that hand had been cut off. One young man – a boy in his teens – rushed to the staircase when he heard Qatrina's voice from up there. He grabbed her by the hair and threw her down the steps all the way from the top. 'Dirty prostitute. Innovator. Living without marriage with an infidel.'

More men came down and reported what they had seen in the six rooms of the house. 'You have both been sentenced to death.' Qatrina and the children were shrieking. 'Children – leave now and if you ever come back we'll burn you alive.' The very air seemed crazed. 'There has been a mistake,' Marcus said, 'we are married.' They pulled Marcus and Qatrina up the steps, Marcus hearing his own cries now also, his arm beginning to bleed at the stump, his body hurting in various other places. 'Your marriage ceremony was performed by a woman so it doesn't count.' They hit him every time he touched Qatrina or tried to block a blow intended for her, because, in their eyes, she was a stranger to him. Outside there was a fleet of pickups with mounted machine guns in their beds, and they hauled them into two separate ones. He heard gunfire from the house: who were they killing in there? He lost consciousness in the back of the pickup and when he regained his senses it was the middle of the night, he was in the orchard, at first not sure what had happened. Not remembering any firm details. He must have escaped, must have walked off the truck, but why hadn't they come after him?

In the darkness he walked to Usha and knocked on the door of the first house. They wouldn't open, just telling him from the other side to go away, but at dawn when they had to emerge from the house to go to the mosque – or be killed – they told him she had been stoned to death yesterday afternoon.

Upon returning from the Pakistani exile, Marcus had revealed to everyone what lay behind the djinn that were said to haunt the area around the lake. David had told Marcus everything Zameen had seen on the night she was picked up by the Soviet soldiers. Two of the cleric's wives were buried there. The myth of the djinn was too deeply ingrained in Usha's psyche so people remained afraid when approaching that part of the lake; nevertheless, when the cleric made his way back to Usha from Pakistan, he was told that he was no longer welcome.

He left, staying away for years, but – Marcus learned now, these hours after Qatrina's death – he had come back to Usha recently, and in order to take revenge, in order to ingratiate himself with the Taliban, he revealed the details of Marcus and Qatrina's life to them. Saying they had entered churches on their visits to Europe. That their daughter had been a fallen woman in Peshawar. That under the pretext of obtaining a sample, the two doctors had once tricked him into urinating into a vessel on which was affixed a label bearing his full name, which included the sacred and beautiful word 'Muhammad'.

He issued an amulet to the Taliban to guarantee their safety when they invaded the house.

Months would go by before Marcus learned the full facts of the raid at his house, how a ghost said to be that of Zameen had appeared in the house to put the men to flight, how the Buddha had bled gold. He learned that they didn't actually kill her through the stoning, had dragged her off in a heap from the field in front of the mosque. Letting everyone think she was dead. They had given themselves the spectacle they wanted but had actually become afraid of the reappearance of Zameen's ghost. She was taken and thrown into a cell at the back of a building, some hidden pocket in a mud-and-brick garment.

That was where she died several days after the stoning. A man at the mosque was sent to see her, to ask if she would beg Allah's forgiveness for a lifetime of sin. She wouldn't respond to him. But as she sat there she some-times raised her burka and pursed her swollen lips and spat out something white into a corner. Maggots had developed in her nasal cavity and were dropping into her mouth.

SHE PICKS UP A BOOK from the table and begins to look through it. It is twenty minutes to midnight. She is sitting on a torn pink divan with David lying half-asleep beside her. She stops at an illustration of a youth tied to the back of a wild-seeming horse, stretched out naked along the beast's spine. The horse he is fastened to is racing through a night forest, the hooves plunged into thick foliage. A moment from the verse of Byron. Its dark eye glaring, the horse has its teeth bared in fury or terror at the six black wolves chasing it. There is very little light. She begins to read the lines printed on the page opposite the image. The helpless boy is Mazeppa, a Polish noble who had become involved with another man's wife, and it was his punishment to have been tied to the back of the wild horse and set loose.

The paths of minor planets. More and more these days Lara's interest is caught by personalities and events on the edges of wars, by lives that have yet to arrive at one of history's conflicts, or those that have moved away from the conflagration – the details of lives being lived with a major battle occurring just over the horizon, or on the mountain above them.

The horse had been captured in the Ukraine and it returned there, carrying the boy half-dead from hunger and thirst, from exposure and fatigue. A warlord named

Mazeppa did exist in reality, someone who as an adult distinguished himself in several expeditions against the Tartars, his bravery causing the Tsar to make him the prince of the Ukraine.

She returns the book to the table. She lowers her own face to his to awaken him or to sink into sleep beside him. Whichever comes first.

DO MOTHS DROWN THEMSELVES in still bodies of water on clear nights? It must happen occasionally. Their mistaking the membrane-thin image floating on a calm surface for the moon itself, the two as identical as a pair of coins from the same mint.

In the room on the highest level of the house, Marcus is thinking, perhaps dreaming, about a night desert he had traversed in search of Qatrina one year, a journey that brought him to a town where she was supposed to be.

Only twenty-nine years in the entire human history had been without warfare, and now here he was too, travelling between episodes of a rapacious civil war. Once there was tracer fire from a night battle in the distance: the swaying lines of brilliant white points that were the glowing 'fire shells' – they had been interspersed with the lead bullets to let the gunmen know where the shots were going.

There was a flat clay bowl before him at chest level during the journey across the desert, the disc of the moon caught in the small quantity of water. He had been advised never to lose the reflection and by the end of the night he would reach the next small town in the desert. He stood still and kept his eyes on the bowl in his raised hands – taking a step when the moon was about to slip out, never allowing it to. He feared he would trip on a rock or an irregularity in the terrain as he moved forwards or sideways without seeing, that he would splash the water onto the ground. His slow overall progress matched the moon's pace across the sky.

Now and then, he thought he would go insane because he could not find the reflection – it had vanished completely from his hands – and he shouted desolately, breaking into short haphazard runs in the pale darkness because he failed to locate the place where the bright likeness had left the bowl. There could not be even a few moments' lack of concentration.

In case of a fall he would puncture a blood vessel, he reassured himself, and collect the dark liquid from within himself to rebuild the strange compass. He set the bowl on the ground and detached several thorns from a cactus for use in such an emergency, securing the large needles on the fabric of his shirt. *Sar-e rahyat bashinum ta biyai. Tora mehman konom har chand bekhahi . . .* He sang out loudly against the darkness. *Until you come I will sit on your path. I will make you my guest whatever the cost . . .*

The song like brocade in his skull.

He saw the first houses on the horizon just as the sun was beginning to rise, his rigidly positioned arms tired from lack of circulation and filled with pain as though he had been carrying not a handful of water but something heavier, as though a long summer had passed since he picked up the bowl at the beginning of the night, a summer that had transformed a weightless flower into a large fruit.

He placed the water carefully on a ledge of rock and continued unassisted towards the half-ruined town, crossing a damaged bridge over a river that had small ferns growing along its bank like a trimming of lace at the edge of a garment. He had pulled out the cactus needles from his shirt and placed them one by one beside the bowl of water. Perhaps the next person was also undertaking his journey because of love and would appreciate the vein-opening thorns should the need arise. All those who love know exactly the limit they are prepared to go to. They know exactly what is required.

She wasn't there and he had to continue onwards to another town. He was waiting at the bus stop in the rocket-scarred central street when he found himself walking back to the bowl he had left behind as a gift. Under the morning sky the water was milky blue as though the hard pill of the moon had dissolved at last, its pigment dispersed. He drank the two sips of water, lowering them into his body. He managed to get back just in time to climb onto the roof of the bus, the metal body punctured by bullets. A man in search of a woman.

7

The Silent Flutes

WITH A SWIVEL, James Palantine leaves the surface and enters the body of the lake, arms opening a diagonal path for him towards the depth. The water heals itself above him.

Within the lake's bowl, he imagines himself in a flooded amphitheatre. His gaze is calmer in this subdued light, after the sun's play on the constantly moving ripples of the surface. The word is 'scintillation'; he remembers David telling him this when he was a child, his father's gem-merchant friend. A word used by jewellers for the light that leaps restlessly from facet to facet on a precious stone.

He is not alone as he travels through the layers of water. His two companions and he are converging towards a point on the sloping side of the bed. In Usha it is said that a crate of bottled water might lie snagged on something at the bottom of this lake.

And here, swimming into the depths, James and his friends have found it.

They could be gem miners themselves, he thinks, as they work away the mud and rotted matter. A funnel of yolk-coloured light shining down from each of the three foreheads. They can run a mile in four minutes, a normal soldier needing about seven, and for the time being they aren't having to fight the water for every second they are in it – the buoyancy that is intent on expelling them. Great forces are present here, waiting to reveal themselves if provoked, in this seemingly contented stillness. When he joined the Special Forces, military psychologists had subjected him to a regime of techniques in case he was ever captured by enemy states. Sleep deprivation, exposure to extreme temperatures, isolation, religious and sexual humiliation, and the procedure of simulated drowning known as waterboarding. Following the 2001 attacks, the CIA, lacking in-house interrogators for the captured terrorists, had hired a group of outside contractors; the military psychologists who had trained James but who were now retired were part of that group.

Nothing is being done to captured terrorists that wasn't done to the interrogators themselves. Nothing the body can't recover from.

The crate is the size of a telephone booth three-quarters sunk into the lake bed. The small amount of air in each of the hundreds of bottles will be enough to lift the entire bundle to the surface once they have managed to loosen some of the lake's grip. The desire of air to meet air will do the rest. But it's too firmly embedded and one by one they surge up to the surface to replenish their lungs, inhaling noisily when they emerge into the air. Bubbles like loops of chains around their necks. From a minaret somewhere in the distance comes the call to worship, the muezzin summoning the faithful to the mosque five times every day. Allah is an insecure deity, he can't help but remark to himself as he gets ready to go back down. Dead leaves from the surface sticking to his face and shoulders like a poultice.

The low bass of the depth is still in his ears. The hum from inside a grave. Before returning to the depths he looks around carefully. Remembering something his father had once quoted. *We in this country*, reads the speech that President Kennedy did not live to deliver in Dallas in November 1963, *are – by destiny rather than by choice – the watchmen on the walls of world freedom.*

'IS IT TRUE THAT YOU AMERICANS shot dead one of your presidents because he was a Muslim?'

Together it has taken David and Casa five hours to stitch the canoe.

'A Muslim?'

'Yes. Ibraheem Lankan.'

'His name was Abraham Lincoln.'

'He wasn't a Muslim?'

'Who told you he was?'

He just shakes his head and looks away.

The edges of the lake are green with the high grass of March, the air above the jade and gold water alive with insects. 'I'll take you out to the other side of the lake when the canoe is built,' David had told Marcus. The boat the family had once owned has been eaten away by insects. It lies under the jacaranda tree, covered by its weightless blossom. The wood almost hollow, brittle as cinnamon sticks or dried-up orange peel. Asking David to remain near by, Marcus has attempted to swim in the lake but the missing hand, he says, makes him feel like a bird trying to get airborne with one of its wings clipped. So he remains in the shallows, the beard running in milky streaks over his chest.

A trickle of blood flows out from the base of David's

thumb and slides onto Casa's wrist. Casa had become distracted and let the blade slip, sending it into David's flesh, the small sound of pain alerting him to the wound.

On the path beside the lake and then along the high wall of the house that is covered with a vine like a child's directionless scrawl – a young woman has arrived on foot from Usha, Casa's eyes following her before she disappears towards the front door.

David looks up from the cut in his skin and follows his gaze, catching the last of the bright veil. A bowl of turquoise liquid flung into the air.

The distraction, the fascination, is short-lived however – the young man has averted his eyes. David read somewhere that if a Muslim doesn't look at a beautiful woman here on earth, Allah will allow him to possess her in Paradise.

'What was that?'

But he seems abashed, having been caught displaying emotion. 'Nothing,' he says somewhat icily, his eyebrows gathered.

'Shall we go and see who she is?'

'Who?'

To not know anything about women is a sign of decency in these lands. Muslim scholars to this day debate the permissibility of a second 'deliberate' glance as opposed to the first 'inadvertent' one.

David resists the temptation to say more.

The boy is serious and brisk, with his own sense of the maladroit, but untested virtue is no virtue at all, and it seems clear to David that his ideas have never been put to the test.

Almost as tall as a harp, the girl leans against the painted wall.

Marcus is preparing tea, and Lara sits at the kitchen table looking at Dunia, the twenty-two-year-old daughter of the doctor in Usha, the young teacher who is in charge of the small school. Thirteen days ago one of her pupils had tied the string of beads around Lara's neck while she was waiting for Marcus at the doctor's house.

'Today is the anniversary of a saint, so there's no school. I thought I'd come see you before you went back to Russia.'

Lara touches the beads, the token of a child's affection. Something is there in children and the young that makes them trust others. The horrors of life haven't yet perfected their aim. At times this seems to hold true even here in Afghanistan, in this land torn as though by God's own hatred. The young everywhere, she suspects, would prefer to live in houses that consist only of doors. And Lara had detected it in Marcus also, in the way he welcomed her into his house, though he has seen the worst that life can offer. With him it's not due to age, it's his character.

Dunia takes the cup from Marcus with a smile. There is a dish containing dry white mulberries. Four years earlier when the doctor had arrived from Kabul to take over the practice here, the girl's trimmed hair could have caused a scandal, but the situation was contained with the lie that she had had typhoid recently, that the hair had fallen out but was now in the process of growing back.

'Before I was born,' she tells Lara, 'an aunt of mine used to work at the perfume factory out there. My father says the money she brought home as wages used to be fragrant.'

'Has your father returned from his trip to Kabul?' Marcus asks.

'No. The day after tomorrow.'

'He took your brother with him?'

Lara knows about the brother, the young man who stole objects from the house to feed his addiction to heroin, trying to take off his sister's bangles while she slept.

The girl nods. 'They say a new clinic has opened there. He could hardly walk when they left. I wished he would stand up straight, as correctly as possible, because I didn't want Satan to make fun of Allah's creations.'

'I hope he'll make a full recovery.' Marcus places his hand on her head, an Asian elder person's gesture of love towards someone young.

Casa enters at this point and greets them all courteously. Lara notices how Dunia's self seems to withdraw, vacating the room and disappearing into her body. Her face slightly lowered. Women in this country are still anxious even though the Taliban are gone.

He says he has arrived to ask for a pair of scissors. 'Something strong enough to snip this.' He indicates the small piece of birch bark that he has brought with him like a letter.

'I thought you were managing perfectly well with the blades and things you already have out there,' Marcus says, 'but let's see if I can find something.' He produces an old pair of scissors whose cutting edges are uneven because Qatrina used it to clip the nibs of pens for calligraphy.

When Dunia asks Lara – not him – about the bark, in a tentative lowered voice, he moves forward and places it before Lara, the gold-like side upwards. 'I am building a boat.'

'Birch bark.' There is something experimental about the girl's smile. 'They found rolled-up pieces of it here in this region, stored in clay jars. The oldest known Buddhist texts were written on them.' She has been looking at Casa but now – suddenly remembering herself – turns her face to Lara and Marcus.

'The discourses of the Buddha,' Marcus nods. 'Among them the Rhinoceros Horn Sutra. The clay jars preserved them otherwise they would have rotted away over the two thousand years.'

'I didn't know they were that old,' says Dunia.

'Yes. Around the time of Christ. A long time before Muhammad.'

The boy takes the scissors from his hand and turns towards the door.

The roots of several trees have grown around a television set. The Englishman at some point must have tried to unearth it but then abandoned the effort, unable to unclasp the woody fingers that can still be seen gripping the half-buried machine. Casa goes past this small ditch in the orchard. Casa and others would sometimes watch Hollywood action movies at the training camps, searching for ideas and inspiration. The burning exploding American cities were their dreams made real on the screen, though later when he was alone the unearthly beauty of some of the actresses and actors would fill him with a disturbing and shameful pain.

The thought comes to him that tonight at Nabi Khan's farm he would have known intimacy with a woman for the first time.

'You said you have made one of these canoes before?' he asks David, returning with the scissors and resuming work.

'I built one with my brother when I was young. And later also with James, the son of a friend, when he was a boy. Do you have a brother, Casa?'

'I have no family.'

'The war with the Soviets?'

'Probably.'

'I am sorry.'

'It wasn't your fault . . . Now I must go and say my prayers . . .' It's still early for worship but he needs to be alone. Who is she? Gul Rasool has sent her to the house to spy on him, he is sure, the Americans from yesterday having told Rasool of their encounter.

Tan butterflies rise up briefly from the muddy edge to allow him to pass and then come down again to settle in slightly different places, as though the letters of a word had been rearranged to spell a new word.

Behind him the radio is on at the lake. A jail being expanded has been bombed by the Taliban and al-Qaeda forces in the neighbouring province. And the driver of a tanker supplying fuel to the NATO forces has been found butchered. The Americans have asked the Pakistani government to control the spread of what they call militant Islam within its borders – as though you can treat the government of a country as a friend but its people as an enemy.

As though, along with mere bodies, you can bomb ideas out of existence too. They have sent a few arrows towards the sky and think they have killed Allah.

As he passes the mulberry tree with its tiers of strong leaves there is a muffled noise from the ground, from the patch of grass where his foot has just landed. He freezes, then slowly shifts his weight onto the other leg, beginning to say in his head the verse of the Koran the believers must recite at the moment of death. Perhaps he felt it instead of hearing it, he is not sure. It is as though two adjacent rooms in Marcus's house have had their common wall removed, the combining of two senses.

He takes a shovel from the glasshouse and begins to dig down. The implement is made of the beaten scrap metal of Soviet planes – faint Cyrillic script is visible at the back. He stops when the plastic sheet comes into view and uses his hands to brush away the earth. It's a thin flat rectangle held in place by fibrous roots. Making a small tear in the plastic accidentally, he rips it all off in frustration. A young woman's face is looking up at him from the pit, the glass in the frame shattered in two places by his weight.

He brings the image out – blowing away two coffin cutters, as woodlice are sometimes referred to in Afghanistan – and overcome with revulsion drops it back into the pit. Allah forbids photography. The only exception to this a Muslim must reluctantly make in today's world is the photo needed for a passport: to go on the pilgrimage in Mecca, or to cross borders for the purposes of jihad. He drops a handful of soil onto her and then turns around, having heard Marcus approach.

'What did you find?'

He quickly pulls the image from the hole, letting the dry soil slide down the glass, and, smiling, stands up. He carries it towards Marcus who tells him the photograph is of his daughter.

It's like a large stone thrown at his breast when he looks up and sees that the girl Dunia is standing at a high window. If she has been there for a few minutes she must have seen him discover and then begin to rebury the photograph.

She is looking directly at him. Their eyes meet briefly and then she turns away.

THE RHINOCEROS HORN SUTRA advocates the merit of asceticism for pursuing enlightenment, as opposed to being a householder or living in a community of monks and nuns. Almost all the verses end with the admonition for seekers to wander alone, like a rhinoceros.

The perils of communal life. The benefits of solitude.

Dunia sits in an armchair in a half-revealed interior. They have persuaded her – she has let them think they have persuaded her – that she should spend the entire day here, stay for lunch and for the evening meal.

She has just said her prayers. When she turned around after finishing, she saw Casa sitting just outside the room. He pointed towards the prayer mat to indicate that he was waiting for it to be free so he could offer his own prayers. Walking away wordlessly when she handed it to him. Perhaps not hearing the apology she murmured for having delayed him.

She closes her eyes against the daylight.

Tomorrow is Friday so there is no school – but in fact classes won't be held the day after either. As there have been none today. The cleric at the mosque has publicly accused her of being dissolute, and the school has been forcibly shut down. It is said that the night the *shabnama* appeared, a man was seen knocking on the window of her room. She doesn't know who he was, but it's the chance the cleric had long been praying for, to uproot the school. He had started a rumour about her which she had disregarded but a group of dog-headed thugs from the mosque had arrived at the school the day before yesterday to tell her they will not tolerate its continuing presence in Usha.

Last month the cleric – he is the son of the old cleric, the one banished from Usha for having killed two of his wives – had expressed the wish to marry her, take her as his third wife, but both her father and she had turned him down. Perhaps this is his revenge.

This cleric's mother was the first woman his father killed – accidentally during a beating because she would not consent to him taking another wife. But after secretly burying her near the lake and spreading the story about the djinn, he realised he had got away with it: so the next murder was deliberate.

He could have just divorced that woman. It's not as though Allah in his inscrutable wisdom has made it difficult for a man to divorce his wife: he just says the words 'I divorce thee' three times and all connections are severed. But the new wife the cleric had wanted to replace her with was her younger sister: her family would not have given him her hand in marriage had he thrown out the older woman. By killing her and saying she had run away from him, he actually placed them under obligation, to supply the substitute.

Dunia defied the people at the mosque yesterday and held classes as usual, but at dawn today she found a bowl placed in the centre of the courtyard of her house.

Someone had broken in during the night. She approached it and saw that it was filled with water and held a single bullet. Her own face reflected on the surface was a warning – a shot in the head.

The Americans want a school here, and therefore so does Gul Rasool, and the cleric and his cohorts have had to put up with it so far – both boys and girls are taught at the school and the cleric often tells the people at the mosque that 'three million bastards are born in Britain every year because of mixed education' – but now they have invented or been handed this excuse. To paint her as shameless and to have the doors of the school locked until a replacement can be found for her. A small victory for the time being.

At the very least they would hold her down and mutilate her face, cut the shame permanently into her features.

She has always tried to be careful, aware that when a woman ventures out of the house she must, upon returning, account for every single step she has taken since leaving the front door.

She cancelled classes today – the other two teachers, both nineteen-year-old girls, had been kept at home by their parents due to warnings from the mosque. Yesterday she went to the homes of her pupils to reassure the parents but a number of them abused her and one even pushed her out of the house. She spent this morning looking up at every flicker in her field of vision. Turned around at every noise. Thinking it might be someone come to punish her, and punish her severely, for having an illicit lover. The thought of Marcus had occurred to her then: she must go to him and stay there – a fugitive from injustice. Others could make up lies about her activities to slander her, could break in tonight to plant evidence. Or they could pretend they have caught her in a compromising situation with a man. But her father, when he returns, would have no doubts when Marcus vouches for her movements at least from this point onwards.

Her father had tried to talk her out of becoming a schoolteacher, saying it was too dangerous. 'I know things have to change but why do you have to be the one to change them?' The legitimate fears of a parent. But she had won him over. 'The bullet that has hit us Muslims today left the gun centuries ago, when we let the clergy decide that knowledge and education were not important.'

With her eyes still closed she lowers her hand to the floor and touches its solidity. Women in Usha have always felt that they could sink into the earth any time. The strata beneath the surface are as insubstantial as the transparent layers of water that form the lake.

'I'LL ASK GUL RASOOL,' James Palantine says after being told by David about the three old men who had visited the house. About what they had said concerning the Soviet soldier and the leaf from the Cosmos Oak.

On the lake the demoiselle cranes are in full uproar at the dust raised by James's car. Those in the second year are beginning their courting displays and all day they have been leaping, airing their wings, flicking pebbles. But, adolescents, they won't get a chance to breed successfully till the third or fourth year.

Consulting his watch, David had walked out onto the path that runs along the lake's edge, to see James arriving punctually.

Christopher had said he would have named him after David had he been born after the two of them met.

When he went to see the family after Christopher's death in 2000, David had thought that recognition would just have to be left to James – not sure how the features of the boy he last saw many years ago would have altered with time. But he had recognised the young man immediately. He had come forward and embraced David, something he wasn't expecting.

And he'd done the same just now, getting out of the car and holding out his arms to initiate a hug.

'So you've seen the Night Letter?'

'It could be just bravado,' James nods. 'Or there may be an attack. But we are prepared.'

'I hear Gul Rasool has acquired a pig, a boar, which he intends to bury with Nabi Khan.'

'Gul Rasool is convinced the *shabnama* came from him.'

'I have a feeling it's him too.'

He remembers this young man as a sandy-haired boy, to whom one morning during a visit to the family he gave the twenty dollars he'd been asked to bring to school. Contribution towards some drive or fund. The child came home in the afternoon and said there'd been a mix-up and the money wasn't needed after all. 'So what did you do with the twenty dollars?' 'I told you it wasn't needed. I threw it in the trashcan.'

Now David asks, 'There's a bounty on Nabi Khan, isn't there?'

'A very small one – but he can lead us to more important fugitives. I would love to have the opportunity to talk to Nabi Khan. Find out what he's got under his fingernails.'

David tries to decipher the impression on the face. Christopher was always hard to read and so it seems is David himself, people always complaining that upon meeting him you feel it's you who is shaking hands with him, not he with you.

Global Strategies Group is a British mercenary company that guards the US embassy in Kabul, and other Western firms provide security all across the country. But

David has just been reading about Americans – one-time CIA contractors, or former Special Forces soldiers – who have set up private prisons in Afghanistan.

He is not sure what James's arrangement with Gul Rasool is. He was among the Special Forces teams – the élite stealth operators whose very existence is denied by the US government – who began hunting for al-Qaeda here in the wake of September 11.

'Are you still in the army?'

'I am still doing what I can for my country and the world.'

'Have you heard about these guys who are going around abducting and torturing Afghans to get information about al-Qaeda and Taliban soldiers? Keeping them in private prisons?'

James looks at him. 'We have to be careful not to use words like "torture" in these countries. It can be inflammatory. When these people hear that word they think of people being raped to death, of limbs being cut off, of six-inch nails being driven into people's heads – that is what the word means here normally. A cold room is *not* torture. Withholding painkillers from someone with an injury is *not* torture.'

Marcus, holding something in his one hand, has appeared on the path from the house and is walking towards their car, Casa a few feet behind him.

'We have a new kind of enemy, David. They are allowed to read the Koran at Guantanamo Bay, as their religious and human right. But have you read it? They don't need jihadi literature – they've got the Koran. Almost every other page is a call to arms, a call to slaughter us infidels.'

James watches Marcus drawing near, and now he indicates Casa with a nod: 'Is he the one my men had a run-in with yesterday?'

'Yes. That's Casa.'

'Sorry about that. But these are strange times. The Pakistanis just helped foil a plot to blow up ten airplanes above the Atlantic. Of course they used torture – they are more straightforward than us – but thousands of lives were saved.'

David himself had had Gul Rasool tortured. And what didn't he think of doing at one time to Nabi Khan, to make him reveal where Bihzad was.

'Who are your men?'

'Two started out in the FBI, one was a Marine, one was in the paramilitary unit of the CIA. The closest things to the robot soldiers the Pentagon has dreamed of for thirty years, from before I was born.'

Robot soldiers will not become hungry, they will not be afraid, they will not forget their orders, they will not care if the soldier next to them has been shot. But it's impossible to teach them to distinguish friend from foe, plainclothes combatant from bystander.

'Look what Casa found in the ground just now.' Marcus has arrived and handed David a photograph of Zameen. 'This is my daughter,' he says to James who gives the image a quick glance.

David introduces them and they shake hands.

'Won't you come in?' asks the Englishman.

'I am in a hurry, sir. Another time.'

Casa has taken a few steps away from them, and then he wanders away towards the lake, stopping to bend down to smell a wild flower. Muhammad used amber, musk and civet as perfume, and spent more money on fragrances than on food. Days later, people would know he had been in a room.

'What a noise the cranes are making!' says Marcus. 'There used to be many more, James, especially on the far shore. They have been passing through here for millions of years, but the war in Afghanistan – all that flying metal in the air, the bullets and planes – and then the war in Chechnya, has meant that they get lost easily, trying to change their paths.'

Marcus takes back the photograph and turns away towards the house, James assuring him he'll visit again soon.

'You're building a canoe,' James says as they walk towards the lake. 'Remember ours?'

'Of course. Do you know who she was, the girl in the photograph?'

'You were my uncle, David, and then suddenly you broke off all contact. I asked Dad why, and when I was old enough he told me, bit by bit over the years.'

'I am sorry.'

'It's okay.'

'So then you must also know that Gul Rasool, the man you are protecting, had tried to kill your father. He had sent Zameen to plant the device.'

The young man nods.

'Make sure he doesn't find out whose son you are.'

'Yes. But we need his help right now in fighting al-Qaeda and the Taliban. Dad would understand perfectly.

My own feelings are irrelevant when it comes to these things.' And he adds after a pause, 'I am not finished with him yet anyway. He too would have paid for everything by the time all this is over.'

'I am here if you need to ask anything.'

'Who is that guy, by the way?' James has been watching Casa, who is busy with the canoe a few yards ahead of them.

'He's a labourer. He's staying here for a while.'

James shakes his head. 'It's such a difficult situation. Why must the United States be the only one asked to uphold the highest standards? No one in the world is innocent but these Muslims say they are. They insist the seven hundred Jews who were taken prisoner after the Battle of the Trench were rightfully and legitimately massacred by their Muhammad. So until everyone admits that they are capable of cruelty – and not define their cruelty as just – there will be problems.'

When they draw near, Casa doesn't look up.

'Watch this, David. What's his name – Casa?' There hasn't been a shared language between the warring sides since the Civil War, so he switches to Pashto:

'Do you think, my dear friend Casa, that everyone on the planet will become a Muslim when the Islamic Messiah appears just before Judgement Day, and that those who refuse will be put to the sword?'

Casa straightens.

'I have never heard that before,' he replies. 'You've been misinformed about Islam.'

AT THE HERMITAGE in St Petersburg, Lara said, glue made from the swim bladders of sturgeons was brushed onto strips of tissue and these were pressed onto van Eyck's *Annunciation* when its wooden backing had had to be removed. When the glue dried and fastened itself onto the picture's surface – onto the angel with his almost neon peacock wings, and the anxious girl – the wood it had been painted on was chipped away carefully with chisels. Leaving nothing but that layer of paint stuck to the tissue paper. It could now be transferred to canvas, the tissue with the sturgeon glue then dissolved or peeled off from the front. And playfully Lara had suggested some days ago that that was what they should do to the walls in Marcus's house. Transfer these images onto canvas or paper, stick large sheets of tissue dipped in some gentle glue.

'Imagine the bricks and the stones have vanished and just the pictures stand – a paper lantern the size and shape of a house.'

Marcus smiles at the thought as he swabs the wall with a wet cloth, clearing away the mud from a painted balcony. There is a girl with a red-and-gold scarf tied over her eyes. Tonight she must have a tryst in the darkness so she's prac-tising going around the house blindfolded during the daylight hours.

On the gusts of wind he can hear James Palantine and David talking down there by the lake. Would there be more fighting between Gul Rasool and Nabi Khan soon? Caught between the two, the ordinary people of Usha have always done their best to survive. Each time there is an atrocity, they go to the house of the murdered party and say that indeed an unjust thing has been done; then they go to the house of the murderers and say that it was indeed an unfortunate thing to have happened.

The hatred between them extends into the past for over a hundred years, innumerable deaths and crimes on both sides since then, because the right to bloody vengeance is demanded by malehood, sanctified by tribal codes, and recognised by the Koran. *Believers, retaliation is decreed to you in bloodshed – a free man for a free man, a slave for a slave, a female for a female.*

The abhorrence, passed down through years and decades and generations, began in 1865 when a woman ancestor of Gul Rasool, named Malalai, had temporarily found herself as the head of the tribe at the age of sixteen, the men around her having perished in an epidemic. The only males that remained alive were either little boys here in Usha or grown men away on the pilgrimage to Arabia, the journey taking several months in those days.

Malalai's new position was regarded as sinister in Usha, people doubting if a woman could ever be counted on to take correct decisions, the cleric at the mosque wondering if Abraham's *wife* would have been prepared to cut their son's throat at Allah's bidding.

After the cleric refused to acknowledge her requests for

an audience, Malalai – hidden in a veil – went to the mosque. The man was incensed when reminded by her that the Queen of Sheba – a female ruler of a state! – was mentioned in the Koran. But he countered it by saying the Queen of Sheba was most probably not a human being, that she was half-djinn and had goat's legs.

His attitude was menacing and so she did not have the courage to remind him that Solomon was aware of the rumours about the Queen of Sheba, and that he had had crystal strewn across the floor when she arrived to meet him. She thought it was spilled water and she lifted the hem of her gown to reveal human feet.

Subtly, Malalai continued to govern her tribe from behind the walls of the large house. After all it was Khadija – the brilliant well-connected forty-year-old business-woman – who had discovered Muhammad, peace be upon him. Khadija had given the poorly educated twenty-five-year-old shepherd gainful employment for the first time in his life, and was the first to believe him when he claimed Gabriel had visited him to announce his prophethood.

One afternoon, when the sun was at its most powerful, a maid woke Malalai and informed her that a traveller was at the door, asking if he might be loaned a mat and the shade of a tree to say his prayers. Those on the road were exempt from worship – not for nothing were *Allah is ever disposed to mercy* the very last words of the Koran – so she was deeply impressed by the traveller's devotion. She had him shown into the men's quarters, and told the servants to point out to him the niche where the family Koran was kept so that, after he had humbled himself before Allah, he may recite a few passages for the recently deceased members of the household, for the safe return of the pilgrims from Mecca.

And later the sixteen-year-old, finding herself drawn to the stranger's voice, ended up sitting just outside the room where he read the holy words, the head of her sleeping baby son resting on her knee. After the recital, seeing as he was a traveller, she began to ask him questions from the other side of the door: Whether it was true that the earth was indeed round. Whether it was true that night did not fall simultaneously across the entire world.

With two servants holding up a curtain between them, she accompanied the traveller into the bamboo grove within the walled enclosure of the large house. The sun was setting and it was cooler now. He regaled her with stories of his travels: how in Baghdad he had come across a treatise on Prophet Muhammad's slippers, peace be upon him; how he had seen Mother Eve's hundred-foot-long grave in Jeddah; how Noah's father, Lam, was buried right here in a forty-eight-foot-long grave near Jalalabad – he'd appeared in a dream to Sultan Ghazni in the eleventh century, expressing regret that his resting place lay unhonoured and forgotten; following the instructions given to him in the dream, the Sultan arrived at a place within this valley and plunged his sword into the ground, from where a red fountain emerged, and there he built a shrine visited and revered to this day.

The bamboos stirred their leaves in the breeze around them, and that was where they were found by the returning pilgrims an hour or so later: she had been overpowered

by the man, and the stabbed servants were lying unconscious near by.

He fled. She told them it was rape but no one believed
her. The cleric at the mosque demanding she produce – as
Islamic law required of a violated woman – four witnesses
who must be male and must be Muslim to confirm that
she had not consented. This was Allah's commandment
and could not be questioned.

The servants fortunately did not die, and they corrob-
orated that they had been attacked – but one of them was
female and the other, though male, was a Turkoman unbeliever so his testimony was void. Women and infidels were
forever plotting against the Muslim manhood. In any case
Malalai and her lover could easily have harmed the servants as a ruse in case they were discovered.

With an axe she entered the bamboo grove one night
and – despite the fact that her body was bruised and her
collarbone was cracked from the beatings she had received
during the previous days – tried to fell the trees. She managed to flatten six before she was discovered and stopped.
She would not explain what she was doing, but whenever
she had the opportunity she went in there with axes and
saws – and once even a small knife – to hack at the bamboos. They knew she had lost her mind when she revealed
that she planned to construct flutes out of the bamboo
stems. The grove had witnessed her assault, *it* knew she
was innocent, and sooner or later there would be found a
flute that would speak with a human voice – announcing
the truth of that afternoon to the world around her.

The traveller, an investigation revealed shortly, was in

fact a man from within Usha, an ancestor of Nabi Khan, a feud beginning between the two houses that would continue through the years and decades.

Malalai herself, sitting surrounded by piles of discarded flutes – they had all remained silent about what they had seen – was eventually sent out of Afghanistan to a far shore of the family, to the Waziristan tribal belt, the area that would one day become part of Pakistan, and where Marcus's father was killed in the 1930s.

The centuries-old Buddhist paintings on the walls of many of Afghanistan's caves were covered in mud to prevent them from being damaged by Muslim invaders, white circles pockmarking the ceilings where soldiers and hunters had delighted in using the images for target practice. The memory of visiting the caves with Qatrina and Zameen was where Marcus got the idea of coating the walls of this house. In the city of Herat lives the only living Afghan artist to have been trained in the style of Bihzad, and he was summoned to the governor's building when the Taliban took Herat: he had laboured for seven years in the building, lovingly painting the intricate scenes recreating the classical glory of his city. He was made to watch stunned with grief as the walls were completely painted over.

The water in the bowl is a deep brown now, mud from a square foot of the wall transferred to it. He replaces it with clean water, looking out of a window when he hears the sound of an Apache helicopter in the sky. He returns to the wall and continues the work. Like Marcus's father, Malalai died in the 1930s. But she was eighty, unlike his father, and she had spent most of her life as little more than a servant, someone abused and worthy of contempt because of that event in her distant past.

A series of aerial assaults by the British was under way in Waziristan at that time, and she died because her masters dragged her from her bed one night, dressed her in men's clothing, and tied her to a post in an open field – to be able to say in the morning that the British were flying around in aeroplanes murdering innocents.

The masters had kidnapped a Sikh girl from India, and despite conferences with the British administrators, and their increasingly ominous threats, had failed to hand her back. At first plainly denying any knowledge of the matter, the kidnappers refused to attend the meetings altogether eventually, becoming belligerent and saying no government had the right to prevent them from abducting infidels – the girls and boys for pleasure, the men to be forcibly circumcised and converted to Islam – or from raiding into India and Afghanistan. All this was a way of life to them, an expression of freedom, as was the shooting of government officials and the patrolling soldiers.

Malalai, tied to the ground in crouching position, could not scream because her mouth had been gagged. There was no one to come to her aid in any case. She had soiled her clothing with terror, knowing that with the arrival of dawn the air raid would begin, if jackals and wolves and the djinn hadn't consumed her by then. She was little more than carrion.

The British had recently begun to use aerial bombardment in the Frontier to curtail some of the tribal wildness, and though there was much outrage at the League of Nations, and in the world press, the bombing was not indiscriminate. Leaflets, printed on white paper, had been dropped from an aircraft all across the tribe's land nine days earlier, warning that aerial proscription against the tribe would result in a week unless the Sikh girl and her kidnapper and a fine of a hundred rifles materialised. The leaflets – a sheaf of them had landed around Malalai when she was fetching water from the well – also defined a safe area, an enclave big enough to hold all the people of the tribe with their flocks, but not big enough to graze the flock or live comfortably in.

Twenty-four hours before the aerial raid, thousands more leaflets were dropped, these on red paper as a last warning. Once the allotted time passed, anyone caught outside the enclave was to be attacked from above with machine-gun fire and twenty-pound bombs, though no buildings were to be targeted unless seen to be used for hostile purposes. Animals sent out to graze were also killed, the corpses attracting wolves and vultures.

The tribes in the neighbouring areas had been warned not to shelter outlaws or join in the fight. But it was clear to the kidnappers that the other tribes had to be persuaded to do just that. That was when it was decided that Malalai should be taken to the forbidden zone during the night, her mouth silenced.

LARA OPENS THE BOOK and begins to read.

> *I think that all people – those living,*
> *those who have lived*
> *And those who are still to live – are alive now.*
> *I should like to take that subject to pieces,*
> *Like a soldier dismantling his rifle.*

It is the translation of a Russian poem she knows. The letter *a* in the word 'alive' is missing – taken away by the iron nail – but the eye supplies it from memory.

She is in the room at the top which is filled with smeared velvet-like light at this hour. The mosaic she had assembled of the two lovers is still here, beside her chair. She lowers her arm when she hears David enter the room, feeling suddenly that it contains no strength, and she puts the book face down on the fragments, imagining for a moment the pages becoming slightly coated with the coloured dust of the plaster.

'Lara?'

She can't look towards him.

'I just spoke to James Palantine. He'll make inquiries with Gul Rasool.'

And he adds: 'I can tell him to forget about the whole thing if you wish.' She looks up to see him pointing towards the phone in his pocket, the thing that never stops ringing when he is not in Jalalabad, echoing off the walls.

'No, I'd like to find out. You would want to know if it was Jonathan, wouldn't you?'

'Yes.'

She stands up and goes to sit on the bed, and he joins her.

'As I grew older my face began to resemble Jonathan's. At nineteen I looked like his photographs when he was nineteen. It was like they'd buried him in the mirror. If they buried him at all, that is.'

This intimacy between them. The moments when any third person becomes a stranger and to talk seems pointless. But they are talking anyway, their voices low, as they do during the nights, he asking her if he can come see her in Russia, whether she would visit him in the United States. There is still a tentativeness on her side, but these are in any case the initial days. He'll wait.

Her head is on his upper arm, and she turns sideways to see his face as he talks.

He has told her how last year he remembered something from his childhood for the first time. He and Jonathan were watching a programme about African wildlife on TV. Their mother was in the room also. The elephants had to set off in search of water because there was a great drought and they risked death if they remained. But one of them had just had a calf that couldn't even stand up properly, let alone walk. The mother kept trying to get the infant onto its feet, pulling it up with the hook of her trunk, propping it against her leg. The rest of the herd was already a mile away in the distance, and Jonathan and he were both shouting at the screen, for the dumb animal to abandon the calf and race towards the others. Their mother became a little involved too, looking over her spectacles at the screen, telling them not to be heartless. 'But she's going to die if she doesn't go!' they told her. She didn't have an alternative but she didn't want the calf abandoned. It took some time but, prodding and lifting, the elephant did manage to get the calf to walk and they set off together in the direction the rest of the herd had gone. And to think that he and Jonathan – a stunned and shamed silence descending on them now – were going to let the calf die in the burning desert. A few minutes later he found Jonathan, who was about thirteen, weeping in the bedroom.

A small restless bird alights on the window sill – its tail and wings and head each shifting into three different positions in little more than an instant – then flies away.

At dawn she had wished him to see her in her one set of coloured garments. She entered the tunic and then her hands disappeared under it to tie the drawstring of her trousers at the navel. She looked down to distribute the pleats evenly around the two legs. She wore the clothes for a few minutes and then carefully put them away. It was as though she had draped herself with some images from the walls in this house. Her face altering against all the hues on the tunic. Her mouth a rich aroused ruby.

Now, beside him, she wears nothing but the thin necklace of beads. Over the previous days the most fleeting contact with her has come as a sinuous discovery. Zameen had taught him about the eroticisation of jewels and ornaments here in the East. Gold. Ivory. Emerald. Even the roadside aluminium and glass. All this against the glory of a woman's bare skin. It is there on the paintings on the wall in this room, as well as in countless statues of temple dancers and goddesses with waist chains and bangles, with jewelled pendants resting between breasts. Brides are covered in jewellery and there is a sexual connection with the night to come. The poetry of these lands is aware of this. *Night arrives and pulls off flowers from the jasmine grove. As when a groom helps his bride take off her ornaments in the bed chamber.*

'In which room did Zameen's ghost appear the day the Taliban came?'

'The one about sight.'

The blind and the seeing are not equal reads the inscription above that entrance, a quote from the Koran in elegant long-tailed lettering.

A blue rectangle of the ceiling stands revealed wherever a book is missing above her. They look like openings onto the afternoon sky. It was to prevent a haunting that in certain parts of Russia a dead body was carried to the church through an open window, or even through a specially cut hole in the roof. The idea was to confuse the dead person's spirit, making it more difficult for the ghost to find its way back home.

Earlier David had received a call to say that the Jalalabad police have found the head of Bihzad at last, flung into a drainage ditch in the bombing. The young man who thought he was on his way to Paradise. To commemorate the baptism of Christ in the River Jordan, the Tsar – accompanied by the entire court and the leading church-men – would emerge from the Hermitage on 6 January every year, descend the steps of the Jordan Staircase, and walk out onto the frozen Neva. A hole would have been cut through the ice, and Tsar and Metropolitan would bless the water. Children were then baptised in the icy river. What amazed the visitors from other lands was the reaction of the parents if ever a child slipped from the numbed hands of the holy men, never to be seen again. They refused to grieve because the child had gone to Heaven.

Stepan knew someone who had lost a distant relative in that manner.

Stepan.

It's almost as though David is listening to her thoughts. 'How soon after meeting Stepan did you know you loved him?'

She slowly turns her face away from him.

'I don't think I married him out of love.' Very quietly. Looking at the wall where a horse and rider have been freed by Marcus from their mud layers beside the bed. The entire horseman except the left hand has been made visible, as though Marcus had forgotten that a person's left arm continues beyond that wrist.

'Stepan pursued me. A small part of me was flattered, but I said no to him many times. I agreed eventually because . . .' Her eyes are still determinedly refusing his. 'How wrong it seems when I say it out loud . . . A secret seen in the full light of day.'

'You don't have to tell me.'

'Would you mind not looking at me right now?'

'Sure.'

'You can't know how bad things were for me, because of my mother's past, and because of Benedikt's defection. I married Stepan, the handsome and well-connected army officer, because I thought he could bring me security. I thought my ill and ageing mother would no longer be harassed by the state because she would soon be his moth-er-in-law. That he would help me get to the truth about Benedikt. Oh, I am so sorry . . .'

An apology to the universe, to her better self, to Stepan.

She is sitting up now, forehead placed on the raised knees. She shakes her head, continues to shake it until she is able to speak again, construct her ever-precise sentences – the singsong voice, the soft *t* and the slightly rolled *r*.

'It was a bad time. I just couldn't see my way through clearly. On the other hand, a quarter of the official world were his father's friends. They had known him from the time when he was a baby. They attended parties at the for-mer palaces of the aristocracy. Had stories of borrowing porcelain and paintings from the collections of the tsars for a function at home.'

'Why did you keep saying no at the beginning?'

'I was falling in love with someone else at the time. But

in the end I controlled myself and buried my feelings –
deeper than the place from where they dig out your gems
for you . . . With him, unlike with Stepan, I had known in
a minute – in a minute – that he was someone I wanted to
spend the rest of my life with. For a long time after rejecting him for Stepan my breast felt like there was a deep
wound inside it. But through it all I did my best to pretend
to be in love with Stepan . . . Oh I am so sorry . . .'

'I can understand your reasons.'

'People marry every day, I said to myself. It should happen once or twice every century if the purpose of marriage
was to find your soul's mate. I kept telling myself my personal happiness was not important – that I should do this
to help my mother, to find my missing brother.'

From the table beside the bed she picks up the little
origami shape she had folded some days ago, before
David's arrival. She turns it in her hands, something material to concentrate on.

'As the years passed I came to love Stepan more than my
life. You ask why I kept saying no. It was partly because I
thought it would be bad for him to be associated with me,
with us. I thought it would harm him professionally.'

'So you weren't completely selfish.'

Folding and refolding the paper for over a minute, she
had fashioned the origami piece – a shape and a procedure
that had lain unremarked-upon in her mind since her
Leningrad schooldays.

'And did things get better because of his connections?'

'Suddenly everything was easy. It was shocking. It
would make me so angry inside. I am here because of his

friends in the army, because he and they began inquiries about Benedikt. But, no, to me what I did remains unforgivable. Other people managed – why couldn't I?'

'Your country made you feel guilty for not being able to fly. They put so much unreasonable pressure on you, so many unreasonable demands. Of course you couldn't cope and looked for a way out.'

'I wonder how much of it is to do with my country. Maybe it's who I am.'

'There's no way of knowing such things.'

'I knew beforehand he wanted to be a father. I kept from him my suspicions that it might be difficult for me to conceive. There were rumours that the state had had me poisoned – I had suddenly fallen ill some years earlier, during the time I was being loud in trying to find information about Benedikt. Now I was too terrified to go to the doctors, in case they confirmed my fears. I decided I would just hope for the best. In the end I did tell him, two weeks before the wedding. He said he didn't care about anything as long as I was his wife. But he did accuse me of deception in later years.'

She places the origami on the table. Four small hoods, hinged together, to be worn on the tips of the fingers. It's a way for children to tell fortunes, the possibilities hidden under four triangular flaps, one of which you are asked to choose. When she made it sitting beside the Buddha, she had turned over each of the flaps even though she knew nothing was written under any of them.

'We can never know how different we could have been,' David says, holding her close. 'This one life is all we have.'

The afternoon is continuing out there. A faint melody from a stringed instrument drifts down from Marcus's room. In picturing what the instrument might look like she recalls the small watercolour of a Persian lutenist in the Hermitage. Marcus said he sometimes sees music as a companion, almost a physical presence.

Pointing to a portrait on the wall he said Ziryab of Andalusia had added the fifth string to the lute in the ninth century and pioneered the use of eagles' talons as plectra.

David's hipbone is like a warm stone against her thigh. A sensation she has not received since Stepan's death two Decembers ago. She had stepped away from everyone, a sleepwalker in a fog, the world ceasing to exist. On many levels she had lived Stepan's life for so long – moving to a new city upon marrying him – and she was only slightly surprised that the withdrawal didn't prove more difficult now. She didn't announce her arrival back in St Petersburg to most of her friends and acquaintances, just letting the darkness increase as the months went by.

But there *was* a world out there. And she was jolted awake to it, to her responsibility to it, when her mother died surrounded by a dozen notebooks' worth of thoughts, all addressed to her. Lara could not be contacted because she hardly ever answered the telephone now or responded to the knock on the door, seldom opened a letter, not wishing to be told *You'll love again*. When her mother died in her sixth-floor flat the first problem for the neighbours was to get the body to the morgue. In the new Russia the men who drive the mortuary vans demand substantial bribes, don't come for days after being called, and sometimes don't come at all. There were stories that in the tower blocks of the very poor the despairing relatives or neighbours simply threw the corpse out of the high windows. There are always bodies in the Russian winter snow in these areas. This did not happen to Lara's mother but there was no loved one in attendance when she was buried, and when by chance Lara arrived for a visit at her mother's flat a fortnight later she found her notebooks scattered on the pavement. Only the first page in each was filled. The rest were blank. She hadn't turned over a new page, had written and drawn on the same one repeatedly so that the feelings and ideas were juxtaposed onto each other, indecipherable, the way a book of glass would be, the eye having access to its depth through the overlapping layers of contents.

As the weeks passed Lara re-established contact with the friends from her youth, reaching out tentatively, reminiscing about those early days when the most important thing for them was owning a perfect smile. 'They say the lips should rest on the line where the teeth meet the gums. And the whiteness of the teeth should match the whiteness of the eyes exactly.' How incredible it seems that until her teens she had ridden in a car only a handful of times. She remembers the thrill, the smell of petrol on a hot Leningrad day, her beloved city with its islands and palaces and its leap-and-plunge arches, its justly loved white nights. There was the garden where Casanova and Catherine had met and talked about sculpture, and there were the cinemas where the ticket seller would for a few roubles extra sell a boy the seat next to a pretty girl.

Her dear Russia. The first boy she kissed at fifteen, the beautiful Mitya, meeting him when his mother called her in out of the street and asked to be shown how to arrange salad on a dish in a pleasing manner: the woman was giving a party and thought Lara, being young, would know about such modern and stylish things. Just called her in out of the street! Pulling her out of the pattern her life had made in the city till then. The sudden rush of blood to the head when Benedikt showed Lara and her friends that a song being played on the radio could be taped, captured on a cassette; until then they had thought you could only record music from LPs, something that cost money. But this was free and it was an electrifying discovery. Back then when everything lay ahead. A life of possibilities and discoveries. Oh the wonder of looking for the first time into one of those mirrors that magnified your face!

As they grew older they discovered that the library copy of *Spartacus* was missing half its pages. They learned that in the past the word 'demos' – the root of 'democracy' – had to be excised from a book on Greek antiquities, and that according to some books certain Roman emperors had not been 'killed' but had 'died' – so as not to encourage among the Soviet populace the idea of the liquidation of unwanted leaders. And, yes, Tatyana Ulitskaya's father climbed into a bottle of vodka every night and began to swim circles in it, swallowing a layer of liquid with each lap so that he was found in the morning lying prone on dry glass. And, yes, while many of them couldn't imagine being able to exist away from Russia, some had dreamed of moving to the West, dreamed of ease, even riches – the dollar trees that would sprout from the palms of their hands once they got there, producing golden fruit they'd store in bank vaults.

But whatever any of them thought, one thing was always certain: even though they suffered, and had to struggle at times to bring meaning and even the most basic dignity into their existence, and even though in their search for justice and truthfulness they were beaten down and met with disappointment again and again – their lives were not available for use as an illustration. Theirs were not stories that could be read as an affirmation of another system.

IN THE ORCHARD Casa is in danger of being engulfed by flames. Mid-prayer, he has rearranged his blanket around him, flinging the loose end over the shoulder, so that one corner has draped itself on the lamp burning on the ground beside him. Just to the left of where he sits on the prayer mat. His eyes closed and head bowed, he has little idea of the change in the quantity of light in his vicinity. The light around a person in prayer is uniform in any case, Allah dispatching angels to hold a four-cornered canopy of rays above him for the duration.

Dunia reclines against the trunk of the tree, hands folded at the spine to cushion the roughness of the bark. Dusk. If she moves forward to pull the thin fabric off the scorching glass and metal she might despoil his worship, introducing a worldly element into his act of contemplation. Perhaps he is aware of the possible fire and deems it trivial. An eventuality he can control.

She'll keep watch over him. Only ten steps separate them, sufficient for her to lunge and slap away the beginning of any flame.

A girl surrounded by red flowering trees.

Her mother died in a Katyusha rocket attack carried out by the Soviets when she was still a child and she has learned that the weapon was named after a wartime Russian song,

316

Katyusha the girl who stood forlorn in an orchard full of apple and pear blossom, longing for the return of the soldier lover. *He will guard the land of dear homeland . . .* 'There is a crescendo in the third line of each stanza,' Lara said when she asked her about it, 'so it must have seemed fitting to name the rocket after it. Why do you ask?'

The mountains soar above the orchard. There are villages in the folds of some of those heights, amid the stone dust and ice glitter, and her father loves to say his prayers up there whenever he visits them. She imagines it's because he feels more aware of Allah up there. They are quite a large and obvious handprint of His.

Casa finishes and she watches him pull the blanket away from the lamp, a strand of smoke just beginning from it. On seeing her he brings the prayer mat to her. All his life is in his glances, making her understand why the first gesture by which a formerly living body is declared a corpse is the closing of the eyes.

'What's wrong?'

'Nothing.'

He is about to leave but stops. 'Then why do you appear so frightened?'

She hadn't suspected that her feelings might be readable.

'I thought you were going to get hurt.'

'The fire?'

She nods.

'But you don't even know me.'

She shakes her head, nods. 'All of a sudden I couldn't move. I didn't know what to do.' Has fleeing Usha exhausted her? If she were to encounter danger here, she suddenly fears she'll surrender.

Touching her eye she brings away a teardrop that has grains of kohl dissolved in it. She is as amazed as he seems to be when her hand advances towards his face and the dissolved kohl is rubbed onto his right cheek. A small daub. A dark bee-wing.

'What are you doing?' he asks in a hollow voice. The forehead is creased in evenly spaced lines that lose all uniformity in the centre like two opposing sets of waves crashing into each other.

'To keep off the bad eye.' Rendering a perfect thing a little less perfect, to stop the djinn from coveting it.

Looking overwhelmed, he parts his lips. She watches the face in anticipation, to see what he would say. It is like watching the tip of a pen make contact with paper: what would that dot become – a poem, a riddle, a letter?

'I . . . I wish I didn't feel alone all the time,' he says at last, very quietly.

'What have you done?'

For reasons she doesn't understand he brings his hands forwards and displays the palms. He thinks she can see something in his lifelines? But what he says next makes it clear that he is someone traumatised by the United States invasion:

'I hate America.'

There is a deliberation before each of his words, which seem carefully chosen as a result. She has the feeling that he is searching for the most stable and most direct bridge between his inner self and the world.

'Sometimes nothing makes sense and I become afraid,' he says.

'There's no need for you to feel alone.'

'There are so many questions.'

'Those questions are being asked by everyone. You have no need to feel alone.'

He lowers his head. 'We'll destroy America the way the Soviet Union was destroyed.'

'The Soviet Union was hated by its own people. The USA is loved by its people so it can't be destroyed.' She moves her fingers towards his lips.

'But how can we let someone obliterate Islam?'

'They can't. And for the same reason. Muslims love Islam. But Muslims hate fundamentalism. *That* can be destroyed.' She touches the corner of his mouth. 'What happened here? This small scar. What we have to make sure is that Muslims don't fall in love with the ways of the fundamentalists – then we'd be in trouble.'

He flinches now and steps away, bringing her out of her own trance too. Even the sound of her consciousness had been stilled. He wipes off the kohl, rubs at it as though it's sulphuric acid. 'Practices and habits of infidels, of star-worshippers.'

She'd rather leave – it's obvious that with him the source of prayer isn't delight, it's fear of Allah's retribution – but she pauses, clutching the folded mat to her breast, because of what he says next.

'And aren't you ashamed of going about the way you do?' There's something thorn-like in his voice now. 'A Muslim woman should keep her face covered.'

'Who told you that?' A shot of furious energy in the blood.

'What?' He clearly wasn't expecting this. It's as though he's heard a heartbeat in a rock.

'You heard me perfectly well.'

'It's in the Koran.'

There was near-revolt in Kandahar when King Daoud's daughters appeared unveiled in public in 1959, obliging the King to send a delegation of clerics and religious scholars – Qatrina's father among them – to debate the issue with the mullahs of the city, asking them to point out where exactly in the Holy Book it said that women must hide their faces.

While he waited for her to finish her prayer earlier today he had been sitting in the corridor, and later she noticed that one-third of a gazelle's neck had been scratched away from the painted wall. The illusion of sun on the creature's fur makes it appear as though clothed in gold needles, and she is sure she would have found bronze and yellow flakes under his fingernails if he hadn't performed his ablutions to say his prayers since then.

'I saw what you did to the wall in the house earlier. You think such things are orphans?'

'I don't know what you are talking about.'

'Who are you, what are you doing here?' She has encountered this kind of behaviour countless times before, from men with nothing but passion where knowledge should be. 'You think no one loves those pictures, and the practices and habits of this country?'

He has no answer.

Although remorseful, because exhibitions of anger displease Allah, she continues to hold his eye until at last he turns away and, collecting the lamp, disappears towards the lake, the suddenly abandoned moths flying off in various directions in search of the disappeared light.

He'll have to meet her again when it's time to say the last of the day's prayers in a few hours, regardless of what he thinks of her. They bow towards the same God.

Before dawn.

At noon.

When the sun is beginning to yellow.

With the first stars of twilight.

In darkness.

Five trysts at the prayer mat. But no, no, she must avoid further contact. What was it that made her touch him? If he now assaults her at some point, he'll say she had encouraged him. She has to think of her dear father's reputation. Though a doctor, he is in debt – the money needed for her brother's treatments over the recent years, and for the bribes that keep him out of prison after his various addiction-driven robberies. The repayments are long overdue, and her father is now open to covert gestures of disrespect from the creditors. The thrill and ecstasy of owning someone. In gatherings he has to listen to humiliating barbs clearly meant for him. Earlier last month at the teahouse one of the creditors had made a comment about how brazen today's girls were, emulating rich modern city women, going about bareheaded, even when the fathers were insolvent, beggars disguised as borrowers, unable to keep their word. The nonchalance accompanying the remark was feigned. Dunia had just walked past a few moments earlier with her scarf off her head – it was of a material that was so sheer the seller had called it 'woven breeze' and it was difficult to keep in place on her sleek hair, requiring constant vigilance. The men, including her father, had taken shocked but wordless note, and the creditor had made that comment a minute or so later. Her father had come home and hit her for the first time in her life.

She begins to walk back to the house, a wave of breeze in the pomegranate trees. Through contrivance she has had herself invited to spend the night here. When they come for her, as they surely will, they'll find her house empty tonight. The caretaker of the school – who was meant to be the nominal male presence and her guardian in the absence of her father – disappeared this morning. Bribed or threatened. 'It's not wise to have a fondness for tussling at your age,' one of the goons had told him when he came to her defence during their visit to the school. 'Old bones don't mend well after breaking.'

Darkness fills the orchard behind her, a chill in the air as there was at dawn. A bird had been singing on a branch in the courtyard and a thin plume of white vapour had emerged with the notes each time it parted its beak to sing.

THE WOMAN WAS FORTY THOUSAND FEET above him. Right at the very edge of the sky. As he talked to her, James Palantine could imagine her clearly. The constellation of Orion was directly over her head and points of light were attached to her fingertips. She was a weapons-systems officer, sitting under the bubble cockpit of an F15 jet. Her seat was equipped with ejection rockets and there was a loaded 9 mm pistol in the survival vest she wore.

Had it been daytime she would have been able to see the earth's curvature from that height. But there was no sun just now and, surrounded by sub-freezing temperature and the deepest of darknesses, she had in her sights the building where a group of men from the Taliban's Ministry for the Propagation of Virtue and the Prevention of Vice was spending the night.

When she wasn't flying above Afghanistan at the speed of sound on these ten-hour sorties, she was at the American base outside Kuwait City, completing course work for a master's degree in aerospace engineering, her professors FedExing her videotapes of the classes from California.

Under cover of darkness, James Palantine had been dropped with three other Special Forces soldiers onto the sawtooth ridges of Afghanistan and left to fend for himself. Living on packaged food or on lizards and insects. The war to punish and destroy the theocratic tyranny of the Taliban and al-Qaeda was under way around them as his team moved back and forth through the icy moonscape of the mountains, refilling their four-wheel-drive vehicles from the giant bladder of fuel that they stored in a cave, getting a fire going by shaving onto the wood a few bits from a block of C-4 explosive. The hardships were immaterial. Perfect mental clarity was needed for the service he was performing for his nation and for the world, and he did not lose focus for a single moment, sleeping on snow, on sleet or cold rock, with the sky above him full of warplanes from the British and American Army and Air Force: so many aircraft that there was a danger of them colliding with each other, of the lower ones being clipped by bombs dropped from a plane higher up.

Teams like his were the eyes and ears of this air assault. As sensitive as wild animals to their environment, noticing the smallest of changes in the surroundings, they prowled deep inside hostile territory, in the vicinity of airports, forts, and enemy troop concentrations. He would use an infra-red laser to 'paint' a target on the ground and, his voice crackling into the cockpit three, four or five miles above him, tell the crew of the warplane to send the bombs down onto it.

The building where the men from the Taliban's Ministry for the Propagation of Virtue and the Prevention of Vice had gathered was destroyed when the five-hundred-pound bomb landed on it. A black splash on the screen of the warplane above. Made of hard metal designed to fracture into hot shrapnel, the bomb would have vaporised anyone within a few yards of its detonation. Then James's team set off on horseback, the stirrups too small for their boots, telling the crew of the jet that they'd be contacted again soon from a nearby village that had come under attack from Chechen and Arab fighters: the Taliban in the village had surrendered to the Americans, and the al-Qaeda fighters were carrying out a massacre in revenge.

As dawn neared, exhausted from the bombing sortie, with the bomb racks empty, the pilot and the weapons-systems officer went back to Kuwait, informing James that they intended to put the plane on autopilot high above the mountain ranges of southern Pakistan and have their Thanksgiving meal, finding the chilled food by the finger-lights on their gloves.

Although the targets that night were legitimate, James knew that others hadn't been. It was James's team that – following the information brought to him from the warlord Gul Rasool – had brought down a bomb onto the house of Rasool's rival Nabi Khan, causing civilian deaths. Afterwards Rasool claimed he had not meant to deceive the Americans, that his own intelligence had been faulty.

And now here James Palantine is, in Usha, a guest and guard of Gul Rasool.

He awakens after the four hours of sleep. He lies still for a few minutes. Directly above his bed is a framed print of England's Prince Edward being attacked by a Muslim assassin in 1272. The time of the Crusades. Sultan Baibar has sent the man – a perfidious servant – into the chamber during the hours of darkness. The dagger is poisoned. The

Prince, awoken from his sleep, is attempting to turn the weapon on the assailant.

He looks along the length of his body, covered by the blanket. If he were in the ground this much soil would be displaced. This is how much earth it took to make him.

When he was younger he had loved listening to David. He remembers watching him as he climbed a frozen waterfall in Oregon during a severe winter, the ice sticking to the mountain side like molten wax down the side of a giant candle. Twice he accompanied David to Hawaii where the woman who became David's wife for some years had grown up on a sugar-cane farm. David gave him the shoulder patch from the uniform of a Montana Highway Patrol officer, the embroidery including the number 3-7-77, the digits that were once a Vigilante ultimatum for the banishing of malefactors, but are now used as an emblem of state-sanctioned law and order in Montana, appearing on the uniforms and car-door insignia of the officers.

Objects were sent or brought to James from around the whole globe in fact, with scrawled notes dropped in the packages. There was a nomad chief's poignard from here in Afghanistan, the postage stamps depicting the one-thousand-five-hundred-year-old Buddhas of Bamiyan. Yes, James knew about Afghanistan – Watson had just returned from there when he met Sherlock Holmes. And David brought him tales collected from Vietnam and Angola. Told him how Shah Jahan's treasury had included four thousand songbirds.

David's voice was like music being played to the

metronome inside the young boy – it had the unhurried rhythm of James's own thoughts.

Now he gets up and meets the others out in the night, going past a locked door behind which – he had discovered when he managed to open it stealthily – are stockpiled several tons of food donated by the World Food Program, meant for the poor of this region but appropriated by the warlord.

They sleep in shifts here. And so, while some are going off to bed, others, like him, woke up only minutes ago and are ready for the night.

The Afghans among them are discussing the latest ruling by the gathering of distinguished Muslim clergymen in the United Arab Emirates: yes, under Islamic law a man can divorce his wife through SMS text messaging.

James tries to maintain a neutral expression. To think that America has had to get involved this closely with people like these.

More or less every day someone asks him about emigrating to the United States. And, while he is willing to help in any way possible, a small part of him does sometimes fear that they – with their fasts and their prayers, and their desire for four wives and the segregation of the sexes, their fondness for crimes of passion and their abhorrence of the very word 'alcohol', not forgetting their belligerent self-pity – will not adjust to life in the First World. Wouldn't it be better for them and for the USA if they just stayed where they were? A group of terrorists – Muslims, and descendants of Muslims who moved to America from these parts – was arrested last month for attempting to set up jihadi training camps in the wilds of Oregon.

He doesn't wish to deny anyone a chance of a better life. He just wishes they were better informed about what they were getting into. There is every possibility that disappointment and rage await them at the end of the journey to the West. Earlier, he had seen them riveted by the DVD of a Hollywood thriller – every scene was full of sleek cars or shiny women or blasting guns – making him understand why the rest of the world thought Americans were crazy. Only minutes later, however, he wasn't too sure. When you learn that the rest of the world thinks this is what life in America is like, that this isn't just throwaway entertainment, isn't *understood* by sane Americans as fantasy or momentary diversion, you realise how crazy the rest of the world is.

Everyone everywhere – including the people who are living in the United States and the West – is allowed to hold any view he wishes about the United States and the West. That is as it should be. The owner of the convenience store near James's house keeps Islamic Radio on all day and has yet to learn more than a few words of English. James has tried to interest him and his family in listening to American stations but without success. Apart from what he sees of it on al-Jazeera, America does not concern him, it seems. When he bought the store he removed vacuum-packed bacon, tinned ham, alcohol, and anything that offended him and his family, even though the neighbourhood is ninety-five per cent white. He refuses to stock Jewish newspapers and has informed James with great pride that at home he watches only al-Jazeera or the Islam Channel. When James's fiancée asked the man's wife and daughters to accompany her to a music recital, they reacted as though she had suggested something obscene. None of that is a problem for James, but when your beliefs lead you to start planning the mass murder of Americans – of your fellow Americans – you have to be stopped. By all possible means.

Two years after talking to her while she sat in a supersonic jet and he crawled or huddled in Afghanistan's dusty landscape, he had met up with the weapons-systems officer – someone who grew up in one-bedroom apartments where she slept on foldout cots, the daughter of an itinerant salesman from Detroit. James proposed to her at the beginning of this year and they'll marry in September. He wants David to be there.

And no, the convenience-store owner's wife and daughters didn't know that she had taken part in the bombing of Afghanistan. But if they did, and if that is why they refused to socialise with her, then they should know she was helping to uproot terrorists, that efforts were made to keep the civilian casualties to a minimum.

And they are not going to learn any of that from things like the Islam Channel and the Arabic newspapers, which teach them nothing except how to invent grievances.

It's hard to appreciate the beauty of a place when you doubt its very validity.

The moon spills its light onto him, a clarity that seems to belong to the beginning of day, rather than the early part of night. Rules are being drawn up in America for space tourism and it is recommended that the tourist companies consult Homeland Security's no-fly list to make sure no terrorists ever get into space. 'So these Westerners intend to keep enraging us Muslims,' one of the Afghans had said in Pashto when he learned about this, 'if they think terrorism will exist in the future too.' Well, today they are angry at wrongs done to them two centuries ago. Who knows when their long memories and their addiction to brooding on ancient wounds are going to disappear?

James pretends to them that he has only minimal knowledge of their language, to let them think they can talk in it freely amongst themselves in his presence.

Within the vast walled compound of Gul Rasool's house is an overgrown lot containing beat-up old Russian cars. Volgas, Zhigulis, Moskviches. Dating from the time of the Soviets, when both Gul Rasool and Nabi Khan had proved adept at kidnapping and murdering Communists. Each to this day claims that the Soviet Union had invaded Afghanistan with the specific purpose of killing just him.

He goes down the corridor towards Gul Rasool's rooms, to ask him about the Soviet soldier who had had an oak leaf upon his person, and tomorrow he'll convey the answer to David. Visiting them at the house should give him another chance to examine that young man they've got living with them. If a person's gestures and comportment speak of the work he does, then this Casa is no labourer, as he is said to be.

A caged *chakor* partridge hangs in the corridor. When he had pointed out to the Afghans back there that loneliness and captivity had driven the unfortunate bird insane – it sits rocking its head back and forth all day – they were astounded. He was unable to see it, they said in English, calling him a 'secular soulless Westerner' in Pashto, but the bird was in fact praising Allah, the way Muslim children keep time when they read the Koran in madrassas and mosques.

They need education, these people, or they'll go on being cruel without realising it.

The response to this is frequently: 'They are like this because the Western powers favour rotten despots, who keep their people in ignorance and darkness.' Yes, the United States is openly friendly towards the Saudi royals: probably the most corrupt family in human history, their kingdom a place where, to pick just one example from a long and repulsive list, hundreds of criminals – women and children among them – are publicly beheaded every single year. But here's the thing. Does anyone really think that if tomorrow the Saudis suspended these barbaric practices the USA would withdraw its support from the kingdom? In fact it would be a cause of delight for the Americans. The savage practices are older than the US support for the Saudi rulers. They are older than the United States itself!

And the people who want to replace the Saudi government these days don't want an end to this barbarism: they want to *extend* public beheadings and whipping, and the cutting off of hands and feet, to other countries. To the rest of the planet.

DAVID FILLS A GLASS with water in the darkness but instead of drinking it he sets it on a shelf. Something has erupted inside his breast. He lowers himself into a chair and begins to weep, silently to begin with but allowing the sounds to escape as first one minute passes and then another. His face contorted and on fire in the effort to keep the sounds to a minimum, the shoulders jolting.

A sorrow the size of the sky.

This has been the principal weather of his soul for a long time.

He stands up when at last the grief subsides and moves towards the glass of water. Qatrina said another explanation for tears is that the body needs to get rid of the trace elements that cause stress, expelling certain metals from the system.

His eyelashes wet, he stills himself when he sees the figure enter the room through the window that stands open to the orchard, sees the black shape leap down from the sill.

Casa enters the three a.m. darkness of the house, the sky outside full of charred clouds. He knows he is being watched by the eyes of the creatures and figures painted on the walls as he moves along the unlit hallway. He can sense her presence in these interiors, the scent from her blue veil. Miles away during these very moments his companions are most probably becoming acquainted with intimacy. A few hours earlier he had said the day's last prayers on his blanket, not waiting for her to free the mat. Since she began using it he hasn't been able to concentrate on his worship on the prayer mat: his feet were where hers had been, his forehead coming to rest where hers was moments earlier. Her breath and scent were in the velvet nap and in the cypress trees depicted in the centre, their tips bent to signal that they too were bowing before Allah.

On his way into the house just now he passed it hanging on a low limb of the mulberry tree. She must have left it there for him to use for the pre-dawn prayers in a few hours.

Just before dinner she told her hosts she would prefer it if they didn't drink wine in her presence, saying the idea and smell of it made her nauseous. The poised ease of her manner had surprised him. Was it really this easy for someone to let others know of his feelings and thoughts? He himself always has to hide things. And then during the meal her candour had actually shocked him: she told them that a part of her is glad America was attacked in 2001, because had it not been for that Afghanistan would still be suffering under the Taliban. Though he hid his own anger about this slandering of the Allah-loving Taliban, he was concerned the others would react with open hostility to the American part of her statement.

Kind though they were, having agreed with unconcerned shrugs to her request about the wine, they had to be supporters of the USA. But their reaction to her comment was even more unexpected. They seemed to give it serious consideration – Marcus with his head bowed and eyes closed, the hair of his head and beard as white as smoke from an incense stick – and they even seemed to understand her position.

Suddenly, yet again, he had been inundated. Feeling tired of walking the endless road of his life, of absorbing the body blows as and when they were dealt and staggering on.

He doesn't even know his own name, doesn't even know how he ended up in the orphanages and madrassas. A nameless child becomes a ghost, he had been told once, because no one without a name can get a firm enough foothold in the next world. It roams the world, making itself visible to the living in order to be addressed in some way – *The Long-haired One, The One who has Green Eyes* – but humans run away from ghosts and won't address them.

But then he was jolted back to himself. He had heard this seductive rubbish about ghosts from one of the people in attendance at a saint's mausoleum. He had gone there to reconnoitre: places like these were contrary to the pure form of Islam and had to be destroyed. And later that week he had helped set fire to the building, after showering it with rockets first.

And so as the evening progressed it became more and more difficult for him to bear her words. Not for nothing had Omar, the second caliph of Islam, said, 'Adopt opinions opposite to those of women – there is great merit in such opposition,' with Ali the fourth caliph maintaining, 'Never ask a woman her advice because it is worthless.'

When David got up during the meal and switched on the radio, the news was that of a martyrdom bombing in Kandahar and of the latest statement issued by the estimable Osama bin Laden. And she had said, 'These suicide bombings don't further the cause of Islam as he claims – they save him and his followers from death, from being handed over to the USA for reward. He is being protected by people who are promised millions of dollars in exchange for him. It is in his interest to keep making and releasing these tapes, to make sure people don't forget about him and his so-called jihad. The moment the Muslim world says, "Osama who?" is the moment that terrorises him.' Adding, 'Stability is the insecticide he fears.'

He had controlled himself then and also later when she said she knew any number of Afghans who loathed Pakistan for having inflicted the Taliban on their country.

And to think that she was passing on such opinions to helpless young children at the school where she taught. Preparing her pupils for an eternity in Hell. She is no doubt immensely proud of her diplomas and certificates, not seeing them for what they are, pieces of paper that say she can function well in Satan's world.

Now he walks under the nailed-up books, a reminder of the feeble-mindedness of women, and silently climbs the stairs. As he opens the glass door onto the landing he remembers that above the door handle on a yellow taxi in Kabul and Jalalabad is always written the word –

آهسته

– advice for all those who reach towards it with their hand: Gently. How far away that other life seems now. Impossible to get back to, Nabi Khan's men on the look-out for him. The radio said earlier that yet another man has been hanged as a spy, by a band of rebels in Kunar province this time, because a USAID identity card was found on his person. Dunia thinks Casa is a labourer but she would scorn a taxi driver as well, wouldn't she? Someone like him will never be good enough for a girl like her. He wonders if she knows what it's like to be slapped. She must have seen Western women behave in unvirtuous manner on televisions and films and decided to emulate them. And, undone by her proximity, he had incriminated himself by uttering those words to her in the garden, by showing her his distinctively callused palms. He places his hand in his pocket now and withdraws the flashlight, having arrived at the door to Marcus's room. He knows where David is, an exact thirteen steps behind him. The American has been trailing him closely through the house. He switches on the flashlight and climbs onto the shelving unit outside Marcus's room, moving the circle of light onto the various volumes for a few quick seconds. He flicks it off and in the darkness raises his hand towards the book that says Bihzad on the cover. He had seen it during the day and he has been curious about it since. The boy who was sent to his death in Islam's name by Nabi Khan in Jalalabad had had that name. Working the tips of his fingers between the book's boards and the wood of the ceiling, he prises it off and makes his way back to that open window on the ground floor, going past David who withdraws into an alcove at his approach.

David climbs the staircase leading to the roof of the house. At times he had been within touching distance. What Marcus's house lacked, he had thought then, was a room dedicated to the sixth sense. Something that allowed you to identify a fragrance that wasn't there. A third eye and a third ear, the second skin, the second mouth.

Only three yards away from him in that deep-blue darkness, he had held his breath as the boy approached the door behind which the two women were asleep. But he had just gone past it, moving along the corridor.

He'd come for a picture book. It was the volume Zameen had craved during her exile in Peshawar. Now he looks down from the roof. He sees Casa emerge from the house in a hurried skulk, holding the big book under his arm. Like a wolf in a fairytale stealing an infant, running on hind legs into the forest, he sees him enter the large glasshouse. His flashlight comes on. During earlier times there had been topiary animals and birds at various locations around the house, trained by Marcus himself. After years of war and absence they outgrew their shapes, though Marcus brought some of them back when the war with the Soviet Union was over. Later the Taliban came and they would have destroyed them definitely, for being representations of living things, had he not transferred them to pots and dragged them into the glasshouse one by one, letting them outgrow themselves safely in there. The ammonite and the panther died from shock but others reverted to being undisciplined shrubs. He told David that he thought of them, the creatures, as hiding for safety in that foliage.

Drought has killed them but they continue to stand dead in their pots, the sap petrifying in the veins. On occasion Marcus still goes in and clips them, trying to remember the long-ago shapes lost in the brown dry twigs and the brittle leaves.

Through the dusty panes he can see Casa in there, holding the yellow light in one hand, the book in the other. There is half a grizzly bear near him. A hoopoe in flight, also unfinished, the untrimmed mass of branches making it seem it is flying while on fire. There is a flamingo. In his journal the Emperor Babur recorded seeing thousands of them in Afghanistan in 1504.

8

The Caliphate of New York

MUHAMMAD ASKED MUSLIMS not to do anything untoward in the vicinity of orchards, as that would offend the angels who are appointed by Allah to protect fruit trees, keeping foraging creatures at bay.

David looks onto the orchard from the highest room in the house, his arms folded on the window sill as he leans out into the breeze. The array of flowers ghostly at five a.m. He's just come out of sleep, having had the dream again. Someone, David can never see the face, walks away from him in a rainstorm. At the moment of separation the falling of each raindrop comes to a halt, each sphere of water hanging in the air. A perpetual and sorrowful present tense for him. But the departed figure has cleared a corridor through all that suspended grey and silver water. David enters this strange tunnel and begins the journey at the end of which lies a meeting. He awakens always before he can arrive.

He looks towards the glasshouse. When he went to bed Casa was still in there with the book, but he's gone now. He must be asleep in the perfume factory, down there where women and men used to work at one time, amid night-blooming night-dying jasmine. Cyclamen. Ginger and rose and cardamom. Coming from Usha and descending the stairs, going down a layer into their country's past.

The mountain range above the house is faintly luminous, dawn not far away.

Back in 1981 Zameen and Benedikt – having escaped from the Soviet military base – had hidden in an orchard during an hour like this. With the first rays of the sun the branches above Zameen had burst into flower. Benedikt would never find his way back to her now. Zameen said she had continued to make her way towards Usha on her own. She hid herself as she neared the house, seeing armed strangers in the vicinity, the flowerbeds trampled. The resistance fighters had taken over the building, but where were her parents? She waited all day and went forward only when the sun vanished. She descended into the perfume factory, and she stopped at the fourth step up from the floor when her foot landed on an object. She leaned down to investigate. A gun. She sent out her arm in an arc and discovered that there were many more. In fact the entire floor of the factory was covered thickly with them, a heap of weapons that – like a flood – submerged one of the Buddha's eyes, one nostril, and a third of the mouth. She stumbled as she walked on the piled-up guns and went past the stone head. In a far corner, digging through all that metal death as silently as she could, she managed to open a cupboard – taking out the small bottle of the perfume that her father had blended for her. A glass world in her hands.

She went to the graveyard in Usha but among the new mounds she couldn't see the grave of the beloved boy who had been shot the night she was apprehended by the Soviet soldiers.

Bihzad was born more dead than alive seven months later, under a thorn tree as she was making her way towards Pakistan. She had discovered she was carrying Benedikt's child during the initial stages of this journey that took her from village to village, a time of slow progress during which she was accompanied by other refugees, the number varying, some picked off by Soviet fire from above, some by cholera or exhaustion or the heat. Pakistan, Pakistan, Pakistan. In their own country the land wanted to strike them dead and so did the sky, and everyone wanted to get to a refugee camp in Pakistan where their suffering would come to an end at last. Scouts who guided refugees to Pakistan – across desert, river, stone, across bandit territory, wolf territory – demanded money she did not have. She gave birth prematurely inside the blue tepee of a burka, planting a long stick in the earth and draping the cloak over it, opening it wide and weighing down the edges with rocks. If the tree above had been shorter she would have detached its long thorns to pin the hem to the ground. Smoke from the candle escaped through the embroidered eye-grille and disappeared into the dead branches of the tree. At that stage of her travel there were no adults with her, only three children who remained on the other side of the tent that night, falling asleep as the darkness increased. She had found one of them a month ago wandering half-mad through the wilderness, having run away from the refugee caravan that had contained his family – he was ten and wanted to go back home to his village and fight the jihad against the Soviets.

Two hours or so after Bihzad was born she heard the helicopters pass overhead. She managed to move her body and look out of the pleated cone. In the darkness something landed on her brow and bounced off. There was a noise of many small objects landing close to her. It was as though someone were throwing pebbles or large twigs in her direction. She lifted the candle out into the night and in the two moments it took for a gust of wind to extinguish it she saw that a butterfly mine was lying directly in front of her, dropped by the helicopters, saw that the sleeping children were covered with them. She could imagine how the night was full of others that were still descending. The Soviets had designed them especially for use in this war. Made of green plastic and shaped like butterflies or sycamore seeds, with a wing to allow them to spin to earth slowly. The Soviets were known to have dropped mines disguised as actual toys onto villages – dolls and colouring pens, bright plastic wristwatches. Things designed to attract children. They fell from the air into houses and streets and the result was meant to encourage parents to vacate a village, a place where children were no longer safe. These villages harboured guerrillas and had to be emptied any which way. And hundreds of thousands of the green butterfly mines were being used to hinder guerrilla passage to and from Pakistan.

For a moment she wondered if the helicopter pilot knew Benedikt, wondered if by chance the two Soviet men had ever met.

The three sleeping children. The butterflies would blow

off a foot or a hand and half a face, maiming rather than killing, though the long distance which had to be traversed to reach a medical facility would ensure that the victim died of blood loss, gangrene or simply shock. Of the three children sleeping outside the burka the first two died instantly, the third she managed to take with her some way towards Pakistan but he too succumbed to his injuries eventually. She had no strength to bury him, the ground being too hard, but still she knew it must be attempted. A branch, a bone – looking for something to dig with she saw the flashing of water in the distance. Drawing near she discovered that hundreds of mirror fragments of various sizes had been placed on a man's corpse, to stop it from being eaten by vultures. The birds perched a few yards away but were frightened off by their own reflections whenever they drew any closer. They flapped their wings as they sat, as though fanning away the stench rising from the decaying flesh. She lifted some of the shards and placed the dead boy beside the original body. After re-arranging the pieces to cover them both, the death embrace, she continued towards Pakistan. For food she had nothing beyond a pouch of almonds, an onion, some honey tilting in a jar. Bihzad and the fragrance her only other possessions. Empty-handed as a ghost otherwise.

THE DAY HASN'T YET fully begun – the flowers are sunk in dew and the lake is lit by the morning star – but Casa and David are already beside their bark boat. A blue greyness is still the chief presence around them. David wonders if he should name the canoe after John Ledyard, the first citizen of the independent United States to explore the lands of Islam, visiting the Middle East in 1773.

It weighs less than fifty pounds. Its base is a fine equilibrium between flatness and curvature so that, even though on the ground, it turns on a dime, an indication of the ease with which it would spin and change direction on water. It seems creaturely now, alive under their fingers, restive as a child being dressed or being given a haircut. The task ahead of them now is the putting in of sheathing – the thin strips of wood which line the inside, overlapping like the feathers of a bird – and then the ribs. As they work their concentration is so great at times that the other man simply vanishes from view, ceasing to exist.

The *Ledyard*?

In a letter written from Egypt, days before his death, John Ledyard had asked his friend Thomas Jefferson to take all those wondrous descriptions of the East – Homer, Thucydides, Savary – and burn them, advising him against ever visiting Egypt.

'What do you think we should name it, Casa?'

But he just shrugs in return. Looking around, as though for the bird whose song with its small piercing explosions is coming to them.

David isn't sure who the first Muslims in the Americas were. When the Spanish brought the very first African slaves to the New World in 1501 they sought to ensure that they were not Muslims. These Spanish Catholics had a particular dread of the Native Indians converting to Islam. One reason was that if African Muslims – who knew about horses – converted the Indians and then taught them equine skills, much of the Spaniards' military advantage would be lost. Let the Indians keep thinking that horse and rider were a single animal which came apart at times to move independently.

And yet only a decade earlier Muslims were the rulers of Spain. When Islamic Spain was extinguished in 1492, Christopher Columbus was months away from his discovery of the New World. Western Christians, not Muslims, would discover North and South America and the great oceans that bind the planet. There would never be a Caliphate of New York.

No wonder Muslims still weep for their Spain. The thought of it is a solace to them, but that too is a tragedy. It's as though England still harboured designs on America.

They work accompanied by the transistor radio, by the sound of frogs from the water, or the whistling wing-joints of a demoiselle crane flying by overhead. Casa is diligent but of course there is no romance in him towards the canoe as there is in David. 'Can a motor be fixed to this boat, at the back?' he asks, looking at the paddle as something frivolous.

'Theoretically, yes.'

'Good,' he nods approvingly, reaching across him for the knife. At times Casa stands or kneels extremely close to David, but David knows that whereas in the West the distance between people is usually an arm's length, here it can be half that. He knows no threat is implied. At gatherings, the Westerners who have yet to learn this can be seen backing away from the person they are talking to, who in turn reads this as rejection.

Casa handles tools expertly and with grace, with perhaps a certain delight, and is an efficient mover in any given area. Of course the Afghan ingenuity with all things mechanical is a myth, encouraged by the United States and the West during the war against the Soviets. Most of the rebels were peasants who had little or no military expertise. They came from villages in distant pathless mountains and, contrary to historical romances, were not natural guerrillas or warriors. They needed training in weapons and technology, they who were still afraid of eclipses and thought communications satellites circling the night skies were in fact stars being moved from here to there by Allah. A mortar crew would fire off its ammunition without first fusing the mortar bombs. They knew little about camouflage or maps and would smash a radio in frustration when it stopped working because the batteries had run out. For amusement they took shots at fireflies, and they played with their weapons until bits broke off. Small arms were fired haphazardly, with the firer keeping his eyes firmly shut. They cut a fuel pipeline with an axe and then set it alight, tried to break open unexploded bombs with a pistol or a hammer. Thousands of men, women and children fell victim to the Afghans' own incompetence and lack of technical knowledge. There were commanders who didn't capture a single town from the Soviets after a decade's fighting.

Afghanistan was known as the Graveyard of Empires, yes, but these and other appellations of ferocity were thought up by British historians attempting to explain the end of the First Anglo–Afghan War of the nineteenth century, the most notorious defeat in British history. During the 1980s male Western journalists enthusiastically revived and embraced these martial stereotypes, to the satisfaction of agencies like the CIA.

'What do you think of the *Bliss*?' David asks Casa. 'There was an American called Daniel Bliss who gave the Arab world its first modern college, in 1866, in Beirut ...'

Casa can tell when a bird is flying out of fright. A useful indicator of danger. And in a training camp in the jungles of Pakistani-occupied Kashmir he had learned to tell if a snake was near him: by listening to monkeys in the tree canopies – snakes attacked these monkeys so frequently that there was a word for it in their language now, a specific sound telling all others to *look down because* he *has appeared*. In that camp operated by the Pakistani military and the ISI he had even witnessed a peacock mating with a peahen, which is – given all the extravagance of the mating dance – an intensely private event, so mysterious that some people believe the peahen is impregnated through tears she drinks from the male bird's face. So now he only half-listens to David's words, paying attention more to his surroundings.

As with monkeys and snakes, the Americans have learnt words like 'jihad', 'al-Qaeda', 'taliban', 'madrassa'.

And in their cunning they know them well enough to be able to undermine Islam, to turn ordinary Muslims against the holy warriors. Instead of saying 'jihadis', the newspapers and radio are being advised to employ the word 'irhabis', which means 'terrorists'. Instead of 'jihad', they are being told to use 'hirabah' – 'unholy war'. Instead of 'mujahidin', it's 'mufsidoon' – 'the mayhem makers'.

He straightens and stretches his back, taking a moment's break from the work, wiping the sweat off his brow. Walking to the water's edge, he removes his shirt and splashes water onto his torso.

'How did you get the scar on your side?' David asks when he returns, buttoning up the shirt.

'Accident.'

During the previous days the two have talked only when Casa has initiated a conversation. He gives quick answers if David ever makes an enquiry, feeling safe only when information about him is concealed. Already he has made the mistake of showing Dunia his calluses. But he won't succumb to her again.

When David asked if his name was short for Kasam, he had said no. The man hadn't guessed the real name, so a yes wouldn't have mattered, but it was important to make these people think their every instinct and independent idea about him was inaccurate. He will tell them what to think. 'It's short for Qaisar actually.'

Now he pretends not to hear because David is asking, 'What kind of accident was it?'

One of the Tomahawks the Americans had sent into the jihad training camp had caused a sheet of corrugated metal to fly into his waist where he was bowing in prayer. The heat of the explosion had sterilised the metal just before it entered him – it was glowing, the entire width and length of it, a vibrating white-red – so there was no immediate infection but the wound had festered later, the stitches coming apart during a training expedition into remote mountains. With the hospital a week away, they had laid him on his side, scratched off onto the wound the ignitable powder from the heads of five hundred matchsticks and lit it, a method of cauterising that has left a disfigurement the size of a hand on his flank.

The look on David's face is intense and yet, paradoxically, unfocused. Casa feels his thoughts are being read.

He wishes the man would take his eyes off him.

'How old are you, Casa? Twenty-one, twenty-two . . .?'

'Yes.'

Perhaps his hostile confusion has seeped into his tone because David lowers his head now and goes back to work.

He remains standing, looking at the carved seat of the canoe – bone-like, smooth to the touch. David had had it made in Jalalabad and Casa had weighed it in his hands many times, testing the heft. It has been fitted in already but he could pull it out without much difficulty. The first blood spilled in Islam was with a camel's jawbone, the idolaters had interrupted the Muslims' prayer and blessed Saad of Zuhrah had wounded one of them with the nearest thing within reach.

David is still bent to his task, the back of his head vulnerable.

If the man is so keen to mark the coming together of the United States and the lands of Islam he could name the boat the *Guantanamo*. If it's the celebration of heroes that is on his mind, how about the *Osama* or the *ISI*?

The voices of the two women – Dunia and the Russian – have begun to drift towards him from the direction of the orchard, and he tries to hide his alarm at that too. The landmine. But nothing can be done, so he continues ladling hot water down each wooden rib – the tough bands that have been soaking in the lake for two days – until it is supple enough and then bends it with his hands, and his feet, to put into the canoe. David said the bottom has to be more flat than circular, more circular than flat, or the craft would be tippy. The ribs will be left in overnight to stretch and shape the bark: tomorrow they'll be taken out for a short time, have their ends trimmed to precision, and be put back in permanently.

He needs that landmine. He will not allow anyone to capture him. Bihzad said that while he was at the Bagram military prison he had tried to kill himself by chewing on an artery in his arm – becoming desperate one night after learning that, back in December 2002, two prisoners there had been beaten to death by their American captors.

The *Bagram*.

Last night in the glasshouse when he had opened the book entitled *Bihzad*, he had found it to be full of coloured pictures. It was like Marcus's house. He had spent almost two hours looking at them and reading the accompanying texts until the battery in the flashlight had gone out like someone blinded. They seemed to be some of the most beautiful things he had ever seen, despite the fact that, against Allah's wishes, they depicted animals and humans. Rustam, the grandson of the king of Kabul, avenged his own impending death in one picture: dressed in his tiger skin, and gored by the lances that had been planted upright at the bottom of a deep pit, he called out to his brother who had set this trap for him. 'Throw me my bow at least so I won't be eaten by lions.' Overcome by mercy, the brother did what he was asked so that Rustam sent forth an arrow and shot him through the tree trunk behind which he was standing. To Rustam's arrow, the thick-boled tree was as flimsy as the bark that is this boat.

The breeze swings and carries to him the sound of the two women again. The landmine is the pit he has dug and lined with spears. He wills the two women away from it. Asks help from Allah.

David has stopped talking because the news is being broadcast on the radio.

Casa always switches it off when the news finishes and music or discussion comes on air, telling David it is to preserve the batteries, but really because these songs and seven varieties of opinion are like stings to him, the Taliban having banned such frivolities during their regime.

How keen everyone is to make this world their home, forgetting its impermanence. It's like trying to see and name constellations in a fireworks display.

The signs of Allah are there but they refuse to see it. After he came back from the moon and was touring the various countries of the world, Neil Armstrong had suddenly stopped in a bazaar one day, his face ashen, and asked what the sound issuing from a nearby minaret was. On being told that it was the Muslim call to prayer, he began to shed tears and told them he had heard that sound while on the moon, that it had haunted him ever since. He converted to Islam straight away.

'David, could you please come to the house for a minute?' Marcus has appeared and is beckoning with his one hand.

'Give me a minute. We'd like to finish as much of the ribbing today as possible. We'll seal it with the gum tomorrow evening and be on the water by early morning the day after.'

'It's rather urgent,' says the Englishman and the tone of his voice makes David look towards him.

'Right now?'

'Yes.'

Casa stays behind for a while but then follows them, standing on the threshold beside the cypress trees and looking into the kitchen where the four others have gathered.

'We thought we should tell you, David,' Marcus is saying.

'And you have no idea who it was who knocked on your window?' David asks the girl.

Dunia shakes her head. 'I wasn't going to tell you anything but the thought of going back to Usha frightens me.'

'There is no question of that,' David says, and Marcus agrees:

'Yes, you must stay here until your father comes back from Kabul.'

Lara and David exchange a few sentences in English. Marcus joins in and concludes in Pashto: 'I am sure there was no one at her window – they just made that up.'

'They want to shut down the school, that's all.' Dunia's words are almost a whisper. 'I haven't told anyone this but I did hear someone knock on the window that night, the night of the wicked *shabnama*.'

Casa remains at the door for a few more minutes, declining the invitation to enter and take a chair.

He steps away and slowly goes back to the water, walking past the spot from where Marcus had yesterday dug out a small idol, saying it was of the Christian saint who protects doctors and who had painted a picture of Jesus' mother from life. Emerging from the glasshouse last night, after having spent the previous hours looking at the Bihzad book, Casa had dropped the book into the now-empty hole and filled it up, throwing the earth in with the sideways movements of his feet, tamping it all down until it was firm, telling himself that when the time is right he'll burn down the animals and birds in the glasshouse too.

THE LATE-MORNING SUN is coming in and illuminating the wall beside Marcus's chair. A spray of pale orange blossoms and grey foliage, the petals and the leaves more or less the same size. He has seen chintz for Afghan women's dresses that has a design of mobile phones interspersed with hibiscus and frangipani flowers. Lara and the young girl are in the adjoining room now, he can hear them talking as he lowers himself into the chair. For a girl from this land, Dunia has long bones. Some of Qatrina's relatives would insist her parents starve her when she was growing up, withhold meat and eggs and milk from her, lest she became too tall for a woman.

He looks up at the ceiling. Both Qatrina and he had been concerned that they didn't really know how the world worked, the various mechanisms of it. Nor did they know much about the many disciplines that allowed the exercise of the imagination. They had trained as doctors but there was a residual shortcoming to their knowledge and they felt they must now teach themselves about history and religions, about paintings and music. So they had slowly collected books, becoming readers. Learning about ancient and modern events. About the best fiction and poetry.

How Gul Bakaoli and Taj ul Maluk were captured and imprisoned by the djinn.

What Xerxes, riding his chariot over a bridge of boats from Asia to Europe, had said.

The immense power of the druids was the weakness of the Celtic polity, Julius Caesar had written in his memoirs. *No nation that is ruled by priests drawing their authority from supernatural sanctions is capable of true progress.*

Aware of these gaps in their own earlier knowledge, Marcus has never really been convinced that the members of the terrorist team that carried out the 2001 attacks were educated men in the real sense. Most of them had a university education but that education wasn't in history or literature or politics. At his university in Germany, Muhammad Atta had refused to shake hands with the professor who supervised his dissertation, because she was a woman. When it came down to it the terrorists' opinions and beliefs were as devoid of nuances as Casa's seem to be. Viewing the world in very stark terms.

There is even a joke about it in Arabic. In Egypt they say the extremist Muslim Brotherhood is really the Engineering Brotherhood. The Muslim Brotherhood itself is aware of this and has tried to recruit students from the literature, politics and sociology departments of the universities but without any luck.

As he closes his eyes for a moment, time seems to distort itself: the kite of sunlight has moved a great distance along the wall when he opens his eyes again, is about to fly out of the room. He rises and approaches the window. Casa can be seen out there at various times of the day, taking a nap under a tree in the bee-filled orchard, stretching and yawning upon rising, his hands disappearing into the blossoming branches overhead. Or, silent as a deer, he'd be saying his prayers somewhere near by, the body compactly folded like the unborn in the womb when he bows, having performed ablutions at the lake beforehand, his face damp and clean. The teeth he brushes with a fragrant twig, selected after experimenting with the trees and bushes in the vicinity, chewing one end until it resembles a brush. He saw the intensity on the boy's face as he listened to Dunia at dinner last night, caught it again and again, his mind straying into a reverie about the two youngsters. Yes, love is still a possibility in a land such as this, though love means an eradication of selfishness and it could easily be assumed that in a country like this selfishness was the main tool of survival, everyone a mercenary.

In the corridor he goes past the statue of St Luke he had found in the ground, not sure how Casa felt as he watched it being lifted into sunlight. 'The Muslims say they revere Christ,' Qatrina had said, 'pointing out the fact that Mary is the only woman mentioned by name in the Koran, and that Jesus is mentioned more times in there than Muhammad. But, according to them, his teachings were made obsolete by those of Muhammad. There isn't a single Christian in the lands of Islam who isn't under pressure to convert – a subtle pressure if he's lucky. A remarkable way of showing respect and reverence towards someone.'

He is sweeping the path outside the house – putting the broom down and giving the lemon tree a vigorous shake to make it drop the weaker leaves, extending the period of tidiness by a few hours – when he looks up to find James Palantine walking towards him.

A rope has been stretched from one side of the room to the other. Lara comes in through the door and sees it, sees the figure balanced on it acrobatically, his toes clutching the thick woven strand secured on a wardrobe at one end and the bars of the window at the other. A young Caucasian. His arms are raised towards the ceiling and he is peeling off a book with both hands, the body in perfect hovering suspension, throwing a corner glance towards her when he becomes aware of her. He tosses the freed book down onto a sofa, where there are others, she now sees. He has obviously been doing this for some time. His khaki clothes are a contrast against the brilliant walls. Khaki: dust-like. A word the British carried away from this region into the wider world, from when they were fighting the tribes here in the nineteenth century – the colour of the terrain, the colour of the hills, the British soldiers dipping their uniforms in vats of infused tea as the nearest available camouflage.

The young man on the single-filament bridge lowers his arms and, holding them horizontally, gives a small leap and spins through the air so that when he lands back on the rope he is facing her. He smiles at her and then once again tilts his face towards the nailed volumes above him.

It is like cold steel, the shock, when she realises that this

359

must be James Palantine – she knows the reason why he is here.

'Are you James?'

He shakes his head near the ceiling. 'I came with him, got bored, and decided to do this. He's out there.'

She turns and slowly takes the two steps out of the room, looking back at the small burst of laughter from the rope-walking boy as he almost loses his balance.

Marcus and David are walking towards her from the other end of the corridor, their strides shortening when they see her.

Suddenly she wishes to postpone the moment, perhaps even cancel it, but she knows she must listen to the words and sentences these men have brought her. This is what she has been journeying towards ever since she left St Petersburg. There is no alternative, any more than streams can flow uphill, any more than smoke can enter fire. For a moment she is so afraid she wouldn't know her name if asked. The whole of her reduced just to a single emotion, a single fact.

The two men have come to a standstill now, their eyes fixed on her, but she continues towards them.

'Lara,' she hears David say. Not the voice in which he had told her that the bulbul's silhouette resembles that of certain American birds, the cardinal and the waxwing. A sound as faint and dream-edged as a word uttered by someone during sleep.

*

Benedikt Petrovich lies on the ground, one eye looking up at the dark morning sky, the other shooting down into dust. The chill sensation of water has awoken him. Either the drops were sprinkled onto his face to rouse him, or it's rain. He flexes his right arm to see if someone or something is near by and then lifts his head off the ground. The movement awakens the pain in his legs and he remembers now, memory too jolted awake, the blade descending onto the back of his ankles just before he lost consciousness. They had hamstrung him. He lowers his head after seeing the white curve of chalk drawn on the earth near him. With great pain he raises his head again and casts a glance towards his feet and sees that, for some reason, he is lying inside a circle drawn on a field. He tries to extract some answers from the confused haze in his mind. How has he ended up here in this field, how old is he, where is he? He remembers his own date of birth and that of his sister Lara. He recalls the day he received news that he had been conscripted, and remembers also the afternoon he learnt that he'd be sent to Afghanistan the following day. This is a photograph of me when I was younger, *someone had said to him once – a new girl at school in Leningrad? A fellow soldier, met at some point here in Afghanistan? – and he had replied,* Technically speaking *all* photographs are photographs of us when we were younger ha ha. *And was it him or someone else who wrote this in a letter to a friend in the Soviet Union,* Mitya, could I please borrow your parade uniform – we'll only be given battle dress so where would we find the badges and other stuff? I hope you have had your teeth replaced by now. And tell Yuri to write to me. Everyone said they'll write but no one does . . .

There is activity somewhere far away, shapes moving, people milling about, but from within his white circle he cannot bring the distance into focus. Seeing just that cracked earth, a grass blade or two dusted with the white powder which describes the line around him. Each of his ankles feels as though it is in a wolf's jaw and he is unbearably cold and only now does he become aware of the sounds of agony issuing from his mouth.

Minutes after leaving the girl Zameen in the orchard, he had found himself staring at an Afghan dukhi, his eyes so fierce Benedikt didn't at first notice the gun he was pointing at him. He raised his hands but the dukhi was unmoving and Benedikt told him in Russian that he was a defector. Sickeningly, he now saw other dukhi on either side of the one he faced, dozens of them, some of them holding lanterns. 'I'll convert to Islam if you wish, and I have Kalashnikovs for you,' he told them across the few yards of pale darkness that separated them, emphasising the words 'Islam' and 'Kalashnikovs'. He pointed the raised left hand backwards, the direction where the girl and the weapons were, and nodded over his shoulder. In the fragmented glimpse he caught of the orchard behind him he saw a line of other men. He turned around slowly – no reaction from the guns in front of him – and saw that there was an equal number of Afghan ghosts behind him, each with his gun drawn.

They were two small armies of about fifty each, weapons pointed at each other, and he stood in the middle. In one place to his left the adversaries were so close to each other their guns crossed. He could perhaps slip away – this battle, this vendetta, had nothing to do with him. But when he took a step sideways there was movement in the guns and a voice said something loudly. He froze, realising he was the prize the two sides wished to possess. The ghosts were talking now, shouting across him, hurling words at each other in obvious rage, pointing at him now and then. The standoff lasted until dawn arrived and then the two groups, still tense, seemed to come to some kind of agreement, wild laughter directed at him occasionally as he was led out of the orchard, the new sun and the uncovered sky making him blink. They had fastened his hands behind him with rope – so tight his collarbones hurt – and now and then they taunted him. Every time he slowed he was made to pick up his pace with a blow, a fist in the face or a rifle butt on the shoulders. 'I'll become a Muslim – a Mussalman. Benedikt Ahmed. Or Muhammad Benedikt,' he told them more than once; but they brought him to a small room and he was imprisoned there, hearing the bolt drive home on the other side of the door.

What happened to Zameen? At the military base she had been chained up in a room like this one. Disgrace and mortification and dishonour had made him enter her room the first time, placing one hand over her mouth where she lay asleep and tearing at her clothing with the other. He and a group of other soldiers had earlier that day gone to the river that flowed beside the military base. They had driven their tank into the water to wash it. Human flesh was caught in the tracks from a week ago when a number of the inhabitants of a village, suspected of harbouring rebels, had been made to lie on the ground and had had the tank driven over them. The meat and bones were decomposing and the unbearable stench had meant that the tank had to be taken to the river. They used sticks to work loose the bits of clothing and bodies. A copper talisman one of the dead men had been wearing around his neck. And that was when they found a girl hiding among the reeds. She said she was from the village whose men had been crushed under the tank, her father and brother among them, and that she had followed the tank tracks towards the military base and had been hiding on the riverbank for five days, waiting. She wanted to collect as much of the remains as she could, to provide a grave for them.

The dead were dead, past caring, but last rites and ceremonies of burial were not for the dead – they were for the living. She was alive and had her responsibilities and her love. She was too weak to have protected them when they were living but could protect their flesh from lying exposed to the elements, to the beasts of day and night.

The girl, who was about fourteen years old, was lifted into the tank and the soldiers took turns brutalising her in there, Benedikt remaining outside to keep watch. When they told him it was his turn he wouldn't climb in – and so they held her underwater and then let her float away. Her bangles could not be heard as she struggled inside the liquid, and the river had also silenced the sound of the gun, and then a fight broke out because the others jeered and began to laughingly speculate as to why Benedikt had refused, touching without knowing on the truth of his inexperience and his fears. In solitude he blushed, feeling wretched. The word had reached the colonel, who, as always, more and more drunk as the day advanced, had called Benedikt out and humiliated him before everyone.

Later that night, the memory of it made him enter the room where Zameen lay chained up.

Now, a prisoner himself, he hoped her ordeal was over, that she'd found safety.

At dawn the next day, three dukhi *came into his cell and twice he heard the word* buzkashi *being spoken excitedly. It was the Afghan national sport,* buzkashi, *he knew. A dangerous and bloody game akin to fierce combat in which the body of a calf or goat was placed in a circle drawn in quicklime in the centre of a field, and the two opposing sides gathered near it on horseback. At a rifle shot, they all launched themselves upon the carcass. To win a point they had to pick it up, carry it to a predetermined turning point about a mile away, and bring it back to the circle without allowing any of the opposing players to wrench it from their grasp, the riders at times literally clinging to their mounts by their stirrups, whips clenched in teeth. The players had been known to number as many as one thousand and when the carcass got ripped apart, as often happened amid kicking hoofs and the slashing whips, the referee decided which team had control of the larger remnant.*

The dukhi *who had entered Benedikt's room took away from him the leaf of the Cosmos Oak he had been holding, the feel of it a comfort to him. They crumbled it away, no doubt failing to understand how it could mean anything to anyone. Then they forced him to his knees, two of them grabbing his arms near the shoulders. The third was behind him, seeming to adjust or position his feet, gripping the tough cord of cartilage above each heel. Light was coming from behind him and Benedikt could see the ghost's shadow on the wall in front of him. He saw the dark blade swing across the wall and disappear downwards – the cutting edge landed on his feet and he lost consciousness.*

Now he lies in the circle, hearing his own cries of pain and the horses slowly coming towards him, a pall of dust ahead of them. He can feel the ground vibrating through his skin, as though listening to thunder below ground. A volcano about to erupt. In the eye that is looking up at the sky there is a distant row of birds, demoiselle or Siberian cranes. The lines appear to be stationary, making him think you could walk from one section of the sky to another by stepping on the back of the birds, a bridge, perfectly suspended there.

Onto his knees and elbows, he raises himself to dog level, but collapses after half a moment. He must try to run, escape, but there is no feeling in his legs other than pain. Weeping, he has begun to scream out for his mother and father and for Lara, for the girl he loved at six, at ten, at sixteen – tugging on any and all conceivable threads of love, summon deliverance from any corner. He is suddenly aware that he is fragile as glass now that the beasts are massed just on the other side of the circle, everything gone a little faint with dust for him. Above the horses' knees many human hands are hanging, now and then the face of a rider reaching down to laugh at him. When the rifle shot comes he thinks they have fired into him, but no, he hasn't been shot, and now a dozen hands grab onto his limbs and hair and clothing and he feels himself being lifted unevenly off the ground . . .

*

'I think I'll leave tomorrow,' Lara says in a dazed faraway voice after David and Marcus have finished speaking, the tale told. What Nabi Khan and Gul Rasool had done to her brother.

Marcus looks at David.

'Yes, I think I will. Thank you, Marcus, for everything, for your hospitality.' She stands up abruptly, eyes full of brilliant energy now, and moves towards her suitcase. David approaches and lifts her hand away from the case's handle, tries to bring her back to her chair, but she refuses to submit.

'First we have to make arrangements – confirm your plane ticket . . .'

'I'll go to Kabul and stay in a hotel.'

'No.' He takes in the smell of her hair, her skin and clothes. Hoelun, the future mother of Genghis Khan, had given her tunic to her husband as she asked him to flee their pursuers, leaving her behind in the wilderness. Her smell in the dress to remember her by. To the peoples of the steppe it is part of the soul.

'I cannot stay here knowing that man, Gul Rasool, is just over a mile away from me. What did they do with . . . the remains?'

'I asked but James says they don't seem to remember.'

She nods. 'It was more than two decades ago. I must go.'

'No, Lara,' Marcus cries out behind them. David turns and sees that Marcus has planted his sole hand on his face to conceal the naked heartache. Maybe there is a ghost here, he had said to David once, because sometimes I get the vivid sensation that I am caressing my daughter's face with my missing hand.

367

Apart from anything else he is afraid of their leaving, David sees now. The fear of being alone is on that hidden face.

Lara goes to sit beside him.

David moves towards the window. Towards free air. He can hear their muffled distressed words to each other behind him. Perhaps she shouldn't have been told. Had he found out about it independently – away from Marcus, at another point in time – he would have kept it from her, he's sure. But she had wanted to know, and he has been quick, sparing her any unnecessary details. *Wouldn't you wish to learn what happened to Jonathan in Vietnam?* A different war – but maybe at some level it was the same war. Just as tomorrow's wars might be begotten by today's wars, a continuation of them. Rivers of lava emerging onto the surface after flowing many out-of-sight miles underground. James Palantine is the age David was when he was here fighting America's enemy.

The sons of the fathers.

Here in this room the three of them are, the old ones. Four if Zameen's ghost is included. And out there are the children. Dunia. Casa. James. The planet's future.

ANGELS CONSTANTLY PRAISE Allah for having created beards for men and long hair for women.

Reciting the Koranic verse against vanity, he looks into the water of the lake.

Locating his reflection he raises his hand to the cheek where she had smeared kohl yesterday. His face. The most important instruction of the Uzbek trainer, who taught him how to carry out a martyrdom attack, was to bend the head downwards when he exploded himself. The head must be destroyed completely or he will enter Paradise with his body decapitated.

Is he thinking of her? If she kept her maddening face and hair concealed he wouldn't be distracted.

If her face had been veiled he wouldn't have been able to see that she was close to tears because of him yesterday, at the thought of possible harm to him.

When they poured wine into a goblet the ordinary goblet shone like a red jewel. And so he saw her looking into a mirror, and walking past it later he realised that without her reflection it was nothing but a piece of glass.

He is thinking of her. No, he can't see why he should feel responsible because her well-being has been jeopardised because of him, because of what happened on the night of the Night Letter. He has no time for such worldly matters.

At certain times of day a small swarm of hornets comes to drink water from this part of the lake's margin. He stops to watch them as they begin their descent, then continues his walk along the edge. So precious are the ingredients used in some perfumes, said the Englishman yesterday, that instead of metal weights a small berry is used to measure them out. The bodies of these small hornets could be used for that purpose too, he's sure, given how very small they are. Something could also weigh as much as one of those red beetles that have black spots on their backs. He's seen them painted in several places inside the house. Yesterday she was saying her prayers beside a vine leaf that held one.

Allah in his compassion understands what he is experiencing. By the time only six generations of Adam's children had passed, corruption and other consequences of temptation were widespread on earth, and the fears the angels had expressed to Allah at the time of Adam's creation began to seem legitimate to them. When the angels repeated their complaints regarding mankind's weakness, He responded, 'If I had sent you to live on earth and instilled in you what I have instilled in them – a passionate nature – you would have acted as they have.'

The martyrdom mission camp was near Kazha Panga village, just where the Durand Line separated the Azam Warsak town of South Waziristan from Afghanistan's Paktika province. There were hundreds of other recruits. Though no girls or young women – it was thought their modesty might be compromised when they exploded themselves and certain body parts came to lie scattered in full view.

Some of the recruits had been brought there from schools, against the wishes of their infidel-in-all-but-name parents, who didn't care that US and other Western forces were occupying Afghanistan. Didn't realise how important it was for Muslims to rise up in revolt against them, unleash a planet-wide lightning storm. The recruiters would arrive at the schools and the children, after listening to their speeches and being shown DVDs of holy wars, would offer themselves up readily for martyrdom instruction. Gun battles often broke out, however, when the principals of the schools sought police assistance, or prevented the children from boarding the buses and vans bound for the secret camps. Once there, they were told to adopt the hairstyle of the jihadis – combed back from the brow and cut straight at the nape of the neck as Muhammad, peace be upon him, is said to have worn it. In addition to the Koran they were taught three books published in Pakistan.

Rehbar ki Shanakhat – 'The Mark of the Leader' when translated into Pashto for those who didn't speak Urdu.

Fidayee Hamlay – 'Martyrdom Attacks'.

Tareekh-e-Shiagaan – 'A History of the Shias'.

All three volumes had been acquired from ordinary bookshops in the Street of Storytellers in Peshawar, fortunately in bulk because – at the behest of the Americans – the Pakistani government had recently banned such inspirational literature. After training they were told to go home and wait to be contacted, Casa being exempt from this because he came back to Nabi Khan in Jalalabad, who intended to use him himself, asking Casa to shorten his hair and also trim his beard to a stubble so as not to appear even remotely conspicuous.

He walks along the water's edge. He had wished to be away from the house as soon as he saw the two young Americans arrive earlier.

He looks up, wondering – as he used to when he was a child – how high Paradise is. Back then when he'd also wonder if his parents had ever been born, had ever existed.

The most truthful dreams occur during the time of year when flowers blossom on the branches, like now. And always at dawn. The prophet Muhammad, peace be upon him, had told his followers that after he was gone prophecy would come only through true dreams, the angels bringing them to the sleepers, creating likenesses and images in their minds to give tidings. At dawn yesterday he had dreamt about being inside the sacred precinct of the Kaaba, taking milk from a gazelle. Waking up he remembered that according to the dream manuals of the believers suckling augured imprisonment. It probably was a false dream, brought on by his encounter with the Americans a day earlier. In any case that was the reason why he had begun scratching away the figure of the deer from the wall as he waited for her to finish praying yesterday. Absentmindedly. He thought he had stopped himself just in time, sweeping the flakes under an armchair, but obviously she had noticed.

Allah is testing the depth of his belief through all this, placing the Americans and the girl in orbit close to him. On which of the two would he focus his truest attention?

He mustn't waver from his devotion or all will be lost. A pious man, someone who had spent his entire life praying, once lived above a dissolute wretch who drank wine and listened to music and indulged in the pleasures of the flesh. One night the upstairs man had the urge to examine the revelries downstairs, while at the same time the downstairs man decided to see what his neighbour was doing. They both died at the stairs. The one on his way down was sent to Hell by Allah. The one going up admitted to Paradise.

Taking the dust path that eventually enters the Englishman's orchard from this part of the lake, he stops on seeing Dunia and the American man James.

Two minutes on this path would lead to where the landmine lies buried.

They are talking. She's presenting her report to him, telling him what Casa revealed to her yesterday when his guard was down briefly. And the story about being persecuted over the knock on her window? A lie to be able to extend her stay at the house?

If it's so then he can only marvel at their shrewdness and elaborate designs. They'll steal the lines from the palm while shaking hands with someone. But really how could he not notice that the devotion she has been displaying to gain his confidence is fake. She who thinks Allah accepts prayers offered within rooms painted with images of living things. That He accepts prayers from a woman in a veil through which her hair can be seen.

Instead of turning around and leaving, he takes a few more steps towards them because they have become aware of him. As he draws near, another American comes into view from behind the rosewood tree – he had arrived with James earlier.

'I am a little tired of having to prove who I am,' Dunia is saying to James in Pashto. 'Didn't I tell you who I was when I was on my way here yesterday?'

James points to the other American. 'He wasn't at the cordon yesterday morning, so he didn't know who you were when he saw you just now. That's all.'

The other white man makes a conciliatory gesture with his hands, saying something in English.

This is just so much play for Casa's benefit, surely, their way of changing the subject because he has just walked in on their conversation about him.

'We are not your enemy,' says James.

'He was extremely discourteous. I am glad you weren't too far behind.'

Or is this authentic? It's something Casa has in common with her, then, being harassed by this group of invaders, these occupiers.

'He has apologised and I do too. You must appreciate how difficult the situation is for us as well. What can we do?'

Submit. Die.

'We are here to help your country. We came to get rid of the Taliban for you . . .'

'Please stop,' she tells him. 'The Taliban regime had been in place for years and no one was particularly bothered about getting rid of it. You are not here because you wanted to destroy the Taliban for us, you are here because

374

you wanted retribution for what happened to you in 2001. I am glad they are gone but let's not confuse the facts.'

The Americans throw glances at Casa from time to time. A rush of delight in him that she is confronting them bravely. The sight is thrilling. Even if she is speaking disrespectfully yet again of the Taliban.

'You can't expect a country to function like a charity,' James says.

'Then why pretend that it is?'

'I am sorry. That was uncalled for.'

'No, I am glad it got said. At last we are on the same page – without illusions.'

'I shouldn't have said that.' There is regret in the voice. 'Our government and thousands of other American organisations do plenty of good work around the planet.'

'Did I say they don't?'

Now Casa sees that her features are in turmoil. These men have distressed her, as though she needs anyone else adding to her consternation and panic. She must already feel like an exhausted and cornered animal, having had to flee Usha.

A brother, a cousin, a lover, he takes a step towards her to signal to them and to her that she is not alone. *Two of their buildings fell down and they think they know about the world's darkness, about how unsafe a place it is capable of being!*

'All I ask is that you do not scare or humiliate me the next time you need to stop me,' she says; and pointing to Casa – looking at him for the second time during all this, and just as cursorily as the first – she adds:

'You are as bad as he is.'

It is as though she has struck him hard in the face.

She leaves, and the Americans too begin to walk away, James raising a quick hand towards Casa – in belated greeting – which Casa doesn't acknowledge, his entire body shaking and gone cold at what she just did. Only seconds after an animal's throat was cut, even as he knelt there pinning down the death throes with his weight, he could feel its body warmth ebbing away, feel it begin to grow cold.

'She has nothing to do with your enemies,' he hears himself say plainly and in a clear voice to the retreating backs of the Americans.

He squares himself but they don't even stop, let alone turn around.

'You sound very sure,' says James, continuing. 'You know someone who *might*?' With his index finger he traces two quick loops around his head. Casa's bandages.

LYING BESIDE THE STONE FACE he moves his fingers absently on the floor, where the few remaining panels of a stained-glass window are casting discs of coloured sunlight from above, the red with more heat dissolved in it than the blue. Then darkness falls and he climbs up and sits motionlessly on the bunched-up hair at the top of the Buddha's head, the bun that sticks out sideways because the head is horizontal. His feet dangling in empty air. What did he expect? What other thoughts did he think would arise in her mind towards him, after his hostility towards her yesterday? She has shown him who he is. He doesn't want to be that. He jumps down and takes a notebook and pen from the alcove. Climbing back up with them he opens the book in the middle. Two large empty pages. A faint scent from them as when someone has cut into a fruit near by. He waits until the darkness is perfect around him and then, having also removed his clothes and cast them onto the floor, he begins to write, beginning at the top right-hand corner of the right page and intending to stop upon getting to the bottom left of the facing page. Sentences about himself. The truth. He can only say it in the dark. Even his eyes are closed as he arranges the small words on the paper. But it is difficult to write like this, and so, after only half a dozen lines, he moves towards the lamp that rests higher up, against the top rim of the large stone ear. When he lights it he sees that the pages are still blank, that for some reason the pen had held onto its ink. He knows the reason. Allah doesn't want him to. Nothing but indentations can be seen in the yellow light. He moves his fingertips over the phantom words. This is the second sign, the dream of the gazelle being the first. Or is it the third? Hadn't Allah arranged for her to spend last night in the house, the night he needed to embrace a female, the final touch in his preparations for martyrdom? Allah is telling him what is expected of him. He knows not to flick or shake the pen to get the ink flowing. He continues to write however – no pigment, just pressure – until both pages are filled and several more. Finishing, he rips them out and folds them carefully – thinking as he goes that the Englishman would not be able to do this as easily with his one hand – and not knowing what else to do with them he drops them into the stone pit of the ear and extinguishes the flame. Words that can't be seen. A silent cry, and an ear that can't hear. Nothing but the maelstrom of his breathing in the darkness now.

'HELLO, DAVID.'

James has returned to the house. The first cold stars of dusk were visible singly and the sky still blue only minutes ago, it seems, but night descends fast in the East. The birds were still airborne but then suddenly their sounds disappeared as the darkness sealed their way.

'I thought I'd come and see how everything was.'

'Come in. Stay.'

'I must go back soon, though. We have to stay ready for the assault promised in the Night Letter, stay sharp especially during these hours of darkness.'

A quarter-century of warfare: a period during which some vultures in Afghanistan have developed a taste for human flesh – whenever there was a dead animal with a human corpse next to it they'd ignore the animal.

Lara has forgotten a cup of tea on the table and David has been intermittently sipping the cooling liquid.

'Did you know C-4 explosive smells like lemons?' James says, indicating the cup. 'Where is everyone?'

'I think Casa is out there . . .'

'I have been thinking about him.'

David looks into his face for a moment then lets his gaze slide off. 'There's nothing to think about. Marcus, if he can, takes in people who are in need. He arrived a few nights ago.'

379

'The night the *shabnama* was posted?'

American fears are huge.

'I understand the need to be vigilant, James, but . . .'

'I am sorry, it's just that he has a wound on his head and several of the alarm guns around Gul Rasool's house had gone off the night of the *shabnama*.'

'I am aware of all that. But let's leave him alone, he's doing just fine.'

David has gone to stand at the threshold. Between two cypresses is stretched a spider's half-completed web like a story left unfinished by the storyteller. James joins him and they walk out into the garden, slowly beginning to circle the house as they talk. Entering and then emerging from the orchard.

'I didn't mean anything much by what I said about him. But this is how al-Qaeda sleeper cells operate in the States. They are like ghosts in front of you, unseen . . .'

'James.'

'Of course, you know.'

Some of these al-Qaeda men may marry into American families and have perfect camouflage as law-abiding citizens, living inconspicuously near the scene of their future operations.

Regretting the harsh tone, he smiles at James. 'In 1953 listening devices were found in the beak of the eagle in the great seal of the United States at the Moscow embassy.'

'There you go,' the younger man laughs. 'Al-Qaeda hiding in the mouth of the Golden Eagle. It's simple – use the laws, freedoms and loopholes of the most liberal nations on the planet to help finance and direct one of the most violent international terrorism groups in the world. They want to do to the Statue of Liberty and Mount Rushmore what they did to the Buddhas of Bamiyan.'

'Do you know about the rumours in Usha concerning that girl we have staying here with us?'

'Yes.'

'Tell me.' The cranes are there at the lake's edge; he sees them in his mind's eye, heads drawn back like the hammers of guns.

'This afternoon in his Friday sermon the cleric denounced her as a –' He throws up his hands. 'Apparently she has a secret lover who was seen outside her house one night – on the night of the *shabnama*. People are full of anger and disgust at her.'

'She'll be safe here.'

'Good. Who knows what they'll do to her if they get their hands on her? Make sure to lock the windows and doors at night. We'll also keep an eye on this place.'

What would they do to her? Christopher said he was shocked in the early years at what the Afghan guerrillas were prepared to do, at how brutal they were, what complete disregard they had for life. The United States and the CIA had wanted courage, but the guerrillas had given them cruelty. 'Yes, we are using their bravery to our advantage,' he would say, 'but I would not suggest half the things they are doing, am disgusted by a third.'

They have completed a circumambulation and are now back at the kitchen door, light arrowing out into the darkness from it. Before entering David looks back into the gathering darkness, into the rustles and other sounds of foliage. The breeze. Or are people advancing towards the house from several directions, as when the king is under threat on a chessboard?

'I have to tell you that Gul Rasool thinks the girl might be involved with the people who put up the Night Letter. It could have been them outside her house that night.' And seeing the look on David's face, he leans back in his chair and looks around. 'He was just wondering, that's all.' He nods towards the photograph on the shelf and, in a changed tone, more considered, says, 'So your Zameen grew up in this house.'

'I miss your father, you know, James. Missed him back then too, and you and your mother.'

'If we catch Nabi Khan I won't forget to ask him about what happened to your son. Bihzad.'

'So he told you everything.'

'Over the years, yes. He never talked much, as you know. Was hardly ever there with us, the work keeping him away. He talked constantly about wanting to see you during his last days but there was no finding you. You were in the will, but that had been there for a very long time. After the doctors said there was no hope and we brought him home to die, he wanted one of your photographs framed and placed on the bedside table next to the pictures of the rest of us. He could never deal with the fact that' – he lowers his voice further and looks towards the corridor, towards the door to the garden – 'he had to let the woman be put to death by Gul Rasool, but he said that at the time he saw no alternative. He thought she was working for the Soviets.'

David lifts the spoon out of the cup and places it on the table. 'What?'

'She was working for the . . . I thought Dad had discussed it all with you. You don't *know* this?'

'Discussed what with me?'

'He thought she was a spy for the Communists. That she was lying to you.'

'Christopher told me he thought she was just someone who had been sent by Gul Rasool to plant a device to kill him. He told me at the World Trade Center in 1993 that he didn't know who she was, that that was why he allowed her death to take place.'

'No, he knew exactly who she was, knew she had a relationship with you for some months. Her behaviour aroused suspicion, so he assigned someone to watch her – he never doubted your own loyalty, not for a minute – and eventually he had her followed. She regularly met a Communist. A young Afghan man. When Gul Rasool wanted to kill her that day Dad was just . . . relieved she'd be out of the way. Relieved or glad, whatever's the word.'

'He said had he known she was the woman I loved he would have done everything in his power to save her.'

There is a pistol taped to the underside of the kitchen table. An act of precaution by him.

'I am sorry, I thought you knew all this.' The young man has an intense stare now, the pupils almost vibrating as he looks at David.

'He lied to me.'

'I thought you knew all this.'

'Who was the man she met, the Communist?' Though

of course he knows the answer.

'It was the man she loved before she met you.'

The man David thought had died in the Soviet bombing raid on the refugee camp.

'An investigation into him was already under way when Zameen died – why was she meeting him? He was questioned after her death. He said they had once been in love but that she was now with another man. He didn't know anything about you – not even your name, certainly not your nationality. She wouldn't tell him. He supposed he saw him in secret so the new guy wouldn't think she still had feelings for him. She helped him financially a few times. They were both from the same place, here, Usha, and she felt connected to him because of all that she had lost. She was not a spy after all. But Dad didn't find that out until after she died and the Communist was picked up for questioning.'

'No. She was *not* a spy. Didn't Christopher think I would have known?'

'Not necessarily. You would expect a spy to be an expert at deception. Even at the best of times we don't really know everything about others. Exactly what I have just said about Casa and Dunia.'

He can see the gun through the table's surface as though it's glass, not wood. The too terrible thing, the truly monstrous thing, is that in the mayhem of those years he had had to make a number of decisions like these himself. He remembers the scattershot speculations, and the collective urgency to grasp opportunities and exploit advantages, to bring the deadlock with the USSR to an end once and for all. *Christopher – according to the best facts he had at his disposal at the time – allowed her to be killed because he thought she posed a danger to the interests of the United States of America* . . . He grips the hair on either side of his head until it begins to hurt. Christopher too had used a bullet to end his life, the pain of the illness too great in the last days.

There is plenty of corruption in the CIA. Christopher was so good at spotting frauds that he discovered before any of his peers that one of the most renowned case officers working in the Latin American division was corrupt – he invented most of his agents and probably pocketed some agents' pay in diamonds and emeralds. But corruption was certainly low in the Peshawar of the 1980s. And he has lost count of the times he has wished Christopher had allowed Zameen's execution to go ahead because of money. Yes, Gul Rasool had lured Christopher to the meeting in order to offer him a bribe. If only this were true. David could have shouted at Christopher then, or had him arrested, fired in disgrace, or yes, perhaps even murdered him and taken the punishment – but no, Christopher was honest in that respect. This was not about greed and personal gain.

Buildings in Pittsburgh and Chicago carry the Palantine family name, there are three-storey Upper East Side apartments with Old Masters on the walls, and there are houses in the Hamptons and in DC and Pennsylvania. Christopher's father helped found the CIA, and there has been a senator in the family of James's mother for three generations. All this against David's own ancestors, who had crossed the Atlantic in the mid-eighteenth century more or less as ballast in the ships that had taken American flax seed to Ulster's linen mills, the human cargo compensating for the buoyancy on the nearly empty return voyage. There is a beloved uncle in Kentucky who charges his customers $10 for a haircut or you can pay him in snakes. But never for a moment had Christopher made him feel that he had an advantage or lead over David because of his background. Respecting his intelligence, his abilities. So no, it wasn't a case of not caring about the happiness of someone with David's roots either.

This was about nations and ideals. About carrying the fire.

He looks at James. 'Was there another reason?'

'No. I have told you all I know.'

'Something I can't help but suspect. There could be another reason why, that day in 1993, he didn't tell me he had known who she was. Looking at that mile-high column of glass and steel with a tower of smoke inside it, he knew I was finished with the CIA. Knew I wanted none of it any more. But the bomb had exploded minutes earlier. He knew the CIA – the USA – needed me now more than ever. My knowledge, my contacts, my skills.'

'He always said you could've made director.'

'Could he have kept the truth from me so I'd keep working with him, helping him understand the new threat to our country?'

'As things turned out you couldn't go on anyway and gave it up,' James says, getting up to leave. 'You shouldn't have left the team, David. Who knows, certain things –

certain events – might not have happened had you been able to bury your personal feelings.'

And from the door he gives a little shrug at David's stare. 'I shouldn't have said that, I'm sorry. But it's possible. And if it came out as me doubting your patriotism, I am sorry for that too. I am sure Dad would have held himself responsible had he lived another year, definitely, wondering how and where he'd managed to make a mistake, and let's just say that he would have regretted the fact that you hadn't stuck around.'

Ornithologists were consulted in the wake of the 2001 attacks because birdsong was heard on a bin Laden video, and David too had volunteered the knowledge of Afghan mountains and cave systems he had accumulated through his gemstone interests. *When Moses commanded Aaron to fashion a jewelled breastplate*, he remembers thinking to himself, charts and photographs of Afghanistan's geographical terrain spread before him, *with twelve stones representing the twelve tribes of Israel, the fifth stone was lapis lazuli and in all probability it came from this set of caves . . .* It was his first contact with the CIA for over two years and it was they who now informed him that Christopher Palantine had taken his own life the previous year.

FROM ENTHUSIASM TO IMPOSTURE *the step is perilous and slippery . . .* In the golden room David looks up from the heavy book in his right hand, the blood vessel in the wrist pulsing beside the edge of the page. *The History of the Decline and Fall of the Roman Empire.* Marcus, Lara and the girl are elsewhere in the house, Casa probably in the perfume factory with a lamp at his side. He looks down at the book again, the smell of dust on the paper. . . . *the demon of Socrates affords a memorable instance of how a wise man may deceive himself, how a good man may deceive others, how the conscience may slumber in a mixed and middle state between self-illusion and voluntary fraud.* The pulse is usually felt where the radial artery lies near the surface of the skin, on the thumb side of the wrist. Before detaching Marcus's hand, Qatrina had cut into his flesh and clamped the radial and ulnar arteries, to prevent excessive blood loss. Can the beat of his heart be felt near the end of his forearm now? The book is heavy. In the Texas of the mid-nineteenth century the illiterate Comanche warriors remembered to take away bibles and other books during raids on farms and settlements. They had discovered that paper made an excellent padding for their bison-hide war shields, absorbing a bullet if packed thickly and tightly enough. Someone came across a shield

stuffed with the complete history of ancient Rome – its
rise, efflorescence and eventual fall to barbarians.

'WHAT IS IT?'

He shakes his head. In their brief past together, this handful of days, he has told her only the most minimal of details about Zameen's death, the barest of revelations about his own activities of the 1980s.

'You have enough on your mind already.'

'Tell me.'

'I don't want to say it out loud.'

He walks to the door and locks it, looking back towards where she stands across the wide room. And returning, he tells her everything. How he met Zameen. The boy she loved, and the Soviet bombing of the refugee camp. How the CIA knew about the raid in advance. His trip to Uzbekistan to deliver weapons and Korans. There seeing the Muslim woman being punished for having taken a lover, and a Russian lover at that. Returning to find Zameen and the child missing, and then discovering how her circumstances had once reduced her to demean herself ...

She listens to all this and more. There is no reaction from her even when the generator is switched on by some-one out there and the room lights up suddenly. They look around, their eyes unsteady. Two day-blind animals exposed to full sunlight. When his eyes adjust he sees how

390

shaken she is by what he has told her, by what he is telling her. As he continues the room becomes dark again, the generator either switched off for some reason or running out of oil.

'The CIA knew about the raid on the camp where her lover was?' she asks through the lightless air.

'Yes. Days in advance. I myself found out about it only a short while before, though.'

'They knew hundreds of people were going to die and didn't warn them. Had you known in advance, you still wouldn't have alerted those defenceless people. Of course.'

He doesn't answer at first but then remembers that he is supposed to be confessing everything.

'We were letting those men, women and children die to expose the brutality of the Soviets. We were saving the future generations of Afghanistan and the world from Communism.'

'I am not arguing with you. But really, I can't ignore the fact that nobody asked them if they wanted to sacrifice their lives. For all I know probably all of them would have willingly gone to their deaths to secure a better future for their land, for the world. But no one asked them.'

'The Soviets would have carried out the raid whether or not we knew about it.'

'But you *did* know about it. That's what I am interested in. God, I had conversations of this type with Stepan . . . When it came to what he called his nation, his tribe, he too suffered from a kind of blindness: he saw what he wanted to. "You think your principles are higher than reality," he'd say to me.'

391

'It makes no difference that I knew.'

She seems to be elsewhere, nothing but silence from her, and then she says, 'You have spent your whole life believing such untrue things. Don't you know how alone you are, David? We are most alone when we are with the myths.'

'America is not a myth.'

And you can't compare me to Stepan, he wants to add but doesn't because the bluntness would be painful for her. *He was the servant of monsters and barbarians, of a system that was an abomination.*

'Believe me, I am not defending Soviet Communism. My father died at its hands and my mother ended up in an insane asylum because of it, my brother was torn to pieces ... I remember how a dissident had asked for his legal rights while being interrogated and the KGB thug had said with a pained look on his face, "Please – we are having a serious discussion here."'

She is on the other side of a barrier now, a branching river of ice suspended in the air between them.

'You let that boy die, Zameen's lover ... He lived but not because of you. Doesn't it trouble you?'

'Of that I am guilty – yes, and I am ashamed that I was that person. I thought she would leave me for him.'

'If you were better than him she wouldn't have. You should have given her the chance to make up her mind.'

'As it was, she *did* choose me.'

Minutes of silence later he sees her walk towards the door, hears her turn the key. To go away and look for light, leaving him to the shadows.

'I wonder about forgiveness,' he says quietly, moving to a chair. 'Whether it's ever a possibility in certain cases.'

She stops, an indistinct shape surrounded by darkness. She comes back to him, advancing and leaning close over him. Her hand moves through the air and comes to rest on the lower half of his face. He can't understand what she is doing – telling him not to speak further on the matter? – but whatever it is, he is soon unable to breathe under that hand. Then he realises that that is actually what she is trying to do. Blocking his nose, his mouth, clamping them shut. He could free himself from the grip easily, could manoeuvre his bottom lip out from under the edge of her hand to take in a gulp of air, but he does not want to struggle against her, against this, wants to be here for ever.

A minute passes, perhaps an eternity, his lungs beginning to burn.

Then she releases him and straightens, looking down as he swallows large gasps of air.

She walks back to the door and before leaving the room she says:

'The forgiveness of the weak is the air you strong ones breathe, David. Didn't you know? You don't see it but you felt it just then. They *allow* you to go on living.'

THE BEAUTY OF THE ROSE is considered a medicine. Healing through sight, through the act of looking with all veils swept aside. Marcus had said this to Casa when he gave him the prayer mat, a row of the blossoms depicted along the base of it.

It's not there on the mulberry branch where Dunia has been leaving it after she herself has finished with it. He stands looking at its absence. The house is locked. It's past midnight and they've gone to bed.

The generator had stopped working suddenly earlier tonight so there was only candlelight at dinner. For some reason David hadn't eaten anything and had sat with them only for a while, and silently, and when Casa suggested they should investigate the generator he said it can be left until tomorrow.

The house is in darkness. Allah has sent her here so he can possess her. It is His command that he do this, then go and find a way of becoming a martyr. When he walks around the dark house he discovers an open weakly illuminated window on the north side on the ground floor. Looking in he becomes aware that something is wrong. It is an instinct long before it is a full sentence in his head. A candle has almost burnt itself to the height of half an inch on a stack of books. The flame squat and blue-tipped.

There is a careless ruck in the prayer mat near by. As though a serpent sleeps underneath.

One of Dunia's earrings lies between the prayer mat and the window. They had carried her out through here.

They must have disturbed her at prayer, while she was unguarded, when the difference between this world and the next is slowly wiped out.

He climbs in.

This house is unhinging him, asking him to look into mirrors he shouldn't. Allah does not wish him to have any ties. Three-and-a-bit days living with them is enough, these people whose very existence is and should be a provocation – to think that he has spent time under the same roof as a Russian, the butchers of Afghanistan, the butchers of Chechnya! – and it is an effort to remain silent all the time. He should steal the keys to David's car and leave. The Americans know him now – if they stop him he'll say he's running an errand, that someone has fallen ill.

He wants to go back to the state of war. For the clarity it brings.

If she is blameless Allah Himself will find a way to save her. Nothing is beyond Him. Casa has heard how a group of the Taliban and al-Qaeda fighters had become trapped here in Usha towards the end of 2001, when the American soldiers were going from house to house, smashing open any door they wished to in their hunt. All escape routes were blocked but then suddenly, out of the room where the fighters stood more or less cornered, ten iron nails had flown out and swerved into the street. Each was six inches long and verses of the Koran written on small pieces of paper had been tied with thread to the head of each. The sharp tips pointing along the direction of travel, the nails continued in a straight line through the moonlight, the rays glinting off the grey iron, took a corner to the left and then to the left again in order to enter the next street, increasing in speed as they approached their targets. Without sound they came and, shattering through the night-vision goggles, lodged themselves into the eyes of the five American soldiers who were keeping guard there, blocking the path to safety.

The miracles of Allah.

Now he goes deeper into the house and finds a lamp and then returns and exits the house and goes to the wooden kiosk that houses the generator. Several of the cables have been cut, he sees. Quick strokes with a blade. The thin copper wires within the rubber insulation shining like insect eyes as they catch the lamp's light. He presses the lever and raises the glass shield of the lamp and blows out the flame. He steps out and stands with his back pressed to the kiosk's door, looking deep into the surrounding darkness.

In the autumn of 1959, Khrushchev visited New York but he kept delaying his departure back to Moscow. When this aroused suspicion, the Western world's listening posts in England, Italy, Japan and Turkey set to work and eventually homed in on signals issuing from a rocket launch site within the Soviet Union. Among the signals was the regular beating of a human heart. The heartbeat grew faster as the rocket reached its first staging point, the cosmonaut experiencing the normal reaction of fear and excitement. At the moment the rocket's second stage should have ignited, all signals ceased abruptly and the tracking devices lost contact. Though the Soviet Union denied it, the owner of the heartbeat had been incinerated in millions of gallons of exploding fuel. It is now believed that important safety checks had been ignored for the Soviet leader to have a triumphal moment while visiting the West – 'The first human being in space is a citizen of the Soviet Union.'

Lara feels along the darkened wall. Her fingers touch the coldness of the lyre-shaped mirror and then journey over its frame, the warmth in the fingertips releasing the fragrance of the wood.

From the shelf she takes the matchbox and strikes herself a flame. In its brief yellow light she picks up the foot-long narrow box that lies on a higher shelf. Five more seconds – and a star bursts before her eyes, the silver brilliance at the centre of it scorching the retina. She turns around with it in her hands, the room shaking with the light. It is a child's sparkler: a small amount of – what is it, surely not gunpowder? – moulded onto a stiff wire. She can't find a candle and has just heard a sound from outside. It's seventeen minutes past one. She moves towards the window with the white starburst. Her shadow is grey tinted with lapis lazuli and it wavers and shifts from side to side, almost vibrating. As when lightning flashes in a storm, entering a room from two different windows. She stands looking out into the night, the five inches of burning powder almost running out.

'How do you think that kind old man out there would feel', she had asked David, stopping him in a corridor, 'if you were to tell him that his daughter's death was needed for the secure and singing tomorrows you were arranging for Afghanistan and the world?'

And he had replied, 'I loved her as much as he did. But Christopher made a mistake.'

He was not innocent but he was not guilty.

She was collateral damage.

'When you are alone at night and your rage takes over – what face do you give it?'

'I am also the man who is privileged to have saved many many lives, Lara.'

Everyone in the house came together at dinner but then she had withdrawn into this room with Dunia. Around midnight the girl said she wanted to pray and went downstairs, Casa's fists sounding on the kitchen door not long after that. He was shouting that the girl was missing, that the electricity had been sabotaged.

There are two possibilities. Either someone from the mosque has taken her, to mete out justice for being immoral. Or – according to David – someone linked with Gul Rasool has, thinking she is involved with the people who put up the *shabnama* that night.

Marcus is in the kitchen now. And she doesn't know where David and Casa have gone.

She takes out the two dozen or so lights that remain in

the flat cardboard box and ignites them simultaneously. She stops herself from shaking. With all the power in her arm she throws the fragments of lightning out into the blackness, watching the thin silver flares slowly drop towards the ground, illuminating the air, the edges of leaves, the boughs of the rosewood tree that is honoured by the three ring-dove nests. They go out one by one in the garden and are a handful of dead moments, bits of time turned to ash.

In the nineteenth century, one of Marcus's uncles in the North-West Frontier Province was in the Duke of Cornwall's Light Infantry. On parade every man of the regiment wore a single red feather at the front of his pith helmet. The regiment had taken part in the successful night attack on the Americans at Paoli in September 1777, the sleeping Americans massacred with swords and bayonets, the place set alight around the screaming wounded. The Americans had vowed vengeance and, in defiance, in order that they should know who had done the deed, the light company stained red the white feathers they wore in their hats, the tradition continuing for a century and more into the future.

He wonders what has stirred this memory as he sits in the kitchen with a small candle, the flame twice as long as the wax. The thought of the red-stained bandage at the back of Casa's head? Or it may have been the small wound David has received while constructing the canoe. The boy and David had just drifted away from here separately, he and Lara alone in the house.

An ammonite rests on his palm. Zameen had found it during a fossil hunt in the Cotswolds. He can hear her upstairs. Lara. Her eyes must not have stopped looking for signs and indications of her brother ever since she arrived at Usha fifteen days ago. He knows this from his own searches for Qatrina and Zameen and the child Bihzad. And from what David has told him about looking for Jonathan in the Far East. At times he thought he would go mad, interrogating the earth and the landscape, alighting on possible symbols and portents. Always telling himself he wasn't looking hard enough. Once he jolted himself upright from partial sleep, the book slipping from his grasp and landing on the floor. Among the clues to Orestes' unknown burial place were

the two winds

that were *by strong necessity blowing*,

and a place where *evil lies upon evil*.

With these clues, Lichas had discovered the bones of the hero in the workshop of an ironsmith. The bellows were the two winds. Hammer and anvil, and the iron being wrought, were the evil lying upon evil. This, Lichas imagined, might be so because iron had been discovered to the hurt of man.

Marcus was in Kandahar when he read this, and in the madness of his mad heart he had wandered out into the night looking for a rickshaw or horse carriage to take him to a place where iron was forged.

9

The Wasted Vigil

QUICKLY, in the brief time it would take the believers to recite the last chapter of the Koran, Casa traverses a darkened courtyard inside Gul Rasool's vast house, going through a plot of land filled with the shells of several dozen cars. There is a weak bulb in an alcove with moths lying around it, each with a few specks of life still in it, the wings damaged on the hot glass. Away from that light there is the absolute darkness. Where is she? He senses the presence of another and comes to a standstill, moving forward only when that second figure mimics his raised hand and he realises it is a dim mirror hanging on a far wall. A dream. But the next moment he is brought back to the present, to the reality of a sound from somewhere near by. A small rustle. He imagines himself to be in the crosshairs of a sniper's gun. A fly held in a spider's web.

He shouldn't have come here.

He is not a good Muslim.

He is not a good Muslim.

Is it any wonder the infidels have taken over the lands of Islam? It's Allah's punishment for men like him who have become distracted by earthly matters. Allah will – is about to – smite him. *I want to dip my finger in a war wound and spell the name of a hero* – this should be his sole preoccupation while the lands of Allah are being invaded by non-believers.

Have they infected him permanently? When yesterday he said he didn't know what to do with the sounds issuing from the radio, Marcus had told him, 'You listen to music with your memories, Casa, not your ears.' Perhaps it is the same with other senses also. You smell, see, touch, and taste with your memory. There have been occasions when he has eaten something sweet and been reminded for the briefest of moments of dynamite, from the time in the al-Qaeda camps when he had been made to recognise various explosives through taste, placing a small amount on the tongue. Certain large flower buds in Marcus's garden reminded him of bullets. Now he wonders if the girl's voice will be a component he'll look for in any piece of music in the future. Many years from now will he be reminded of his experiences in the Englishman's house – the six rooms, the perfume factory? The two places of safety.

He presses the button on the side of his flashlight and sends the thick ray into the air of the room he had entered a moment ago. Held within the light's circle, the bird's head remains motionless, though its eyes are open. Perhaps peacocks don't close their eyes when they sleep. He lets the light flow down the body, leaving the diademed head and arriving at the blue and green tail. A quiver full of stiff jewelled arrows. As though the heat from the beam has brought it to life, the creature now sends a shiver into the long feathers, and the head flickeringly turns to look at him when he brings the beam back up. The bird has been resting in a deep niche and now stands up, making Casa think it is about to step onto the rod of silver light issuing from his hand. The diameter of light when he moves it around the room reveals other smaller birds, asleep on perches, on dead branches and dozens of wire swings. Every colour is represented, and there are various shapes of beak, various lengths of tail. Eyes like pearls. Some are mistaken by him at first glance for toys – the carved and moulded objects banned by the Taliban. As a child at the madrassa he had learned to whistle, much to the displeasure of the teachers who saw it as a kind of music, his mouth a sinful musical instrument they wanted to but could not find any way of destroying. Though he himself had no wish to be separated from the newly acquired skill, he became careful about when and where he practised it after repeated warnings to desist – imitating bird calls, the rhythm of the Koranic verses, the call to prayer. Inevitably he was caught and they sewed his lips together with needle and thread for four days.

He touches the scar on his upper lip. The place she had touched.

He knows why these birds are here. Gul Rasool, he has heard from Nabi Khan, keeps falcons and likes to feed them on the meat of elegant birds, enjoys seeing them tear into and scatter the brilliant feathers. Paying a high price to the owner if a bird is particularly beautiful. At one time there were three hundred falcons and a hundred thousand white doves to feed them.

At the brief sound of a chain he moves towards the far corner and finds a large wild boar tethered to the wall there. He had hunted them in the villages around Peshawar, lying in wait all night for them to raid the peanut fields, the eyes glowing amber in the darkness. The beast turns its thick neck and looks at him. Gauging the length of the chain, he maintains a distance of just over two and half feet from it. The memory coming to him of the times when, from the forests around an al-Qaeda training camp, he would capture jackals and yellow-gazed lynx and hare, and bring them to the camp laboratory where they died strange deaths in gas chambers.

Now there is another noise and he turns to see that the peacock is jumping out of its high niche and onto a log on the aviary floor. It disappears from the circle of light, Casa not following it because something else has caught his attention. There, behind a log, is an octagonal box with crescent-shaped brass handles on its sides. It is covered in white streaks because of the birds, but he can see that the Paradisal tree under which the throne of Allah is to be found is painted on it. The box in which the Englishman said his wife had kept her paintings? He opens the lid and finds the rolled-up tubes of paper, each held together by dusty, rotting Chinese silk. The box – its eight sides echoing the shape of the Throne – is filled to the brim with them, perhaps all ninety-nine names of Allah are still in here, discarded amid logs and branches and various useless items in the corner. With the light in his mouth he unrolls a picture. *The All Seeing.* He carefully puts it back, and as the tubes shift he sees that something else is also in there, an object of different dimensions. The hundredth name? A landmine detonating at this range would kill him certainly. It's something spherical wrapped in a dark torn shirt, and when he sees that it is a man's head he lets it drop in shock, the desiccated skin, the empty eye sockets, the dried-up nerves and blood vessels issuing from the torn neck, falling towards the floor out of the light beam. He is not sure whether he has let out a sound, a shout, but the torch is still there in his mouth, directed now at the wall, now at the ceiling, as he loses his balance and falls backwards, dust motes floating in the bright shaft. Somewhere in the darkness near him is that parchment-like face pasted onto the skull, the lips pulled back to reveal blackened teeth. Adrenalin still in him, he propels himself backwards with his feet, knees rising and falling, to be as far away as possible. With his back against the wall he manages to bring order into his breathing. The shirt is a Soviet soldier's. He recognises it from the many bloodstained ones that can be found for sale in the bazaars of Peshawar and Kabul. He has heard how in the 1980s, convoys of ten-ton trucks filled with automatic rifles, with machine guns and grenade launchers, bought secretly by the United States, would come into Peshawar daily from the Arabian Sea docks of Karachi, and then move on towards the Afghan interior. In return, bloody fur hats and Red Star badges taken from dead Soviet soldiers were taken out of Afghanistan on mules for sale in Peshawar. When the Afghan guerrillas returned a prisoner to the Soviets in exchange for one of their own, they axed off his right hand so he would not be able to fight again, and these trophies too could be found in the bazaars.

He has often wished he had been alive back then, to be

able to kill a Soviet soldier. But, he reminds himself on those occasions, I am alive now and able to kill Americans, infidels all.

The shirt is still in his hands. It's just the front panel really, a rag black with blood, the sleeves ripped away, most of the back too, the collar hanging off. Throwing it sideways into a corner he moves towards the three steps that lead out of this room. They are made of rough wooden planks and each board had tried to make a different noise underfoot when he came in. He steps out without making a sound to find James Palantine and three other Americans looking at him. One of the Kalashnikovs is his. He had written onto its strap the verse from the Koran which lavishes praise on iron, the metal of swords and warfare.

The cloud is thickening above David as though someone wishes to hinder his progress by hiding his surroundings from him, by cancelling the meagre light from the thin moon. There's barely a landmark for him as he drives towards Usha, the path firing a spray of pebbles at the car. Cloud cover and fog banks are to be some of the weapons the United States plans to use in the wars of the future, a summoning of hailstorms and lightning strikes against the enemy on the ground, the owning of the weather. Monsoon clouds above Laos and Cambodia were drenched with chemicals during the Vietnam War in order to prolong the rainy season, rendering Vietcong supply lines impassable.

He parks the car some way before Gul Rasool's house and gets out and stands looking at the building from a distance. Those guarding it will make themselves known any moment. He can feel the weight of their eyes on him.

Who has her? Dunia told Lara that a man had come forward two days ago to claim to the people of Usha that she had once tried to seduce him. And yet it had been she who had rebuffed him after he, a toymaker, had attempted to gain her love with a doll he had sold her, a figure moulded from clay in which he had added his semen.

He walks along the high wall, towards the door behind which a light burns, showing through chinks, and he shouts out his name when he is told to halt.

'I am here to see James,' he tells the American man in the group that has gathered before him.

'That's far enough. He called you?' This young man was at the house during the day, pulling down books while standing on a bridge of rope.

David moves towards that door, taking the others with him, their weapons drawn. He pushes at the door but it won't yield so he slams into it with his shoulder.

'Wait. I am getting James on the phone for you.'

But David is already through the door.

Casa is on his back on the floor in the centre of the room, his legs being held by an Afghan man, his chest pinned down by the knees of an American who also grips his hands. Another American, beside Casa's head, is holding a blowtorch, its blue jet directed into Casa's left eye. This young man straightens up on seeing David, and just then James comes in through a door on the far side of the room. Casa's mouth is open in a twisted soundless scream, that eye erupting black blood. The boy with the blowtorch stands up with a glance towards James, the blue fang-like flame briefly touching Casa's hair so that a patch of it catches fire with a crackle. It goes out by itself, reduced to wandering scarlet points. The smoke rising threadily into the air.

And now suddenly the other two have released Casa, and Casa rises, covering with one hand the absent eye, but he cannot stand up and, lurching sideways, hits a wall after three faltering steps.

James, the features perfectly composed after the briefest of initial frowns, walks towards David and stands facing him.

The blowtorch, still on, would explode were David to fire a bullet into it.

No words from anyone until David says, 'Tell them not to go near him.'

'Put the gun away, David.'

'Did you fucking hear me?' His voice like a canine's bark.

Casa is bowed on the floor, as he has seen him many times during prayers, but this is pain and a groan is now coming from him. There is a short length of rope tied to one of his ankles.

James, without turning around, flicks his head to the right and the men move to that side of the room. His jaw muscles working. Holding David's gaze he says, 'He confessed he is with Nabi Khan.'

'Bring that thing near me and *I'll* confess to that.'

'No, you wouldn't, and neither would I. And he came up with Nabi Khan's name by himself. We didn't suggest it.' He takes a step towards David. 'He can bring us to Nabi Khan – and Khan will tell you where your son is. Think about it.'

'You think you are going to get away with this.'

'He told us the exact details of the raid that was promised in the Night Letter. The exact date. It's next week – next Thursday. He said Nabi Khan wants to take his time with the attack, that he had said, "We mustn't rush history."'

'James, are you listening to me? I am going to have you all arrested for this.'

'Gul Rasool is in the government,' one of the Americans says.

'He's not in the United States government.' He feels faint as though someone has decanted a pitcher of blood from his body.

'He's in the government the US installed here,' says the Afghan who'd been holding Casa.

James raises a hand to silence his companions. 'I did what needed to be done, David. These people have been trained in how to survive interrogation techniques. For some of them true jihad starts at capture. So we have to be extreme, go beyond their trained endurance. I am just searching for our country's enemies, David. It's nothing personal against this man.'

'Nothing personal? You are holding a flame to his eye.'

'It's not between him and me. It's between them and us.'

411

They don't need to watch jihadi DVDs to become radicalised: they'll just watch the evening news on the TV – with things like these being reported.

'And when I say *us* I include the majority of the Afghanistanis, who want to get shot of sons of bitches like these. I include the majority of the world, not just Americans.'

'Have you any idea how much damage you have done *us* by your actions here tonight?'

'None, if you keep quiet about it.'

To the side of him Casa makes a lunge towards the open door. David hears sounds of a scuffle from out there. If he had died they would have buried him somewhere under cover of darkness? No one would have been any the wiser.

'Tell them to let him go,' he tells James.

'No. He could run off and warn Nabi Khan. And I want to know what else he knows.'

'You know all this is illegal?'

'Illegal? This is war, David. You've been looking into the wrong law books. These are battlefield decisions.'

'Tell them to let him go. You do not have the authority to do this.'

'Suddenly you are an angel.'

'Whatever I did or did not do, I was an employee of the government of the United States.'

'How do you know I am not?'

'I intend to find out. This is not over.'

He looks at the others. The long thick veins on the arms of the one holding the blowtorch are like cables or tubes that feed the blowtorch, the instrument a part of him. And

David sees that on his white T-shirt is printed the sonogram image of a few-weeks-old foetus. A black rectangle filled with grainy strokes. His future child back in the United States, no doubt.

He turns and leaves the room with James following. Casa is on the ground out there, in the rectangle of light falling from the door. And when they release him and James moves forward to lift him to his feet, Casa makes to stab him in the face with the canoe maker's awl he has produced from the folds of his clothing, the barb as thick as a porcupine quill moving past James's shoulder. James wrenches it out of the weak grip and steps away.

'They are the children of the devil. They have no choice but to spread destruction in the world.'

'He is the child of a human, which means he has a choice and he can change.'

James throws the spike into the darkness. 'Just look around you, David. Look at the devastation all around you. These people have reduced their own country to rubble and now they want to destroy ours.'

'Where's the girl, James?'

'I don't know.'

'She's missing.'

'Wasn't us. Must be the fellow countrymen of this man, the people you are so keen to protect. Do you know what is probably being done to her by them right now?'

When Lara said she was very brave to have taken on the responsibility of the school, the girl had replied, 'I pretend I don't exist. It's easier to be courageous that way.' As Zameen used to say at the Street of Storytellers.

Casa has stood up and begun to stagger away, trailing that bit of rope.

David now moves in front of James to block direct access to Casa, just in case. There are only a few inches of space between their faces, the eyes staring at each other. The gap widens as David backs away in Casa's direction. 'This is not over,' he says firmly.

Like lightning arriving a few beats before the roll of thunder, James's face tenses and his eyes flash and then the noise of his rage comes out. 'We are not responsible for this. If he is half-blind or if he dies of his wounds – it's not our fault. And those hundreds who died by chance in our bombing raids, and those who are being held in Guantanamo and in other prisons – none of it is our fault. Osama bin Laden and al-Qaeda and their Islam are answerable for all that. We are just defending ourselves against them. This is not over? You bet.'

David turns his back to him and looks for Casa. His ruined face. The water in the eye gone, the colour too turned to smoke and ash in the cindered socket. He glances around but there is no sign of him. Occasionally when he is in Asia he visits the site where Zameen's death took place, on the outskirts of Peshawar, around where she possibly lies buried. The first time he went he felt her presence there, a hint of her like an unevenness in a sheet of glass. Has she been accompanying him since, the unanchored dead? Before leaving he had bent down and picked up a handful of earth from the ground and closed his fingers around it and he took it with him to the USA. This is among the few things that can be said about love with any confidence. It is small enough to be contained within the heart but, pulled thin, it would drape the entire world.

It's almost dawn and Lara has been here at the table with a book, surrounded by the painted vistas and processions on the wall, for many hours. Marcus is in an armchair in the next room, in a state of alert exhaustion no doubt, like her. She can see part of his body next to the plum blossom printed on the chair's fabric. Can see part of his lengthy comet-like beard. 'This land and its killing epochs,' he had been saying earlier. 'The Soviet invasion took away Zameen, the Taliban era swallowed up Qatrina. I fear that this new war will take someone else away.'

She had gone to sit on the floor beside him. Her head on his lap.

'You have to go away, Marcus. Go far away from this place.'

'I live here.'

'It's called waiting.'

'Do you think?'

In both of them there was a wish to conserve energy so it was a whispered exchange. A drowsiness, and little or no inflection behind the words. He began stroking her hair but soon stopped even that, the hand just resting there.

'I am waiting for my grandson, yes. All this' – the hand was lifted a fraction off her head because he probably wished to wave it around the room, the house, what she thinks of as the ruin of golden Islam, a destroyed *markaz* perhaps and a

'Zone of Peace' with him as the Sufi – 'is his and must be passed on to him. Having all of you here has made it even more clear to me that this is my life and my home. I don't just live here because I don't have an alternative.'

'I inherited everything of Stepan's. But I want nothing to do with it, the wealth he left. I don't really want to know the methods by which it was accumulated. You could buy a trainload of Siberian timber for one dollar during the financial crash of 1993. No, I don't want it. Who would?'

'Me.'

'As children we heard a story about the tin-based Russian currency. How one particularly cold winter, when temperatures fell below minus eighty-six degrees, the nation's entire coinage had turned to white powder, as tin does under such conditions. I am sure the story is untrue, but I don't want to touch what Stepan has left me, I will let it turn to dust. I have come to hate money.'

'Not me.'

She had straightened at that, shocked even within her tiredness. 'I can't believe what I am hearing. You wish you had money?'

'A vast amount of it. Why not? It could be used to build schools and hospitals, parks and libraries and community centres. I am not saying the only way to save someone is through money, or that life should be reduced to quantities of wealth. The rich have this idea that they have paid off their debt to the world by becoming rich. No, I am talking about the difference between greed and need. And not just this country, there is a world out there that I would try to help.'

She had felt ashamed. 'You are good.' *It all depends on how big you think your family is.* The words of her mother.

'I didn't say that to imply you were being self-centred.' He cupped her face in both his hands. Or got as close to doing it as was possible for him. He attempted it and she understood the attempt. If the left hand was missing – well then, it was missing.

The touch of his hand was tough in some places, fine in others. A gatepost weathered by departures.

He said, 'You must go back and take charge of these matters intelligently. You must delve deeper into Stepan's death, try to discover what your country's government and your country's army is doing.'

'I am too weakened, Marcus.'

'You are going to let them go unchallenged?'

'They are very strong.'

'Then you'll fail. But so what? At least you will have tried. The goal is to have a goal, honesty the striving for honesty.'

A dependable clarity dissolved out from him. An aura. It was as though she had been able to make out each of the pages her mother thought she was filling her notebooks with in her last days.

Now she rises and drinks a few gulps of water, which after the thirst feel immensely pure. It is like being a bowl of dew.

From the orchard she looks out at the lake. During the night she had gone down the path towards Usha several times, always turning back because of fear, but starting out again later, covering this time a distance greater or shorter

417

than earlier. At the dacha they had hurt Stepan to make her reveal herself. She had heard his screams from the hiding place where she sat whimpering. And so, during the course of the night that is ending, she kept hearing Dunia's voice, calling to her.

Now she moves along the path again, trying to gather her nerves as she goes. The sky above her is still dark but there are many hints of light, almost everything visible. A sound like a shower of broken glass and she looks to her left, into the trees that are populated by the djinn, catching sight of the peacock just before it disappears with its waterfall-like tail. The retractable trim of long feathers on each wing was glowing with the reddish orange of rust-covered knives. She enters the contained and muffled solitude of the trees, the silence so heavy it is as though her ears have been sealed. Here could be another explanation for the painted rooms of Marcus's house: it could have been built to provide an education to the djinn about what it means to be human. Each interior a classroom, the djinn moving upwards within the building as their knowledge increased sense by sense, arriving finally at the topmost golden space.

She notices small birds flitting around and above her. Bee-eaters, parakeets, orioles and goldfinches, who received their red faces when they tried to remove the crown of thorns from Christ's head. They are too many and too different for it to seem natural. It's as though the door to an aviary has been left open somewhere. Minutes later, lost and unable to find a way out onto the path, she is leaning against a tree when she becomes aware of an intense fragrance. There is no arrival or gradual rise in intensity – it is there suddenly like music released. There is movement beside her, the faintest of stirrings. She turns her head and sees the ten figures, bowing in two rows towards Allah. All their attention on their Maker. They are not aware of her even though she is only two metres away from the end of the second row. This beautiful brown-skinned boy is little more than fourteen. How close she is to the pulsating energy field that this innocent-looking child exists within, the grand realm of spiritual events in which his real life occurs, Muhammad and Gabriel more real to his passioning eye than she.

He has Pakistani features and colouring. Recruited from a religious school for this cause? Terrorist groups in that country buy and sell boys as young as twelve for suicide missions. Once they receive training they can be barred from returning to their families, becoming virtual prisoners. The groups have been known to accept 'ransom' for their release, justifying it by saying that neither the boys nor their training had come cheap.

Or is he doing this willingly? In the months to come his mother or father, sister or brother, would be scouring this land for some word of him.

Hundreds of Russian mothers wait along Chechnya's border with Russia, women of advancing years who have decided to come and discover the fates of their conscripted sons, brought there by the news that his military card has been found or a locket with his name on it. They move from town to town and search the train carriages heaped with the dead boys, looking for a birthmark or asking one another if eye colour is the same in death as in life, untangling one boy from the press of the hundred others and pulling him out, already unrecognisable, bitten by dogs and rats or cut to pieces.

A few birds are singing in the branches overhead. The song much more powerful than the fragile body of the singer.

In America they would have to face the east in order to say their prayers, and so, David said, the early Muslims in America were thought to be worshippers of the sun and the moon.

They have straightened in unison – it's like opening a child's pop-up book – and are now standing up, hands folded neatly on the stomachs, on the suicide belts, faces lowered in obedience. Today is the day of reckoning promised in the *shabnama*. There is a slope in front of them where the tall grass is tiger-striped with paths. They must have come down through there to perform this final act of worship before going on to meet Allah, and other battalions must be elsewhere around Usha.

How long, she wonders, before they finish and see her? They'll perform the two motions that are the last acts of the Muslim prayer: the head is rolled first to the right, then to the left. *Allah, I wish well-being and peace for all those on this side. And, Allah, I wish well-being and peace for all those on this side.* She had seen Casa and Dunia do this at the house.

She is sure they can hear the noise her heart is making. She steps sideways, the support of the tree disappearing from along her spine. And she takes a step back. The corner of her eye is fixed on them and now she sees David at the other end of the rows. He hasn't seen her: he is moving towards the back row, eyes fixed on the third boy along from his end.

Casa.

David inches forward and comes to stand directly behind Casa, carefully raises his right hand towards the boy's waist and his left towards the head. As the other boys move forward to bow again, David clamps shut Casa's mouth and with the other arm fastens the boy's arms to his sides. A tight grip. He lifts him out of the rank just as the others fall to their knees and then make their bodies foetally compact on the ground. The combined rustle of the others' clothing hides any noise that the two of them have made. *Why is Casa's eye bandaged?* she wonders. David drags the struggling boy away from the two bowing lines of the death squad, away into the trees, managing to raise him off his feet so the thudding cannot alert the others – their ears so close to the ground in their prostration. Her hands are wet with the tears she has wiped off her face, her vision slipping in and out of focus. Their clothing has drenched the air with perfume here. Jihad handbooks warn terrorists not to wear fragrances in airports, as it gives them away as devout Muslims. They have, of course, become aware of the disturbance, reacting as though in a dream, unable and unwilling to interrupt their prayer. By religious decree they are not even allowed to look sideways until the act of worship is complete. But in ones and twos around the gap that Casa has left behind, they come out of their trance, look back, see her, see David and Casa in that terrible embrace. All this takes place in a matter of seconds but to her it seems so slow that buds could appear and break into blossom and then wither around her. Coins of the realm and the names of cities could change. Governments and empires fall.

David's mouth is next to Casa's ear, and he is whispering something fast.

He is hoping to win over his murderer with an embrace.

THEY HAVE FALLEN BACKWARDS onto the earth. Managing to free his right hand from David's grip, Casa feels along the belt tied to the waist. Through gritted teeth he says something, his face parallel with the sky visible through a gap in the foliage. The last words David hears.

The blast opens a shared grave for them on the ground.

TEN OR SO BUTTERFLIES go past Marcus's knees and they double in number when they begin to fly over the lake's reflecting surface. The sky has a milky lustre above him, the pale blue of lines ruled on the pages of a child's exercise book.

He is dragging the canoe to the water's edge, the various woods of it gleaming in the late-morning sun. The water seems to take it out of his hand, attempting to uncouple it from his grip. He has to make sure his feet don't slither sideways. It looks raggedy. The ends of the ribs protruding where they haven't yet been trimmed. It has not been sealed – with that gum sticky to the touch like certain leaf buds before opening – but it floats. Keeping his hand on the prow he walks with it into the water until he is submerged up to the navel, standing on rocks within the water. He lets go and with his one hand tries to lift a heavy rock out of the lake. Failing, he takes a deep breath and crouches. His head is in the liquid now. He manages to work one round stone out of the bed and then slides it up along his thighs, into his lap. Cradling it, he stands up out of the diffused shimmer and then carefully sends the black stone over the edge of the canoe. The bark vessel sinks half an inch deeper into the lake, the water sieving in. This was how the Native Americans stored the canoes when they were not in use, burying them in the water.

He looks towards the house, the balcony of the room where Lara is. He saw her walking from the direction of Usha earlier and took her into the house, helped her upstairs, stopping on the seventh step of the staircase to pick up the book that had become dislodged and landed there. The blood on her clothes was, she said, that of Casa and David. She wouldn't bathe in the house, rejecting the idea of the drain, and had stood in the lake instead so that all the redness would become part of the roaming water. The sun-dazzled surface. One year soon after the Soviet Army invaded, the air around the house had turned yellow, thick billows of the colour arriving on the breeze, falling from the sky, every heart fearful at the sight because there had been reports of attacks with chemical weapons. In the end it turned out to be the pollen-rich droppings of a large swarm of wild bees. The colour settled on this water thickly enough for Zameen to be able to write her name in it.

He knows Dunia will never be found. Her face of unstudied nobility. The silent earrings she was still wearing from the time of the Taliban regime, when women would hold up a piece of jewellery and shake it to see if it made a noise. No one will know what happened to her. The talk in Usha will be that she must have run away with a lover. Her father will hold Marcus responsible for her disappearance. Perhaps violence will come from him towards Marcus.

He goes down into that water again, amid the drowned

rays of the sun, and brings out another rock. Then another. He does this carefully, imagines the boat tipping and pouring the stones onto him, a landslide of his own making. Now and then he is forced to look towards Usha, the sound of an explosion. Rockets. Gunfire. Street fighting in the sewers and alleys of Usha. He imagines flattened homes, with hands protruding from the rubble as though still trying to grab hold of and stay the rampaging storm. The heroes of East and West are slaughtering each other in the dust of Afghanistan.

Both sides in Homer's war, when they arrive to collect their dead from the battlefield, weep freely in complete sight of each other. Sick at heart. This is what Marcus wants, the tears of one side fully visible to the other.

Over the next ten minutes the boat sits lower and lower on the water. There are small insects on the lake not far from him like words suspended on the surface of a page. When the water is just three inches from the lip of the canoe he walks away from it, the lake falling from him in dense liquid sheets.

He stands watching it as it takes in an increasing amount of water and eventually disappears. He feels he has driven seventeen nails of various sizes into a book to make it stay on the ceiling.

Nothing but a set of oval ripples is on the surface. They become more and more circular as they travel away from the centre.

10

All Names are My Names

A BREEZE comes along the migratory route of birds and enters the orchard. The Buddha's head slowly rises off the floor in the perfume factory, the first movement it has known for several centuries.

The knitted harness of chains, almost a net, lifts it through the gap in the glass roof and brings it out into the September sunlight, the avenue of Persian lilacs – the chinaberries – thrashing in the wind that is being generated by the aircraft's two mighty sets of rotor blades. In March there had been flowers but none of them remain, so only the foliage and the clusters of green berries are being dismantled onto the Buddha.

The stone face hangs from the twin-rotored military helicopter. As they hover and then move sideways and gain in height, Marcus looks down and catches glimpses of the head. The features smiling above the suddenly visible vista. His own body – the portion of earthly dust assigned him – feels insubstantial in comparison with all this. The soldiers have strapped him to the metal wall beside a window though they themselves know how to move with confident safety within the hulking machine. The mountains and hills rise and fall on either side of them. Sometimes the shadow of the flying machine is tiny – moving like a gnat along the floor of a deep valley – but at other times it is almost life-size, projected onto the side of a mountain that has suddenly appeared beside them.

'Do you live alone?' one of the soldiers had asked Marcus.

His family and friends are gone. He is alive but has been buried in many graves.

A letter came from Lara in July. The fragments of painted plaster she arranged on the floor in the golden room are still there. Looking at the mosaic after she went back to St Petersburg, he realised that one piece was missing, the piece on which the faces of the two lovers made contact. She had taken it with her to Russia. That and one of the perforated books. A kinship of wounds. It was *The Golden Fleece* picked at random. *The dead may speak the truth only, even when it discredits themselves.*

Rivers and small bright lakes pass under them – pale-yellow light held together by water. Some of the hills down there are dotted with red: the rocks have been daubed to warn that the vicinity hasn't yet been cleared of land-mines.

Marcus and Qatrina had informed the National Museum at Kabul when the head was discovered during the building of the perfume factory decades ago, and they had attempted to take it away but hadn't managed it. In the end Marcus's house was officially designated an annexe of Kabul Museum, a dozen or so visitors managing to make it to the house every year to see the colossal Gandhara sculpture. During this summer Marcus has persuaded the Museum to make another attempt to transport the statue to Kabul, most of the priceless collection once housed there having disappeared or been smashed during the wars.

He can see a shepherd resting under a tree in the plains below. His animals have spread themselves out in such a way that they form a living imprint of the tree on the ground, making maximum use of its shadow.

From the folds of one of the hills in the next valley a rocket is fired at the aircraft.

Marcus watches it climb, almost in staggered time, incrementally. Its low speed seems unconnected with the massive tail of white smoke issuing from its rear, hinting at its great weight, at the effort involved in raising it – the many deaths it contains. Then another comes, both of them missing the target.

The American boys around him lower the Buddha onto a low hill, and he too alights. The metal bird rising and veering away to investigate, the soldiers telling him they'd prefer it if he weren't with them. He watches them disappear towards the possibility of a battle.

He is alone with the smile. Suddenly now it feels perishable, hard stone though it is, without the protecting walls of his perfume factory. He can see all around him, the arid dusty plains, the walls of green or blue but mostly khaki hills, the mountains beyond, and he can hear the sounds of a skirmish from the other side of the nearest hill. He sits in the shade cast by the statue head, his back leaning against the chin, his ear next to the mouth.

The school has remained shut since Dunia's disappearance but it's reopening soon.

'Majrooh?'

A man had approached him last week and called him by the name he had taken to be able to marry Qatrina.

'You won't recognise me, sir, but when I was much younger I used to come to your house to borrow books. Your daughter and I . . .'

Marcus nodded and, encouraged, the man took a step towards him.

'I have come back to Usha to take over the school.' He smiled, and pointing to his motorbike on the other side of the street – a child with an artificial leg was sitting on the back seat – he added, 'I was riding past just now and thought I recognised you . . .'

Marcus sets out in search of water, finding a patch of dampness at the base of a hill and knowing how to use the very tips of his fingers to gently persuade the spring to come out into daylight. The water quivers in the curved palm of his hand, as frightened as a small captured lizard. Nabi Khan's raid on Usha had been unsuccessful but he has promised another in a recent *shabnama*. That day American soldiers engaged in a fire fight near by had got involved and had requested aerial assistance, the giant bombers arriving like lions roaring in the sky. Making the earth shake as they dropped bombs from above. Afghan officials speculate that conservative Saudi Arabians, as well as certain rogue elements within the Pakistani government and military, are financing the attacks. Pull a thread here and you'll find it's attached to the rest of the world.

The human eye is trained to look for symmetry, so the fact that someone has a missing limb is obvious.

Seventeen ordinary citizens of Usha died in the battle that morning in March, and twelve people – including James Palantine – lost their legs or arms. Ringing from Western countries, families and lovers always ask the soldiers about their limbs first, about their hands and feet.

He comes back to the statue and waits.

The stars – one for each life lost during the wars of the previous decades – are out by the time the young men come and lift him out of the landscape. A deep indigo evening. Half a moon with a coloured halo. There is an up-pouring of glow from the land as though in response to the moonlight.

The Buddha is lowered in the grassy field beside the Museum, the building now secured by the British Army. There are three tonnes of Afghan antiquities in a warehouse near Heathrow, reliefs, bowls and sculptures that were illegally removed from Afghanistan at the behest of various warlords and chieftains, waiting to be brought back to these impoverished galleries.

Near by are the two ruined horse carriages once used by the royal family, the insignia and medallions still bright on the otherwise weather-beaten sides and doors of the larger carriage. The six-petalled moulded flower at the very hub of the wheels is surrounded by the words *PETERS & SONS LONDON* arranged in a circle.

A few hours of sleep later, he looks out from the window of the room he has been given inside the museum but he cannot see the stone face.

A dawn made of mist.

When sunlight appears and the soldiers allow him out

he walks through the lit haze, feeling his way towards it. He stands looking at the giant lips as though waiting for the answer to a question. Apollo, the lord whose oracle is at Delphi, who neither speaks nor keeps silent but offers hints.

He enters the building and asks if someone would be kind enough to take him to the city centre in a while. He is meeting someone there who could be Zameen's son.

June 2003 – August 2007

Acknowledgements

This is a work of fiction. The characters and organisations depicted in it are either the author's creation or are used fictitiously. No resemblance is intended to any persons living or dead, to any organisations past or present. When a fictitious character is present at a real event – for example, David Town at the Islamabad embassy siege in chapter three, or the child Casa at the burning of the Ojhri Camp ammunitions depot in chapter six – the results are fiction.

The verses on page 304 are by Yevgeny Vinokurov (tr. Daniel Weissbort, *Post-War Russian Poetry*, Penguin Books, New York, 1974). The poem on page 16 is *Note on the Terazije Gallows, 1941* by Vasko Popa (*Collected Poems*, Anvil Press Poetry, London, 1997). The italicised line on page 403 is from Aamer Hussein's *Turquoise* (Saqi Books, London, 2002). The two lines that end the section on page 415 are a paraphrased couplet by Jigar Moradabadi. *Casabianca*, the poem, is by Felicia Hemans. Mark Bowden's essay 'The Kabul-ki Dance' (*Road Work*, Atlantic Books, London, 2004) informs the paragraphs about the flying sorties over Afghanistan in chapter seven. Another helpful book was *Inside the Jihad* by Omar Nasiri (Basic

Books, New York, 2006). The author is grateful to Beatrice Monti della Corte of Santa Maddalena Foundation in Italy where a section of this book was composed in 2005. Thank you to the Lannan Foundation, Dr Naeem Hasanie, the gentlemen at ICUK, to Muneeb and Mughees Anwar. A special thanks to Victoria Hobbs and A. M. Heath. And to Salman Rashid – *Khizr* and guide during travels in Afghanistan's cities. Kathy Anderson. Diana Coglianese. Maya Mavjee in Toronto. To Angus Cargill in London and Sonny Mehta in New York.